D0934226

From the
Ashes of Ruin

From the
Ashes of Ruin

by Miriam Freeman Rawl

Summerhouse
Columbia, South Carolina

Published in Columbia, South Carolina
by Summerhouse Press

Copyright © 1999 by Miriam Freeman Rawl

Summerhouse Press
519 Huger Street
Columbia, SC 29201
(803) 779-0870
(803) 779-9336 fax

ISBN # 1-887714-39-1

First Edition

Library of Congress Catalog Card Number

99-70777

Dedication

To all women of courage and strength.

At clouded dawn of peace
they faced the future undismayed
with conviction
that from the ashes of ruin
would come resurrection.

—Monument Inscription by William E. Gonzales
"Erected to the Memory of the Women of the Confederacy, 1861-65
Reared by the Men of South Carolina, 1909-11."

One

South Carolina, February 8, 1865

From a front window, through slits of light between tightly closed shutters, Ellen Heyward watched the two approaching horsemen. They rode slowly, pausing often to search the roadside. The dreaded blue of their uniforms was clearly discernible in the bleak February afternoon sun.

A faint tremble of fear shook her as she observed them leave the main road and turn toward Oak Lane. They advanced beneath the canopy of live oak branches, passed the huge magnolia trees, and neared the camellia garden. Fear was no stranger to Ellen, but she had silently prayed that the soldiers would ride on. Facing the questions they might ask was going to be difficult.

The sound of quiet commands to the horses carried across the verandah, invading the darkened parlor. With growing alarm Ellen saw Randolph, the house boy, hovering near the wide front steps.

The taller man spoke to the boy.

"I know this is the Heyward plantation. I want to speak to the missus. I see that she's at home." He pointed to the female clothing flapping on a clothesline, and to a drift of smoke rising from the wide kitchen chimney. The acrid stench of charred wood hung heavily in the air. He looked toward the pile of burned rubble off to the left.

"Missus dead," the boy volunteered.

"Then I want to speak to the person in charge here. There has been a recent fire."

"Yes, suh."

Ellen resolutely turned the key in the brass lock, pulled open the heavy front door and stepped outside in the chilled air. The faint rustle of skirts alerted the men to a slender, proudly-poised woman of indeterminate age quietly standing on the verandah. She focused clear hazel eyes on the intruders. Only the pallor of her face and tightly clenched hands at her sides betrayed signs of emotion.

Both men dismounted with the muscular ease and lean strength of campaign-hardened veterans.

She waited.

The larger of the two, an officer, approached her. Ellen judged him to be in his late thirties, weathered, dark and tall. From a chiseled, expressionless face granite-hard eyes studied her. Then, with practiced grace, he removed his black slouch hat and nodded slightly.

"Miss Heyward?" A quirked eyebrow made it a question.

"Yes." Her low-pitched voice was barely audible. Knots of fear gripped her stomach. He knew her name. He had been asking questions. What else had he learned?

"This is Sergeant Kelly and I'm Major John Arledge of the Western Campaign on special assignment to General Sherman's Fifteenth Corps."

The cultured tones of his deep voice surprised her. His long dark hair and deeply bronzed face made him appear more raw plainsman or buccaneer than educated gentleman.

"I'm sure you are aware that small advanced parties of the Union army have moved into this area."

Ellen, feeling the stab of his piercing gaze, nodded but did not reply. She noted his slow, deliberate manner of speech.

"I'm conducting an investigation into the disappearance of three soldiers from one of these units. The men were detailed as foragers to procure supplies from the surrounding area."

"The Union army can't supply its men?" she coldly inquired.

He ignored the taunt.

"I have already talked with your neighbors. These soldiers were at the Taylor plantation and were last seen headed in this direction. They were mounted and had two pack mules with them. Were you at home last Thursday?"

"I am at home every day. Travel and social life have been rather severely curtailed for southern women." Cold resentment colored her voice. Reddened hands pressed against threadbare clothing attested to a dull, work-filled existence.

"Kelly," he addressed the man beside him, "please look about the grounds while I ask the lady a few questions."

He turned his attention back to Ellen. "You've had a fire. The stables?"

"Need you ask? Your soldiers were indeed here, Major. The sergeant is free to examine the ashes," voice resigned and bitter, "but neither of you may enter my home. My young sister is ill. I don't wish her to be disturbed or frightened."

"I'm sorry," he replied curtly. "I hope it will not be necessary to bother your sister, but I must locate the troopers."

"Why are these particular men so important?"

"An exchange of letters between your General Hampton and General Sherman has precipitated a crisis. I have been detailed here to conduct a formal military inquiry."

She could detect traces of a southern dialect.

The sergeant, small, wiry and seasoned by years of soldiering, ambled toward the distant pile of blackened wood. He stopped to converse easily with Randolph, who still cowered behind a boxwood, near the corner of the house. Ellen watched anxiously, afraid of what the boy might reveal.

"Miss Heyward, the men I'm asking about seem to have completely disappeared. A good bit of preliminary investigation has already been done. The information we've received has led us here."

He paused, then added with deliberate emphasis, "Here, and no further. We feel the party met with foul play. We intend to find out exactly who was involved and why."

Ellen had seen few men in the past four years. She was aware of the stranger's strong male physicality. Though frightened by his presence, she determined to show no trace of emotion.

"Any criminal acts uncovered will be punished," he continued. "General Sherman is very explicit about that. I hope you have nothing to hide. I shall expect you to answer my questions truthfully." He spoke with quiet authority, every word a military command.

Cold winter wind whipped around the big chimney on the north side of the house, fanned across the brick porch floor and out between the row of slim white columns. His gaze never strayed from Ellen's face.

Clutching her mother's black wool shawl close around her body, she continued to face him squarely. "Proceed, sir, with your interrogation." Her stoic tones lacked animation, but angry defiance was clear in the stiffened set of her narrow shoulders.

"Please tell me exactly what happened." He placed his right foot on the bottom step and leaned casually on his knee, one hand loosely holding the horse's reins.

Ellen took a deep breath, gathering courage.

"It was after noon when the men arrived. Earlier we had seen smoke at a neighboring plantation and were alarmed. We could see the men coming from a distance away." She faltered.

Keen blue eyes, sharp and assessing, stayed focused on her.

"The news of Sherman's march through Georgia has been very… disturbing. Naturally we were apprehensive. I locked the doors and shuttered the windows. Most of the hands who have remained on the plantation were working in the fields. Only Randolph," she gestured toward the boy whom the sergeant was questioning, "who is twelve years old, was here."

"And what happened?"

"It became clear that the men were coming to the house and that they were a raiding party." She felt panic rising and swallowed painfully.

His gaze shifted to the stable area. An indication of sympathy and understanding? She thought not.

"Father keeps whiskey in the cellar. I told Randolph to slip out to the camellia garden and pretend to be working. If the men asked, he was to tell them that the family was living in Columbia with relatives until the end of the war." She paused, nervously biting her bottom lip, for the first time uncertain. He watched while she foundered in chaotic silence.

"The men argued, cursed, and searched around outside the house. One of them noticed the cellar door and asked if meat and potatoes were stored there. Randolph told him that only the master's whiskey was left in there, and that no one was allowed to enter. The other two heard what he said and rushed forward. When they couldn't break the lock, they shot it off. They brought jugs outside and sat in the sun drinking."

Again she stopped talking.

"Continue." He straightened his tall frame, and frowned.

"I had hoped that the 'bummers'," she viciously spat out the word, "would take the whiskey and go back to camp. Or, if they spent time drinking, they would soon realize they must start back to their unit before dark. Instead they stayed, and as the afternoon wore on, they became more boisterous. There was a great deal of loud laughter, profanity and obscenity."

"You provided the whiskey for them, Miss Heyward," his voice accusatory. "What did you expect?"

She ignored his sarcasm.

"A young heifer with calf was penned in the stable. In the afternoon Randolph was to take them to graze down in the pocosin... the swampland on our plantation." She paused.

"I know the word. Please go on."

"The heifer began lowing and the men grew increasingly annoyed. They determined that it was too late to walk her back to their encampment and too much trouble to butcher her here. In their drunken stupor they decided to burn the stables. Our last remaining horse was also in there... as well as the buggy, the big wagon and our farm implements. The men staggered across the lot and began pulling down hay from the loft."

Tears started to course down her pale cheeks.

He looked away until she could regain her composure. For a moment he watched the sergeant examine a two-wheeled cart in a shed beyond the stable site. Kelly was questioning the boy. The major's glance, cold and unreadable, shifted back to Ellen.

"Dusk was falling. I smelled smoke. There was a great deal of noise and confusion." Her voice was low and controlled. "We... I couldn't let them burn the cattle and horse. We did not want to lose our stables. I ran out of the house to try to stop them. There was shouting and gunfire. More men on horses arrived. Additional shots were fired. It was still light enough for me to recognize Confederate uniforms... three, perhaps four men. I... they..." Her face contorted with pain as she recalled details of the afternoon.

"Were there injuries?" he prompted.

"A bummer grabbed me. We were struggling. The others attempted to run for their horses. The stables were ablaze. By this time our people were coming in from the fields. I'm not certain exactly what happened next. I tried to save our animals. Several men were down… drunk, wounded, dead. I can't say. They fought… they all rode off, or were carried away. I don't know who was in pursuit of whom. The field hands and I were busy trying to control the fire." Resentment and hatred were clear in her tear-choked voice. "That is the story."

Arledge stepped up on the verandah, closing the distance between them. Towering over her, he blatantly studied her face. She was younger than she had at first appeared, and prettier, a high-cheeked, fine-boned aristocrat, and under thirty, perhaps.

"Which direction did the men take when they left?"

"I don't know. South, I assume. I wasn't looking, and except for the light of the fire, it had grown dark."

"Who lives that way?" He pointed east, toward Columbia.

"About a mile down you'll find a small cabin. Adam Heyward, a free Negro lives there. My father gave him his house and some land many years ago. Beyond Uncle Adam's there is timber and swampland for about four miles until you reach the Goodwyn land."

Arledge unbuttoned the wool flap on his uniform blouse and withdrew a small notebook. He checked notes recorded on a page.

"Don't bother to go there," she hastily added. "No one is at home. The men are in the army and the ladies are in Columbia for the duration of the war." She recited the facts woodenly. "And I have been told that just beyond there is the first enemy encampment in the area. Yours, I presume, in advance of the glorious main army."

The major bypassed her scorn and forged ahead.

"You said that shots were fired, men hit. Which army? Were any of them killed?"

"I can't say. Men from both sides were wounded, I think. I wasn't concerned with the fighting. We were busy with the fire."

"What about bodies?"

"There are none here, if that is your question."

"You said 'we'. Who else was present?"

Ellen felt her blood start to freeze. He must not learn about Pam's involvement. "Aunt Mariah, Randolph... some of the field hands."

"You said 'We ran out of the house', I believe."

"Did I? Perhaps. My sister Pamela is here, but she stayed inside. She is young... and not well, as I told you earlier."

"What is the age of your sister?"

"She's a child."

"Exactly how old?" he persisted.

Ellen hesitated, then snapped angrily, "Fourteen years old, though I fail to see why that should be of interest to you."

A sardonic smile darkened the major's handsome face. "In an investigation, Miss Heyward, you never know what information may later prove to be important. Am I to understand that the two of you live here alone?"

"Certainly not! An aunt lives with us... and we have a number of former slaves who have chosen to remain here."

"May I ask your aunt's name?"

"Mariah Heyward." She set her chin stubbornly.

The jingle of spurs halted further inquiry. Wearing a noncommittal expression, Kelly strode up.

"Evening, Mam," he dipped his slightly grizzled head.

"Do you have questions for the lady, Sergeant?"

"Yes, sir. I want to know about the dark stains in the cart under the shed. Could be blood. What's the cart used for, Mam?"

His eyes narrowed suspiciously.

"For chores about the plantation," Ellen replied calmly.

"Why is it so clean?" He turned his head toward Arledge. "It has been scrubbed lately, Major."

"Your people burned our buggy," she reminded the two with haughty contempt. "The cart had to be cleaned. It's now our only means of transportation."

The older man nodded solemnly. "And that red mule in the pasture, is he yours?"

"No, but he appears to be an ordinary mule. There are several like him in the community. He wandered in several days ago. I had Randolph put him in the pasture. I intend to work him in return for his feed and care until someone claims him."

"Looks to me like one that left with that group of foragers."

"Perhaps it is, but wouldn't an army mule be branded?"

Arledge was watching the exchange. The slight squint in his sharp eyes indicated that he was taking note of Ellen's quick responses and her constant struggle to show no signs of fear.

"No, Mam, not necessarily. Lately there's been a lot of real hasty requisitioning," Kelly answered dryly. "Could be anybody's mule. I guess that's all for now, Major," he added, preparing to mount.

Ellen could feel the officer's penetrating gaze still on her face. His cool observant eyes reflected dissatisfaction with her story. There was a hint of something more. Provocation? Suspicion? Grudging admiration?

"Miss Heyward, your losses are unfortunate."

She greeted his remark with proud disdain. "May I expect to receive reparations?"

"That is unlikely. Your providing whiskey for the men was most unwise. I shall need to trouble you again. I want to talk with your sister. When may I see her?" He would not be evaded.

Years of plantation responsibility and authority had taught Ellen to be assertive. "That is entirely unnecessary, sir. Pamela is a child. She can add nothing to what I've told you. I consider this interrogation to be concluded. You may not...."

"Miss Heyward," he interrupted sharply, "we are not having an idle drawing room conversation. I have told you that

General Sherman personally ordered this investigation. I can further assure you that both he and General Hampton consider this to be a very serious matter. I intend to uncover the truth. Now, with or without your permission, I must question your sister. What is the nature of her illness?"

She stared at him with lethal calmness. "She suffers from what we all suffer from here... fear, loneliness, despair, cold, lack of proper food and medicine. We think she may have influenza. We pray that it isn't pneumonia. I cannot allow you to disturb her."

He saw wariness in her face, heard a slight tremor in her voice. He moved closer. "Are you afraid of me, Miss Heyward, and of what I might learn?" he asked softly.

"Should I be?" she countered smoothly. Though she felt threatened by his nearness and the male strength of him, she lifted her head and looked boldly up into his face.

His height was intimidating. His broad shoulders, the long, lean look of him, the alien blue of the uniform, they were all unsettling. She endured his inspection, feeling his gaze linger on her trembling lips, sweep boldly down her body and return to her frightened face. No gentleman, this one. She refused to flinch.

"Perhaps you should be." His voice was low, almost sensual.

Suddenly breathless, Ellen stepped back. Arledge hastily reached forward to steady her. Feeling her pulse quicken, Ellen shrugged away from his hands.

"Don't you dare touch me, sir," she commanded fiercely.

"No, Mam." The remark sounded courteous, faintly patronizing. "You looked as if you might need help," he explained. "I should have known better."

"Help from a Yankee soldier? Not likely! A southern turncoat one at that, I suspect," Ellen lashed out, furious that he had the power to upset her.

A muscle tensed in his jaw. He visibly stiffened, wheeled around and strode to his horse. "You can expect to see me again very soon, Miss Heyward."

Everything about Arledge's set features suggested bridled anger. He spoke with quiet authority, a man accustomed to issuing commands and expecting them to be obeyed unquestioningly.

Ellen remained on the verandah for a long while watching the retreating backs of the two men, one narrow and slightly rounded, the other broad and ramrod straight. Alarming thoughts raced though her mind. Did he know more than he had revealed? Had she been careless and contradicted herself? If the Yankee major had been less authoritative, less confident, less observant, less intelligent... or less handsome, perhaps she might have lied more convincingly.

At the far end of the shadow-draped lane Arledge paused to look back. He lifted his black hat and nodded toward her in mock salute before again proceeding.

After the men were out of sight Ellen sank down to the cold brick steps. For the first time she began to weep with complete abandon, head down on her knees. The horror and despair she had denied for the past week engulfed her. When her breath no longer came in anguished gasps, she looked up to find Randolph quietly observing her.

"Miss Ellen, how come you crying? Them soldiers hurt you?"

"No," she replied steadily. "I feared they might burn our house." He would believe her. "Is Benjamin in from the fields?"

"Not yet, but he's coming," the boy answered. "Crossed the back pasture a little while ago."

Ellen stood up, smoothed the wrinkles from her faded dress and, with the backs of her hands, wearily wiped the last traces of tears from her face. She must check on the cattle. Benjamin had to be warned that the Yankees might be asking him questions.

Two

Light rays filtered through the window panes and bounced weakly against the washstand mirror in Ellen Heyward's frigid bedroom. Buried deep in a feather bed, she lay sleepless. Two days had passed; the Yankee major had not returned. If he didn't come today, they could get away. Pam was well enough to travel.

The war news was bleak. Word had come from the Taylor plantation that Sherman's main army was meeting little resistance moving up from Georgia. Hardeeville, Barnwell and Blackville had all fallen. The state seemed prostrate at the Union general's feet.

Discouraged and heartsick Ellen threw back the heavy quilts, removed her flannel nightgown and pulled on a yellowing pair of men's woolen underwear. She poured cold water from a china pitcher into the matching bowl. Would she ever again awaken to crackling fire, kettles of warm bath water and a real cup of hot coffee?

After a few quick splashes she donned two petticoats, layered on one of her mother's frocks, and was dressed. She and her sister were fortunate that old family clothing had been packed away in the trunk room. She stooped to lace on sturdy, flat-heeled shoes, the kind no lady would wear, and shuddered to think what her mother would have said about her appearance.

Ellen brushed back her hair and secured it in a net, hiding soft waves that glinted brown in the growing sunlight. Before

the mirror she noted that winter pallor had faded the sprinkling of freckles on her nose. Worked better than buttermilk!
Tiny wrinkle lines were beginning to gather at the corners of
her eyes. Her lips were cracked and peeling. Despair and drudg-
ery were taking their toll, but what did it matter how she looked?

She turned, walked across the room to the hall and started
down the graceful curving stairway. Descending past the old
portraits of unsmiling ancestors arranged along the wall always gave her the illusion of stepping into another era. She
paused before Grandmother Jayne's likeness to wish again that
she had the lady's legendary strength. She also lacked her
grandmother's charm and beauty.

I am responsible for my sister, for this plantation and for
more than twenty black people, she thought. With no money
for supplies and no hope for the future, how in heaven's name
will I manage? She closed her eyes, silently praying for courage. Then, with shoulders resolutely squared, Ellen went down
the remaining stairs to the kitchen at the rear of the house. The
almost forgotten odor of frying ham filled the air.

"Aunt Mariah," she exclaimed, "what are you cooking! It
smells like decent food. Surely I am dreaming."

"This some good meat I been saving." A broad smile sliced
the ebony face. "I thought ham and eggs this morning might
pick up Miss Pam. That child losing all her strength. She got to
get up and get out of her room. It's been a week. What's done
is done. Fretting ain't going to change nothing. Us got to face
that."

Ellen's sigh was deep. "When will she begin to recover?
You don't suppose that... Surely God will be more merciful!"

"No, mam, Miss Ellen. She ain't going to have no baby. She
be all right. Miss Pam a fighter. She going to get over it."

"We have to leave for Columbia tomorrow. We can stay
with Aunt Sophie until the Union army moves past — we'll be

safer there with other women and children. I want you and Randolph to go with us."

"You know I ain't going to let you all go no where without me. I been looking after you since the day you was born." She slammed the iron skillet down on the stove indignantly. "Go off by yourself! Two girls! I never heard of such."

Ellen dropped a quick kiss on the old lady's cheek. "How would we ever do without you?"

"Miss Pam going to be better before long, honey," the old lady comforted. "The body, it heals. Heals whether you want it to or not. The mind sometimes heals more slow-like, but it heals. Forgets, too. Good thing for womenfolks it does," she muttered. "We all got plenty we just as soon not remember. Now sit yourself down and eat."

"We have a lot to do today."

Aunt Mariah looked up at Ellen. Worry and weariness were apparent in her drawn face.

"We sure do, honey, and we going to get that little girl upstairs stirring and busy. I'm going up there right now and tell her you need her help. Her Papa depending on you two."

Ellen stared at the plate of breakfast. The pungent aroma of smoked ham made her feel vaguely nauseated. It had been so long. She hoped her father would have a decent breakfast this morning. Countless men and boys would go hungry today.

Unlike most southern women, Ellen admitted to herself that the Confederacy lay dying. That glory year, May 1862 until May of '63, the high water mark, had ended. Glowing memories of the great victories in the Shenandoah Valley, around Richmond and at Fredericksburg, and First and Second Bull Run had long ago faded.

Antietam, where nearly twelve thousand men on each side were killed, had made the horrors of war soberingly clear. Alexander Gardner's stark pictures of the battlefield dead, so widely circulated by Matthew Brady, had made the carnage agonizingly real, even to firebrand non-combatants. Since that terrible day at Antietam war news for the south had rarely been encouraging.

Ellen ate the food and rose to prepare a breakfast tray for her sister. A camellia might cheer Pam. While Aunt Mariah scrambled an egg, Ellen went outside to the flower garden and cut a Jarvis bloom, velvet red and still luminous with morning dew.

"I done been up and told her today's the day she's getting out of that room," Aunt Mariah announced as Ellen returned.

"And what did she say?"

"She didn't say nothing, but she knows I mean business." Ellen placed the flower beside a delicate china cup and saucer, hoping it might convey the love and concern they were feeling. She grimaced as she filled the cup with the disgusting drink made from parched acorns they were reduced to drinking. At least acorns made better tasting coffee than burned peanuts. She covered the tray with a napkin and carried it up the stairway.

There was no reply to her insistent tap on Pam's door. She turned the knob and entered. "You must get out today, Pam."

"Yes, Ellen," she answered, voice hollow and lifeless.

"I brought your breakfast. It smells heavenly."

"Thank you, but I can't eat. I'm not hungry." One hand plucked listlessly at the bed covers. Dark circles ringed her eyes. "Aunt Mariah has already been up and issued my orders."

Ellen placed the tray on a small table near the bed and looked down at her sister's pale pinched face. The bruises on her cheek were fading to greenish yellow.

"Good. Sit up, Pam, and I'll put a pillow at your back."

The girl quietly complied. Bed covers fell back revealing, beneath the flannel nightdress, the slender form of a mature young woman. Soft ash blond hair trailed down her back. Like a wooden doll, Pam waited while Ellen arranged the pillow and then tucked the quilts securely around her.

"Pull the collar of your gown high around your neck. It's cold this morning. I'll light a fire while you eat. We have a million things to do and I need your help." Though she spoke quietly, her manner was firm and matter-of-fact.

Pamela took the tray, placed it on her lap and lifted the cup for a cautious sip of the brown liquid.

"We can't continue to stay at the plantation. Tomorrow we are going to Columbia and visit Aunt Sophie for a while."

The younger girl recoiled. "Must we go?"

"Yes. We must. That would be Father's wish." Ellen's pronouncement was deliberate and unequivocal. She knew she sounded harsh. She had to find a way to rouse her sister.

"Tell me what to do." A strange response, for resigned acceptance was not Pam's habit.

"First, we have to figure ways to secure our valuables. I'd like you to tell Benjamin exactly how to care for the cattle. You know more about them than I do. Pack whatever clothing you will need."

"Oh, Ellen, no," Pam begged. "I can't go to Aunt Sophie's. Let the damn Yankees come. What worse can they do? Why didn't you let them kill me?" Sobs began to shake her frail body.

Ellen took the weeping girl in her arms.

"Hush, Pam. You are strong and you're brave. You must have courage. Father is depending on us."

"Ellen, I saw you with the pistol," she whispered shakily. "Did you kill the men?"

"Of course not!" Ellen protested with more vehemence than certainty. "I intended to. I shot, but one of the scurvy brutes knocked me down before I could take careful aim."

"I remember so much gunfire. Who was doing the shooting?"

"I was… and some Confederate scouts. A reconnoitering party came. They spotted the smoke rising from the stables. When they saw me struggling with the bummers they began firing."

"I can't remember much after the two men pulled me to the ground and began tearing at my clothes." Pam's voice trembled.

"One of the Yankees had struck you so hard you were unconscious. Benjamin ran up from the pasture. He and I carried you back to the house. It was dusk, almost dark."

"I keep remembering noise, so much noise."

"The hands were coming in from the fields. The Confederates started shooting. When the bummers saw them, they scrambled for their horses. Some of them were probably taken prisoner or killed. Soldiers of both armies were firing. The barn was burning, the animals were screaming, and everybody was shouting."

"How did you and I suddenly become part of the war?"

"I don't know. Pam. Our area is a no-man's-land now. Small forward parties of the Union army started arriving a week ago. Remnants of Confederate units are still around. The ones who came here saved our lives... but they didn't know about you."

Ellen feared her voice lacked conviction. She was fiercely determined to protect her sister.

"But I know about me." Pamela fought for self-control.

"Pam, that rabble cannot be allowed to affect our lives. You are eighteen years old, a young woman. We won't dwell on this incident. We are both alive. We still have a house to live in. Starting right now we are putting it all behind us."

"How? Awake or asleep I still smell those awful men... and feel their filthy hands on me... How can I go on living?" She covered her face with her hands. Tears slipped through her trembling fingers and dropped unnoticed on the bright patchwork quilt wrapped around her.

"Pam, we have no time for this." Ellen's voice was deliberately stern. "I should have stayed with you instead of coming back inside for the pistol. I failed to protect you."

"Don't blame yourself, Ellen, please."

"That band of scum is not going to defeat us, Pam." Each word was deliberately emphasized. "Do you hear me?"

"You sound like mother." Pam's smile was feeble. She picked up the fork and began trying to eat.

Ellen watched her sister's brave efforts to choke down the breakfast. Turning to the fireplace she knelt to kindle a blaze, continuing to talk as she arranged the lightwood splinters.

"This is our story. Yankees were here to steal food. They burned our stables. Confederate soldiers chased them away. That is all we know. We will tell Aunt Sophie that and nothing more."

Pam nodded mutely.

"I have another task for you. Pack the family china in burlap bags. Get Benjamin to help you take it to the swamp. Lower the sacks in the water and fasten them to stumps. The mud can't hurt the dishes and that's the best way I know to hide them. Don't let anyone else see what you're doing."

Ellen dusted her hands together and then wiped them on the sides of her skirt. She looked back to make sure her sister was following all she had said. Pam appeared to be listening.

"I don't mean to be ordering you about," Ellen's voice was husky, "but I need your help today."

"Give me instructions. Keep me busy, Ellen. I don't want time to think."

Her automaton manner of speaking was heart-wrenching.

"Use the farm cart to move the china. Cover the sacks with straw before you leave the house. Tell Benjamin we may have to stay in Columbia a while, and warn him to keep the cattle in the back pasture until we return. They must not be where they can be seen or heard from the road. Even if Sherman's main army doesn't pass by here, foraging parties and deserters might."

The fire began to crackle. Ellen stretched out her hands to warm. "There is sunshine today. We can hang laundry outside and wash our hair. Have everything ready. We will leave to-morrow at first light. In the farm cart we can't carry much or move fast."

Pam forced a watery smile. "It's into father's drawers for a hard day's work, I guess." She threw back the bed cover, rose and walked unsteadily to stand by the growing warmth of the fire.

Ellen gave her a fierce hug.

"There's something else," she warned. "Two Union soldiers were here last Wednesday investigating the disappearance of their foragers. I told them the men came here, searched our cellar, stole whiskey and set fire to the stables… and, that there was a skirmish with a Confederate patrol which came to our rescue."

"Yankees back here again!" she gasped. "What will we do?"

"Behave the way all women are expected to," bridled anger heightened Ellen's voice, "flee to safety with older relatives."

"Some protection Aunt Sophie will be. Probably offer us smelling salts." Her forced laugh sounded more like a sob.

"Yes, I expect we'll be looking after her, but it's the right thing to do." Ellen moved toward the door. "Pam, the men who came asking questions were very persistent. I was forced to tell them I have a sister. I insisted that you are a child, and because of illness, know little about the incident."

"Were the men satisfied with your answers?"

Ellen frowned and shrugged her shoulders. "Not entirely. The officer threatened to return. He says he must question you."

"Is that why we are running?"

"Partly. If he does come back, we'll reveal as little as possible. He said that this investigation is important… a feud of some kind between Sherman and General Hampton. While he was talking to me the other man questioned Randolph. I don't know what the boy might have said."

"Not much, I'm sure. Randolph's not a talker." A slight smile tilted the corners of the young girl's mouth. Randolph practiced word economy to an annoying degree.

"Thank heaven for small blessings! I hope we get away before the man returns." Ellen closed the door as she left.

Pam started dressing, then crossed the room to the long pier glass mirror. She stared at herself with apparent loathing... soft body, fragile. Reaching for her mother's sewing basket, she took out scissors. One by one she lifted the long coils of shining hair and snipped. Task completed, she shoved the remaining short stubble behind her ears and trimmed girlish bangs across her forehead.

By early afternoon most of the work was completed. Ellen sat in the sunshine on one of the wide brick steps that spanned the length of the front verandah. She had unbuttoned her dress at the neck and turned the collar inside. With forehead on her knees and her long hair spread forward to dry, she allowed the sun's heat to soothe her tired shoulder muscles.

She reviewed the morning's work. The flat silver had been wrapped, taken to the cellar and buried beneath stacks of empty glass jars. In past years the jars were always filled with canned fruits and vegetables. Silver bowls, trays and candlesticks she had taken outside, knowing that if the house was burned, heat would ruin these pieces.

The soil in the flower bed was sandy loam and the garden spade sharp. Working alone, she had buried the family heirlooms. Task completed and hole refilled with dirt, she gathered oak leaves and pine straw to cover over the freshly dug earth.

In former days her mother and grandmother had reigned over the silver pot with queenly elegance. Southerners drank coffee, never tea, a habit dating to before the Revolution, when tea drinking was denounced. North Carolina's Edenton Tea Party predated the more famous Boston one.

Ellen was usually a misfit at social gatherings. She had never been overly concerned about the fact. Her mother repeatedly warned, "Young ladies never take part in political discussions. They do not have heated opinions, and they certainly do not disagree with men."

"Horse feathers," she usually replied, "who cares! Men only want admiration and submission from women. They certainly won't get that from me."

Five years ago she had dutifully tried to bite her tongue and stay aloof from the talk of secession. She was rarely successful. Eligible young bachelors, boasting about the certainty of a quick decisive war, were not attracted to women who coldly reminded them of the scarcity of gun and ammunition factories in the south.

"No one wants to have you tell them that shoe companies and textile mills are more important in winning a war than brilliant leadership and inflammatory rhetoric," her father had said, and he was right. She did come across to others as disagreeable and unpleasant. Her father did not attend any of the secession meetings. He, too, had not favored the cause, but after Fort Sumter was fired on, he volunteered.

Now, at twenty-seven, Ellen was, by all local standards, at least eight years beyond marriageable age. Worse, she was known to be outspoken, independent and headstrong, each quality was one not likely to endear her to any of the neighborhood swains. That mattered little to her, for none of the men she knew had stirred her interest. Nor, she ruefully reminded herself, had she been aggressively pursued by any of them, once they began to know her. Perhaps it was just as well. Most southern women her age were now widows.

She thought again of the bold Yankee major. His confident manner and air of sophisticated worldliness were unsettling. Where was his wife? How many broken-hearted women had he left strewn behind? His searching gaze had stirred uneasy feelings.

"Are you afraid of me?" he had asked.

Absolutely! That fear was causing her to seek sanctuary in Columbia. She dared not face his cold scrutiny again. To dismiss disturbing thoughts, she forced herself to concentrate on the matters at hand. She must be well prepared for tomorrow.

Earlier she had caught a glimpse of Willie lurking near the slave cabins. Willie was one of the few of their blacks whom she disliked and distrusted. How much had he seen? He was skilled at instigating trouble and having others bear the blame.

"What are you doing back here, Willie?" she had called out.

"I done come home," he whined. "I can't find work nowhere. I got hungry and cold. I want to stay here on the plantation with you all, Miss Ellen. Please, can I come back?"

In early 1863, at the first news of Lincoln's Emancipation Proclamation, Willie had left Oak Lane. A few others followed, but having never known any home except the Heyward plantation, most of their people had returned. Of late, Willie had been seen slipping in and out of the slave quarters at nightfall.

"You weren't here last spring when we wanted you to help with the planting. We don't need you now. There's hardly enough food to go around as it is. I intend for the people who have worked and been loyal to get what little we have."

"What done happen to the stables?" He slyly changed the subject.

"As you can see, there was a fire."

"How come you out here digging with that shovel, getting your hands all dirty?"

"We can't spare anyone for yard work now." She cast about for a more plausible reason. "I have been looking in the rubble for anything still usable... hammer heads, axes, chisels... iron things that we can repair. Big John can put in new wooden handles. We need the tools."

"Let me help you."

"No thank you, Willie." Her voice was firm. "I think I have looked thoroughly. Go to the kitchen and see if Aunt Mariah had some hominy left. After you eat, I expect you to leave."

"Yes, mam. Thank you, mam."

She heard resentment, rather than gratitude in his reply.

The whole family had despised his sly, ingratiating manner. Ellen hoped that what she feared was craftiness in Willie was really shiftlessness and density. She watched until he disappeared behind the shrubbery at the rear of the house.

The cart was back in its place in the nearby shed. That meant that Pam and Benjamin were finished hiding the china. From the height of the sun, she could tell that it was past noon. Dinner, once a lavish mid-day spread was so monotonous and meager anymore it was hardly worth the effort of appearing at the table.

After Willie left she had gone to the kitchen well in the side yard and turned the creaking wheel to draw water. She knew that drinking water helped dull hunger pangs. She had taken a long, cold drink from the metal bucket, another act her mother strongly disapproved. When she poured the remainder of the water over her dirty hands the February wind blowing on the icy dampness sent her scurrying inside to the warmth of the big kitchen.

"Come in here, child. Your dinner been waiting. What you doing out there at the well freezing your little self?" Aunt Mariah's scolding words were always filled with loving concern.

"Just washing up for dinner."

"You better eat your food. Both you girls ain't nothing but skin and bones. If I can't get no meat on you, I ain't never going to get you no husbands. I promise your mama I look after you. All the young men done gone off getting themselves killed. Ain't nobody having parties no more, and people don't hardly even go to church now. I don't know what this world is coming to."

While she worked Aunt Mariah usually muttered aloud to no one in particular. "I can't get me no sugar. If I had some sugar I'd cook up a mess of cakes and pies fair bug your eyes out. I bet you all would eat them." As the old woman grumbled she doled out small servings of dried peas and collard greens on a plate, then added a hot square of cornbread.

"Thank you, Aunt Mariah. Looks good. You are a wonder." Ellen tried to voice her love and appreciation. "Did Pam eat?"

"That baby come in a little while ago. She eat like a bird. Look like death warmed over, but she got her work done. Said she was going to wash her hair and then rest some."

"Do you think she's better?"

"Some. She trying and that's good. She done mess up her hair though."

"What do you mean?" Ellen became instantly alert.

"Chop it all off. She looks a sight."

Ellen felt her eyes fill with unshed tears. She put another kettle on the stove so there would be enough warm rinse water for her hair and sat down to eat. Since their father left for the army, she and Pam ate most of their meals in the kitchen.

Later, work done and hair washed, Ellen sat on the front steps in a relaxed haze. She stirred restlessly and tried to shift her thoughts to the present. Sheltered from the wind, the warmth of the sun penetrated her clothing. She was beginning to feel drowsy.

Sounds of the hands at work drifted up from the nearby woods. She could hear a tree being felled and the chopping noises as axes split firewood. The occasional muffled lowing of cattle assured her that the herd had been moved deep into the swamp.

She turned her head to the side and idly watched several black children as they played in the lane leading to the slave quarters. The pine boughs stirring overhead smelled fresh and clean. Her ears picked up the steady hoof-beats of an approaching horse. Had a trace broken she wondered, or did one of the hands finish work early today?

She continued to listen as the sounds drew nearer and then stopped. The noise must have come from the front of the house instead of the side. She lifted her head. Her stomach knotted with fear. Less than twenty feet away stood the Yankee major.

Everything about him projected raw virility.

She tossed back her hair and sprang up with a start. There was no time to escape. She hastily fastened the top buttons of her dress and rolled down the sleeves. Embarrassed, she could feel her cheeks reddening like a school girl's.

"A gentleman would not approach unannounced," she snapped.

A slight smile hovered about his mouth. His probing glance assessed her, sweeping up her body, lingering for several long moments on her flushed face and locking into her hazel-eyed glare. He tethered his horse to the iron hitching post.

Ellen watched as his hard, lean legs moved with animal grace toward her. He approached silently, walking leisurely between the ancient green boxwoods that lined the front pathway. Confident and assured, he reminded her of a strong mountain lion stalking helpless prey.

She refused to show fear.

"I didn't wish to startle you, Miss Heyward." His voice was low, his tone too familiar. "I waited quietly until you became aware of my presence. As the enemy, I hardly expected to be made welcome, but I don't believe I have done anything particularly offensive yet."

Ellen felt violated by his bold look. Her pulse began to beat erratically. She made no attempt to smooth her hair or further improve her unsightly appearance. To face him again was unsettling. He knew he had caught her unaware.

"Don't feign shocked surprise, please. I told you that I would be returning."

The insolent familiarity was infuriating. "Why did you approach so stealthily... and alone?"

"The element of surprise is often of benefit in my work. I find that I uncover," his voice seemed to drop suggestively, "some fascinating information at unexpected times and places."

She itched to slap his insolent face.

"For instance, Miss Heyward, the story you told me is most intriguing. Or is misleading a better word?" Again the bold stare made her feel uncomfortable. "As for alone, Kelly will be here shortly. He's asking questions in the neighborhood."

Neighborhood? At Adam Heyward's place? Uncle Adam would never betray her. Down in the slave quarters? She would have seen the sergeant pass. How much did the two of them know?

"What further questions could you possibly have to ask me?"

"Many. Are you an enemy spy? Or worse, a murderess?"

He was standing too near. His presence so dominated the space that breathing had become difficult. No man she had known in the past had ever crowded her. Barbed words had always made them recoil.

"On what do you base such outrageous speculation? I certainly hope," she spaced her words evenly, emphasizing each one, "you don't think I am a simple-minded maiden easily intimidated by your magnificent presence."

"No, mam, not guilty." The slight rumble in his broad chest seemed to indicate that he was amused.

She was not.

"You behave as though you've had wide experience with women, Major. I'm sure you realize that I'm no match for your sophisticated sarcasm."

"On the contrary, you seem to cope rather well, Miss Heyward," he countered pleasantly. "I've known many southern women. I have always found them more than resourceful where men are concerned, and especially adept at repartee."

"Now I presume that you have switched to the charming man-of-the-world approach. What has happened to your campaign of terrorizing helpless women?"

His low chuckle was not what she had expected. "A frightened innocent, are you? Not very convincing."

Inexperienced she might be, but Ellen recognized arrogant male self-assurance. She would try a different tack. "You said your name is Arledge, Major. Surely you are not one of the northern Virginia Arledges?"

His quick look told her she had caught him by surprise.

"I've heard that South Carolinians know a person's origin as soon as they hear the family name."

She had struck a nerve.

"Yes. We've made it into a science. Dare I ask why the northern uniform?"

Let him deal with difficult questions for a while.

"I believe that I am the one asking the questions, Miss Heyward." The fierce blue of his eyes had turned to ice.

She waited, heartbeat still irregular.

There was an awkward silence.

"Few people have had the nerve to ask me that question for a long time." The words were ground out between clenched teeth.

"Is it a question you can't answer?" she taunted softly.

"I'm not sure why I should bother to reply… but I shall. Yes, I'm a Virginian. My family's land is in the Shenandoah Valley. Our rolling hills and grassy meadows are very different from your Carolina fields." He looked briefly across the flat, weed-infested cotton land and pastures bordering the house and then back at her. "I had little interest in raising livestock or becoming a gentleman farmer." His voice trailed off, as if searching for words.

This tall, threatening stranger seemed different when he spoke of home. Without seeking permission, he had walked up to the step below her and was standing only a few feet away.

"Naturally my parents were disappointed," he continued, "but I have a younger brother who has more affinity for the land. He was more settled... a disciplined man. I entered the university to study law and later had the opportunity to attend West Point. By that time I was ready for more adventure than the classroom provided."

"So you decided to make the army a career?" Using woman's time-worn strategy, she encouraged him to talk about himself.

His knowing half-smile told her he recognized her ploy.

"No, not immediately, but soon much to everyone's surprise, my own included, I adapted to the routine and rigor of the military. I was assigned to the western campaign and I liked the challenge of frontier life."

For an unguarded moment the inscrutable mask fell from his face. In a gray uniform he would likely be the dashing kind of man whom she might foolishly have let break her heart. Ellen dismissed the ridiculous thought and looked away.

"And so," he leaned casually against one of the tall column posts, "ten years passed. I was isolated from the political talk back east. I had no strong feelings about state's rights. I thought it was a damn fool notion for Southerners to think they were equipped to win a war. A decade earlier I might have rushed out to swagger about with the most hot-headed of the firebrands. Older and far removed from the scene, I was able to see the folly of it all." He straightened, indicating that the subject was closed.

Ellen bristled at his detached analysis, but she made no comment. She had often voiced similar thoughts.

"The legal training has brought me varied assignments. I served, for a long while, on General Grant's staff. I am currently attached to General Sherman, at his personal request. Both men are excellent soldiers, tough but skilled. They believe my southern background can be of some assistance in the tangled negotiations going on now concerning the treatment of prisoners of war... and the acts of hostile civilians."

"I have heard rumors of General Sheridan's harsh treatment of the Shenandoah area. Are you not concerned about your home?"

"I am concerned."

"And it gives you no problem... serving the Union, I mean?" She persisted in her assault.

"You seem to brand me a traitor," his low voice was deadly calm. "I'm a citizen of the United States... all of them. You must know that the war is nearly over. The Confederacy has bled itself to death. I expect to be involved in peace negotiations. And later in the military occupation of the southern states, that will likely follow. I believe I can function well in that capacity."

"Occupation! Surely that won't happen." She was aghast.

"Of course it will," he asserted, studying her face, "and in South Carolina it will probably last quite a while."

Ellen had not considered this possibility.

"I serve both my country and my heritage honorably. I am not the only man from the south in the Union army, Miss Heyward, nor," he took a deep breath, "the only soldier with a brother fighting on the opposite side."

Seeing raw pain in his eyes, Ellen began to sense the depth of his personal struggles.

"And you can't begin to imagine how the West Point men I was in school with are torn asunder. I have good friends serving on both sides, but I am sure that, ultimately, I'll be of greater service to my country wearing a blue uniform than a gray one."

He could deny conflicting emotions, she observed, but he could not bury them.

"And so, despite our personal differences, I hope you won't have occasion to question my patriotism again." His grim visage told Ellen that he rarely felt it necessary to explain himself.

"Do you not find your present assignment difficult?"

"A soldier's life is always difficult," he answered dryly. "That's part of the challenge. But, as to my present assignment," he shifted his gaze back to her face, "it's by far the most interesting one I've had lately."

"Am I to understand that you are here to arrest me?"

"Possibly. What crimes have you committed?"

The glint in his eye, was it a threat? Mischief, perhaps or amusement?

"Am I expected to make some kind of confession? I repeat, foragers came here and burned our stables. A Confederate patrol chased them off and possibly took them as prisoners. There were likely casualties on both sides. I was too busy trying to save our livestock, our buildings… and my own life, incidentally, to know exactly what happened between the soldiers."

"There are discrepancies between what you have told me and what I know to be true."

"I find that hard to believe," she declared firmly, thoughts racing madly back to their first meeting. Had she slipped up?

"First, you are reported to have had a pistol."

Oh, God, by whom? Randolph must have told the sergeant.

"Did you kill those men? What did you do with the bodies?"

Ellen turned a frightened face away from him. "Why do you think the men are dead? Perhaps they are deserters."

"I have considered that possibility... and others," he courteously agreed. "However, their horses returned to camp. The men are not among our injured, nor have they been reported captured. Were they in uniform?"

"I'm not sure. Uniforms are such a mottled assortment now, it's difficult to know. They may have been renegades instead of soldiers, but they clearly were here to rob us. I know that Sherman's bummers have been to the neighboring plantations."

"And your rescuers? Were they uniformed?"

"Yes, one of them, a lieutenant, wore a recognizable uniform. It was growing dark. Why are you asking me this?"

"Because, Miss Heyward, you referred to the men as scouts. Although the forward groups of Union soldiers may technically be behind enemy lines, the Confederates are withdrawing. We regard this area as captured territory. Your so-called scouts can be shot as spies if they were out of uniform... and so can any or all accomplices who committed hostile acts."

Ellen shook her head in disagreement. "No. Who is in control of this area is arguable. Men from both armies are present and no decisive battle has been fought. You overstep your bounds, sir."

"The Union army is definitely here and in control." He was explicit. "You are being evasive. Three Union soldiers on an army mission have disappeared. The trail leads here. Your people do not fully support the story you tell. Civilians are not supposed to be armed. I shall have to examine the weapon you had at the time of the incident."

"Incident? What an insipid word! Atrocity, assault, or arson are all more accurate. My father left a pistol with me for our protection. I'll get it. And, Major, please include this statement in your official report 'though the lady was clearly affronted, she was cooperative'."

"First, there are a few more matters to settle. Why did you indicate that your aunt lives with you when Mariah Heyward is, in fact, one of the household slaves?"

"Surely," outraged dignity in her voice, "you understand my position. After what we've already suffered at the hands of Union soldiers, I had no wish for you to know that my sister and I are here alone."

"Why are you alone? Where are your parents, your brothers, the men in your life?" He stared pointedly at her left hand, noting the absence of a wedding band.

"Father volunteered as soon as war was declared, but he was both over age and frail."

"And did the Confederacy accept him?" As he talked Arledge unconsciously fingered the brim of the big slouch hat he was holding. There was a tan line across the top of his forehead.

"Not until two years ago. He was a student at the Medical College when he and mother married. He is serving as a doctor. My sister and I run the plantation. We have no brothers."

He nodded, not surprised at what she had told him.

"My mother manages our place alone, too. I've always admired the courage and stamina of southern women."

Ellen sensed sincerity. She steeled herself against softening toward him. "I believe my father may be back in this area. General Beauregard's men still hold Columbia, don't they?"

"Are you asking for information or giving it?" He quirked a dark eyebrow.

"Sorry, I did not consider that. I'm only concerned about my father's health and safety."

"Miss Heyward, if you have relatives or friends in Columbia I strongly suggest that you and your sister join them. If you were my..." he hesitated, "sister, I would want you surrounded by other women right now. You should leave here immediately."

"Thank you, Major, but my welfare is not your concern. I'm quite capable of making decisions for myself."

His short laugh was derisive. "I doubt that. It's apparent to me that you are too headstrong for your own good. However, until this investigation is completed, I intend for you to remain where I can locate you. If you persist in being difficult, perhaps I will pack your things for you and deposit you in a safer place on the outskirts of town."

"You wouldn't dare," she spat.

"Wouldn't I? Try me." His lips were pressed tightly together, firm with determination.

"I find you presumptuous and rude, sir."

"And I find that you show every indication of being a mean-tempered shrew. In addition, you are likely an accomplished liar." He straightened up, eyes regarding her with quiet force.

She glared back, beyond intimidation.

"But," he continued, "with your hair down around your shoulders, cheeks flushed in anger, and those marvelous green eyes flashing fire, you are even lovelier than I remembered."

She gasped, out of her league momentarily. Lovely? No man had ever thought she was lovely. Intelligent, perhaps. Or spirited, but lovely? Horse feathers!

"In fact, Miss Heyward, I find you completely captivating."

"You are hardly conducting a military investigation, Major Arledge," she sputtered. "It's time for you to leave."

"Perhaps," he murmured, ignoring her command, "it's the flashing eyes I like best, or maybe the vitriolic temper. At any rate, I'm rather enjoying the confrontation. You and I do strike sparks off each other."

"If you have quite finished with your assessment, I'll get the pistol for your inspection. Then you will have no further need to remain here." As Ellen turned to go inside she was conscious of his amused glance following her every move.

She took the pistol from the desk drawer in her father's office. The weapon had been carefully cleaned. Ellen knew the man would not be able to tell whether it had been recently fired. She went to Pam's room and knocked.

"Are you awake?"

"Yes, Ellen." Her voice was clear.

"I'm sorry, but that Yankee officer is here asking questions again. I have told him you are ill, but he may insist on seeing you. He doesn't know what really happened here. Could you come down? Remember, you never came outside that day and only know that there was a fire. Maybe, after he sees you, he will direct his attention elsewhere."

She hoped Pam wouldn't detect fear in her voice.

"Oh, Ellen, I can't see him," she pleaded. "I just can't."

"Please, Pam, it's the only way to make him stop hounding us. Let him do most of the talking. Pretend you are afraid of him… act childlike. I have told him you are only fourteen."

There was silence. Then a muffled reply came. "I'll be down in a few minutes."

Ellen returned to the verandah and solemnly handed over the gun. Arledge reached to take it, his warm fingers brushing hers.

"I fired above the men's heads, no time to take aim. One of them knocked me down before I could shoot a second time. They were torching the stables with our livestock locked inside."

She faced him squarely, not denying having shot at the men.

"I have the right to try to protect our property. I only intended to threaten or wound the men, but I was forcibly denied the opportunity."

"The weapon has been cleaned recently," he observed. "I assume you know how to use a gun and take care of it properly?"

"Yes." Her reply was confident. "Now, perhaps you are ready to be on your way."

"Not so fast. I shall have to talk with your sister."

Ellen heard the big front door behind them open cautiously. An awkward, frightened-looking young girl stood stiffly in the doorway. Stubby shoulder-length hair bristled where ashen curls had recently hung. A usually trim waistline was obliterated by the apparent shapelessness of adolescence. From beneath a full skirt two stockinged skinny legs protruded. A pale Pamela squinted up at the officer through her mother's steel-rimmed sewing spectacles.

"You wanted to see me?" she piped in a shrill, nervous voice. "I hope you are not here to set fires like the other soldiers did."

Arledge appeared to be surprised at her appearance.

"There is no cause to be frightened, miss. I have a few questions I'd like you to answer for me." He kept his voice even, his manner polite. "You are Pamela Heyward?"

"Yes."

"Do you have another sister... about eighteen or older?"

Tears began to course down the girl's cheeks. "Only Ellen. There's no one except Ellen and me."

He frowned slightly at her reply. "Please tell me what you remember about the day the Union soldiers were here."

"Nothing." She swallowed painfully. "I can't tell you anything. I have been sick for nearly two weeks. I had fever and was in bed the day the men came. They burned our stable, and they killed our horse and my favorite baby calf." Her shoulders started to shake and her face contorted, tears very near.

"Thank you, Pamela." He sounded mystified. "I'm sorry it was necessary to bother you. I hope you'll soon be well."

Pam fled into the house.

"I apologize, Ellen." His tone was sympathetic. "The child doesn't look well. Was another young lady visiting that day?"

"Of course not. Why must you continue this questioning?" Arledge's familiar use of her given name surprised her.

He was frowning impatiently.

"There are pieces of this puzzle which don't fit. I warn you, I'm thorough with my work and doggedly persistent. I hope you have nothing to hide, and that you have told me the truth. Three men have disappeared. Atrocities are being reported which are of grave concern not only to me, but to

General Sherman, himself. This incident could have serious consequences."

Ellen drew herself up to her full height, five feet four inches. "Major Arledge, you continue to try to intimidate me. I hope that you and your general are not in South Carolina to make war on women. Unless you have some damning evidence against me please depart."

He did not stir. "You are truly exasperating! We both know that you have spun for me a web of half truths. Your obvious attempts to anger me further convince me that you are hiding something. For both our sakes I hope my suspicions are wrong."

"You hypocritical blackguard," she lashed out, "who cares what happened to three drunken scoundrels! My father would have had them horse-whipped... or shot. Surely you don't condone, as legitimate acts of war, the criminal deeds that have taken place all across the south. You have seen my sister and me. What danger do we pose to your advancing troops?"

"Ellen," he replied harshly, "You know very well I don't approve of every action of either army. Sherman's men aren't professional soldiers. Most of them are conscripted boys with little understanding of what the whole mess is about. Some hardly speak English. Many have been hired to fill someone else's enlistment. They are anxious to go home. They all know the war started here. Some of them will want to take revenge on the people they believe helped to cause their misery."

"My sister and I did not cause their misery, sir."

"I am aware of that. Feeling the way the men do doesn't excuse what is happening, but it sure as hell helps to explain it. Why do you think I'm urging you to go to a safer place?"

He started to stride angrily toward his horse, but halted abruptly and wheeled around. "I have told you this investigation is serious. We are caught in the middle of it, but that doesn't alter a thing. You and I are not at war. I have no desire to persecute you, far from it... but I intend to do my duty."

His eyes held hers, making sure she understood his position.

She refused to acknowledge his words or to look away. Damn the man! Threatening, yet drawing me to him like a magnet, arousing a riot of reckless and disturbing feelings.

"Thin, pale, disheveled and opinionated as you are, since the first time I saw you, Ellen Heyward, I haven't been able to get you out of my thoughts."

She felt his smoldering eyes fix on the throbbing pulse at the base of her throat. Her face remained passive.

"I have rarely felt this nagging attraction to any woman... a suspected criminal, at that," he smiled thinly, "and certainly not to a female as exasperating as you are. There are strong undercurrents between us, lady, that neither of us can deny. I know these feelings aren't convenient for you right now, and they sure as hell aren't for me." He looked at her pointedly. "So what are we going to do about them?"

She finally replied.

"You have taken leave of your senses, sir. I am appalled by your conduct. I don't know what you are talking about."

"Again, my dear, you are lying, but I don't intend to let you drive me away. Apparently you have always dealt with boys, but not this time. You have met your match."

So infernally sure of himself, practiced and domineering. "Major, what kind of game do you think you are playing? As you so ungallantly reminded me, I am not a young debutante plagued with swarms of suitors. Neither am I a simple farm girl who swoons over swaggering males. I will not be threatened."

With one powerful arm Arledge reached out and swept her close to him. Held firmly against his broad chest, Ellen could feel the thundering of his heart.

"God, you provoke me," he swore through clenched teeth. "We haven't seen the last of each other, little lady. Don't bother to try to escape from me either. I'm good at my work and I will find you. I just hope I don't have to see you hanged."

"You are hurting me," she whispered. Her racing pulse was betraying the strange excitement she refused to display. She was not a frivolous, emotional female.

He released her. "I do beg your pardon, mam," he baited, bowing mockingly. "Although I'm sorely tempted to break your neck, right this minute hurting you is the last thing on my mind. I'll be back. I expect to find you waiting here for me."

Ellen stiffened, defiantly ignoring his bold words.

He grinned at her with handsome audacity. "And when I do return, I want you to look exactly as you do this minute, all breathless, wide-eyed and receptive."

He walked to his horse, untied the reins and mounted the huge roan with effortless ease. She watched him turn expertly and prepare to ride away. The horse nervously snorted and reared. Firmly seated, the enigmatic Virginian spoke gently to calm the animal. He turned and looked back toward Ellen. "I like my horses spirited, too." Smiling rakishly, he tipped his hat, large even teeth flashing white in the late afternoon sun.

Her traitorous heart skipped a beat. His arrogance repelled her. His strength was overpowering. His lightning quick mind and calm assurance frightened her. She felt smothered by the veiled passion in his brilliant blue eyes. She had no experience with this new kind of inner turmoil she was feeling. She didn't need the aggravation, but she had never felt more alive!

Sergeant Kelly waited at the end of the lane. Ellen watched Arledge rein in the big horse and listen intently to something the older man was saying. He looked back, nodded to her once more, and the two men rode away. By this time tomorrow, Ellen promised herself, I will be safely hidden from you, John Arledge. She had no intention of fighting a battle that she might lose.

Three

Ellen rose at daybreak and shivered into her clothing. Though she had sponged and brushed carefully, her dress showed signs of years of hard wear. The once vibrant green material, chosen originally because it was her best color, looked faded.

She checked the valise... wrapped in ruffled pantalets was the pistol, its sinister ugliness comforting. The last of the family cash was stuffed in a stocking. Two dresses, a dowdy moiré and her mother's old black wool, constituted her wardrobe. She closed the bag, buckled the leather straps and took it downstairs with her.

The windows revealed a gloomy, leaden sky. Cold air permeated everything. The Heywards had seen little of the light-heartedness that supposedly accompanies youth, and the war dragged on. They had been in Columbia on the day of secession. Tumultuous joy reigned then. Church bells across the city rang in unison to celebrate. Almost all of the student body at the South Carolina College had formed a cadet corps to enlist. Since that day the youthful romanticism had gradually faded and harsh reality had settled in.

Downstairs Aunt Mariah poked at the fire in the cook stove. The chill was not yet off the kitchen. "What you doing up so early in this pneumonia air, Miss Ellen?" she scolded.

"Things to do, Aunt Mariah. May I have one of the candles?"

"Sure, honey, but your breakfast going to be ready before long. You get back here to eat while it's hot."

"Don't worry. I wouldn't miss it."

She picked up a candle holder, walked outside to the root cellar and stepped hesitantly into the yawning blackness. At the bottom of the steps she placed the light on an empty shelf and reached for a small market basket. Since early fall she had hoarded corn, dried beans, dried okra pods, a teaspoon of turnip seed wrapped in a bit of paper, and a few shriveled potatoes. She put them in the basket, picked up the candle and climbed back outside. Ignoring the broken hasp, she pushed the heavy door shut with her foot.

Pam came into the kitchen in the same clothing she had worn for the major's interrogation. Her short hair was pulled severely up into a girlish topknot tied with narrow navy ribbon.

"Your appearance will shock Aunt Sophie," Ellen observed.

"I suppose so," she replied listlessly. "I've thought about what you said, and I am determined to stop dwelling on the past. My first step is the altered appearance. As long as Yankee soldiers are around, I shall remain a dumpy adolescent."

"That may be a good idea for the present," Ellen approved.

"And, Ellen, watch that Union officer. He seemed to be displaying more than a casual interest in you."

Avoiding Pam's direct gaze she placed the candle back on the table. "What have you done to your waist line?"

"Stuffed a small pillow in my corset. Lacing myself up alone in semi-darkness with cold-numbed fingers was no easy task." At last, the hint of a smile was on Pam's face.

"You look a bit young for a corset." Ellen studied her appearance. "You will be warmer though, and more comfortable."

The two girls sat down to eat the meager breakfast before them. Ellen was first to break the silence.

"I'm concerned about going to Aunt Sophie's without taking food. I don't know how we'd manage if four people descended on us for an indefinite stay. I imagine it's the same with her."

"Surely not. We still have some money. We can buy what we need. If Sherman comes to Columbia his men will steal or destroy everything there. And," Pam added dismally, "who knows how much longer merchants will accept Confederate currency?"

Ellen was amazed at her sister's mature acceptance of reality. She rose from the table. "I'll call our people together and tell them we will be gone a few days. You should stay inside. They would take notice of your changed appearance."

Outside daylight tinged the horizon. Ellen walked to the big iron plantation bell, mounted high on a cedar-post frame. She reached for the hemp rope hanging below. The clear tones of the bell pierced the morning air, reverberated through the wooded countryside, and echoed far down in the swampy bottom land.

A small group, accustomed to the summons, assembled. Ellen looked from face to face as they quietly waited. She counted those present, Willie, not to be trusted, Timothy, who had not been with them many years, and John, Luke and Benjamin, the three who had been born on the place and seemed to be the most loyal to her father. In the background stood several women.

"Is this everyone who will be working this morning, John?' She addressed a big gray haired man.

"Yes'm," he answered apologetically. "All 'cept for Esther. She keeping care of the children. Some more our people run off."

"That's all right," Ellen replied. Then speaking louder, she addressed the group. "I have told you that you are free to go. Mr. Lincoln, the Yankee president, made a law saying nobody is a slave anymore. We need you to work, but I don't have money to pay you. I must also warn you that work off the plantation will be very hard to find."

"Yes'm, Miss Ellen. We done heard that," John said.

"No one is going to give you food. You will have to work for it. If you choose to stay here, you will be safe. We will share with you what we have and what we can raise. When my father gets back I hope things will be better. I expect everyone who stays to go on working, as you have been taught to do."

She looked from face to face but the blank stares were inscrutable. "My sister and I are going to Columbia for some supplies. You are to carry on with the work here. John is in charge. He knows what to do. Does everyone understand?"

There was nervous foot shuffling, a few nods, and several voices could be heard answering, "Yes'm."

"There is no money for seed and fertilizer," Ellen continued, "our best hope is to clear and plow new land. Get the fields ready. We will grow corn and peas, no cotton. Think about your own cabin garden. Save some of your dried bean ration to plant. Gather any other seeds that you can and hold on to them until spring. You'll need to raise food, if you are to eat next year."

"Naomi," she looked past the men to a tall, stately woman in her middle years standing in the back, "Aunt Mariah is going with us. You are to be responsible for the house and yard. There are eleven chickens. All eggs you find are to be divided among each family, unless one of the hens starts setting. In that case, all the eggs go under her." Looking squarely into the face of each person present, she added with emphasis, "I expect to see ten hens and a rooster still walking around here when we get back."

Some laughter followed her statement.

"Snare rabbits, catch squirrels, fish the creeks for extra food. You know what to do. We believe in you. I hope that you won't disappoint us. Father is near here and may be home soon."

A few people nodded approval, saying nothing.

"Remember that as long as you stay on the plantation you will be safe," Ellen continued. "There may be fighting near here.

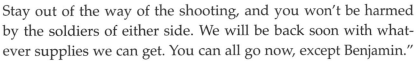

Stay out of the way of the shooting, and you won't be harmed by the soldiers of either side. We will be back soon with whatever supplies we can get. You can all go now, except Benjamin."

Benjamin, a youth of sixteen, waited as the others moved silently away. She and Pam placed great dependence on him. He was Aunt Mariah's grandson and had been brought up at the big house. Ellen's mother had taught him to read when he was seven years old. Now he and Ellen were teaching Randolph each night at the kitchen table.

"The cattle are in your care. You know how important they are. The hay is gone, and we need our corn for spring planting. February is the hardest month on cattle, but ours are a tough breed. Graze around from place to place. Try rushes, cattails, honeysuckle, dried weeds, broom sedge…whatever you can find. Grass should put out soon. I wish we had more to feed them, but I think you can keep them alive. They are our future, Benjamin, and our only cash crop for the next few years."

"Yes, mam. I know."

"When any of the men have time, they are to cut trees and split rails to use for more pasture fencing. Some heifers may calve soon. Watch carefully, and if one of the young ones has trouble birthing, call John. He is good with the horses and he will know what to do."

Benjamin listened quietly, not surprised by anything she said. "Miss Pam told me yesterday that I was to care for the cows until she gets back. I know every one by name, Miss Ellen. Looked after them since I was a little boy. I'll do my best."

"I know you will." Working to stem the tears that began to gather in the corners of her eyes, she put her hand on the boy's slim shoulder. "God bless you, Benjamin, and thank you. We have great faith in you. Your grandmother is going with us and I know you'll be lonely. I'll leave one of my school books for you, and a sheet of paper so you can keep a daily journal.

We will want to know what has happened while we were away."

"Yes, mam. I'll stay out with the cattle deep in the woods and only come up at night to cook me some supper."

"That will be good." She turned back toward the house.

Randolph, with John's help, had hitched a mule to the cart and was waiting by the kitchen door. Aunt Mariah loudly berated him. "Boy, why you fix a whole load of pine straw? I told you just enough to make the cart ride soft. You never listen right!"

Long accustomed to the old woman's grumbling, Benjamin was oblivious to what she said. Ellen passed the two unnoticed and entered the kitchen.

"It's good I decided to be a child," Pamela solemnly said. "I found four good dresses among our old things. I don't have that much adult clothing left! And our lunch is ready, boiled eggs and corn pone. Once we would have thought that revolting."

"Wouldn't we though!" Ellen took the package. "A proper picnic lunch was fried chicken, potato salad, brandied peaches, cold melon, and little lemon custard pies. I can hardly remember how they taste."

"Will the world ever be right again, Ellen? When is the war going to end?" Pam's voice trailed away plaintively.

"Soon, very soon," was the older sister's grim reply. "People said everything was going so well at first."

"That was a long time ago. Now our soldiers have to rely on captured horses, and enemy guns and ammunition to equip themselves. Our money is inflated beyond belief, and cotton sits rotting in warehouses or on docks all over the south because of the Yankee blockade."

"And nothing can be done?"

"Not any longer, I fear. Fresh Union troops and supplies pour down from the north, in from the west... and now up from the south while our army slowly starves. No, it will all soon be over."

Pam tried to choke back the tears. "You always see things with such cold clear logic, Ellen."

"And that ability rarely brings me any happiness."

"Mother said that a quick mind and a smart tongue won't help ensnare a man." Pamela's smile was feeble as she tried to joke.

"True, but I don't want one right now. Men don't always mean happiness. Mother and Aunt Sophie placed great store in men, counted the number of proposals a girl had as a measure of her beauty and success."

Pam's face took on a stricken look.

Aunt Mariah bustled in and ordered Randolph to put the bags in the cart. Ellen checked the front door bolt, picked up the basket of seeds and, with one last look about the house, walked out. While the old woman hung the iron kitchen key on a nail outside, Pam got into the high cart. Then, amidst great pushing, pulling and groaning, Aunt Mariah was hauled into position beside her. She settled into place, plump legs and big shoes dangling out the back of the cart. Ellen grabbed the cart side and climbed nimbly in beside them.

Standing in the front of the cart Randolph snapped the reins smartly and they began to move slowly down the tree-lined lane. Columbia was twelve miles away, and the mule was pulling a heavy load. The road was rutted, and the sky dull and threatening rain. Pam dug under the quilt into the straw behind her and hid their food package.

"Unappetizing as it is," she explained, "I would hate for someone to take our lunch from us." She smoothed the quilt back down over it.

As they creaked out onto the main road each sister took a long look back. Would their home be standing when they returned? Shuttered windows and smokeless chimneys looked

strange and forbidding on the big brick edifice that several generations of Heywards had called home. Spanish moss swayed
eerily from the limbs of the giant live oaks that lined the road to
the house.

"Randolph," Ellen called sharply, breaking the spell, "when
we get to Uncle Adam's road, please turn in. I need to talk
with him before we leave."

After nearly half an hour of slow, steady movement
Randolph turned down a narrow overgrown path and approached a small cabin. Ellen jumped to the ground and reached
back for the seed basket. "Uncle Adam," she called. There was
no reply. She shouted again, her breath creating white vapor
in the cold, still air. A thin wisp of smoke hovered over the little
cabin's brick chimney. "It's Ellen Heyward, Uncle Adam. Are
you home?"

The plank door of the house scrubbed against rough wooden
flooring as it was pulled back a few inches. An ancient man,
hair snow white, peered cautiously out, then swung the door
wide.

"Lord, Miss Ellen, I'm glad to see you," he said. "I didn't
know who that was coming here so early. How you folks
doing? Since them two Yankee soldiers been by here asking
questions, we been fair scared to open the door when we
hear somebody."

"We're fine, Uncle Adam," she assured. "Soldiers were
here?" Her face paled. She didn't want to cause him trouble.

"Yes, mam. Two times, but don't you worry none. I told them
I saw smoke down your way a few days ago, like something big
was burning, and that's all I know. They was satisfied."

"Good," she nodded. "Miss Pam and I are going to Columbia to stay with Aunt Sophie a few days." She handed him the
basket. "Father says you are the best farmer he knows. This is
all the garden seed I could save. Please take it and get it started."

"Miss Ellen, I am much obliged. I ain't hardly got nothing to plant this spring neither. Just a little corn and sugar cane. I'll watch over this seed you brought careful-like and bring you some nice little plants later on," he solemnly promised.

"Just make them grow so we can have food this summer and seed for next year. When we get back home, I'll send you word."

"I will be right here ready to help. We family, Miss Ellen. You heard anything from Mister Henry lately?" he inquired.

"No, we haven't," Ellen wore a worried frown. "I was sure there would have been some message before now."

"I been wondering. That no-good Willie stopped by here a few days ago. He been in Columbia and he say he most sure he saw Isaac there. Isaac wouldn't be nowhere 'cept with Mister Henry."

Isaac was the old man's only son. When Henry Heyward went to war, Adam, knowing he was too old to accompany him, sent Isaac to care for his former master. Adam had been responsible for the white man since his birth. The two had been slave and master, teacher and pupil, for many years. As adults, they were devoted friends and neighbors. When Henry Heyward inherited Oak Lane one of his first acts was to free Adam and his wife and give them a tract of land of their own. Though there had been some criticism from neighbors at the time, the plantation owner had remained steadfast.

"I talked with Willie, but he didn't mention seeing Isaac. You never know when to believe what he says."

"That's sure the truth," Adam cackled. "I put you all and Mister Henry in my prayers every night," he told her as they parted, "and I keep an eye on your place 'til you come home."

After Ellen was back in the cart, Randolph headed to the main road. Once underway they were soon startled by the sharp command, "Halt!"

Randolph jerked the reins to a stop. A raw lad in Federal blue, clutching a new Springfield rifle, stepped from the woods.

"What you got there, boy, a load of Rebel spies?" he called out sharply in a nasal midwest twang.

"No, sir, got me a load of women," was the frightened reply.

The young soldier walked to the front of the cart and looked closely at the waiting animal. "Ain't this one of our mules?"

"No, sir," Randolph assured him. "This the Heyward mule. Him and me been part of the same family a long time."

"Advance a few feet and let me see what's in the cart."

The boy complied.

"Well, I do declare," the recruit gasped in mock surprise. "You do have yourself a load of women!" His scrutinizing gaze swept across Ellen and Aunt Mariah and then fastened on Pam.

Ellen's heart gave a sickening lurch. She stole a quick glance at her sister. Pam was sitting stiffly upright, thin legs and clumsy shoes stretched straight in front of her. The stubby topknot of blonde hair bristled in the air. Both hands were clutched at her sides and her beautiful eyes were squinted and blinking rapidly behind the sewing glasses.

He stared a moment longer. "What you got hidden under that quilt you are sitting on?" he demanded to know.

"Ain't nothing but pine straw," Aunt Mariah explained loudly. "This cart gets mighty hard on ladies' bottoms when they jogging up and down this here bumpy road."

The soldier lifted the corners of the covering to check her story. "Where are you headed and why?" He addressed Ellen.

"We are on our way to Columbia to stay with relatives."

"You live around here? I hear the city is already crowded."

"A Yankee major came to our house and told us we must go into town. We have to join the other women and children there."

"You heard that Uncle Billy Sherman's whole army is coming, and you are running. I bet you been starved out... burned out, too, maybe. You live around here?" he repeated, trying to look menacing.

"Soldier, please contact Major Arledge. He is stationed near here. He told us to go into town. I am sure he will clear this up." Ellen was horrified to hear herself invoking the Yankee major's name and insinuating that he was her protector.

The recruit backed away. "You one of the major's lady friends?" he sneered knowingly. "You could be better off in the city and, then again," he observed philosophically, "you might be worse off. I hear the Reb army has already pulled out. They were scared, too. Likely hightailing it up to Virginia."

Everyone in the cart remained silent.

"Move on." He stepped back, motioning with the rifle.

Ellen breathed a sigh of relief.

"And, lady," he added impudently, "that daughter of yours ain't never going to be the looker you are."

"Young man," she admonished, smothering the hint of a smile, "shame on you! That is a very unkind thing for you to say."

Randolph urged the mule forward. The soldier disappeared between a thick tangle of trees.

From time to time the Heywards got out of the cart and walked to lighten the mule's load and to stretch their stiff limbs. The sky remained overcast and a light drizzle fell intermittently. Their shoes soon became muddy, the soles soaked through to their stockings. The hem of Ellen's damp dress dragged heavily around her ankles. Aunt Mariah sat stoically in the cart. At midday they stopped briefly beside the road for lunch and to let the mule rest.

By late afternoon, as they neared Columbia, other vehicles were on the road. Several faster rigs, loaded with large trunks, barrels of china, feather beds and small pieces of expensive furniture, passed by them. They were soon following behind a long line of wagons filled with bulging baskets of produce, bundles of clothing and odd assortments of prized possessions.

"Thank the Lord it's fairing off some," muttered Aunt Mariah. "These quilts and all my clothes done wet clean through."

From time to time whole families, who had obviously traveled long distances, drove past them. Family portraits protruded from one buggy. Inside another glints from pieces of a silver service caught their eye. In a wagon ahead Ellen could see a gilt-framed mirror flashing in the sickly rays of the setting sun.

"The traffic is getting heavy, Randolph. Would you like me to help with the driving?" Ellen asked anxiously.

"No, mam, can't go fast nohow," he assured her, "all us packed tight together and all going in the same direction."

"Apparently other people think they will be safer in Columbia, too." Pam tried to take an interest in the congestion.

"What do you suppose this mass exodus from the countryside will do to the city?" Ellen asked, not expecting an answer.

The weary group reached their aunt's Laurel Street house after dark and waited anxiously outside. Dark shuttered windows, the untracked waxed glassiness of the gray porch flooring and the stout unyielding front door all seemed to indicate an empty house. Ellen knocked and called to her aunt. There was no answer. She and Pam looked at each other with real apprehension.

"Aunt Sophie," she called again. "It's Ellen and Pamela." Finally the tap of feminine heels could be heard inside the darkened house, and the door opened. "Girls, oh, girls," their aunt exclaimed, tearfully embracing them. "Thank heaven you're here. I have been so worried about you way out there in the country by yourselves. I'm here alone, too, and so glad to see you. Bring your things in."

"Thank you, Aunt Sophie." Ellen hugged the stout little lady tightly in relief. "We would like to visit you for a while until things are more settled," she explained.

"I have been expecting you. Randolph can take the mule around the back. I have hay. To think I was afraid to answer your knock! I peeked through the parlor shutters before I dared open the door. I never locked my house before this week. The rumors I've heard lately have been enough to turn my hair gray."

Sophie's hair had been gray as long they could remember.

The older woman stood in the doorway chattering nervously as they emptied the cart. "You girls out after nightfall without a man's protection, and me locked up alone in a servantless house scared out of my wits. What would my dear late husband say!"

"Life is very different for all of us, Aunt Sophie," Ellen acknowledged as she placed the valises inside.

"Wagons and buggies have been coming and going all week. Riffraff, white and black, are strewn over the town. It's down right dangerous to be outside." She paused for breath. "Mariah, I am so glad to see you with the girls. Their mother wouldn't want you to let them out of sight under conditions like these."

"Yes, mam, I know it and that's how come I'm with them."

"I hope you can teach that good-for-nothing Hattie how to manage a kitchen, if she bothers to show up."

"I'll be proud to, mam. I'll go on to the kitchen now."

After unloading the last of their belongings, Randolph went back out to the street, opened the iron grillwork gate to the side yard and led the mule and cart around to the carriage house.

"Come to my bedroom, girls. That's the only fire I am keeping. Miss Gilham, my roomer, left me two days ago. Poor thing. She was concerned about her brother's children over in the

Lexington District. She had word that her sister-in-law is sick. We both cried! She has lived with me ever since your Uncle Marion passed away, and she's like a member of the family."

Ellen, relieved at not being pressed into explanations of their presence, was happy to have Sophie continue to talk.

"Everybody thinks Columbia is about the only safe town left in the state. You can't imagine how many people have poured in here. All week I've heard wheels rolling down Laurel Street the whole night long. I haven't slept a wink. I have hardly had the nerve to look outside for fear the Union army is moving in."

She ushered the girls into the warm comfort of her bedroom. A fire was burning in the fireplace and a single candle flickered in the half dark. "Why haven't I heard from you two lately? Is anything wrong at the plantation? You know your father would want you to come into Columbia and stay with me at the first sign of danger." She stopped talking to look from one to the other.

"We know, Aunt Sophie. That's why we are here," Ellen rushed to answer. "We are both fine, but the plantation is so isolated. We are like everyone else, food scarce, money dwindling, clothes worn out, slaves deserting. And we hear little good news and lots of frightening rumors."

"Pamela, my goodness!" Their aunt was dumbfounded. "What have you done to yourself?"

Before the younger girl could speak Ellen hastily replied, "It was my idea, Aunt Sophie. There have been a few Union soldiers camped near the Goodwyn plantation, some of Sherman's advance foraging parties coming up from Georgia. Pamela is young and pretty. No need to invite unwanted attention. I thought we could travel more safely if we looked like mother and daughter."

"Have the soldiers tried to harm you?"

Ellen saw the muscles in Pamela's face tighten. Again she rushed to reply. "Bummers came and set fire to the stables. After that a Yankee major showed up asking questions about deserters. Pamela was not well that day and I wouldn't let him talk to her. I led him to believe she is a child. He's still in the area. It seemed a good idea to continue the deception."

"I expect you are right, dear. The stories we have heard from Georgia! You are both too lovely to be out and about. A Yankee major. How awful! Was he insulting?"

"No. He was a legal officer, a West Point graduate, a man who has chosen soldiering as a career. He was originally from Virginia… an Arledge," she added, knowing such information would divert her aunt's line of questioning.

"A Virginian! Good Heavens, I am sorry for his poor mother. Why isn't he in the Confederate army?"

"I asked that. He has been out west for years. He's here now on special assignment to General Sherman and probably on his way to Charleston right now."

"Do you suppose Sherman is going to Charleston, or will it be Columbia? I am so thankful that your Uncle Marion doesn't know how things are." Tears began to gather again.

"Surely some of your house servants stayed with you, Aunt Sophie." Pam tried to head off the storm.

"Albert," she sobbed, "and Hattie. Albert has been here for forty years. He promised Marion he would always look after me. He is getting weak and sickly, but there is little to be done anyway. Hattie is his daughter. She stayed because of him. My other two house servants left. Just as well, feeding them would be a problem. Oh, supper! Will hominy, yams and fried bacon be all right?"

"All right!" Ellen exclaimed, "sounds like a banquet to us."

"Anymore it almost is," she agreed. "Most people take only two meals a day now. Imagine fine, proud old families reduced to wondering where the next meal is coming from." Sophie sighed and looked about the room to see what else needed to be done.

"Please get another candle from the top bureau drawer, Pamela. The gas lights ceased to function months ago. Nothing is dependable lately. I want you girls to take the small room adjoining mine. You'll be warmer and I'd like to have you near. You can hang up your frocks while I go see to supper."

"Thank you. We appreciate all you are doing for us."

"There's plenty of room for Mariah and Randolph over the carriage house with Albert and Hattie. When we are ready to eat, we'll move a table by the fireplace and have supper in here."

Pam found the candle, lighted it from the one already burning and placed it in a holder. She picked up her bag and led Ellen into the tiny area that had once been the dressing room for the master chamber. A big spool bed had been pushed near the fireplace. Though the hearth was cold, the thick brick chimney radiated some of the warmth of the fire in the adjoining room. "Imagine sleeping and dressing in a room with the chill knocked off the air, plus meat and sweet potatoes for supper. I feel like visiting royalty," Ellen remarked lightly.

Lifting her valise on the bed, she undid the straps and began taking out the clothing she had brought with her. Pam placed the candle on a table and stood silently, arms crossed, clutching herself.

"Once I came to Uncle Marion's and Aunt Sophie's for a week's visit before the war. I was about your age." Ellen talked to fill the void. "Assembly Ball. Remember? Mother enjoyed it all so much. I felt like a prize race horse being displayed at an auction. I'm afraid I wasn't a great success. No charm."

Pam listened mutely.

"This same oak wardrobe hardly held all my dresses," she reminisced. "Now here we are, the two of us for an indefinite stay with most of the clothes we own, and there is space to let."

"Why did you bring mother's old funeral dress? She would never let you wear black and you certainly can't dye it."

"It's warm and made of better material than anything I have. I can redo it to fit me. Lie down for a while, Pam. This was a hard day. You've been brave and wonderful." Ellen's voice choked. "I'll fix the table and help Aunt Sophie."

"Take the candle. They're scarce and I don't need it."

"I can see. It's not dark yet. Bring it when you come."

Ellen waited until Pam sat on the bed, removed her damp shoes and slid her cold feet under the feather comforter.

In the next room Ellen sank wearily into a big platform rocker by the fireside. The red velvet upholstery was soft and comforting. The flickering light of the fire helped to dispel the gathering gloom. She closed her eyes for a minute. Poor dear Aunt Sophie, Pam and I are rescuers instead of the rescued, she thought. I'm glad we are here. I don't want to admit weakness, but I need to feel safe and hidden from the world for a while.

Thoughts of John Arledge had haunted Ellen all day. There was a hard edge about the man, a dark, ruthless inscrutability that fascinated her. She thought of his parting words. He indicated that he found her sexually attractive. She knew she was neither young nor beautiful, yet Arledge's bold eyes had lighted with interest. Strange and disturbing.

Fatigue engulfed Ellen but thoughts of Arledge persisted. Had he been so long deprived of feminine company that he could be enticed by anyone? Perhaps she was not sufficiently experienced to read a man's intentions. Was he a womanizer, a veteran of countless flirtations and affairs? Was she a misguided spinster romanticizing about something she had imagined? How ironic that an insolent Yankee should be the first man to stir her senses.

Soon the tinkling of dishes and the sound of light footsteps in the hallway roused Ellen from the reverie. Enough of this foolishness, she told herself, I'll never see the man again. She opened the door, took the tray of china and flatware from her aunt and placed it on the marble-topped bureau.

Sophie shifted books and candlesticks from the library table and together they moved it before the fireplace. While her aunt continued her birdlike chatter, Ellen spread the white damask cloth and laid out thin porcelain china and heavy sterling flatware. She half listened to the monologue. "...Weather has been so cold, incessant rain, much sickness in the neighborhood, Mrs. McMaster's nephew in the hospital at the College, nobody knows the whereabouts of General Beauregard or whether Wade Hampton will come to Columbia's rescue..."

Ellen moved three ladder-back chairs to the table and the older woman sat down to continue talking.

"Oh, Ellen," she gushed. "If only you could have been here three weeks ago when our bazaar opened at the State House. The ladies had been preparing for weeks. We were determined to raise a large sum of money for the war effort and we did. I arranged tables and helped sell goods every afternoon and night. It was almost like old times." She wiped away a tear.

"Did the bazaar go well?" Ellen tried to show interest.

"Oh, my goodness, yes! We had seven marvelous booths set up in the House of Representatives for the different states. South Carolina was at the Speaker's desk. Virginia, Mississippi, Missouri, Louisiana, Texas and Tennessee were all represented."

"Why only seven states?"

"There were more. They all had booths. On the Senate side North Carolina was at the desk and Georgia, Florida, Alabama and Arkansas nearby."

"I wish we could have been here to help." Ellen finished spreading the table. Aunt Sophie continued about the bazaar.

"Every booth was draped with Confederate flags and damask and lace... the curtains and tablecloths from our homes, of course, but it was so festive and lovely! Elaborate decorations of evergreen everywhere, tables loaded with fancy items. You wouldn't believe the splendor."

"Where did it all come from? Are stores still stocked?"

"Why, yes," her aunt confirmed. "Almost anything can be had, if one can pay the prices. Most of the bazaar articles were either brought through the Charleston blockade or made by the ladies. And sweets... cakes, jellies, creams, candies. One slice of cake, and not a generous one, sold for two dollars. A spoonful of Charlotte russe brought five. Can you imagine?"

"What I can't imagine is anyone being able to afford those prices," Ellen laughed.

"There was such a crowd of people! One could almost forget there is a war. It was like at the beginning. You were here. Do you remember the optimism and the good times? Now nobody knows what is going to happen next. Perhaps our brave boys will never benefit from the money we took in. That monster, Sherman, may get it."

"No, Aunt Sophie," Ellen comforted. "Confederate money won't mean much to him. Tell me more about the bazaar." She wanted to preserve her aunt's gaiety a little longer.

"There were several beautiful imported wax dolls. They were raffled off for five hundred dollars each, and I heard that one of them brought two thousand. We kept the bazaar open until last Saturday. Only rumors of Sherman's proximity forced us to close. We heard that the contemptible devil said he would personally attend the Columbia Ladies Bazaar unless we ended it earlier than we had planned."

"How awful! Do you have dependable news sources now?" Ellen sat down in the velvet chair to listen.

"Who knows? There was no mail for most of January. Rains washed out the bridges over the Edisto River, the road to Greenville is under repair, and the one to Danville has been impassable for more that two weeks. General Lee depends on that road for his supplies. Trains are running less often than they did and schedules are erratic. Many people are saying that Columbia is doomed."

"But others believe it is the safest place in the state."

"Yesterday I heard that Sherman will march to Branchville, where all of the railroads meet. That little town is equal distance from Charleston, Augusta and Columbia. No one can prepare. All we can do is wait to see which direction he chooses. How long that will take, nobody knows."

Ellen looked thoughtful. "The general is wily. Delaying in Branchville is a clever maneuver to tie up our defense forces. He will stay there until his men wreck the rail system."

"But while he waits he has the whole state on tenterhooks. There is wild speculation everywhere."

"Since his bummers were at the plantation over a week ago foraging for food, I think that means that the army will come through here."

"Oh, Ellen. I have heard such bad things about those bummers! They scout miles to each side of his army scavenging and stealing and destroying everything... and Branchville is only seventy-four miles away."

"Some of his men could be in this area without the army following. We can't be sure where the main force will go."

"Most people think Charleston is his target. Since Fort Sumter is located there, to capture Charleston would seem a greater victory to the North, don't you think?"

"For propaganda purposes Charleston may be better known, but I expect it's also better defended. There are fewer troops here. Don't they say Sherman runs from battle?" Ellen asked.

"Oh, yes, dear. He makes his war on women and children, and on the property of brave soldiers who are away from home. I've heard that he is quite mad. The stories my neighbor had from her relatives in Milledgeville, Georgia, have convinced me that he is depraved. He lost his command early in the war because of insanity. It runs in his family. He would have been completely finished, except that he is a friend of that drunkard Grant."

"Do we still have any troops stationed in Columbia?"

"Not many. I hear that Butler and a few thousand men are to remain here. With the recent influx of people, we at least have the protection of numbers. Wade Hampton is supposed to be coming."

"Does anyone seem to know when? I want news of Father."

"No. Everything is rumor."

Ellen picked up the empty tray. "I'll go get supper. I hope bringing Aunt Mariah won't cause trouble. She'll take over, you know. She thinks she is the world's best cook."

"Compared to Hattie she certainly is. That girl has been such a trial. Our meals alternate between being undercooked and burned, and food is expensive. Corn is forty dollars a bushel. Lately Hattie has been so sullen I don't dare to complain."

In the kitchen Aunt Mariah's dark face beamed as she turned small slices of sizzling meat. She reined supreme in front of the wood stove. "Honey, this here smells like eating, don't it?"

Ellen smiled and nodded in agreement. Hattie sat on a stool in the corner. She did not speak to Ellen.

"Hello, Hattie," Ellen said. "Is Uncle Albert well?"

"Yes'm."

"Please tell him I will be up to see him tomorrow."

"Yes'm.

Ellen looked closely at the young black woman. The downcast eyes, frozen features, abrupt answers, and sullen attitude were symptoms southerners had learned to know and dread. Hattie sat watching as Ellen spooned hominy into a bowl and prepared the food to be taken to the other room.

The spicy odor of cinnamon from syrup-coated yams made Ellen realize that many hours had passed since they had last eaten. The meat platter held three small slices. Four more for the black people were cooking in the iron griddle. Ellen picked up the tray and started to the door. Hattie sat, made of stone.

"Girl, get up from there and open that door for Miss Ellen," Aunt Mariah stormed. "Your pappy raised you better than that." Hattie rose reluctantly.

"I know Randolph is tired and sleepy, Aunt Mariah," Ellen said as she left the room, "but please see that he looks after the mule and feeds him. We'll need him to take us back home."

Ellen gently bumped the bedroom door with her elbow. She could hear the rustle of taffeta as her aunt crossed the room.

"You don't know how happy I am to have you girls with me," she said once more.

"It's nice for us, too. There is little visiting between plantations. With the men all off at war, most of the women and children have gone to visit relatives who live in safer areas. Pam and I have work to keep us busy, but we've been lonely. I'll call her."

"Has the child been ill, Ellen? She doesn't look well."

"Yes, she has." The girl answered carefully. "Influenza, I suppose, and malnutrition and fatigue. We have carried on with the plantation work since father has been gone. I supervise the house and fields and Pamela looks after the cattle and pastures."

"Four years of war. What girlhood has the poor dear ever had! No debut, no parties, no young people around who are her age. Most of my friends who have daughters have placed them in the Ursuline Convent right now. And you, Ellen, there have been no opportunities for you either."

"Are there non-Catholic girls at the convent, too?"

"Certainly. The nuns provide a good educational program and I hear that they have an adequate supply of food. That's more than some parents have. If the enemy should enter the city, then surely there's no safer place for girls than a convent."

"One would think so," Ellen replied, trying to shove the recent horror they had endured to the back of her mind. "You sit down. I'll go get Pamela and we can have supper."

Four

As dawn began to light the windows Ellen slipped out of bed and dressed quietly. She had not slept well. She stared for a moment at Pam's face and left the room. Aunt Mariah was in total charge of the kitchen. She reached in the cupboard for a cup, poured pale hot liquid into it and handed it to Ellen.

"This ain't got good color, honey, but it sure got the smell of coffee," was her greeting. "You sit down and sip on it while I take up the corn muffins."

"Pam is still asleep, Aunt Mariah. Please see that she eats something after a while. I hope she'll stay in bed and rest."

"Yes'm, I'll tend to her. You go on about your business today, and don't you worry none."

"Ellen, dear, you are already up," twittered Aunt Sophie, bustling through the doorway. "You can't imagine what a joy it is to have a good cook in the kitchen. Mariah, did I tell you how delighted I am that you came with the girls?"

"Yes'm. Thank you. You done told me." The old negress glowed with pleasure as she set another place.

"Ellen, did I tell you that the newspapers predict England and France will recognize the Confederacy by early March?"

"That's good news, Aunt Sophie. We've waited a long time. Do the Columbia and Charleston papers still come out regularly?"

"Fairly regularly. The casualty lists are so important."

"What are you and your friends doing for the war effort now that the bazaar is over?"

"Until recently we had a neighborhood sewing and knitting circle, but we can no longer get the materials we need… not even cloth for rolling bandages."

"Tell me about the wounded in this area. Any field hospitals? I want to see if I can find Father."

"I don't know much about the hospitals, dear." The two sat down at the end of the kitchen table. "Wounded come in by train. Some women work with the wounded at the South Carolina College. The walk over there is too much for me, so I try to help in other ways. Miss Gilham was nursing there for part of the day. She says there's a great deal of suffering for want of simple medicines. I think she would have seen Henry, if he's there."

The older woman tasted the coffee, frowned slightly and continued. "And measles! Ordinary childhood measles. Can you believe that more men are dying from measles than from battle wounds! There is talk of opening private homes to the sick."

Muffin eaten and coffee finished, Ellen rose from the table. "Please excuse me, Aunt Sophie. I want to speak to Uncle Albert. After that Randolph and I will walk to the College and volunteer to help today. Perhaps I can get news of where Father might be."

"Ellen, hospital duty isn't suitable for you. Young unmarried ladies do not bathe sick men and dress wounds."

"The war has changed things, Aunt Sophie, including what constitutes proper behavior for ladies. I'm accustomed to work, and while I'm here I want to serve where I am most needed."

"Miss Ellen," Aunt Mariah interrupted, "Albert told me Isaac was here day before yesterday asking for you and Miss Pamela. Miss Sophia was gone. He didn't get to talk to nobody but that trifling Hattie. Isaac didn't tell her nothing, just that Mister Henry told him to see if you girls were here with your aunt."

"Father is in Columbia! Please stay at the house all day, Aunt Mariah, and watch for Isaac. If he comes back, tell him I'm at the hospital looking for them. If he can't find me there, ask him to meet me here at dark this evening."

For the first time in weeks Ellen's footsteps sounded light as she rushed from the room. "I'll get a wrap while you give Randolph some breakfast," she called. "We may be gone all day."

Ellen started the nearly two mile walk at a brisk pace, Randolph trotting behind. They moved steadily across the city, down the wide majestic avenues, all named for Revolutionary War generals. Choosing Bull Street to avoid the congestion on Marion and Sumter, they reached Pendleton, paralleled the high brick wall around the campus to Sumter Street and walked on down to the front gate.

Once inside the College grounds Ellen paused to decide which of the structures would most likely be the headquarters building. Though people rushed about and ambulance wagons rattled in and out the gates, the campus was quieter than the streets outside.

The College had served as a hospital for so long now that limping soldiers were as familiar a sight on the horseshoe-shaped green as young students had once been. Efforts were being made to gird the area for battlefield conditions. The hospital, already filled with sick and wounded, was preparing for siege.

The first building on the left was the library, built fifteen years earlier. Many people believed it to be from designs of the brilliant South Carolina architect, Robert Mills, though there was no proof. She looked past its stately columns and beautiful windows to Elliott and Harper Colleges, then to DeSaussure and around the curved drive. Her attention settled on Rutledge.

Since all former dormitories housed patients, the college chapel seemed a likely choice to locate hospital administration.

The entry hall was already crowded. The lieutenant sitting at a desk just inside the doorway seemed buried under an avalanche of paper work. He was being bombarded by mothers seeking sons, wives hoping for news of their husbands, and orderlies and nurses asking for records and information. Lists of arriving wounded, and of the dead being removed, were piling up on his desk.

As he tried to deal with a room filled with people clamoring for his attention, the line outside steadily lengthened. When Ellen was finally able to talk to him she learned nothing.

"Miss Heyward," was his distracted reply to her questions, "I can't tell you whether your father is here or not. These files haven't been put in order or brought up to date in weeks. More men are arriving hourly. My advice is, look for him. The Chief Surgeon is begging for more help. Volunteer as a nurse. You are needed. If you don't locate your father, you may find someone who has seen him."

Discouragement settled heavily on Ellen.

He lowered his voice, strain showing in his face. "I suggest you begin looking immediately. Rumor is the hospital will be moved to North Carolina. Scouts place Sherman's main force less than twelve miles out of town on the Lexington side."

He stood and pointed across the green. "That is Hospital Number One. Start there and someone will tell you what to do." He attempted a thin smile.

When he rose Ellen noticed that the left side of his pants was split to the knee and his leg was swathed in bandages. His face was lined and haggard. He was probably twenty-five years old or less and he looked fifty. "I'm sorry I can't be more help to you."

Ellen thanked him, called to Randolph and together they walked through the cold mist back across the horseshoe. As they entered Building One, an elderly man carrying a worn leather medical bag was leaving.

"Sir, I'm a new volunteer. Where should I begin?"

"My dear," he smiled tiredly, "start at the first bed. Some men want water. Many need a bath. Beds should be made, bandages changed, letters written. Help wherever you can. Many of the men are beyond help."

His stooped shoulders and weary face attested to long hours of overwork. "I have completed my rounds here and I have to go on to the next ward. Do whatever you are able to. When you are needed in the operating room, one of the doctors will call you." He clutched his coat together, pulled his hat low against the cold February wind and hurried to the next building.

Ellen pushed open the door. From every direction pleas, groans, and requests assailed her ears. "Randolph, wait outside on the grassy area." She was attempting to shield the boy.

"Yes'm." The usually taciturn boy looked frightened.

"Do not leave. I will be working inside with the sick soldiers, but I want you to stay out here. You are to watch for Mister Henry or for Isaac. They are here some place and we need to find them. If you see either one, ask them to wait and you come back here for me. I won't leave this building. I'll come to get you later, unless you come for me first. There will be plenty for you to look at. Find a sheltered place out of the wind to sit, but don't you go to sleep. I am depending on you to stay alert."

Time passed slowly as Ellen moved down the endless chain of cots. After three hours her back began to ache. Her eyes smarted with unshed tears. She was revolted by the sickly lead smell of blood and the putrid odor of gangrenous wounds. Methodically she worked through the sea of unknown faces, pausing to wipe perspiration from men burning with fever and to cover others shivering with chills. She adjusted bandages,

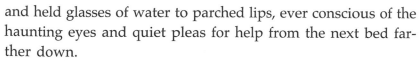

and held glasses of water to parched lips, ever conscious of the haunting eyes and quiet pleas for help from the next bed farther down.

"Miss?"

She glanced up at the young soldier on the next cot. He was propped up on one elbow, the other shoulder covered in bandages.

"I have been watching you," he said weakly. "I'm sure we have met some place before."

She focused tired eyes on the speaker, ready to be the sister, mother or girlfriend of still another delirious soldier. The color drained from her face. She recognized him immediately from that terrible day the barn had burned.

"I am James Milton from the Beaufort area, one of General Butler's lesser lieutenants." He smiled weakly. "And now that I am wounded, of even less service to him." He suddenly stopped speaking.

There was an awkward pause.

"You have remembered how we met," she observed quietly.

"Yes, I'm sorry. Please, mam, forgive me for reminding you of such a painful incident."

"I can never thank you enough for helping us... me," she substituted quickly. "You and I might have met under other circumstances. Let's pretend we did. How were you wounded?"

"It happened late that same night. After my patrol finally left your place, we tried to skirt around the Union encampment to get back to our lines. We were ambushed by another small party of Yankees. One of my men was killed."

"I'm so sorry."

"I was hit, but I managed to escape and work my way to our picket lines. We were separated and the third man in my group might have been taken prisoner. Later I was brought here."

"Which of the men do you think was captured?" Ellen asked uneasily.

"Mills, the older man, the one from Georgia. Don't worry. If he was captured, we have nothing to hide. General Hampton has issued orders that we are to shoot any Union soldiers caught firing dwellings or private property. If nothing else had occurred but the fire, the killings would be justified, but under the circumstances…" He paused in embarrassment.

"A Union officer has questioned me twice about the disappearance of the foragers. I told him the men rode away pursued by Confederate soldiers. I don't think he believed me."

"You mustn't be frightened. The worst thing he can prove you guilty of is not revealing the full truth. Surely he will understand that, if the entire situation ever comes to light." He leaned back weakly on the hospital cot. "How is it that you are in Columbia? I hope more raiders didn't come to your place."

"No, none… other than the two Yankee investigators. After what happened, and the stories I kept hearing, we decided to join relatives in town until the Union army moves out of this area."

"We?"

She had revealed too much.

"My sister and I. She… is much younger." Ellen quickly rushed on. "I am thinking of entering her in the Ursuline School for girls. She's not well. Being among young friends might help her."

"And the other young lady involved in the incident?" he inquired softly.

Ellen busied herself with the pitcher of water in her hand. "A friend who was visiting… a terrible experience for us all."

Hoping to protect Pam from any blundering sympathy in case the two should ever meet, she groped for convincing words to substantiate the lie. "Her family came and urged us to come

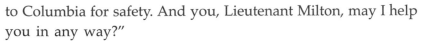

to Columbia for safety. And you, Lieutenant Milton, may I help you in any way?"

"Thank you, no. I hope to rejoin my unit soon. The doctor says I'm healing well, no infection. I can't seem to regain strength, though."

"The wound, the loss of blood and the other hardships you have endured for years have caused that, I expect." She stated the truth that he refused to utter.

"I don't want to fall into enemy hands. I have to get away somehow before Sherman's troops arrive. About the last thing any soldier wants, Rebel or Yankee, is to be taken prisoner."

"I have heard that General Hampton is here, or coming soon."

"Only to help in mounting and putting General Butler's division in the field, though. General Butler is currently serving on Beauregard's staff. He is supposed to defend the city, but a handful of battle-weary men aren't going to be able to put up much of a defense against the most seasoned group of veterans in the whole Yankee army."

"Sherman's troops? They are that strong?"

"Those men have been together a long time. They've done little actual fighting, mostly pursuit and mop-up... but they have marched hundreds of miles. They have stolen enough provisions to feed and equip two armies." His voice was filled with despair.

"Have we no hope of reinforcements?"

"From where?" He lifted the good shoulder. "Only great effort and good strategy have sustained us this long. Georgia fell for want of defenders. South Carolina is nearly helpless, and there are few troops in North Carolina. The audacity of General Lee is the single miracle still holding Virginia."

"It's difficult hearing my own fears confirmed." She sat on the straight chair by his cot, her eyes brimming with tears.

Lifting his good arm he reached toward her. Ellen placed her small hand in his large one. They comforted each other for a few silent moments. Then she stood, preparing to move on. "Lieutenant Milton, you know where our plantation is. If you can get there, you can recuperate a while longer and perhaps be safe from capture. Tell John, the black man I left in charge, I sent you. He will open the house and look after you. Pam and I will return as soon as it seems safe. You are welcome at my aunt's home on Laurel Street, but if the city falls it would be better for you to be found in the hospital."

"You are kind, Miss..." It was a question.

"Heyward. Ellen Heyward. I wish I could help get you to Oak Lane. Yesterday there were Union soldiers still camped on the road between here and home. I would ask Randolph to take you in the cart but you'd never get through."

"And you wouldn't get your mule and cart back either! If my legs will function I'll make a try. The Union men out there will likely come in to join the main force. Perhaps I can make it safely."

"Good luck," she whispered. She started to move away and then turned back. "My father, Major Henry Heyward, is with Butler's medical staff. Do you happen to know him? Have you seen him?"

"No, I'm sorry. The unit is widely scattered."

"I'm hoping he's near here. I should move on now." She smiled and looked toward the next cot.

"Some of Butler's men are in the hospital. Perhaps I can find someone who knows him for you."

"I would appreciate your help."

His eyes implored her to not to go. "I'll start to ask about. Will you come back?"

"Yes. I'll be back tomorrow." She walked away. Tomorrow she thought. Tomorrow will be February 14th, Valentine's Day.

Poor, gallant, disillusioned boy. Wounded, sick at heart. Hardly more than twenty years old, he was now a burned out shell.

Two days had passed and still no news about her father. Ellen straightened up wearily from the floor she was scrubbing. The dark oak planks of the college building were not suited to a hospital. Randolph, on his knees behind her, rinsed sloppily with a pail of cold water. She dried her hands, red from hours of immersion in hot water and homemade lye soap.

Outside the weather was cold and disagreeable. Dusk was gathering and she and the boy must soon make their way back to the house on Laurel Street.

"Randolph, please take the buckets outside and rinse them. You know where to leave them in the hallway for the night nurses. I'll visit Lieutenant Milton a few minutes and then meet you at the main gate. Don't be late. It's nearly dark."

"I be waiting, Miss Ellen."

She crossed the lawn, brown from the winter's cold and worn by the constant traffic back and forth. Her breath steamed white in the frigid air. Ellen wondered if her face reflected the same despair that she read on the countenance of every other person that she met.

Army ambulances and farm wagons and carts were bringing more sick and wounded. The stream of relatives who came to search for, care for, or to claim their loved ones continued to grow. Gloom and chill permeated everything. Yesterday it had rained again. February seemed to be stretching to forever.

She pushed open the heavy door and pasted a smile on her face. Most of the men now recognized her. Several waved weakly or called out greetings. Milton's cot was empty and Ellen turned to leave.

"Miss Ellen, please wait. I was looking for you." The lieutenant started walking toward her from the far end of the building on legs too weak for his skeletal frame. Perspiration glistened on his white forehead, despite the chill of the room.

"Sit down, Lieutenant Milton," she entreated. "I'm glad to see you up, but your legs are as unsteady as a newborn calf's."

"I'm trying to build strength," he explained, breathing hard. "Every hour or so I take a short walk. I have talked to some of the men and I have news for you."

Her face brightened.

"It's about your father." He paused. "Not good, I fear."

Her eyes met his bravely.

"I found a man who knows him. He was in a bed beside him. Your father was here. He is sick, influenza or pneumonia. He remembers Dr. Heyward, because, when he was not feverish, he took care of the seriously ill men around him. This was more than a week ago."

"And where is he now?" Ellen asked anxiously.

"When your father could no longer help in the hospital he began to make arrangements to go home. He said he could recover faster at home, and that would free his bed for some other soldier."

"Was he able to get someone to move him?"

"There was a big black man named Isaac who slept on the floor beside him at night. He helped with night nursing in the ward when your father didn't need him. Several days ago… the man couldn't remember exactly when, Dr. Heyward realized he had the measles. He was moved to the contagion ward. Since I am not allowed in there, that's all I have been able to learn." Milton reached his cot and eased himself down slowly.

Ellen put her hand on his good shoulder. "Again you have helped me, James. My indebtedness to you continues to mount."

He shyly smiled. "It has meant a lot to me these past few days knowing that you would be coming by to see me. I have been away from home three years. I miss my family... my sisters."

Ellen looked down at the earnest young face.

"I admire you very much." He looked up shyly.

Warm tears rushed to her eyes. "Thank you," she whispered. "I have been without father and friends, too. I understand. I hope you will accept me as an older sister. You risked your life to help me. I've grown very fond of you."

"I don't have a girlfriend," he blurted, reddening slightly. She stooped to kiss his forehead.

"I wish I were eighteen. I'd surely fall in love with you. Your mother must have hated to see you go to war! You can't be more than twenty years old."

"I'm twenty-two," he replied defensively. "I have had a year in college and almost three in the army. I'm not a boy."

"I know that! You are a fine, courageous young man, the kind young girls adore. If only I were young and beautiful!"

"You are a young and lovely woman, Miss Heyward. You will be when you are ninety." He smiled thinly.

"Alas, few others share your opinion," she countered gently. "My sister and I have always wanted a brother. Let us be your family until you get back to Beaufort." She reached down, squeezed his hand briefly and released it.

"Will I see you tomorrow?" he asked hopefully.

"I'm not sure. If Father is at home, Pam and I may try go back there. If Isaac doesn't come tonight, I'll ask for permission to work in the measles ward tomorrow."

She prepared to leave. "I will get Randolph to come and tell you where we are working if I don't come tomorrow."

"Please do. I'll look for men who have been recently released from the contagion ward and try to get more news for you. Your father would not want you to go back to the plantation with Sherman's army near."

"When I get to my aunt's tonight she'll have the latest rumors. We will decide what to do. I won't leave the city without letting you know."

"I hate feeling so helpless," he apologized.

"Nonsense. If you still want to try to get out of the hospital before the Union forces occupy the town, we'll take you with us. I don't know how far we'll get, but we'll surely try."

"No, if you were caught smuggling me out, you might be in trouble. Without me, the enemy will let you pass."

"We can tell them you have the measles," she replied. "That would help. We'll talk again tomorrow. Good night, Lieutenant."

"If I am to be your baby brother," he scowled in mock disgust, "you will have to start calling me Jim."

"Goodnight, Jim," She kissed her forefinger and placed it on his cheek.

Ellen's footsteps dragged as she turned the corner onto Laurel Street. Every night this week she had returned to the house bone-weary and gone straight to bed after supper. The street was deserted. She was later than usual getting home.

As she neared the house, what had appeared to be a dark shadow by the hitching post moved. A big man stood in her pathway. Fear wrapped itself around Ellen's heart.

Words boomed out of the darkness. "Miss Ellen, that you?"

She immediately recognized Isaac's deep musical voice. "Isaac," she breathed in relief, "I have been looking for you all week." She hurried toward him. "How is Father? Where is he?"

The big Negro waited silently until she was beside him. When she could see more clearly, Ellen searched his face. She saw tears begin to course down his cheeks.

"What? Is it that bad?" she asked holding her breath.

"Yes, mam, bad."

"Randolph, please go and tell the others that I will be in shortly." She sat down on the granite carriage block and breathed deeply. "Now, tell me about it."

"Mister Henry, he had a bad cough and cold. Bad. He been outside too much helping with the wounded. He got so bad off he had to come to the hospital. He keep right on doctoring there. Him and me work until he come down with the measles."

"I had heard about that." Ellen waited, afraid of what he would say next.

"When he wasn't able to be up no more he want to go home, be in his own bed to get well. He start looking for a way to get back to Oak Lane. He sent me here looking for you."

"Yes, I know. Hattie told us. Did you leave a message?"

"No, mam. No need to mess with telling that girl nothing. When she say you ain't here, I went back and told Mister Henry I go to the plantation and get the wagon and fetch him home myself. He was some happy to hear that." Isaac stopped talking.

"Go on," she prompted.

"I left early the next morning walking. I had to go way round through the deep woods so them Yankees near the Goodwyn place wouldn't see me. I come up the back way, through the pocosin and found Benjamin. He tell me about the fire and that you all done took the only cart when you left to come to town."

"What did you do then?"

"I didn't hardly know what to do. I went by to see Papa a few minutes and let him help me figure out the best thing to do. We make up our mind to get a wagon, don't say nothing to nobody, go get Mister Henry, and bring him home. Then Papa could nurse him while I come back and hunt for you and Miss Pam."

"When was this?"

"Three, four days ago. So much happen, I lose track. Next morning we get a farm mule from John and borrow a wagon from off the Taylor plantation. Ain't nobody there now. I took Mister Henry's own feather bed and pillows and fix up the wagon nice. I even got some of Mister Henry's regular clothes to put on him so the Yankees wouldn't know he was a soldier when we pass by them."

"That was a smart thing to do."

"Then Papa and me started back. We had to circle behind the soldiers. They weren't paying attention to the road that night, but it was hard dark before we got back here." Isaac paused to breathe and wipe off tears with his coat sleeve.

"Soon as we get to the hospital Mister Henry ready to leave right then. He was mighty bad off. Papa told him the night air be bad for him and the mule had to rest. Finally he say wait for daylight. The doctor came by to look at Mister Henry and just shake his head. Fever high, chest rattling. Doctor say take him on home, if that make him happy. So many sick in that place, Miss Ellen."

"I know, Isaac. I have been working in the hospital all week. I had thought I might find you and Father there."

"Next morning we get Mister Henry dressed in his clothes and carry him out to the wagon. Heap of folks coming and going. Don't nobody ask us no questions. Papa sit in the back and hold Mister Henry's head so the bumping don't bother him. He don't hardly even know Papa and me. He talking out of his head."

"I am glad Uncle Adam was with him."

"Around noontime we stop to rest the mule. We move quick as we can because we got to get home before dark catch us. We use the main road. Mister Henry so sick them soldiers couldn't worry him none. We most home when one of them Yankees stop us. We told him Mister Henry been visiting in Columbia and got sick, and we bringing him home. The soldier look at him and say 'Take him on home, boy. That's one old Reb that ain't going to give nobody no more trouble.' So we go on." Isaac's voice drifted away.

Ellen waited.

"Time we get to the house it's black dark. John and me take Mister Henry up to his room and fix him in his own bed. About the middle of the night he wake up and see Papa nursing him. He say 'Adam, go get Miss Elizabeth. Tell her I am sick and I need her.' Papa wipe his tears and say 'She be here directly.' Mister Henry close his eyes, smile nice and don't say no more."

"Father is dead, isn't he, Isaac?"

The big man nodded his head sadly.

"Yes'm. Miss Ellen, Papa and me sit with him rest of the night. About daybreak Mister Henry gone. I was coming to get you, but Papa and John say you and Miss Pam ain't got no business out there in the country by yourself with all them soldiers around. And, besides, there ain't nothing you could do for Mister Henry now nohow. Nobody to tell at the Taylor plantation and nobody at the Goodwyn's either. John and me built a nice pine box for Mister Henry. Esther cleaned and pressed his uniform and Papa dressed him just like he used to when he was a little boy."

"Bless you, Isaac."

"Yesterday we put him in the ground beside Miss Elizabeth. Papa prayed like Mister Henry's Papa taught him long time ago, and we testified what a good man he was. Then everybody sing some hymns." His big voice choked.

Ellen was too weary to shed more tears.

"After we get through with the burying, I go back home with my Papa. We ain't hardly had no sleep for two days. This morning, come light, I start back to town to find you."

Ellen sat quietly until she was able to speak. "You did the right thing. Thank you for being so good and faithful to my father, Isaac. He loved you and your father. I am glad he was at home with you when he died and not among strangers."

"If you need me, Miss Ellen, I stay. If you don't, I want to go back home and help Papa and John with the field work. They mighty shorthanded and I am tired of war."

"I understand. There is one thing I want you to do for me, if you think you can."

"Yes'm, I sure will try."

"There is a young soldier in the hospital. He was hurt helping Miss Pam and me. He's not able to get back to his unit. He doesn't want to be captured. I told him to go to Oak Lane and stay until he's stronger. He can never make it alone. Will you try to take him back with you and look after him for a while?"

"Yes, mam. Which building is he in? I go get him now. If he can't walk, I carry him til we get out of town. Outside, I might can find somebody let me borrow a horse. Don't worry. We make it sure."

"Thank you. Look for Lieutenant James Milton. He is in the third cot on the left in Building Two. You and Father worked in the building right beside his, so I know you can find him. He will recognize your name. I'll be coming back home as soon as I can."

Five

For more than a week Arledge and Kelly had been camping ten miles east of Columbia in the narrowing stretch of no-man's-land between the two opposing armies. Their tent was pitched a short distance from the small forward unit of scraggly, undisciplined Union scouts and foragers who had been dispatched weeks earlier to begin amassing supplies for Sherman's slow-moving main force.

"Kelly, these men have told us all they know about the three missing bummers. Why is there no further trace of them?"

"Could have deserted. Scavengers are a wild bunch. Questionable absences for men like them ain't uncommon."

"On foot? You don't think that."

"Naw. Ain't sure what I do think."

The two of them were accustomed to working alone on assignments, and miles ahead of headquarters. Both men were thorough and skilled. The major's continued preoccupation with these particular missing men was unusual.

John hunkered down on a camp stool beside a small fire. He sipped coffee from a tin cup, long legs stretched out toward the heat. Reaching for the notebook in his breast pocket, he began to carefully leaf through, scanning once more the pages of neatly written script.

Kelly, squatting on the other side of the fire, dipped hard-tack into his steaming cup and absently chewed on the softened dough. They had long since become inured to life in the open, but the past few days had been particularly nasty.

"I thought the South was supposed to be warm, Major."

"Not always. Gets cold here, too." He would not be distracted. "Those men are dead, aren't they?"

"I expect so, Major. Been missing two weeks now. Too long for a drunk, too far from home for them to desert. There ain't enough Rebs around to have captured them. Anyhow, having to retreat ahead of us, what would Rebs want with prisoners?"

"So the answer is here. Why haven't we made any progress?"

"I've scouted the whole area between here and town. Right now there ain't no soldiers around but this group we are with. The only people moving are women, children and old folks scurrying into Columbia with what possessions they can carry."

"You have been into town?"

"No, but some of the boys have. They saw a few military there, wounded and the like, but if the Confederate army ever was here in any strength, it has pulled out now. Don't you think we ought to get to working on something else?" Kelly searched Arledge's face, watching for some reaction.

"Kelly, we have a job to do and we are going to do it. The locals may be foundering in a sea of uncertainty, but we are not." Fierce blue eyes squinted at him through the pungent smoke.

"So with nothing happening here, General Sherman is going to head for Charleston, huh?"

"No, he's coming here. I know the old man. Next to Richmond, he'd rather capture Columbia than any other city. The rebellion started here. He won't let anybody forget that fact."

"What about Wade Hampton?" Kelly probed. "With him and the general feuding right now, and this place being where his home is and all, don't you expect Hampton to come and put up a defense?"

John rose from the stool, carefully buttoning his blouse. "Sergeant, General Hampton might posture and threaten, but he's too far away and his men are spread too thin. They don't have the equipment or supplies to be coming to anybody's rescue."

"Yep, I reckon the only thing coming this way is Uncle Billy Sherman and that bunch of tough, mean bastards with him," agreed Kelly. He rose to his full height. The sergeant was a head shorter than Arledge, and fifteen years older. The two men had soldiered together for nearly ten years, first in the west, then just beyond the Mississippi River, and now through Georgia and South Carolina.

"And they'll be here soon, so let's get on with it, Kelly."

Kelly delayed. "I'm thinking that mouthy little woman at the plantation back yonder killed the men and hid the bodies."

The younger man looked at him sharply. "It occurred to me."

"I wondered if it had. Now, I ain't saying the men didn't need killing," he continued, "but as you always tell me, Major, we ain't the ones to decide that." He watched for reaction.

Arledge contemplated him in icy silence.

"I guess you just don't want to arrest a woman." He knew exactly how far to push his superior.

"I'll arrest anybody who should be arrested, Kelly, and you know it," he barked. "We don't have proof of anything yet, except that the men were there. We'll keep working. The general wants hostile civilian acts punished, that's what you and I will see done."

Same as usual. Stiff-necked and determined. Kelly knew what to expect from the quiet Virginian. "You went back out there yesterday, didn't you. You know she's gone."

"I know."

"Ain't saying much, are you?"

"No."

"One of the boys told me he stopped some women on the road Sunday. Could have been her."

"I heard."

"She get under your skin?"

Another sharp stare. "Why do you ask that?"

"I been with you a long time, Major. You don't usually pay a whole lot of attention to the women. This one you did notice. And," he paused for emphasis, "you don't run across many women who ain't kind of taken with you either. I saw some of them rebel ladies down in Savannah eyeing you. This one didn't."

"Any women in Savannah that were encouraging Union soldiers weren't ladies, Sergeant."

"I'd say that would be even better." He grinned wolfishly.

"Well, I'm not quite the womanizer you are."

"But this one, this Heyward lady, different, ain't she?"

"Not 'taken' with me, you mean?" The Virginian grinned.

"I ain't saying that. There's encouragement and there's encouragement. She got your attention, didn't she? Sometimes a spitting tiger can be a heap more interesting than a tame house cat. You know what I mean?"

"No, but I'm sure you will tell me."

"There's more to that lady's story than what she told us."

"Could be. Anyhow, we'll keep at it." Arledge positioned his hat on his head and turned to go.

A soldier from the adjoining campsite approached and saluted. "Major Arledge, a courier just rode in. He says General Wood's boys are coming in from across the river. Strung out a long way, moving ten or twelve miles a day, but coming."

"Good, I've been waiting on further instructions. I'm ready to see the man as soon as he gets a cup of coffee."

A slender young soldier strode up, saluted and handed Arledge a dispatch case. "Good morning, Major. The general sends his regards. Things are moving slow. With all this rain, General Wood's men have been having to lay corduroy roads most of the way for the supply wagons following behind them."

"What about the bridges from the other side. Been burned?"

"No, sir, not yet. Civilians are still pouring into town."

"And our main army? When will they be getting here?"

"Hard to tell. General Sherman has put his men to tearing up rail lines, wants cross ties and rail sections dug up and set on fire. The engineers got some kind of special claws to twist up the bars when they get hot. He's fixing them so they can't be relaid, calling them 'Sherman's neckties'."

Arledge listened to his commanding officer without comment. The general's policies were harsh. Sherman's successes since the capture of Atlanta in September had not only boosted Union morale, but had also assured President Lincoln's re-election in November.

Arledge did not always agree with his general's decisions, but he understood his strategy. Leaving Atlanta in flames on November 13, William Tecumseh Sherman, forty-four years old and in his prime, had moved one hundred thousand men over three hundred miles to the sea in a path of destruction sixty miles wide. He was proud of his march.

In old newspapers, John had read that Jefferson Davis was calling this victorious Atlanta campaign a 'Moscow disaster.' While northern editors wondered where Sherman was, southern newspapers claimed that he was trapped, beaten and fleeing for his life toward the coast. Editors accused him of pursuing only territorial objectives, reminding their readers that Sherman had never once commanded in a battle where he engaged his whole force. Nor had he, they claimed, ever won a resounding victory.

"Uncle Billy ain't never going to let nobody know where he is and what he's going to do next," the young courier boasted.

"I expect you are right, soldier," Arledge agreed.

John knew Sherman was an enigma, secretive and suspicious where the press was concerned. It was evident that Sherman felt he had been maligned by them in the past, so the general made it a practice to bar all newspapermen and photographers from his inner circle.

Arledge found his general an intriguing commanding officer. A light sleeper and a constant cigar smoker, the man was always anxious and ill-at-ease. At times he was somber and morose. Then these spells would be followed by periods of explosive energy, during which he talked rapidly and incessantly. Few people understood Sherman, and among the generals, only Grant truly respected his ability.

Following the destruction of Atlanta, Sherman's primary goal had been to scatter Confederate forces, devastate the countryside and demoralize the civilian population. His display of overwhelming strength, and the use of economic warfare were having the psychological effect of making battle unnecessary. Tough strategy, but totally effective, Arledge grudgingly admitted.

"I reckon the old man's about ready to send the President another telegram," Kelly observed.

"Probably."

They recalled the general's delight when he sent the highly publicized message to the President, 'I beg to present you as a Christmas gift the city of Savannah.' It was Sherman's supreme moment. He despised reporters, yet they were attracted to him. He was now one of the most written about generals of the war.

"The way things been going lately, the old man's bound to be happy."

Arledge grimaced and nodded.

"Probably, if he knows how to be happy. I'm sure he's glad to be moving. He thought we stayed in Savannah too long, worried that the troops would soften up. The general gets impatient when the local women start complaining and asking for protection."

"But you the one who has to handle most of that."

"Usually turns out that way."

Arledge read the orders he had received. His job was always one of dealing with civilians... interrogation, negotiation, amelioration, pacification, and the myriad of administrative details that the lank, red-haired Sherman so detested.

"Looks like we'll be in Columbia within a day or two doing the same old things again, Kelly. He wants us to prepare to set up office." Arledge consoled himself with the thought that each task completed moved the war closer to the final conclusion.

"Sir, I brought you some fairly recent newspapers." The courier handed him a package.

Arledge reached hungrily for the papers. "I'll pass these on to the men. What seems to be happening inside the city?"

"Confusion mostly, Major. I hung around a little while and listened to people talking. The stories the refugees coming up from Georgia and the lowcountry are telling have people real scared. People say street lights been out for the last few weeks. Crime in town is increasing. Folks are afraid to go out at night. There's over twenty thousand extra people packed in the city and less than five hundred of them are men."

"How about military inside the city?"

"Practically none, and General Wood and our Fifteenth Corps are sitting over yonder right now less than six miles away on the banks of the Little Congaree."

"Did you notice any apparent plans to defend the city?"

"I heard some worrying about ammunition being abandoned. Seems General Beauregard ordered Hampton to have all the cotton stored in warehouses rolled out into the streets. I don't know why. They sure got no way to move it."

"Perhaps they plan to use it as barricades."

The courier shook his head. "No, they are bound to know the main enemy force is bearing right down on them. They can see them, if they look across the river."

"Get some rest, soldier. Any food left over there, Kelly?"

"Yes, sir. They got potatoes and bacon. Plenty of coffee. Roast chicken for tonight. They been finding food all right, but they waiting to round up hogs and cattle until after they know where to set up holding pens. They asking me what you think."

"Wait another day or two. We need to be nearer, probably inside the city. They'll be able to find some areas already fenced in when we get there. I expect we are going to have a bunch of civilians to feed, too, soon after we arrive."

The loss of her father was not a surprise to Ellen. Since their mother's death ten years earlier, he had been a distant and lonely man. Day-to-day management of the plantation was left to Ellen. He took little interest in the decisions made. Though he still pored over his farm journal his heart was not in it.

Henry Heyward lacked the physical strength for the hard life of an army doctor. He had, nevertheless, volunteered repeatedly and, once accepted, totally buried himself in the work. He had been home rarely since.

The choice to serve in the army was his. Ellen tried to reconcile herself to his death, but, in truth, she knew that her life would be little changed.

"Aunt Sophie," Ellen announced at breakfast, "Pam has agreed to go to the Ursuline Convent. I'm going with her to talk to the sisters and then on to the College. Will you be all right?"

"Yes, dear. Mariah is here. All any of us can do is wait."

"I don't know when for you to expect me to be back. I'll be safe at the hospital, so don't be concerned. If I'm too badly needed on the ward tonight to leave, I'll try to let you know."

By eight o'clock the Heyward sisters were struggling to weave their way through the four crowded city blocks to the convent. Already people were rushing to and fro in a seeming frenzy of indecision. Randolph, carrying Pam's bag, was warned he must keep up with them.

"Yes, mam." The boy was still awed by city sights. "Ain't wanting to get lost here."

Groups of people were gathering on street corners talking excitedly. Several unescorted women, a sight never seen on the streets before the war years, were hurrying about.

Civilians wearing grave expressions huddled in tight knots and whispered quietly. Occasionally, soldiers uniformed in gray or butternut could be seen. The men tried to avoid questions as they pushed their way through the crowd, bent on some mission.

The convent, a large two-story building, was on the southeast corner of Richardson and Blanding Streets, Formerly the America Hotel, the structure could house two hundred pupils.

Ellen's knock on the street door was answered by one of the younger sisters. They were shown into the reception room and asked to wait for the superioress, Mother Baptista Lynch. Ellen looking about at the obviously valuable furnishings, noted several beautiful French tapestries and original oil paintings.

Within a few minutes the mother superioress entered the room. She waited for one of the girls to speak.

"Good morning, sister. I am Ellen Heyward and this is my sister Pamela. Do you have accommodations for Pam to stay temporarily in your custody? We are not from Columbia. We live on a plantation outside of town, and we're not Catholics."

Ellen made it a habit to be direct.

"Welcome to the Convent of the Ladies Ursuline Community." The clipped words, spoken rapidly, were in a midwestern dialect. "We do not require that our students be Catholic."

"I urged my sister to come here because I thought she might be safer. We have lost both of our parents." She stopped to clear her throat. "I am staying with an elderly aunt, but Pamela is young. Considering the rumors about and present uncertainty, we prefer that she be in your care."

"Of course, my dear," the sister replied softly. "We have plenty of room. Only about forty girls with us at present. They range in age from young children to adults. Sister Agnes can acquaint your sister with our school and with the other girls."

She gestured to Pamela to follow her to meet the other nun.

"Please wait here, Miss Heyward. I will return in a moment and we can complete the other necessary arrangements."

Pam took her bag from Randolph and prepared to leave.

Ellen wrapped her in her arms. "Pam, nobody knows what the next few days will bring. I'm sure it's safe here. I have read that Sherman himself is Catholic. He will see that the nuns and their pupils are protected."

"He will," the superioress said with certainty. "His daughter Minnie was a pupil of mine in a convent in Ohio. I'll remind him, and ask for his protection. I anticipate no trouble."

"I plan to keep working at the hospital, if the Union forces allow me to. I may even stay there at night for a while."

Pamela nodded mutely.

"I'll ask Aunt Sophie to go to a friend's house, or have someone stay with her for the next few days. Large groups of people will likely fare better than small. As soon as the crisis is over, I'll come for you and we'll go back home."

Pam clung for a moment, seeking strength. "Don't worry about me, Ellen. I will be fine," she mouthed woodenly.

Ellen watched her go, straight back and narrow shoulders disappearing down the hallway behind the nun.

The mother superior returned shortly. "I think Pamela will find contentment with us. We have several girls with whom she should be compatible. Our pupils are kept busy and as sheltered from the outside trouble as we can manage."

"Do you have adequate food for everyone at the convent?"

"We have enough. We converted our money into provisions. We thought food would be of more value to us than cash. Of such as it is, we have plenty." She spoke with calm authority.

"I don't know how long my sister will be with you, nor if I will be able to pay for her board right away."

"We can discuss that later," she assured Ellen comfortingly.

"Pamela can help with the younger girls. She is mature… for her age," she added, "and accustomed to responsibility."

"My dear, you need not make explanations or tell me anything you don't wish to reveal. I have worked with girls a long time. It's apparent to me that Pamela's school girl appearance and her actual age are incompatible. With all the stories circulating, I don't wonder that you tried to disguise the fact that she is a young woman and quite beautiful."

"Our plantation was recently raided by a party of Union soldiers. That's why we fled here. We had a painful experience, and we have recently learned of our father's death. Pamela hasn't been well. I'm not sure how much more she can withstand. I hope Sherman will not make Columbia into another Atlanta."

"Miss Heyward, your sister may stay with us until you come for her. I don't think you could find a safer place for her."

Randolph rose from the bottom step of the convent doorway the minute Ellen came out.

"Scary out here, Miss Ellen," he observed. "Real scary."

"I know it is. Too many people rushing around. Let's go to the hospital. They need us this morning."

She breathed a prayer of gratitude that Pam could stay cloistered while the rest of the city seemed to be going mad.

Randolph solemnly trailed behind as they began the long walk down the street toward the State House.

Despite the crowds Ellen was able to move fast. Bales of cotton lined Richardson Street from Richland to Laurel. She counted two hundred more stacked at the intersection in front of City Hall. There was cotton at Blanding, Plain and Washington Streets. More bales were concentrated near the capitol square.

"What all this cotton for?" Randolph asked as he continually lagged behind, watching the crowds mill about.

"I don't know, Randolph. Maybe they plan to move it. Anyhow, we have to keep going," she reminded him.

They covered the mile down the street to the capitol and soon reached the location of the new capitol building that the state had begun to erect a few years earlier. It was still largely a construction site. Snatches of several conversations reached Ellen's ears. She paused to rest and to listen.

"Sherman will demand surrender of the city… Hampton can't fight, outnumbered sixty to one… cotton on nearly every street in town, might use it as a barricade… Hampton ordered it there in case they have to burn it… thousands of Yankees on the Lexington side of the city right up to the river's edge… heard the town is full of whiskey… our soldiers are pulling out…"

A crowd had gathered on the State House grounds. The people were looking and pointing westward to the hills across the river. Ellen's eyes followed the upraised arms. Clearly discernible on the New Brookland Heights was the enemy. The entire area was alive with men. Trees were being felled, ground leveled, tents set up and bivouac established. The smoke of countless campfires climbed into the air. Drum and trumpet signals could be heard.

The crowd around Ellen was speculating as to whether the enemy troops were getting settled for the night, digging in for a long stay, or girding for an immediate all-out attack.

"Our army is coming back. There will be a major battle."

"No, I heard our troops are retreating. Columbia is to be declared an open city," contradicted someone.

"Orders to burn the cotton were in the paper this morning, but the major who gave the order left the city yesterday."

Ellen realized that the mass confusion was paralyzing. Coordinated effort by any group, military or civilian, would be virtually impossible. The same air of disorganization and panic observed at the other end of town existed here, too. Moving farther down the street, she could see that the railroad depot was awash with people... jammed almost to the point of suffocation.

To stand and listen to rumors and allow feelings of anxiety and despair to well within her served no useful purpose. They would not linger. Work at the hospital would be sufficient to keep mind and body fully occupied, both hers and Randolph's.

While they waited at the street corner an army wagon train at least half a mile long rumbled slowly through the unpaved street toward the Charleston depot. Something important was being moved out. The drivers quietly urged their teams on. It was as if they were trying to steal unnoticed from a doomed city.

"Randolph," Ellen instructed as soon as they were inside the hospital compound, "I want you to move through the ward from bed to bed looking for Lieutenant Milton. He may be gone, but we must be sure. If any of the men ask you for a cup of water or something, get it, but keep looking for Lieutenant Milton. Isaac may be with him."

"Yes'm. I rather be inside with you today, anyhow."

"Good. You can help me with the nursing."

On and off all day they could hear the thunderous booming of enemy cannon. The occasional noise of trains indicated
that some were still running, though schedules were erratic.
Whistles blew and wagons continued to rumble through the
streets. With each new person arriving at the hospital came
fresh conflicting rumors.

"That soldier you looking for ain't here, Miss Ellen."
Randolph made his report at midday. "I done looked everywhere in both buildings."

"Good. Perhaps that means they have gone to Oak Lane."

"Somebody told me that every soldier able to walk done
skedaddled."

Ambulances continued to bring wounded to the college
grounds. The sky had resumed its incessant drizzle. Flags pro-
claiming the college buildings to be hospitals had been raised
at the gates of the campus.

All day Ellen worked with stoic determination. She tried
not to think of personal concerns. Where was Arledge today?
Would all the new activity divert his interest from her? Surely
he would be too busy for continued pursuit.

By nightfall the thunder of the cannons sounded nearer.
When that noise subsided, the sharp crack of musketry claimed
the silence. Alarm bells clanged a warning of fire somewhere.

"It's real late. Ain't us going home, Miss Ellen?"

"No, Randolph. They need us at the hospital." The relief
nurse was late. She did not add that it sounded too unsafe
outside to be on the streets. The whole Union army had surely
arrived. Ellen passed an outside window and could see that
the western horizon was lit with the glow of fire. There were
no curtains for her to close. She had to fight to still her own
feeling of panic.

A terrible lull-before-the-battle kind of calmness settled over
the ward. Randolph sat down in a corner near her looking anxious. Some of the men were quietly reading. During the late

afternoon she had been asked to write several letters to loved ones. Now there were no requests. The atmosphere filled with mounting tension. The night nurse did not arrive. Ellen knew the woman had children. She had not expected her to come.

"Randolph, we have to stay here tonight. Please go to the kitchen area and see if they have some supper for you. Try to bring me back something." While he was gone she hunted for a blanket and a place on the hospital floor for the boy to sleep.

"Got you some soup, Miss Ellen. All they had." Randolph carefully handed her a bowl of lukewarm gruel, the same they had served patients earlier. She showed him where to sleep. After ten o'clock the ward grew quiet.

Ellen stepped outside to look around. She turned the oil lamp down low and opened the door on the horseshoe. Smoke and the odor of gunpowder in the night air was stifling. She could hear muffled shouts from the few able-bodied Confederate soldiers still left in the compound as they assembled for formation on the street ready to march out.

After a few minutes she closed the door and started her late rounds. She carried a sputtering candle. There was no more gas for the lights. There had been no fuel until someone cut down one of the beautiful old trees on the campus. She moved nearer the fireplace, and stood before the flickering flames. What would the next day bring?

In the early morning the scene abruptly changed. Men from Butler's cavalry, who had been harassing Union troops from the Lexington side of the river, retreated into Columbia burning the bridge behind them.

Ellen overheard a soldier say that Generals Slocum and Sherman arrived just in time to find the bridge in flames. Across the Broad River from them Columbia lay in plain view. Union troops could easily identify the granite outlines of the unfinished state house. A Union officer unlimbered a section of twenty pound Parott guns and began sporadic shelling of the town.

Ellen's ward was startled awake by the noise. The thick hospital walls felt the reverberations. Wounded veterans, long familiar with the sound, knew the waiting period had ended. The city was being fired on by the Union army from across the river.

Ellen had drifted into a disturbed sleep about three in the morning. She had spent the night in a wooden classroom chair, her head resting on a table the hospital staff had brought from the college science laboratory. Her body felt stiff. She was cold and hungry. The joints of her fingers were swollen. Her vision was bleary, eyes dry and gritty. She needed a bath. Rising gingerly, she made her way to the outside door.

In the chill morning air Ellen took a deep breath. She had hoped that fresh air would clear her head, but the smell of gunpowder was too strong. At the well she drew cold water to splash on her face.

Looking through the campus gates across the river, she was able to make out troops up on the hilltops. As she stood watching, a shell whirred past her head. It fell and exploded close by. Stunned, she darted back inside the hospital building.

Randolph had been asleep on the floor near Ellen's chair. He was awakened by the sound of the explosions. Frightened, he was looking anxiously for her.

"Them Yankees here, Miss Ellen. Our folks be worried. Us got to go home," he pleaded. Unusual behavior. Randolph rarely said more than three words at a time.

"We'll leave as soon as we can," she promised. "Don't be frightened. This is a hospital and the Yankees will not fire on wounded men. Some of their own soldiers are in here. Get us some warm water and we will help the men wash their faces."

"Yes'm, but us got to go home."

The regular routine of activity was changed. Doctors and orderlies were out on the green preparing for immediate evacuation. Concern for the safety of the wounded was uppermost.

A Confederate officer's head appeared in the doorway.

"Miss," he called, motioning to Ellen. "Please tell the doctor in charge that walking wounded who do not wish to be captured must prepare to move out now. We plan to bring the litter cases from other parts of the city to be concentrated here."

"The hospital has been fired on several times, sir. Aren't the wounded as safe in private homes as they will be here?"

"No, Miss. Shelling of the hospital has stopped. There was a small contingent of cavalry in the street near the college chapel. We realized they were drawing the fire and they have dispersed. These buildings will be safe now."

As he spoke the Union battery could be heard still firing, though a yellow flag signifying a hospital building floated above the chapel. After breakfast time there was a two hour lull in the shelling. Throughout the city indecision and nervous waiting were replaced by crisis planning for personal safety.

"Government stores in the main part of town have been thrown open to the people. There is a big scramble out there for supplies," an orderly reported. "I heard that all Confederate soldiers will be out of the city by nightfall."

The sick and wounded from makeshift hospitals and homes in the area began to arrive. Soldiers unable to travel were concentrated in College Hospitals One and Two. When activity began to slow, the Chief Surgeon issued orders for all army doctors on duty in Columbia to report to points beyond the city. They were to prepare to move out with the troops.

After another thorough search through the wards, Ellen was certain that James Milton was no longer there. Isaac must have been able to move him to Oak Lane.

Several times during the day she wondered what role John Arledge was playing in the fall of Columbia. She hoped that he would be too busy with other duties to go back out to Oak Lane. If he should find Milton there, he might connect him to the investigation he was conducting.

"Randolph, you can go on back to Laurel Street now," Ellen told the boy at midday. He was tired and there was little he could do to help with the new patients being brought in. "Tell Aunt Sophie what has been happening at the hospital and that I'm fine. You know the way home, don't you?"

"Folks shooting out there, Miss Ellen. I'm scared."

"You will be all right. You are a big brave boy, Randolph. Remember you drove the cart all the way here for us. Leave now. Don't stop to look at things or talk to anyone. People who see you out will know you were entrusted with an important errand."

"Yes'm, but when you coming?"

"I'll stay here again tonight. Come back for me tomorrow. Wait by the well in the early afternoon. Get here in plenty of time for us to make it back to the house before dark."

"Yes'm," he replied doubtfully. He stuck his head out the door, quickly looked in every direction and departed at a run.

People continued to straggle into the wards all afternoon with more wounded. Ellen was kept abreast of the latest rumors and news. The cots, so recently emptied, were soon filled.

She was told that women and children, fearful for their lives during the shelling, had rushed to the State Hospital for the Mentally Ill. The high brick walls surrounding the institution, more than two feet thick, afforded a measure of safety. Despite hunger and cold they had remained huddled behind the solid fencing all day. What would Robert Mills, the architect, think of such use for his beautiful building and grounds?

"Union prisoners of war were confined in the barred-window cells at the asylum, weren't they?" someone asked.

"They were, but this morning they were released. I heard they went downtown to wait for their army to cross the river."

For three days now Columbia had been under martial law. Though Federal troops occasionally shelled from across the river, there had been no demand for surrender. Hurried war councils were meeting to plan how they should handle Sherman's actual entrance.

In late afternoon, according to rumor, the governor and his officials left the city. Elderly Mayor Thomas Jefferson Goodwyn was informed that the last of the Confederate soldiers would evacuate by morning, and the city would then be officially under civil authority.

Ellen continued to work throughout the day. She had attended to her responsibilities the best she could. The convent was a safe haven for Pam, and the others were at the house on Laurel Street.

She was accustomed to using work as an antidote for worry. The ward grew quiet around midnight. A second night would be spent in the straight chair, with her head resting on the lab table. By tomorrow they would surely know what Sherman planned to do.

Six

Day dawned on the 17th, murky and oppressive. When Ellen stepped outside the hospital door, a dramatic change in weather was immediately noticeable—dry, finally, and warm for February. A high steady wind reminiscent of March was blowing from the northwest. Acrid, smoke-filled air stung her nose and soon had her sniffing. All plantation hands were alerted to watch for forest fires. Tightening her shawl, she walked to the well to freshen up. There was no time for indulgence in nervous apprehension.

Ellen saw Emma LeConte, precocious daughter of the mathematics professor, standing on the green nearby.

"You're out early this morning, Emma," she called. Through the years she had seen and talked with the young girl at campus lectures and concerts.

"I barely slept all last night, Miss Ellen. I perceive that distressing events are occurring in the city. A noise awakened me and from the window of my room I saw an alarming fire."

"I heard it, too." Ellen cupped water in her hands to splash on her face. Even under duress little Emma's speech remained precise.

They later learned that after daylight the city had been jolted by a loud explosion. New arrivals at the hospital said plunderers, knowing that quantities of valuables were still in the South Carolina Railroad depot awaiting shipment, had broken into the building. Torches had touched off ammunition which was to have been shipped to Charlotte. Several men were killed and the depot caught fire. The fire, some distance away, was not a threat to the city.

"Aren't city officials taking charge?" Ellen asked.

"Yes," an orderly replied. "Mayor Goodwyn was summoned early to the Town Hall to meet with aldermen and prepare to surrender the city. There is a white flag raised above the market steeple. At nine the mayor and three aldermen, in a carriage bearing a white flag, proceeded to where Sherman's troops were beginning to cross the river."

The burning of the Columbia to Charlotte rail terminal was the last official act of the evacuating Rebels. By ten o'clock Butler's division, the cavalry rear guard of Beauregard's army, began to assemble. While the remnants of the defending force, fewer than five thousand men gathered, the skirmish line of the Federal advance troops was approaching the city suburbs.

On Laurel Street Aunt Sophie watched as the Confederate soldiers moved out. Staunch little family groups waited on nearly every piazza and watched through tears the silent orderly retreat. They waved and tried to call hearty farewells to the men they recognized. For the first time in the long war those left behind felt that their own need to be heartened might be as great as that of the men filing past.

She was positioned alone on her porch watching and waving bravely. The woman had hardly slept all night. Pamela, she felt, was safe at the Ursuline School for Girls, but Ellen was still at the College hospital. One of the departing soldiers rode up on the sidewalk in front of the Whilden house in the next block. Sophie recognized Captain John Lanneau, a neighbor's son, an engineer on Hampton's staff.

Captain Lanneau paused, raised his cap and called out to those who stood proudly paying respect to their retreating army, "God bless and protect you all."

Bits of information, often conflicting, reached Ellen with each new arrival. The surrender delegation had presented a written statement requesting that 'citizens of Columbia be given the treatment accorded by the usage of civilized warfare' and that 'sufficient guards be sent in advance of the army to maintain order and protect the persons and the property of the citizens.' Colonel Stone, acting brigadier, met them and accepted the surrender. He guaranteed protection until the general arrived.

Across the river Arledge waited while Sherman sat on a log quietly watching his troops prepare to enter the city of the Secession Convention. "It is no small thing," the general remarked, satisfaction evident on his face, "to march into the heart of the enemy's country and take his capital."

As they delayed, Sherman received a note from a Catholic sister claiming to be a former teacher of his daughter. The nun was requesting protection of her convent.

About midday, formal entrance into the city began. A detachment of soldiers was sent ahead to remove the barricades blocking the wide thoroughfare. The carriage of the mayor turned around and drove back to city hall. Behind Mayor Goodwyn rode Sherman and his staff. They were followed by blue-coated regiments of infantry, cavalry and artillery, many of whom were from the northwestern states of the Union.

Near-gale winds were blowing cotton from the torn and cut bales lining the streets. White wisps lodged in lifeless tree branches along the way, giving the city an ethereal ghostly appearance. Like tumbleweed, little bits of cotton rolled about the streets gathering dried leaves. By late afternoon the trees and streets of the city, covered with this highly combustible mixture, looked as if a northern snowstorm had struck.

Through closely curtained windows frightened citizenry peeped at the man that a Cincinnati newspaper had labeled insane. They looked for the flaming red hair and the fierce shaggy beard. They also knew about his nervous, sanguine temperament and fiery snapping eyes.

Behind the general, Arledge could hear the measured tramp of soldiers. The endless, heaving multitude of fearsome Yankees made an awesome sound. The troops, in highest spirits, sang and yelled boisterously. Except for a group of jubilant, recently-released Federal prisoners of war and a few curious Negroes, the streets were deserted. The agonizing immediacy of defeat had settled upon the people.

"Damn! Folks here are all holed up in their viper's nests!" the colonel riding beside Arledge swore.

"Nobody left here, Sir, but women, children and old men."

"Where are they all hiding, Arledge? You are a southerner."

"Most of able-bodied men are in the trenches around Petersburg and Richmond."

The entire Fifteenth Corps entered the city and distributed themselves along different streets and lanes. There was not enough room for them all. Some units had to make camp on the outskirts of town.

In early afternoon Ellen heard rumors that the first troops had left ranks and broken open Mordecai's and Heise's liquor shops. Streets and roads throughout the city were soon reported to be filled with drunken soldiers.

Sometime later, while wearily making rounds from one hospital building to the next, Ellen first heard the shouting of enemy troops. As she walked from Legare College to Pinckney she again saw seventeen-year-old Emma LeConte standing in the doorway. Her home, the stately faculty residence house, was beside the front gate, just inside the college walls. Lovely, brilliant little Emma was a favorite on campus.

"Miss Ellen," she called, "what recent news have you had?"

"Not much, Emma. Nothing since Mayor Goodwyn's surrender."

"Come upstairs with me," Emma invited. "We can see the whole city from there."

Together they climbed the tall narrow stairway that ran beside the stairs of the adjoining house. Through the high top-floor bedroom windows the two had an unobstructed view of the panorama below. Already the United States flag was flying over the State House. They sensed the terror gripping the city.

"Oh, what degradation," sobbed Emma in her very formal and precise manner, "after four long years of bloodshed and hatred, to see that symbol of despotism once more."

Ellen looked across the city in grim silence.

They watched as a Yankee contingent arrived to guard the hospital. The soldiers began building a makeshift shelter next to the gate. Sentinels were posted and preparation of their delayed noon meal began. The men had to keep chasing their hats which were constantly being blown off their heads by the high wind.

"Other than the wounded men and occasional prisoners, this is the first sight I have had of Union soldiers," Emma remarked.

Ellen thought of the drunken foragers, now dead, and of the coldly handsome Arledge. Was he among the invading horde?

"Thank you, Emma, for sharing your vantage point. I must go meet my escort home. The streets may soon be dangerous."

"Oh, yes. I fear they will be." Emma, preoccupied, studied the scene below. "I shall record all I see in my journal."

After the formal entry into the city had ended, the higher ranking Union officers sought comfortable quarters. Many houses had already been abandoned by owners looking for safer shelter. The better homes were ordered evacuated for officers. Enlisted men were bivouacking in the streets or taking possession of unoccupied buildings. Some were setting up lodgings in the front yards and on porches of inhabited homes.

Visitors to the hospital, filled with anxiety and disgust, declared that Sherman's troops had surely been collected from the lowest orders of humanity. Except for Midwesterners, the men they had seen were predominantly Irish and German immigrants. Contact with them so far had not been pleasant.

From three o'clock on Ellen could hear elements of the army passing down the streets by the college campus to encamp in the woods behind. She watched long wagon trains roll past. The men looked strong and well-fed. They wore sturdy shoes and warm dark blue woolen uniforms, a great contrast to the varying shades of gray, brown, blue, and French butternut that she was accustomed to seeing Confederate soldiers wearing.

The shouts of soldiers as they converged on the State House grounds sent waves of fear through Ellen. She was thankful to be too far away to see the arson and pillaging begin. Shadows were gathering. Soon it would be dark.

The wooded area south of the college was dotted with campfires of soldiers preparing their supper. A huge orange glow dominated the sky a few miles away in the direction of Millwood, General Hampton's plantation. She spotted a fire on Main Street. A house on Sumter was burning so brightly that she could feel the heat.

Ellen found Randolph waiting on the horseshoe near the well as he had been instructed. Several older black boys were sitting with him.

"Thank you for coming, Randolph. We need to leave right away," she said quickly, trying not to reveal the relief she felt to know that he was there to accompany her.

"Yes'm, bad out there. Met these boys on the street and they came with me." He nodded to a knot of slightly older youngsters. "Yankees out there setting fires and tearing up things awful. Ain't you scared?"

"The soldiers are either busy or drunk. They won't pay any attention to us. We'll be all right," she assured. "Let's go."

Randolph turned to the boys. "We got to go way cross town. Don't you all want to walk with us? Where your house is?"

The largest of the four answered. "Don't live here. Ain't got no house here. We come to see what Yankee soldiers look like. Don't know nothing about this place."

"Come with us," Ellen suggested. "You can sleep at our home tonight. I'll see that you get supper."

There was greater safety in numbers. She buttoned her coat and pulled her shawl over her head to cover her face and disguise her identity. Surrounded by the boys she moved toward the front gate. The posted sentry squinted through the gathering dark at the group.

"Where are you boys going?" he challenged.

"Tell him we are going home," Ellen whispered.

"Us going home," Randolph answered. "Our folks be worried."

"All right," the guard answered, "but you better stay clear of the drunk soldiers. It sounds like a lot of celebrating is going on out there."

He signaled them through the gate and the group moved around the high brick wall to Sumter Street.

"Boys, we should walk as fast and as quietly as we can," Ellen instructed. "Let me lead the way, but stay close around me. Don't be talking and causing anyone to take notice of us."

The little band headed north toward Laurel Street. They could cover the distance in half an hour if they traveled fast and were not stopped. In the red glare from a burning house, she could see soldiers staggering toward their campsites on the edge of town.

Ellen, head down, walked rapidly and the boys trotted along easily, clustered about her. Flames were rising from other areas of the city. A few white citizens, probably those already homeless, were out on the streets, too. A gale wind still blew and sparks were scattering wildly.

Finally, she was able to make out the tall pointed roof and white frame porch of her aunt's house in the distance. They passed the Whilden home, where all was quiet. She breathed a prayer of thanksgiving that their street seemed safe.

"Randolph, take the boys around to the carriage house. I'll send you supper in a little while."

Breathing hard, she stumbled up the porch steps. The door was locked. She rattled the knob and called softly to her aunt. Finally she heard footsteps.

"Ellen, is that you?" her aunt answered hesitantly.

"Yes, Aunt Sophie, please open the door."

Ellen entered the hallway, breathless from the blustery wind. The normally quiet house had been transformed into a beehive of activity. Her aunt was frantic.

"I have been so distressed. Randolph left to get you hours ago. You should not be out alone. I am at wit's end. Things are so distressing."

"This time I certainly was not alone! Randolph and I brought four boys home with us. I told them they could sleep in the carriage house tonight. I was glad to have them accompany us on the walk back, and they may be of some help tonight. I hope we can find a little supper for them."

"Oh, dear, I don't know. Two Yankee officers have billeted themselves upon us. I don't know if that is good or bad."

"How did they even know about you, Aunt Sophie?"

"My neighbor across the street went to General Logan's headquarters early in the afternoon to request guards for his home. I asked him to leave my name as desiring protection.

Then these two men arrived about an hour ago saying that they had been assigned to this address."

Ellen wondered if asking for protection had been wise. As she unwound the shawl from her head Sophie added, "They were sent here by a friend of the family, a Major Arledge. How in the world could two northern strangers know a friend of ours?"

Ellen was visibly shaken by the remark. He knows where I am! He will find me. Her aunt immediately saw the stricken look "What is it, dear? Do you know Major Arledge? Is he a friend of yours?"

"He is not a friend, Aunt Sophie." She tried to make her voice sound calm and disinterested. "He's a Union soldier. Remember I told you about the officer who came to the plantation a week or so ago to ask questions about the fire?"

"How could he have associated my simple request with you? He probably had hundreds of applications today."

"He probably did, but he would remember. The man asked me if I had relatives in town. He said it was too isolated for women alone out in the country and advised Pam and me to come to Columbia. He must have heard the request for protection for you, and he remembered the Heyward name."

"Despite the fact that he's in the Yankee army, he shows good breeding. I am glad he is concerned about our safety. I hope I will have the opportunity to thank him."

"I would have preferred that he not recall our name."

"The men are in the bedrooms upstairs. I had no choice."

Ellen saw that the fireplace in the dining room had been lit and Hattie was noisily arranging plates and silverware on the table. Candlelight flickered softly on a white damask cloth.

"You are exhausted, dear. I know how hard you've been working. Rest a few minutes before you change clothes," her aunt advised. She seemed concerned by her niece's wan appearance. "We won't be ready to serve dinner until seven."

Ellen went to the kitchen for a kettle of hot water. She must have a bath first. Inside her little room she undressed slowly, bone weary and apprehensive. Her arms felt too tired to remove the soiled clothing she had been wearing for two days and nights. She poured water into the china bowl on the marble washstand and began to scrub the dirt and soot from her grimy face. He knows where I am, she worried. He knows where I am!

After she completed the sponge bath and put on clean undergarments Ellen took her mother's black wool dress from the wardrobe and slipped it over her head. She went into her aunt's room and stood before the mirror tucking and pinning until the garment looked less like a shapeless bag. Fortunately the length, though short, would do. She removed the dress, sat down on a needlepoint stool by the hearth and, by the firelight, sewed the pinned seams. Not professional work, but adequate.

Had Arledge been back to the plantation looking for her? He was definitely in the city. Would he seek her here? Was he still bent on pursuing her as a criminal? Surely recent events had caused him to drop the investigation. No, not likely.

Arledge professed to be persistent and thorough, not a man to forget duty. Nor, despite the fact that some of his remarks had sounded flirtatious, was she the kind of woman to interest a handsome, worldly man. Exasperated by the direction of her thoughts, she rose hastily and put the altered dress back on.

She vigorously brushed her hair back, twisted it into a tight coil and pinned the shining mass into a small stiff bun, high on the back of her head. She was careful to ensure that no loose tendrils softened her face. Now, there was the sensible, level-headed woman she took pride in being. No need to be fearful. She could look after herself. She had proven that.

The matronly lines of the black dress, the severe hair style and the chalky pallor of her expressionless face combined to make Ellen the picture of withered spinsterhood. No sane man would be attracted to me, she told herself with grim satisfaction.

Shortly before seven Ellen went into the kitchen. Aunt Sophie, Hattie and Aunt Mariah all looked up. Surprise at her altered appearance was evident on their faces.

"You ain't fix up yourself very pretty," Aunt Mariah grumbled with her usual loving tactlessness.

"We don't know anything about these men that have been imposed on us, Aunt Mariah, and we don't want to invite unwelcome attention. This way will be safer."

"Every lady suppose to look the best she can. Your mamma always tell you that," the black woman scolded.

"I don't think we have anything to fear from these two men, dear," her aunt comforted. "They are both well past middle age and they behaved in a gentlemanly manner."

Sophie was filling a cut glass pickle dish with the last of her artichoke relish. She surveyed the food on the serving table, a small bowl of dried black-eye peas, a dish of collard greens, four baked sweet potatoes and a plate of cornbread. There was no meat. Parched acorn coffee boiled on the stove.

"Since they are older men, Aunt Sophie, perhaps you are the one most in jeopardy." Ellen wanted to lighten the atmosphere.

Sophie, never one for teasing, regarded her with a puzzled expression. "What do you mean? I am sure we can rely on the protection of the officers." She examined the food table agitated. "However, unless they furnish the food, theirs will not be a lengthy stay as our boarders." Ever the gracious hostess, the meager meal concerned the proud aristocrat. Enemies or not, the men were guests in her home.

"Hattie, ask the gentlemen to join us in the dining room."

The scarcity of food was disguised by a lavish display of china and crystal. A centerpiece of exquisite pink camellias had been placed between the silver candlesticks. Habits of southern hospitality were deeply ingrained in the older woman.

Aunt Mariah poured water in tall glasses, and assuring everyone that she would send Hattie in with the coffee as soon as dinner was served, she padded back into the kitchen.

Ellen could hear the guests descending the stairway. She stood silently watching, eyes suspicious and hostile, as they entered the dining room. The first man was slight in stature and had silver hair. He was closely followed by a tall colonel, florid and thick through the waist. There was an air of quiet dignity and soldierly bearing about them both.

The first officer approached Ellen. "Good evening. I am Dr. Calahan and this is Colonel Corley. You must be Miss Heyward." He looked at her, politely awaiting her reply.

Ellen nodded slightly but did not answer.

"We do not wish to presume upon your aunt's hospitality. We hope our being in her home will be of mutual benefit. Major Arledge, whom I believe you know, suggested we come here."

Ellen did not acknowledge acquaintance with the major.

"Your aunt's request for protection came to his attention," he continued, "and since the two of us had not yet been assigned quarters, it was his thought, and ours, that perhaps Colonel Corley and I might be of some assistance to you ladies."

"Thank you," she replied coldly. "Surely a town filled with helpless women and children will need no protection from troops who serve under an officer with the reputation of being so strict a disciplinarian as your General Sherman." The lengthy sentence left her breathless. "We have his assurance that we are safe, do we not?"

"Yes," he replied gently. "Let us hope so."

"Shall we take our places at the dinner table?" Sophie interceded, waving her arm to indicate where each man was to sit.

Once they were seated and the dishes passed, Colonel Corley cleared his throat noisily and in a booming voice announced, "When we came our supply trains had not yet arrived. By tomorrow we should be able to draw rations and contribute to our upkeep. Or perhaps we could pay you, Mrs. Heyward, for our accommodations. We know that it may be difficult for you to acquire provisions."

"Oh, no…" the older woman began.

"Yes, Colonel," Ellen cut in smoothly, "although South Carolina is an agricultural state, our men have been away for over four years… not just those of conscription age, but all men from sixteen to sixty. We haven't be able to produce much food lately."

There was an awkward silence.

"And," Ellen continued, "at the present time we have no seed or fertilizer, little help from the Negroes who have chosen to remain with us, and no way to import what we cannot raise. We accept your offer of provisions." Color mounted in her cheeks.

The elderly doctor nodded. "I quite understand, Miss Heyward, I am from Maryland. I know the hardships you have been suffering. My wife is a southern sympathizer."

"That must make things at home difficult," Sophie observed.

"No," he replied quietly, "like many others, we have relatives on both sides. As a physician, my war is with injury and death. When I treat a young man, I try to save his life whether he is dressed in blue or gray. Mrs. Calahan knows this."

He was a man much like Henry Heyward, the same sympathetic eyes, the slender ascetic build and kind smile. He seemed to share the same lack of passion about the political arguments that had precipitated the war.

"However," he continued, "I do know the hearts and minds of these Union soldiers. They blame the south for starting the war. And South Carolina they fault most of all."

"That was made clear to us quite recently, sir. Our stables, hay, farm equipment and some livestock fell victim to a party of foragers," Ellen said bitterly.

"We are aware," the colonel cut in, "that both Sherman's bummers and Kilpatrick's troops are openly seeking vengeance. Sixty thousand men, jubilantly celebrating an important victory in a city this small, are apt to get out of hand."

"That's why Colonel Corley and I are here with you. You may have need of our protection. Young Arledge seemed anxious for us to be posted with you. Have you been friends long?"

Ellen ignored the question. "We appreciate your help, sir," she replied, teeth clenched, "and hope it will not be needed."

"The men in my command are from Illinois," Colonel Corley continued loudly. "Most of them have never been concerned with slavery or state's rights. I doubt they have given any thought to preserving the union either. Their only interest is getting back home to their families. They have been away a long time."

He helped himself to another serving of collards. "You are intelligent ladies. I'm sure you can understand that the doctor and I feel there might be danger."

"We are aware of the mood of the men. I walked home through streets filled with drunken rabble less than an hour ago. They have already set numerous fires. I even saw some destroying the fire fighting equipment." Ellen fought to keep her voice level.

"I have been extremely concerned about the large quantity of whiskey in the city. What were your commanders thinking of to leave it here?" asked the doctor.

"I presume that your armies moved faster than was expected," Aunt Sophie defended. "In addition to the whiskey that was not destroyed, I understand there are cotton bales in every street. They were to have been moved, also."

"Certainly irresponsible behavior on the part of someone."

"We had not thought that Columbia would be a Yankee target, Colonel," Sophie countered. "There are three times more people in the city than usual… not counting the Union army."

Ellen was proud of Sophie's uncharacteristic near rudeness.

For a while they ate in silence.

"I have known John Arledge for some time, Miss Heyward. Served with him in the western campaign. He is a fine young man. Brilliant mind. Virginian, I believe. Were you acquainted before the war?"

The colonel had returned to his earlier question.

"No," she answered, eyes downcast as she fought to control spasmodic trembling deep within her. Ellen was conscious of his scrutiny. She knew the men were wondering what the major's interest in so plain a woman could possibly be.

"We met briefly recently." Then, as casually as she could manage, she inquired, "Is he posted in the city, too?"

"I believe he has been temporarily assigned to headquarters. This afternoon he was handling civilian requests and complaints."

They ended the meal as the grandfather's clock in the hall was chiming eight. Excited voices were spilling from the kitchen. Loud footsteps sounded in the hall.

Aunt Mariah burst into the room shouting, "Lord, Miss Ellen, 'scuse me, but the boys been outside. Randolph say them drunk soldiers done set this whole town on fire. Ain't nobody trying to put them fires out, just setting more. I look outside myself… everything bright red. We going to burn up for certain."

Colonel Corley rose. "Surely the report is exaggerated. Is there some place that is high enough to look out over the town?"

"Yes," Sophia replied, "a small set of windows in the attic. Ellen, take a candle and show the gentlemen the way up there."

In a matter of minutes they reached the balcony and stood surveying the scene below. On west Gervais Street they could see the smoldering remains of the row of low wooden buildings which had been the red light district. Toward the eastern outskirts of town they spotted numerous small fires burning.

"Soldiers are camped in that direction. Those little lights are likely campfires," the colonel speculated.

"The big blaze farthest away is surely General Hampton's home," Ellen's cold voice contradicted. "Secretary Trenholm's house is that one on our far left, and Colonel Wallace lives beside him."

They could see as many as twenty fires flaming brightly in almost as many different quarters of the city, all being fanned by the high February wind. Cotton Town, the northernmost limit of the city, became alight as they watched. Then fire sprang up on Main Street near Hunt's Hotel.

"I'll get my bag, Colonel," the doctor announced with resignation. "We must go. We will be needed down there."

The men rushed to their rooms.

At the front door, as he buttoned on a huge military cape the colonel advised, "Keep all doors locked, ladies. Your street doesn't seem to be a main thoroughfare. I think you need fear only occasional wandering drunks, but they can be dangerous."

"I will, Colonel," a visibly shaken Aunt Sophie replied.

"I'll try to locate some of the men in my command and send a small contingent here to guard your house until morning. They will knock and call you by name. It might be best not to answer anyone who does not identify himself. I do not wish to frighten you two ladies, but precaution is wise."

"We are not afraid," Ellen answered calmly, "but I have a young sister I am concerned about. She is at the Ursuline Convent on the corner of Main and Blanding. Fires are beginning in that area. The sisters and their pupils may need protection. Will you please see that a guard is posted there?"

"Yes, my dear." The doctor placed a hand on her shoulder. "The colonel and I are both Catholic. We will go immediately."

Ellen closed the front door and locked it behind the two men. She went to the kitchen. Randolph and Aunt Mariah huddled together and Hattie was talking excitedly.

"Hattie, hush that screaming," she ordered. "If you are frightened here, you are free to go. Yankee soldiers are not going to hurt you."

Ellen heaped the leftovers from the table on a plate and handed it to Randolph. "Take this to the boys when you go out. Aunt Mariah, you and Randolph finish your supper quickly and go back to the carriage house. Bolt the doors. If you hear noises, it will probably be soldiers wandering about lost. I hope they'll think no one is home and leave. Miss Sophie and I will be in our bedroom. Unless I come and call you, stay inside."

When the servants had gone the lull inside the house seemed ominous and foreboding. The lone candle Ellen carried scarcely cut the thick darkness. In the bedroom she found her aunt seated beside the flickering fire reading from her large family Bible.

"You are wise, Aunt Sophie. It's early. This will be a long night and sleep is out of the question. It is best not to voice our fears. Reading will help to pass the time."

Ellen placed the candle on the bedside table. She picked up a slender volume of poetry and began to calmly leaf through the pages. The evening dragged interminably. The pall of deathly quiet in the house magnified the alarming sounds outside.

After an hour the two women climbed the stairs to look out from the high attic windows. The heart of the city was bathed in garish light. They could hear the crackle of flames and the chilling crashes made by charred falling timbers three blocks away. What appeared to be small family groups, dazed and moving slowly, were wandering around in the streets below.

About nine-thirty they were startled by loud knocking on the front door. Sickening fright washed over Aunt Sophia's face. Ellen held her breath and listened. The banging became more insistent. Above the frightening night noises they could hear someone shouting, "Mrs. Heyward, Mrs. Heyward!"

"Perhaps it's the guard the Colonel sent," whispered Sophie.

They heard the call again. Clearly this was not a chance looter. "Mrs. Heyward, come open the door. I am here to help you."

"Stay here, Aunt Sophie," Ellen said. "I'll go investigate. I won't open the door unless whoever it is identifies himself."

Ellen moved noiselessly toward the front hallway. Glare from the bright copper sky reflected through the fan window above the door, lighting the vestibule. She hovered close to the wall.

"Mrs. Heyward, Ellen... for God's sake open the door."

For a moment she stood frozen, heart racing madly. John Arledge's deep voice was easy to recognize. Her heart filled with conflicting emotions. Fright? Elation? He shook the door more violently and called out again. He might attract attention.

"Major Arledge, is that you?"

"Of course it is. Open the door, Ellen," he commanded.

She turned the key and pulled the door back a few inches. He thrust it open with such force she nearly fell against the frame. He strode inside, quickly closing the door behind him.

"Thank God," he muttered, anxiously examining her face. "I had the devil of a time finding this place. Why didn't you answer me, Ellen? You knew I would be here as soon as I could."

He studied her face, intense concern darkening his eyes. "Are you ill?" he demanded. "Come closer. I want to see you."

She could see the granite-chiseled line of his jaw. He quirked an eyebrow. A slight smile hovered around his mouth. He took Ellen's arm and drew her toward him.

"I prefer your hair down. If with that severe hair style you are trying to make yourself unattractive, you have failed." He gathered her in his arms and held her firmly.

His nearness was overwhelming. She could feel his hard body and the warmth of his breath on her cheek. She must gather the resistance to fight.

"It's all right," he whispered. "I'll take care of you."

"I usually take care of myself," she stiffly informed him.

"I'm well aware of that," he acknowledged. "I went back to the plantation. I wanted to find you again. There is so much I want to know about you. I haven't had time since to search for you. When that request for protection was presented today, I desperately hoped the lady would turn out to be your aunt. I came as soon as I could get away."

The intimate huskiness of his voice was both soothing and alarming. Ellen pulled away from him, fighting the urge to stay and lean her head against the corded muscles of his chest.

"Come back to me," he commanded. "We don't have much time."

"Stop ordering me around, John Arledge." A sob caught in her throat. "You are not a conquering hero on a rescue mission." She was disgusted to feel tears trembling on her eyelids.

With one of his lean callused fingers he brushed away a glistening tear as it began to course down her cheek. He traced the outline of her face, gently lifting her chin. His touch was that of a man accustomed to expertly caressing women. Tenderness was a new experience for Ellen. She felt weak and helpless.

He bent slightly forward, his breath warm on her neck. Passionate fluttering seized her heart.

His mouth hovered hungrily over hers. He softly covered her lips with his and she began to succumb to the intoxication of his kiss. His lips became more demanding.

She wrenched away from the shelter of his arms, glad that the semi-darkness hid the flush of humiliation on her cheeks.

"You Yankees," she accused, voice sharpened with fury, "arson, thievery, rape. What else do you excel in?"

"Ellen, honey," he laughed softly, pulling her back into the cradle of his arms, "rape is not my style. My women come willingly. I'll wait. I am sure you did not intend it," he mocked, "but your lips were warm and responsive. They were just the way I desire. And, lady, how I do desire!"

Shock and fury lit her hazel eyes. Her breath came raggedly. "Keep away from me, sir," she sputtered.

"Not a chance," he boldly assured her.

She felt the sexual magnetism of his masculine confidence.

He stepped back with reluctance and removed his hat. An unruly lock of dark hair fell forward. "Are you here alone?"

Ellen flinched at his sharp question. The tense maleness about him was intimidating. Dare she trust him? Or herself? She had no intention of falling victim to his practiced charm.

"Of course I'm not alone. My aunt is here… and her family. This is her home." Ellen's voice trembled despite a brave show of defiance.

"Oh, another aunt?" he said, reading her thoughts, "genuine, I hope. Where is your sister? I told you I will protect you."

"I took her to stay with the other school girls at the Ursuline convent until the present crisis is over."

"Did the officers I billeted here arrive? I saw no guards."

"Colonel Corley and the doctor came, but they left nearly two hours ago. They promised to send someone back. That's the reason I answered your knock."

"You and your aunt can't stay here alone. I have been assigned to the hospital for the night. Get your coats and let me walk the two of you to a neighbor's, or to the convent, if you'd rather. Half the army seems to have turned into a crazed, drunken mob."

"Our servants are out back. We can't leave them."

He impatiently shoved his fingers through his hair. "Go tell them that you are going to a neighbor's for a while. They will be all right. I will not leave you in this house unprotected. Please hurry. I have to report to my post."

Ellen went for her aunt. When they returned she made no introductions. He bowed slightly, hat in hand. "Mrs. Heyward, I am John Arledge. I was concerned about your nieces and you. I am here to escort you to a safer place." His commanding manner and the sound of his southern speech reassured the older woman.

"I hope you will send a guard here, young man. I have never witnessed such wild disorderly behavior in my life."

"Yes, Mam. I'm sure Colonel Corley will send troopers." He guided her firmly through the door. The women waited while he locked the door and placed the key in Ellen's hand. She dashed around back to tell Aunt Mariah they would be at the Whilden home.

The major's horse was tethered at the hitching post in front of the house. The night noises were chilling. "I will walk with you to your neighbor's, but I'll have to lead my horse," he explained. "He might get stolen while we are gone, and I am on duty tonight."

Although Mary Whilden lived less than a block away, without the usual street lamps the way in front of them stretched like trackless wilderness. The glow of the fires in the distance failed to penetrate the murkiness ahead.

As they neared the house Ellen could see tiny shreds of light splintering the darkness around the front windows. They climbed the piazza steps. The excited voices of children could be heard inside.

Arledge took Ellen's hand and held it briefly. "I'll be near the main gate of the College hospital all night, if you should need me." He turned, mounted his horse and disappeared into the night.

Seven

Ellen watched him ride away, a poignant sense of loss engulfing her as Arledge's broad shoulders vanished from sight. Her mind warned against believing his words, but her body still tingled from the warmth of his touch. Reason had always ruled her life, and caution. She would not take leave of her senses.

At the Whilden house, the door was open. Mary Whilden, a lady in her late thirties was much loved and respected. She managed a busy household, her grandmother, and five children ranging from Frank, age twelve, to the small baby. Her husband had been in the army for over two years; her only brother was killed at Secessionville. She helped with the war effort, the church and the hospital, and she always had an open door and a warm heart for everyone.

"Miss Sophie and Ellen, I'm glad you came," she exclaimed. "Help us decide what we should do." She ushered them inside.

"Mr. Richards," Mary motioned toward an elderly gentleman standing in the hallway, "is concerned about his invalid daughter, Rose. He feels they are not safe inside their home and less so outside. What do you think?"

The four older Whilden children raced noisily about and Mary's grandmother was trying in vain to soothe the crying baby.

"Bring Rose here," Ellen immediately replied. Her voice was firm in the prevailing indecision. "She must be frightened alone. We can all take comfort in the nearness of each other."

"That's wise," Mary agreed, anxious to comfort her old neighbor. "Can you arrange to move her here, Mr. Richards?"

"Yes, yes," he answered, obviously relieved. "Thank you, ladies. I can't seem to think clearly. We have a stretcher and two servants on whom I can rely. We'll be back soon."

"Would you like me to go with you?" Ellen offered. She walked out behind him and firmly closed the door.

"No, thank you," he replied, "that won't be necessary." He spoke with the quiet dignity of a man humbled by age and circumstances beyond his control. "I live across the street."

He descended the stairs and looked back. "Mrs. Whilden is a trusting lady, but I think she should be gathering up the things she will need for her children if the worst should happen."

Ellen nodded, knowing that Mr. Richards was probably right.

"I fear she doesn't realize the gravity of the situation."

"Yes, sir. I'll wait here until you get home. Then I shall insist that she take the precautions you suggest."

Ellen had closed the door behind her so the family could not see how much nearer the fires now were. As she waited on the porch she could hear people passing by in the dark near the house. The voices of several men talking loudly became clearer. They were coming toward her. Ellen, breath held, pressed against the door. The men approached, paused near where she stood, then walked past on down Laurel Street toward her aunt's home.

"That damn house must be near here," muttered one in the dialect of an Ohio farm boy. "We followed his directions."

"But we are going to miss the fun. Let's tell the colonel we couldn't find the place," a companion pleaded.

"Tell him, hell! I served with that old man too long. No excuse is good enough for not following his orders. This ain't the only night we will be in the army. There's plenty more time for celebrating. Right now we still got to answer to him."

"Damn right," added the farm boy. "Anyhow I'm already half drunk and getting tired. I hope the house we are supposed to guard has some of them soft feather beds. I could sleep a week."

"Not me. Fast as we been moving, this war will be over in another week. I want to be the first soldier back to Illinois."

When the men had moved out of earshot Ellen sighed in relief. They must be guards Colonel Corley sent. She went back inside, where the anxiety was continuing to mount.

"We should prepare for the worst. Let's pack necessities," Ellen insisted. "The wind is still high. If the fires get closer, we will need to spend the night outside. Mary, please name the items the children must have. Frank, Walter and I will gather them. Aunt Sophie will care for the baby and Little Mary can help Grandmother. Do you have a large box or basket?"

Ellen barged ahead with plans, not waiting for a reply.

"Tubs," Mary said, studying Ellen's serious face. "This afternoon our servants brought home washtubs filled with plunder from the streets... ribbon, hardware, useless junk. Frank, empty a tub and bring it back in here. Get buckets, also, if you can find them."

Frank sped toward the rear of the house.

"Grandmother's rocking chair has to go wherever she goes, and we may need a mattress," Mary continued. "We can put it on the ground, if necessary, so the children will have a place to sleep. I'll send a servant to get one and several blankets."

"Mother! Come!" Frank's terror-filled voice screamed from the kitchen. Ellen's eyes met Mary's for one stricken moment and they both rushed to answer the adolescent's frightened cry.

"Look," he shouted, pointing. "Men outside setting fires."

The women peered through the rear window and were alarmed to see several soldiers shouting and drunkenly careening about. One carried a lighted torch, another bundles of cotton. A third with a box of Lucifers cursed each failure of the matches to flare.

"I am afraid this is what that nice captain meant," Mary said as they helplessly observed the nightmare outside. "There is nothing we can do. This afternoon two Union officers came up on the piazza and asked if I could give them supper. I felt I must comply. They introduced themselves as Captain James Crosier of the Twenty-first Illinois Regiment and his lieutenant."

"Had you ever seen them before?"

"No, they wanted to be with a family they said. They saw the children outside. After they ate we talked in the parlor."

"Aunt Sophie had two men for supper, too."

"Around eight they thanked me and got up to go. Captain Crosier handed me some medicine and a bottle of glycerin, 'You will have need of these before morning, as we have orders to destroy the city.' I couldn't believe what he was saying."

As they watched, a soldier flung turpentine against the rear wall of the house. Flames began to crackle and spread.

"We got this one," he yelled. "Move on to the next."

"I must get my family to safety." Mary spoke with horrified resignation and began making hasty plans to leave the now burning house. Once outside in the street they saw the Richards family approaching. Two black men were bearing a stretcher. Ellen looked at the pale face of Rose Richards in the light of the flickering fires. Already she was homeless, her house, too, was ablaze.

The frightened group was wondering in which direction to flee when a voice spoke out of the darkness. "Mrs. Whilden, I thought you might need help, so I have come back." A lone Union soldier moved into sight. They could not see his face clearly. "You must not risk staying here. The children are in danger."

The adults looked at one another dumbfounded. Here was kindness and an offer of help where they had expected none.

"You think this may be an attempt to rob you," he said, "but you are wrong." He spoke calmly. "My name is Crosier."

"One of Mrs. Whilden's supper guests?" Sophie asked.

"Yes. The Whildens are the only people I know in the city." He looked toward Ellen who seemed to be in charge of the group.

"Mam, I suggest that you get everyone to move farther down the block and out into the middle of the street. At least you will not be among falling sparks there while you decide what to do."

Mary Whilden made a quick decision. "Thank you, Captain. All of us are grateful for your help."

Four generations were represented within her family, the oldest over eighty-one and the youngest an infant in arms. Old Mrs. Whilden's rocking chair was placed down in the intersection of Marion and Bull Streets. Without complaint she stoically sat and rocked, though a bitter northwestern gale blew relentlessly. The mattress was placed down for the three smallest children.

Noticing sparks falling on the blankets covering the children, Ellen realized they should have a pail of water handy. "The blankets need sprinkling. Frank and I are going for water."

"It's too far back to our well and too dangerous for you to go alone. Perhaps Captain Crosier will get it for us."

"No, Mary, I would rather he remain here," Ellen protested. "He can protect those who are unable to do for themselves. Frank and I will be careful. You can hear us from here. We can call if we need you to send the officer to rescue us."

With one of the buckets they had brought, Ellen and Frank ran, hand in hand, toward the flaming house. They halted a short distance away to look. The arsonists had apparently moved on. They hurried to the well in back of the house and Frank drew up water to fill the bucket Ellen held. They saw a drunken soldier stumble from the darkness and up the steps of the burning house.

"Miss Ellen," Frank whispered in awe. "He won't be able to get out of there alive if he goes in. What should we do?"

"We must shout a warning... even though he hardly deserves help from us," she grimly replied.

"Soldier, soldier, come back," Ellen yelled.

"The house is burning, mister. Don't go in," Frank's shrill voice persisted. "You will be hurt. Come back! Come back!"

Their calls fell on deaf ears. As the man staggered in, parts of the roof were already beginning to fall. Knowing he was beyond help, they returned with the water. All through the night the Whildens' two servant women were kept busy wetting down blankets and extinguishing falling sparks.

Repeatedly the group was subjected to taunts and insults from passing soldiers. The presence of the Union officer enabled them to hold on to the few possessions they had piled in the street.

Around midnight Aunt Sophie suggested that they move farther down the street. "I haven't seen my house burn. It's too dark to be sure, but it may be still standing. Shall we risk going there?"

"No," was Mary's decisive reply. "I believe we are better off here. At least we can watch on all sides. This way we don't have to wonder whether someone is sneaking up behind us."

All of Main Street was now a mass of flames. They could no longer determine exactly which buildings were burning or distinguish between the separate blazes. Ellen watched the fire gnaw nearer the north end of town. The convent was only four blocks away from the burning area. Were the girls safe? And if they were, how much longer would they remain so?

Little knots of people straggled past. Occasionally Mary recognized a passerby and they heard snatches of news. Soldiers had burned the church where they thought the Secession Convention had met. All the business section of town was in ruins. The old State House was gone, and the College buildings were threatened.

Ellen looked closely at each passerby. She hoped to see an acquaintance going toward the convent. They heard the sound of footsteps on a dark street near them and wondered whether foe or friend approached. A small man in formal civilian dress came into view. He paused, panting for breath. He inspected their group huddled around the mattress full of frightened children. He eyed the Union soldier suspiciously, then advanced haltingly.

"May I stop a moment with you? I am August Conrad, the Hanoverian consul." His guttural German accent sounded strange to ears long accustomed to the soft drawl of the Carolinas.

"How do you happen to be out alone, sir, and in flight?" inquired Mr. Richards. "I should think that the flag of Hanover would afford protection for you."

"I, too, sir. Alas, I have suffered the same outrages that all Columbians have had to endure." He drew closer to the circle.

"Early this afternoon I went out to procure a traveling bag in which to pack my own valuable papers and those of my government. As I returned to my lodgings, I was accosted by a mounted soldier. He ordered me to hand over the bag. My firm remonstrance that it did not belong to him, and that I would like to keep possession of my own property went unnoticed."

Mr. Conrad paused to catch his breath.

"The rascal drew and brandished his saber, and remarked that rather than waste his valuable time, I should save my arm. I saw the wisdom of his good advice and gave up the bag, which fortunately was empty."

The stiff, stilted sentences, coupled with his look of righteous indignation, brought a smile to Mary's drawn face. Ellen glanced back and was thankful to see that even the old grand-mother wore a look of restrained amusement.

"And did that satisfy the scoundrel?" Ellen asked.

"Ah, no, madam. That was but the beginning of the out-rages I have suffered." He shook his head in disbelief.

They gathered nearer to listen to Mr. Conrad air his griev-ances, forgetting their own troubles for a short while.

"I survived the first highway robbery," he continued. "Back in my room new horrors awaited. Upon entering the yard, I found the contents of my trunk, so far as they still existed, scat-tered about and mixed up with a vast collection of strange ob-jects. Little Negro children were amusing themselves with the damaged pictures of my dear relations. Letters from loved ones, which I had so carefully preserved, were broadcast about the street. Many valuable and irreplaceable objects were entirely lost. I tried to gather those remnants that were most dear to me and gave up the others to utter destruction."

"Have you lived in Columbia long?" inquired Aunt Sophie. She took pride in knowing all city residents. He was a stranger.

"No, madam. My offices are in Charleston. I arrived here only a few days ago and took up abode in the residence of a German lady whom I had known in Charleston. She had es-tablished herself here as a teacher of music and singing."

He removed a linen handkerchief from his breast pocket, wiped his forehead, then carefully folded and replaced it.

"She, in anticipation of coming events, had asked me, by virtue of my office, to protect her. I betook myself and bag-gage to her home, displayed the banner of Hanover from the window, and mistakenly believed the residence to be well protected."

"And there was more trouble, I presume," prompted Ellen.

"Indeed there was," he continued indignantly. "I learned that my landlady had fared no better than I. The loss of her silverware, which she had so prudently buried in the garden, was affecting her most seriously. Because of the spread of fire around us we were obliged to leave the dwelling."

"That is what we have all had to do," explained Mary.

"Each valuable we brought out to save," he continued, "was seized upon by a hungry pack of vandals and carried off or divided before our very eyes. With pleas delivered on bended knees, enough to melt stone, the poor frightened widow besought the commander of the troops bivouacking in the streets near us to conduct her and her children to a place of safety."

"Well, I certainly hope he did." Aunt Sophie was aghast.

"He agreed to extend his personal protection to her, but not to her baggage and they departed. I then loaded myself with a few bundles and packets made up of the contents I had salvaged from my trunk and left the house, already on fire." The German gentleman was exhausted and overcome by the telling of his experiences. He spoke so rapidly and with such agitation, they had experienced difficulty following his lamentations.

Mr. Conrad sat down on the ground beside Mr. Richards. No one spoke for a while.

Over the sounds of distant noises they heard the clock in the tower of Market Hall strike one. That was its last hour, for even then the spire was brightly lit by the fire within the building. Five minutes later the tower crashed to the ground.

Ellen, who had been listening intently to Mr. Conrad's recital, pointedly asked, "But, sir, did not your country sympathize with the north in this war?"

He nodded his head slowly. "Alas! yes. I fear that the English and the French may have been wiser. They favored the South." He sighed heavily and rose to his feet. "I realize that many of you have been visited with far greater misfortune than I. My family and my home are not here, and my life I have thus far managed to save. I shall now proceed to the home of my friends the McCullys on Arsenal Hill in hope of finding there a small measure of peace and rest."

"Sir, may I accompany you?" Ellen requested. "My sister is at the Catholic convent and I'm anxious about her. You pass the school on your way to the McCully home. I am not asking for your protection," she hastily assured him, "merely to walk with you."

"Of course, young lady," he responded gallantly, "I delight in the pleasure of your company. We will have no baggage to tempt robbers, and they should be tiring of their sport by now."

"Allow me to tell my aunt and I'll be ready to go." Ellen went to where Sophie sat beside old Mrs. Whilden's rocker.

Her aunt jumped up with surprising alacrity. "I shall go, too. The protection of an older woman might help." Her determined manner indicated that she would not be dissuaded.

The three said their farewells.

"Mary," Sophie was fighting tears, "if tomorrow I have a house, so do you for as long as you need it. And, Rose," she reached down to take the girl's hand, "the same thing is true for you and your father. Please tell him that for Ellen and me."

Tears spilled down Mary's cheek. "I appreciate your thoughtfulness throughout this night. I have relatives I will want to see tomorrow. None of us can know what we will do until we survey the damage in the light of day and can collect our thoughts. I shall keep in mind your generous offer."

Through the evening the Union captain had maintained his vigil on the outer fringe of the group. Though he could surely hear the conversations, he had not joined in nor made comments.

"Captain Crosier," Ellen called as she was leaving, "I am glad to have met you. In later years it will give us all consolation to remember that on this dreadful night there were a few men like you among the Union soldiers."

He quietly replied, "Thank you, Mam. I expect many people will long remember this night. I shall stay with Mrs. Whilden and the children until dawn."

John Arledge's powerful horse picked his way through the streets toward the College campus. The rider held the reins carefully. The animal snorted, excited by strange noises and the movement of soldiers and townspeople in the streets. Visibility was no longer a problem. The orange glow from hundreds of small fires haloed the city. Chaos reigned.

He saw no other officers about. No visible effort was being made to halt the spreading fires, none to control the rioting. Disgust with the scene consumed him. The blowing wind was hot on his skin. Jaw clenched, he rode doggedly toward his assignment.

Arledge was still plagued by his lack of progress in tracing the missing bummers. The lapse of time since their disappearance convinced him that the men were dead. Long experience told him that Ellen Heyward was deeply implicated. As his prime suspect, he rationalized, he must keep close surveillance over her. Through the years he had conducted hundreds of military investigations without personal involvement. Why had he allowed himself to become so concerned about this one aggravating and unpleasant female? He had known women, too many, he grudgingly admitted, but had rarely remained interested in the same one long. Other things took precedence. He knew this was different, but why was Ellen Heyward so different?

He had never court-martialed a woman, nor recommended that one be hanged. He could do it, and would do it, if the situation warranted. So, why did this one haunt him? And why had he told her he would protect her? Her seeming lack of guile and slender body were a far cry from his mental picture of a deceptive siren. There was no coquettishness about Ellen Heyward, no veiled-eyed hinting, no throaty promises, none of the characteristics with which he was all too familiar. Her skittishness might be the real allure. Certainly different.

Arledge meticulously organized the facts. Ellen's complete lack of sophistication seemed out of harmony with her keen mind. A ruse? Her air of innocence and naiveté were both appealing and difficult to understand. And when he did catch her off guard, her face had a heart-wrenching look of vulnerability. Hiding something? She might be a murderess. He might have to arrest her, but she was one intriguing woman. Was he so starved for the softness of a woman, any woman, that he was forgetting duty?

He could remember every barbed word she had flung at him and the flash of her eyes as she uttered them. The stiff pride and spirit with which she rebuffed him were admirable. She was likely capable of skillful deception. So many women had schemed and fawned, openly inviting his attentions, that, rather than being put off by this one's resistance, he was attracted.

A slight smile hovered about his mouth as he thought of her aura of ladylike purity. God help him, Ellen Heyward was the kind of girl his mother would have selected for him. He sighed resolutely. His interest went deeper than a military inquiry. As soon as the night ended, nothing short of direct orders from General Sherman would keep him from seeking her out again.

Arledge had scouted the area. He knew the front gate at the Hospital was the only opening in the eight foot high brick wall encircling the College. He identified himself to the young captain and the eight-man guard detail posted there. Cautioning them to be alert for arsonists, he entered and rode the distance around the horseshoe compound to ensure that all was well within. The buildings now housed only Union sick and wounded.

He dismounted, tethered his horse to a tree on the green and walked toward the steps of Hospital Building One. He pushed a table and chair into the doorway for maintaining vigilance. He had been on virtual twenty-four hour duty for three days. He watched and waited in a state of exhausted stupor as the night wore on.

Early in the evening sentries repelled several parties of revelers. At midnight Arledge was called to the front gate. A large group of civilians was milling about outside. Burned out of their homes, they had no place to go. He ordered the guards to allow them to enter and stay the night in any faculty houses available or on the campus grounds. A great sea of flames was slowly making its way from downtown up toward the College walls. He began patrolling his area on foot.

Before four in the morning the old State House, only a few blocks away, was a roaring inferno. The night was transformed into daylight brightness by the blazing glare. Columns of black, rolling smoke streaked the sky. Glittering sparks and flying embers showered about him. The shining glass in the tall windows of the College library gleamed golden and ruddy. Bits of fire rained on the buildings on the north side of the campus.

Arledge ran from ward to ward alerting the staff inside. Soon physicians and orderlies were climbing to the roofs to extinguish sparks as they fell. Every patient who could muster the strength came out to quell possible fires. In the eerie light, men who could barely walk were beating out falling cinders. Gravely wounded patients, left to themselves, struggled outside.

From a rooftop, on which he had climbed to stand guard for the remainder of the night, Arledge could see that the Common opposite the main gate was filled with homeless women and children. The more fortunate among them had blankets wrapped about them.

Around five o'clock a large group of drunken soldiers assaulted the main College gate, threatening to overpower the guards. Arledge could hear them boasting and swearing that they would allow no buildings in the Rebel city to be spared.

"Fools," he shouted down to them, "this hospital is filled with wounded Union soldiers. Can't you see the yellow flags?"

He stood on the roof edge, his dark uniform silhouetted against the sky. "I am a Union officer and I will see every one of you in front of a firing squad if you set fire to these buildings."

His commanding voice carried clearly over the mass confusion. Earlier he had dispatched Dr. Thompson, head of the hospital, to General Howard's headquarters on Gervais Street to ask for reinforcements. As the gate guards struggled to turn back this latest siege, he heard the new troops arriving. Together they were able to avert disaster within the College walls.

Toward dawn the last of the riotous soldiers disappeared. By seven o'clock the flames in the city had died down. The sun began to show sickly red through the stagnant, hazy atmosphere. It reflected dully on blackened hulls and smoking ruins. John had thought daylight would be a welcome sight, but the unnatural calm of daybreak was more disturbing. The soldiers who forced their way on campus before dawn were now under guard and quarreling noisily among themselves. The grounds and buildings were secure.

John untied his horse, led him to the well for water, then made his way out the gate. The strain of the night showed on his grimy, haggard face. His eyes burned. He needed sleep, First, though, he had to make sure that infernal Heyward woman was safe.

When Ellen, Sophie and the dapper little German finally reached the corner of Main and Blanding Streets it was after two o'clock. They walked single file on the inside edge of the streets, keeping to the shadows and shrubs. They listened for voices and were careful to avoid intercepting anyone.

At Main they saw that the separate fires were losing their identity and becoming one giant flaming wall. Illumination from the firelight was so brilliant that minute things could be seen in detail at great distances. They walked past several yards where small groups of soldiers were probing the ground with bayonets and iron ramrods hoping to discover buried treasure.

The convent was a sheath of roaring flames. The students had been moved. Already the plunderers had moved on, too. Hidden in the shadows, the three watched helplessly. Ellen noticed an elderly couple standing not too far from them. She nudged her aunt and they moved toward the man and woman.

Ellen spoke first. "I wonder if you could tell me where the nuns sought refuge. My sister was one of the pupils."

"Yes," the old man studied her sadly, "Our granddaughter is a member of the community, too. Mother Ursula took them to St. Peter's Church. Thank God they were moved in time."

"Yes, thank God," Ellen echoed.

"Our home was destroyed early in the evening. Since then we have wandered to the home of one friend after another, only to find them in our same predicament."

Ellen reached out and touched his arm. "I'm so sorry. I don't see fire in the direction of St. Peter's. Is it standing?"

"The Church is safe, the children are hiding in the cemetery. We walked near to make sure. The sisters have faithful guards now. We didn't want to alarm our granddaughter, so we didn't make our presence known. The children have had enough trauma for one night."

"Ladies," Mr. Conrad called anxiously, "I have peered up and down the street. I think we should proceed. My friend's home appears to be as yet unharmed. My present state of exhaustion and depression makes rest almost a necessity. If you wish to continue, I assure you the McCullys will make you welcome."

Half an hour later they wearily approached the McCully doorstep to find the family in great alarm. They had thus far escaped the night's madness, but were unsure whether to feel thankful or to continue to expect the worst. The appearance of Mr. Conrad and his two friends was greeted with joy.

Ellen immediately realized that the McCully family was not equipped to deal with the realities of the situation. The husband, disabled and mentally ill, sat buried in silent brooding. An aged grandmother lay sick. The frightening events of the past few days had been carefully concealed from the two.

The German consul was appalled. He nervously recounted his experiences and urged Mrs. McCully and her two daughters to make evacuation plans. "You must take measures for collecting and securing your most valuable objects," he insisted in high excited tones. "You may need to take flight momentarily."

"Surely that won't be necessary," Mrs. McCully reasoned. "We have the good fortune of having a very fine young man among the soldiers quartered with us. He has repelled several attempts to rob the house and set fire to it. You should have heard his denunciations of his comrades for their vile and shameful acts."

"You are indeed fortunate, madam, but one man is not sufficient to deal with the rabble we have seen tonight."

"But he insists that these horrible deeds are being committed contrary to the orders of higher authorities, and that most of the thieves and arsonists are illiterate immigrants."

"Mrs. McCully," Ellen interrupted, "don't be lulled by a false sense of security. Your lone defender can be overpowered. Do as Mr. Conrad suggests. My aunt and I will be glad to assist."

As the night progressed so, too, did the terror. The onslaught of plunderers and arsonists at the doors and windows of the house was soon more than they could ward off. Frenzied soldiers, maddened with the desire to destroy, entered the house.

Family portraits were slashed, books thrown from the shelves, and the grand piano chopped into with an ax. Bedding and curtains were ignited, china shattered. In the kitchen the attackers emptied sacks of sugar, salt, flour and meal, sorely needed food, on the floor and poured molasses over it in wanton destruction.

The powerless family ceased pleading for reason. Flames took hold in several parts of the house. There was no hope of saving it. As they were struggling to move the grandmother outside two passing Negroes stopped and helped them lift the bed.

After the old lady was safely outside Mr. Conrad noticed a soldier about to set fire to her mattress. Indignation made him lose all fear. He rushed to grab the offender by the throat.

"Is no deed too shameful for you, you wretch?" he shouted. The two began wrestling. As Ellen ran to assist the overmatched little consul, the soldier extricated himself, grunted a few unintelligible words and fled into the darkness.

Mr. Conrad looked dumbfounded.

"Are you injured?" Ellen asked anxiously.

"No," he moaned. "Do you realize that beast was a German? He could not even speak English. What can he possibly know about this war?"

"Nothing, Mr. Conrad. He has probably just arrived in America and needed a job. I am sure he was hired to fill someone else's conscription."

"Such a son my good fatherland sent for the extirpation of slavery!"

Once again without shelter, the group began the search for a place of safety to wait out the remainder of the night. While the older family members waited in the street, the two McCully daughters came with them hoping to locate shelter for their older family members. Mr. Conrad, scanning the city skyline, observed that above them, higher on Arsenal Hill, the area was still dark.

"Perhaps," he said hopefully, "the bands of incendiaries have not forced their way up there yet."

"The houses are smaller," Sophie said, fatigue weakening her voice, "they may look unworthy of the army's attentions."

"I am acquainted with some residents there, the Goings family. Shall we try to make our way to them?" he suggested.

"We have cousins living up there," Jane McCully said. "If they can take in Father and Grandmother, we can manage."

"What do you think, Aunt Sophie? Can you keep going?"

"Let's move on, dear. Anything is preferable to standing here," answered the gallant old lady.

They were stopped several times. The valuables the McCully girls had saved were wrested from them.

From the top of the hill Sophie looked down. "Now we know what hell looks like."

The McCullys located relatives and went back to rescue their family members. The other three moved on to the Goings home. Mr. Conrad's friend was an energetic, exceedingly acid-tongued New Englander. She made them welcome and confidently told them she had fended off numerous bands of intruders during the night.

The sharp words of Mrs. Goings apparently had a powerful effect upon men who heretofore had been meeting only terror and entreaty as they pillaged. The severe reproof shouted through her locked door sent arsonists off in search of easier prey.

"The human will to survive is strong. I never imagined I had the physical endurance I've shown tonight," confided Aunt

Sophie. "Everything has been too ghastly for me to have time to worry!"

Every bedroom was already filled to capacity. The women, in wordless agreement, lay down on the parlor carpet and sought rest for the short space of time until dawn. They were awakened later by the McCullys seeking shelter on the floor beside them.

Finally the night of February 17 ended. They were surrounded by desolation. Thirteen hundred homes had been destroyed. More than seven thousand dazed women and children were cold, hungry and homeless. Hundreds of Columbians waited where they had sought safety on the edges of town. Others were gathered at the Theological Seminary, in Sidney Park, behind the walls of the State Insane Asylum, on the College horseshoe green and in any other sheltered spot where they could find refuge.

Eight

Ellen awoke, body aching from having slept on the hard floor. Disoriented, she struggled to remember where she was and why. Reality, stark and painful, returned. Saturday, February 18. Outside in the dim light there was silence. She touched her aunt's shoulder.

"Aunt Sophie, we must not burden these people. I think we should go now," she said, voice hoarse, throat parched and sore. Sophie raised her head slightly and nodded. She reached back to rub her stiff neck.

The McCullys were stirring too and preparing to leave.

"We thank you for taking us in last night," Ellen said gently to Mrs. McCully. "We are sorry about your trouble."

"You and your aunt helped us get through the night," she replied. "I must go and see to my husband and his mother right away, but if you are alone and homeless, perhaps you would like to join us as we seek lodgings."

"We're uncertain about everything, too." Sophie tried to conceal how badly she was shaken. "Last night Ellen and I went to a neighbor's around ten, but they were soon burned out." She swallowed with difficulty, adjusted her wrinkled clothing and tried to organize her thoughts. "We were promised guards for my home," she continued, "but they had not arrived when we left."

"I pray that they came in time, Miss Sophie."

"I live on Laurel, several blocks removed from downtown." Aunt Sophie pulled at her wrinkled skirt in a vain attempt to make herself look presentable. "I'm hoping the house is still intact. If not, I have a grape arbor which will offer some protection. You are most welcome to stay with us until you can make more satisfactory arrangements."

They found Mrs. Going in the kitchen, thanked her and started the trek down Arsenal Hill through the blackened, gutted city. The spirited little German counsel was with them. Each person silently studied the horizon.

The cluster of small houses above them, and those on the outskirts of town, seemed to be all that remained of the city of Columbia. Places that a day earlier had been busy streets and intersections were filled with blackened debris and no longer passable. Smoke hung heavy in the air.

They walked in silence. Though the aftermath of the night of rioting was visible everywhere, the revelers had disappeared. The group picked their way around charred, smoking timbers and piles of fallen brick toward what had been the downtown area.

"Mr. Conrad, we have reached Main Street. My aunt and I have to go up some distance to Laurel, and then three blocks over. Would you like to accompany us?" invited Ellen.

"Thank you, no," the consul was still determined to seek justice. "I wish to learn the fate of my office and my dwelling place. I shall certainly lodge a complaint at army headquarters about my losses and our dreadful treatment. Your kindness, ladies, has been most gratifying to one so far away from home." He executed a courtly bow and departed in the opposite direction.

Ellen and Sophie watched briefly as he purposefully marched away. They finally located their street, and on both sides could see only desolation. The two walked past the brick foundation and mounds of rubble that had been the Whilden house. Ellen thought of the intoxicated soldier who must surely lie dead among the ashes. Had others perished the same way?

In the next block they passed two houses only partly destroyed and were heartened. Further ahead Ellen caught a glimpse of the black slate roof of the Heyward house. She took her aunt's hand and they ran the remaining block. Sobbing and out of breath Sophie sank down on the steps of her house.

"Thank God," she wept, "oh, thank God!"

Ellen walked up on the porch. The door was splintered where the bolt had been forced. Inside she found disorder, but no signs of the malicious destruction they had witnessed all night. The parlor sofa had been pulled into the doorway and its burgundy velvet upholstery was mud stained. Chairs had been rearranged and pipe ashes were strewn on the floor. She looked more closely about the room. The drawers of the big walnut secretary stood open, showing unmistakable signs of having been ransacked. The house had been searched and the pantry rifled.

"Come in, Aunt Sophie, things are better than we dared hope. Someone spent the night here. Those men I heard go past in the dark last night must have been sent by Colonel Corley."

At the rear of the house everything was shrouded in a death-like stillness. Ellen called and waited. The door moved slightly, then was flung wide open.

Mariah peeped around the door frame, then rushed out shouting, "Lord, Miss Ellen, I am so glad to see you. This the longest, most scarifying night I even spent in my life."

"Yes, it was. We are glad to see the house still standing."

"About the time you and Miss Sophie left, some of them Yankee soldiers broke in here. I could see candles moving around in all the rooms. I expect every minute they going to set the place on fire, never did. Must have left at first light."

"I went inside. There's nobody there."

"I been scared they might come back. All us wait here quiet, like you said. Let's go home today, Miss Ellen. Randolph and me done had more than enough of this town life."

"We will, Aunt Mariah, soon. We'll find Pam, and after we make sure that Aunt Sophie will be all right, we will go."

"God knows I sure be ready!"

By the time John Arledge finally left the College it was full day-light. He had not had time to secure quarters for himself since arriving in the city. He wondered wearily if he should seek a place within the College, but the area was already crowded. Homeless refugees, black and white, were continuing to file into the compound.

Outside the gate, stark chimneys marked where buildings had stood. Crumbling masonry walls and gaping windows of warehouses and stores helped him identify his way. Arledge rode past the foundation stones and chimney which had been the old State House. His head throbbed dully. He had shared boiled coffee and hardtack with the gate guards. The acrid stench of the smoldering damp cotton was sickening. A variety of emotions assaulted him… anger, frustration, disgust, despair.

His soldier's mind was trained to remember landmarks, but everything familiar had been obliterated. He forced himself alert and studied the horizon. Many of the houses on the outer fringe of the city were still standing. He headed north in the direction of Laurel Street and continued riding.

Far down a side street he spotted a black youngster sitting on a granite carriage block in front of a brick house. He had not seen the Heyward home by daylight, but the location seemed right. As he neared, the boy jumped from his perch and dashed to the rear of the house.

Dismounting, Arledge tied his horse to one of the scorched pecan trees planted to shade the packed red clay avenue in summer. He walked wearily to the house and knocked at the door.

"Mrs. Heyward," he called, voice strained and tired. He waited and listened. "Mrs. Heyward, Ellen, it's John Arledge."

Ellen pulled open the damaged door. He examined her patrician features, all high cheek bones and fine hollows, sensitive mouth, a glorious cloud of reddish hair… all beauty and refinement, exactly as he had remembered.

Accusing eyes stared straight into his. He felt a spasm of longing and desire wash over his body.

"Thank God," he croaked hoarsely. "It was a terrible night."

"I couldn't agree more." Her eyes glittered icily. She permitted herself to see only the blue uniform and her anger mounted. His handsome face froze.

"Stop looking at me that way!" he barked.

His eyes were like winter lightning. They showed the ambiguity he was feeling.

"I have had enough for one night, Ellen. I refuse to be castigated for things for which I was in no way responsible. I am here out of concern for you."

She endured unflinchingly his glacial stare. Her face was defiant and her manner distant, withdrawn, and taciturn.

"There is unfinished business between us, but I can see that it must wait," he snapped. "I won't trouble you further."

"Your investigation of me still continues?" she inquired with carefully calculated sarcasm.

"That, and other things," he replied and turned on his heel. Strong lean legs, fueled by the frustration he was feeling, carried him to the waiting horse. He swung into the saddle, relieved to have found her, infuriated by her haughty attitude.

The animal, aware of the sheathed anger of his rider, sensed danger and shied nervously before he galloped away.

Seething with bitterness and wrath, Ellen watched him go. The anguish of the night tore at her throat. She fought for control. She would never weaken. This day must be endured, and tonight, and tomorrow and a thousand more tomorrows after that. She would survive.

She stared down the street after him. All was desolate, and lifeless. In that aching place where her heart should be, Ellen felt a strange yearning for things that could never be. She shrugged off the pain, and scorned herself for indulging in girlish fantasy.

Reality had to be faced. Back in the kitchen, her aunt had decided to cook whatever food was available, and to offer shelter, for the night, to as many of the city's wandering homeless as they were able to accommodate. Collards from the small vegetable garden which Uncle Albert had maintained through the war years must be gathered and cooked. The last of the hominy would be prepared. Every quilt, blanket and piece of bed covering of any kind was being brought out and stacked in readiness.

In another part of the city morning had dawned on a soot and tear-stained group of homeless nuns and children. Their convent had been burned, their church repeatedly threatened and, during the night, they had been forced to hide in the cemetery. Gravestones made poor windbreaks and they were cold and hungry. The sympathetic and curious were beginning to gather around the churchyard fence.

Food was sent to the children by families nearby whose homes had escaped the torch. The two Union officers who had faithfully kept vigil with them through the night were preparing to leave.

"We can never fully express our gratitude," the mother superioress said. "We owe our church and perhaps our lives to you. I am proud to number you gentlemen among our faith."

"Please do not thank us," the doctor replied. "We are sorry we couldn't do more, and that you should have cause to need us."

"How will this night be explained to the world!" the old sister agonized. "That so much private and religious property could be burned... quantities of badly needed food destroyed and raiment wantonly ruined, innocent children needlessly frightened, and all imposed on us by the Christian army of the most Christianized country in the world. I wonder how another soul can ever be converted." She walked to the street with the men.

As they were leaving Colonel Corley asked, "Is the young Heyward girl still with you?"

"Yes, do you wish to speak with her?"

"No, but you might tell her that her sister sent us here. We are lodged in the Heyward home and I'm sure that her family is safe. I sent guards to protect them."

"Please express my thanks to Miss Heyward for sending you."

"I know she and her aunt are anxious about the little girl. I will pass the word on that she is safe with you."

"Tell them, please, that I am not sure where we will go from here, but our group will be easy for her to trace. Pamela can remain with us as long as they like. God will provide a way."

They heard the hoofbeats of approaching horses. One rider, easily recognized as General Sherman, detached himself from the group and came forward. As he neared he removed his cigar, hesitated, then quickly restored it to his mouth, and chewed on it with an exaggerated air of irritation.

The nun drew herself proudly erect. Her sharp eyes and the flowing robes of her sacred order had great power to intimidate.

General Sherman stopped before her, shifting his balance nervously from side to side. He removed the cigar and held it behind him.

She lifted one arm and gestured to the shivering group of nuns and children among the tombstones. Then in carefully calculated words began to speak. "This, sir, is how you kept your promise to me, a cloistered nun!"

"A most regrettable accident, Sister," Sherman said. "The Rebels were foolhardy to leave so much whiskey in the town. It would have been impossible for anyone to maintain strict discipline over a drunken army, particularly one in the temper of my men."

Her eyes flashed. "Perhaps you can't control all of the soldiers in your army, just as Father O'Connel and I can't be responsible for the conduct of all Roman Catholics, but we did expect that a few of the principles of human decency would be shown by your men."

He did not miss her barb about the conduct of Catholics.

The angry nun continued, "I assured the parents of these children that I had a personal tie with you. Having known and loved your daughter made me feel that I could rely on your promise of protection. I wonder, sir, how you would feel if one of these frightened faces were that of your daughter Minnie?"

He appeared to consider her words. "I need not remind you of the high wind. There was no way to control the fires."

"No doubt the fires were wind-fanned, but thousands of witnesses, half of them your own army, can attest to the fact that most of the blazes were man-made. I have been told that within two hours after you issued the order to extinguish them this morning the fires were all out."

"It was never my intention that private homes, most of all your convent, be burned. You may choose another among any of the buildings left standing. It shall be yours as a gift, and I assure you it will be protected."

"I do not think that the houses are yours to give, sir, but when I do make arrangements for my community and our pupils, I will thank you to move us. I will also expect you to provide food for this large number, which I shall now find hard to feed."

He turned to go. Then, looking into her penetrating eyes he remarked, "I have often said that war is hell."

"There could be no more fitting description for the war you visited upon us," she agreed. "I shall pray for you, General. I hope that you can reconcile your government and your conscience to this holocaust, for it is certain that your God and the people of Columbia will have cause to long remember this night."

The nuns were first taken to the Methodist Female College on Plain Street. Colonel Ewing came with ambulances and transported the group. The sisters soon discovered they were overcrowded, and the kitchen facilities were inadequate for their needs. The Mother Superior, remembering Sherman's promise of any home in the city, asked Ewing about Confederate General Preston's mansion.

"That is where General Logan has his headquarters. Orders have been issued to have that building burned tomorrow morning before we leave the city. If you choose it for your convent I will go now and apply to the general to countermand the order."

When the sisters arrived before the stately mansion on Blanding Street the next day fires had already been kindled and servants had begun to carry out furniture and bedding. The burning was halted. Titles to the property were executed and signed, and the mother superioress was deeded the house.

As the sun climbed higher in the sky, the morning became bright and clear. Arledge prepared for a busy day. Thousands of requests and complaints would come across his desk. Compared to the previous day, the city was quiet and orderly. Outside gloom and silence weighed heavily until well past noon. The bummers had been ordered to spread out into the countryside in search of cattle and provisions. Other soldiers were set to tearing up and destroying the railroads for miles out of town. Depots, supply houses and public buildings of military significance were systematically destroyed. The gas and water works were blown up.

Though the robbing and burning within the city had ceased, the search for buried treasure continued. Soldiers sifted ashes, rummaged through blackened timbers, and dug in the private grounds and yards of the remaining houses. Citizens petitioned vainly for guards. They were told that double guards would be posted throughout the city and no individual sentries would be needed at private homes.

By late afternoon Ellen began to wonder how they would accommodate all of those seeking shelter with them. A note had been delivered earlier from Colonel Corley assuring them of Pamela's safety and saying he and the doctor would return that night. Torn between thoughts that no Yankee deserved to sleep indoors and the realization that, without the help of the two men, they would be homeless themselves, Ellen and Sophie had assigned one of the upstairs bedrooms to the two officers.

Mr. Richards arrived. Apologetically he informed them that he had been unable to find temporary lodging. The Richards family, father, daughter and servants, were established in the second bedroom. One of the McCully girls stopped to ask if they might return to stay the night. They were to sleep in Sophie's room and she and Ellen would share the small dressing room.

As evening shadows began to lengthen Ellen began arranging the parlor furniture so pallets could be spread on the floor. She looked up and saw young Frank Whilden coming up the walk.

"Frank!" She hugged him warmly. "We have been watching for you and inquiring about your family. Where is your mother?"

"We are staying in the Theological Seminary. We were in time this morning to get one of the rooms there. Mother sent me to tell you that we are safe, and that she can make room for you and your aunt with us. Is Miss Sophie all right?" His young eyes were dark circled. His shoulders were carrying burdens too great for his years.

"We are all fine, son. We have heard from my sister and she is safe. Tell me about your grandmother. Is she well?"

"Yes, mam. Grandmother usually has a lot to say about everything. Today she has not even mentioned the troubles we had last night." He thrust a small package into Ellen's hands, "Here, Miss Ellen, Mother told me to give this to you. These two books were all she was able to hold on to last night. She wants you to put them away safe for her."

Ellen recognized the Whilden family Bible. She remembered seeing Mary grab it from its customary place on the bedroom mantelpiece as they were leaving the flaming house. The Bible contained the only records the family now had. There was a marker toward the middle of the book. Ellen opened it and her eyes fell on several pages filled with Mary's fine script:

"This little record of my experience I write so that my children, some of whom were too young to remember, may refer to it in years to come, when the incidents of the war shall have passed into history and the burning of Columbia be attributed to other causes than the incendiary torch of Sherman and his brutal soldiers.

I record this in my Bible where aught but truth dare not be written, that my eyes saw the United States soldiers, under the command of General W. T. Sherman, set fire to and burn not only my own but other houses in my immediate neighborhood. This Bible, together with a small Episcopal prayer book, were the only books left me after the fire, and I desire to bear record to the circumstances under which it was saved, and how it is that so high a value is attached to this volume."

—Mary Stephens Whilden,
Columbia, S. C., February 17, 1865

Ellen went to the end of the walk with Frank and waved goodbye. Mr. Conrad shouted from the opposite direction.

"Miss Heyward," he called, "I have found you. May I be so presumptuous as to intrude upon your hospitality for the night? I realize that you have far more friends than beds, but please know that I have now accustomed myself to sleeping on the floor. I shall require no more than a roof over my head, if you can allow me that."

"Certainly, sir. You have arrived in time to claim our parlor sofa. You may have to sleep with your knees tucked under your chin, but I know that will be more comfortable than the drafty floor." She admired the little German's spirit.

"Oh, dear lady, how delightful to hear a kind word. Be glad you did not accompany me to the general's headquarters today!"

"And how fared you there?" she inquired.

"Neither as well as I had hoped, nor as badly as I had feared," was his quick reply. "I went to lay complaint about the treatment to which I had been subjected, and to be indemnified for my losses. I was politely received by General Howard. He is second in command to Sherman and reputed to be a fine soldier."

Mr. Conrad drew a deep breath in preparation for launching into another colorful rendition of his experiences. "General Howard, a former clergyman, lost an arm in the Mexican War. Distinguished himself further in the Indian Wars, I have been informed."

Ellen nodded and waited for the gentleman to continue.

"I gave him my complaint, as consul of a neutral nation, and he listened courteously. He expressed regret about last night's occurrences, and declared that if I would point out the captain who robbed me, he would have him shot before my eyes."

"Which of course you could not do."

"You are quite correct. And what indeed was the guilt of this one single individual in comparison to the innumerable and far greater crimes of thousands of others? I informed him of all I had witnessed."

"General Howard must have had a busy day," Ellen responded.

"Indeed, yes. While in his office I heard charges of breast pins being snatched off ladies and rings jerked from their fingers. I myself talked to a lady who had the lobes of both ears torn asunder when her earrings were grabbed. What other outrages in word and deed the female sex had to suffer I can only imagine."

Ellen averted her eyes. "Let's go inside, sir, before it gets dark."

"I am most appreciative of your kindness, Miss Heyward. I have money secreted on my person and I shall pay your aunt."

"I am sure she will not accept it. So many people are more in need than we are."

"Mayor Goodwyn came to see General Sherman while I was waiting at their headquarters. He is suffering from an enflamed eye caused by a burning cinder. He was summoned, received cordially, and informed that the destruction of the city was his fault for having suffered ardent spirits to be left in the city."

"And all of the fires were accidental, I suppose?"

"Indeed, yes, and all most profoundly regretted."

"I find that most infuriating," she said wearily.

"General Howard told me that the army will remain in Columbia only a few days, They do not plan to leave a garrison behind. They are to march in a northeasterly direction, arriving at a seaport in about eight to fourteen days. If I wish to avail myself of the opportunity of reaching that point in safety and try to embark from there for Europe, he informed me, I might partake of all the comforts and or privations of himself and his staff, which I was invited to join."

"Perhaps you should do that, Mr. Conrad. This is not your war and you are a long way from home. There is little hope of your sailing except from some northern-held port. I don't know how you would find transportation to the seacoast except with the Union army. They have taken or destroyed all the horses and carriages and you know the condition of the railroads."

"At first I had the inclination to view the situation as you do, but upon closer consideration I renounced the alluring opportunity. If I should do this, the Confederate territory would be closed to me. One of my superiors is still, so far as I can ascertain, in Charleston. I feel that it is needful for me, before everything else, to lay before him a full account of my experiences and of the losses sustained."

Agitated and indignant, he continued. "For transportation, the general expected me to perform clerical work for him!"

Ellen regretted that Sophie was busy elsewhere. She knew she'd never be able to describe all the outraged mannerisms and remember the details of Mr. Conrad's continuing saga.

"I would not like to return to my country and later be brought before authorities on suspicion that I had pretended this robbery or neglected my duty. This way I can, with his consent and a clear conscience, pursue my design of seeking my home, to which I am now drawn with redoubled longing."

"You have chosen the most honorable course, sir. I admire you, and bid you welcome to remain within the now failing confines of the Confederacy." She smiled and curtsied.

They entered the house together.

"How may I be of service to you and your aunt?" he inquired.

"There are a number of colored people in the yard. Our servant's quarters and carriage house are filled. We have told the others that they may sleep under the grape arbor. Most of them are frightened. Perhaps you can help by reassuring them and organizing a fuel-gathering force. We have need of fire-wood."

"I shall be happy to be useful."

Ellen was wondering how they would manage supper when she was again summoned to the door. The Masters family, mother, aunt, and three children asked permission to spend the night on the piazza. Sophie gave them the fourth and last bedroom.

Dark was gathering. All day Ellen had pushed thoughts of John Arledge into the back of her mind. How much should she read into the stormy passion in his eyes? What caused the magnetic attraction between them? If there were no war, would the tempestuous relationship still exist? He would be leaving soon.

The loud voice of Colonel Corley intruded upon her thoughts. "Miss Heyward, your sister is safe. The doctor and I were at St. Peter's with the nuns and children until dawn. General Sherman is giving the mother superior the Preston home for her community. They were transported over and food has been provided."

"That is welcome news, Colonel Corley. Thank you."

"Mother Baptista personally assured me of Pamela's safety. Your sister helped with the smaller children throughout the whole ordeal. You are invited to allow her to remain there. She will be cared for, better perhaps than anywhere else in the city."

Dr. Calahan entered the house behind him. Following them were two enlisted men carrying a number of large bundles.

"Miss Heyward, these men are our aides, Sergeant Watkins and Corporal Johnson. We have drawn our rations for the next few days. You shared with us, now we share our provisions with you."

The soldiers filed into the kitchen and deposited a side of beef and packages of salt, dried peas, potatoes, dried apples, flour, and, most rare of all, rations of sugar and coffee.

Ellen, Sophie and Aunt Mariah stared in disbelief. "Truly, gentlemen, we in this house would have had little supper had you not brought this food," acknowledged Sophie.

"We want to repay your kindness," Dr. Calahan informed her.

"The house is filled with hungry people. Aunt Sophie and I thank you and we will see that dinner is prepared for you, but we cannot dine in such plenty."

"Ladies, I know food is scarce in the city and this is intended for everyone here. Stretch it as far as it will go. We will secure more. If each house still standing is accommodating as many people as you are, that will alleviate some of the suffering."

Aunt Mariah set about happily cutting beef, peeling potatoes, soaking peas and stewing apples. Tomorrow there would be rice and gravy, broth for soup and perhaps even an apple pie. Soon the almost forgotten aroma of boiling coffee filled the house. Hattie had been gone all day so Ellen prepared the table. The good china and silver had been safely hidden away. Ellen laid out a medley of ill-assorted makeshift settings.

Hard dark closed in. There was no movement in the streets. If someone else should seek sanctuary with them, only floor space was available. Where had Arledge found quarters, Ellen wondered.

At seven they sat down for dinner, the two officers, Mr. Conrad, Mr. Richards and the two Heyward women. The Masters family politely declined, insisting that they had eaten at the home of a relative earlier. Rose Richards had been taken a tray and, upon her insistence, her father sat at the table.

Mr. Richards ate and said little. Pride made it difficult to be seated with the Union officers, and harder still to be forced to accept their generosity. Breeding, good manners and the knowledge that he and his daughter hardly knew where their next meal was coming from, forced him to accept the invitation.

No comparisons were drawn between the crude assortment of unmatched kitchen dishes and cooking utensils and the fragile porcelain and silver of the previous evening. No apologies were made. The conversation, though strained, was polite and general, and carried, for the most part, by Mr. Conrad and the colonel.

Only the two men in blue were served coffee full strength and sweetened with sugar. Theirs was real South American Rio brewed from the whole berries. The coffee the others drank had been diluted to make it go further.

"Before secession," Aunt Sophie informed them, "we were accustomed to drinking Brazilian coffee three times a day. In most households the pot boiled on the back of the stove throughout the day. When the Yankee blockade first denied us coffee, many people complained of headache, dizziness, and other withdrawal symptoms."

"My wife is partial to hot chocolate." The doctor carefully sipped his hot brew.

"Since the blockade," Sophia continued, "ersatz coffee is always a popular topic of discussion at all ladies' gatherings. The beverage has been extensively written about in southern magazines and newspapers. Every imaginable seed has been parched, dried, toasted, pulverized and served as a coffee substitute. Sugar cane, okra, seed from sea island cotton, acorns, and melon seeds had all been pressed into service."

"Professing that these drinks are delicious," Ellen added stiffly, "is regarded as an act of patriotism among Confederate women."

Dr. Calahan noticed the others hesitantly sipping their coffee. "We have a generous coffee ration, Mrs. Heyward, which we are happy to share while we are billeted with you. General Sherman is much addicted to coffee."

"We have become accustomed to our substitutes."

"The general believes that coffee satisfies a yearning more powerful than the theory of 'habit' can account for. He makes sure that his men are well supplied. He has ordered that each soldier carry his own coffee and sugar with him, even at the expense of bread. He feels there are many substitutes for bread, but none for coffee."

"Thank you for sharing your coffee with us." Sophie spoke with great pride and dignity. "We have been able to develop a few hot drinks that we find to be quite satisfactory."

As soon as courtesy permitted, Mr. Richards rose and asked to be excused. He explained that his daughter was suffering the effects of a night of exposure. When Dr. Calahan offered to see her the old man insisted that it would not be necessary.

"If you should need me at any time during the night, sir, please do not hesitate to call. I can appreciate the fact that you do not want to be obligated to a Union army official, but I am a doctor and I want to be of service to anyone who is ill."

There was no mistaking the sincerity in his kind voice.

"Sir," Mr. Richards assured, "my love for my dear daughter is far greater than my pride. I do not wish to make unnecessary demands, but if Rose should need you, I would ask for your services, even if you were not the man of honor and integrity you have shown yourself to be."

Colonel Corley rose. "Before you go I would like a word. My men are not those of the Fifteenth Corps."

The room was suddenly very quiet.

"Few of them participated in last night's fracas. I in no way condone what happened, but I am not sure it could have been prevented. Hatred and vengeance are powerful forces, hard to control. To many Union men, this state stands as the symbol of the conflict. Retaliation was on the minds of most of them."

"There were no rebel soldiers in the city," spoke up Ellen. "Why should they seek retribution on helpless civilians?"

"Emotion unchecked runs riot. Many men must feel ashamed and penitent today. I am sure that is why so few were on the streets. Men died for having lost their sanity last night. I talked with one officer today who said he lost more men in the sacking of Columbia than he did in the battle of Atlanta. We estimate that as many as two hundred soldiers perished in the flames."

"Victims of their own evil doings." Ellen regarded the two with open hostility.

The doctor interceded softly.

"There are many by-products in any life and death struggle, especially a war. I am sure your army could not have wished for so many Union prisoners to die as have been lost at the Confederate prison camp in Florence for lack of medicine and attention. The starvation diet, lack of shelter and deplorable sanitary conditions at Camp Sorghum, just across the river, have cost numerous Union officers their lives. I do not say that the north's record is any better, but who can be sure what is and is not justifiable, if the desired end is achieved."

"You have not heard us plead for quarter." Ellen remained defiant.

"No, Miss Ellen, we have not."

To lessen the tension Sophie rose and said, "If you gentlemen will adjourn to the parlor I'll have Albert make a fire. Ellen, would you take some coffee and biscuits to the Masters family. I'm afraid not wanting to accept what they have no way of repaying prompted them to refuse dinner."

"Yes, Aunt Sophie, I plan to. I wonder where the McCullys are."

"Pride again. They won't arrive until supper is well over. We can stretch the coffee and biscuits. I'll save them some."

"We can only stretch things so far. We served most of our greens and grits to the blacks in the back yard this afternoon. We must have fifteen or twenty people out there now. I told Frank their servants could sleep under the grape arbor. Mr. Richards has two maids and the Masters family brought two. The McCullys may have a servant with them. We have food for one or two more days, but I don't know what we will do after that."

"By Monday the mayor will have things organized," the colonel assured them. "We plan to get emergency relief stations set up. Food will be provided. The city will not starve."

Sophie and Ellen helped Aunt Mariah with the dishes, while the two orderlies ate in silence at the kitchen table. Mr. Conrad and the officers talked in the parlor by the fire light, the rumble of Colonel Corley's bass tones interspersing with the German consul's stilted pronouncements. As they worked quietly by candlelight, the monotonous drone of voices was hypnotic.

Ellen heard the clock strike nine. Time had come to divide the quilts. To stay warm, everyone would have to keep on most of their clothing. Fortunately the four Yankees had brought their own blankets. Someone knocked at the door. Ellen opened it and found the McCullys standing at the threshold.

"Come in, girls. We have been expecting you for hours. Where is your mother?"

"Oh, Ellen, today has been a nightmare. Grandmother is very ill and Father is much worse. We had trouble locating a doctor."

"Perhaps Doctor Calahan can help."

"We found our doctor, but it is all so distressing, no medicine, no nourishing food. We can't let them know how bad things really are... the house they are in is crowded. Mother wouldn't leave. Father doesn't want anyone else to look after him and Grandmother may not last the night. None of us knows which way to turn!" Sally looked as if she might dissolve into tears.

"You must be brave, Sally. I understand. My father died recently, and I was unable to help him. Come inside. I know rest will help."

She pulled them into the hallway and propped the door shut.

"Tomorrow you can take over for your mother. Things will look better then. Aunt Sophie will show you your room and I'll bring you some coffee. Would your servant like to stay, too?"

"No. He is to return to help mother during the night."

When the McCully girls had knocked Ellen's first thought was of John Arledge. He would not come this late. Perhaps he would not come at all. Would he persist in the investigation? Perhaps she had finally discouraged him and seen him for the last time? Anxiety and distress had taken their toll. By ten o'clock the house was quiet. Ellen lay down beside her aunt and almost immediately fell into a deep, exhausted sleep.

Nine

Finally, a clear balmy day dawned. Sunday, February 19, no church bells rang in the city. Columbia residents, after a quiet night spent in uneasy slumber, rose and began to take stock of their situation. Their town lay in total ruin. Travel was impossible, and they were occupied by a vengeful enemy.

Stores, shops and offices throughout the city had vanished overnight. There was less than a two-day supply of food on hand, and the countryside for miles around had already been robbed, pillaged, burned and virtually devastated. Prior to the fires most homes were already crowded to overflowing. Shelter was available for fewer than one-tenth of the newly homeless roaming the streets.

At sunrise the Union army began mopping-up activities. Poe's Engineers were sent to remove the munitions in the State Arsenal and dump them in the Saluda River. Arledge was ordered to supervise the destruction of the presses in the factory which printed Confederate money.

"Kelly, get a few sober recruits. We have a job to do in town." Arledge waited while his sergeant rounded up four men to accompany them.

When they arrived, the plates had already been removed, but fifty presses still remained. Money, in various stages of manufacture, was gleefully seized and tossed about by the soldiers in Sergeant Kelly's detail.

"Boys, get hold of yourselves. You have done enough hell-raising." Kelly spat the words with disgust.

At Laurel Street the occupants waited. Sophie rose before daylight and moved about the house restlessly fretting. "Ellen, someone came by and said the men in town are meeting to form relief committees. I wonder what the ladies are doing?"

"Most women have children and older relatives to care for, Aunt Sophie. I doubt they are free to do much for others."

"You're probably right, dear. We're doing all we can now."

Mr. Richards as a member of the citizen's group went with the mayor to call on Sherman at his headquarters on Gervais Street. They requested provisions for the twenty thousand women, children and elderly men now stranded in the city, and for some means to defend themselves.

Food was necessary, but the general seemed to eye with surprise their request for arms and ammunition. After solemn consideration, he agreed that civil officials would need to be able to enforce law and order. Bands of stragglers and plunderers always followed in the wake of an army.

"Gentlemen," he told them, "Your requests will be honored."

Later in the day the committee was notified to be at the College horseshoe the next morning at six to receive five hundred head of cattle. The College fence was the only enclosure in the city still intact and large enough to hold a herd of livestock. The guns requested were to be issued from the State Asylum. Committee members were instructed to prepare to take over the city by two o'clock on Monday as Federal troops would soon be moving out.

Ellen could not shake her uneasiness. She missed the hospital work. The McCully girls left to help their mother. The Masters family was preparing to leave to stay with relatives.

The two Union officers and their orderlies went to take up duties in other parts of the city. The black people who had spent the night departed on their separate ways. A servant was with Rose. Her father and Mr. Conrad were attending a men's meeting. Ellen offered to sit with Rose.

"That won't be necessary." The frail girl never made demands. "I shall read and then take a nap. Lilly is with me and Father will be back later. After his meeting, he plans to check on some rental houses he owns. We hope to find one undamaged that we can move into. Poor Father, all of this is very difficult for him."

"He is showing remarkable strength, Rose. He has been a great help to Aunt Sophie. You must be very proud of him."

"If only I were not such a burden." Her face was anxious.

"Oh, do hush. You are a complete joy to everyone who knows you. Since Lilly is here, I think I'll walk over to the Preston home this morning. My sister is there with the convent pupils."

"Today is Sunday, isn't it? Is it safe? I've not been out much in my life, but that night in the street was horrendous."

"Today is abnormally quiet, Rose, even for a Sunday. It's eerie out there. I was told that the only soldiers about are the few on special work details."

Ellen found Sophie and Aunt Mariah busy folding blankets and putting bedding out to air. When her aunt heard her plan to visit Pamela, she immediately cautioned that she must take Randolph along.

"If anyone should inquire, I will be back in about an hour."

"Yes, dear," Sophie replied. "Stay as long as you like."

Though the weather was not cold, Ellen felt chilled through. Melancholia had descended upon her. The view in every direction was oppressive. Ellen turned to wait on Randolph, who always lagged a few steps behind. He intently observed everything, but was inclined to say little. When he had caught up she continued. The distance was short, and once there, they located Pamela easily.

The sisters exchanged news of the past two days. Ellen skipped rapidly over the frightening events of Friday night, told of the many guests at the house and did not mention having seen John Arledge again.

Pam made little reference to the hardships the group at the convent had suffered. She assured Ellen they had adequate food, and that she was busy and needed. She asked to remain at the convent until time to go back to the plantation.

When Ellen returned no mention was made of callers. They had beef bouillon for lunch. Ellen was restless and at odds. Knowing that much of her problem stemmed from the conflicting emotions she felt about John Arledge was also disturbing.

"Have you made plans for the afternoon, Ellen?" her aunt inquired. She was pouring bouillon into a large Mason jar.

"No, is there something I can do? I need to be busy."

"If you plan to be here, I'd like to go out for a while."

Ellen knew the jar of soup was for some needy friend. "Should I unpack the china and put it away? The danger of theft seems to be over. The colonel says strict discipline is being enforced."

"Yes, but let's wait a while on the silver. Thank goodness Aunt Mariah kept it in her bed in the carriage house. I want to walk over to the Seminary and take soup to the Whilden children."

They both knew life had to be hard for them now.

"By tomorrow I think we'll have room for Mary and the family. I will urge her to come and stay with us. Since you are here, Rose won't be in the house alone. I'll take Randolph along."

After Sophie left, Ellen put a kettle of water on to heat. She removed the stovewood from the bin beside the range and lifted out the box of china. A saucer on top had broken, the rest was undamaged. She had seen her aunt wince each time Randolph brought in an armload of wood recently and carelessly dashed it in the bin. They had not dared caution him.

Ellen methodically washed each piece of china, glad to be occupied with the task. She was looking for dish towels when she heard someone knocking. Heart skipping erratically, she hastily removed her apron, then pulled her sleeves down and buttoned them. Her face felt flushed as she walked to the door.

Through the beveled glass of the sidelights she could see John Arledge waiting outside, immaculately uniformed and more breathtakingly handsome than she had remembered. When she opened the door he towered above her, eyes searching her face.

Ellen's pulse quickened. She tried to appear unruffled.

He made no move to touch her.

"Would you like to come in?" she invited, anxious to end the long, uncomfortable silence. Upon closer scrutiny she saw that his face looked tired. Dark shadows under his eyes emphasized their startling blueness. He seemed ill at ease.

"May I speak with you alone?" he asked hesitantly.

"Certainly." She led him inside.

Where was the arrogant confidence? He had never asked permission for anything. He followed her into the stiff parlor and stood awkwardly in front of the cold fireplace. She waited for him to say something.

"Miss Heyward... Ellen," he began, speaking in a low voice, "I am here to apologize. I regret having caused you anguish. I am sorry that..." his voice trailed away.

"Major," she interceded, "I don't hold you personally responsible for all of the atrocities that have been committed. You made your decision long ago about where your loyalties lie."

"Ellen, you know very well I didn't come here to discuss the war. I'm here to beg your forgiveness, to try to make amends."

171

"If you are trying to tell me that you regret having kissed me, that you lost your head, that you were carried away in a moment of passion, or whatever it is that men say at times like this, please don't bother. I, too, failed to maintain my reserve. Shall we forget it ever happened?"

He reached out, wrapping strong arms around her and pulling her close. "Not on your life, lady. You're way off the mark!"

Ellen stood stiffly in his embrace, unsure how to reply.

"I have walked around the city all morning despising myself and aching to see you. When I first questioned you about the disappearance of the Union foragers it was easy to see that you weren't telling all you knew. I tried to make it clear that I had every intention of getting at the full truth."

"I believed you, major. You were most explicit."

"Since then, I have worked constantly to solve the case and close it. I hoped you would not be criminally implicated. I wanted to see you again, but under different circumstances."

She stirred in his arms. "And what are you trying to say?"

"You are aware that one of the men in the Confederate patrol was captured. He has steadfastly refused to reveal information about what happened. I knew he must be protecting someone."

Arledge continued to hold her, his face against her hair.

She did not pull away from the warmth of his arms.

"Something more than a skirmish between two enemy patrols must have taken place." He was choosing each word carefully. "This morning I showed the prisoner two recent dispatches. It was most important that he understand why a statement from him is so necessary."

He released her, his face deadly serious, and with his right hand pulled two folded papers from inside his tunic. He held them out to Ellen. "Please read these letters."

His clear blue eyes burned into hers as she reached for the papers. Recent events had almost crowded from her mind the original horror that had brought them together. She looked down. He had given her two military letters. The words swam before her eyes. Knowing that, to him, they were vitally important, she began reading.

HEADQUARTERS MILITARY DIVISION
OF THE MISSISSIPPI

Lieut. Gen. WADE HAMPTON
Commanding Cavalry Force,
Confederate States Army General:

It is officially reported to me that our foraging parties are murdered after capture and labeled, "Death to all foragers." One instance of a lieutenant and 7 men near Chesterville, and another of 20 near a ravine, 80 rods from the main road, about 3 miles from Feasterville. I have ordered a similar number of prisoners in our hands to be disposed of in like manner.

I hold about 1000 prisoners, captured in various ways, and can stand it as long as you can; but I hardly think these murders are committed with your knowledge, and would suggest that you give notice to the people at large that every life taken by them simply results in the death of one of your Confederates. Of course, you can not question my right to forage upon the country. It is a war right as old as history. The manner of exercising it varies with circumstances, and if the civil authorities will supply my requisitions I will forbid all foraging. But I find no civil authorities who can respond to call for forage or provisions, and therefore must collect directly of the people. I have no doubt that this is the occasion of much misbehavior on the part of our men, but I can not permit an enemy to judge or punish with wholesale murder.

Personally, I regret the bitter feelings engendered by this war, but they were to be expected, and I simply allege that those who struck the first blow and made war inevitable, ought not, in fairness, to reproach us for the natural consequences. I merely assert our war right to forage and my resolve to protect my foragers to the extent of life for life.

> I am, with respect, your obedient servant,
> W. T. Sherman
> Major General, United States Army

HEADQUARTERS IN THE FIELD

Maj. Gen. W. T. Sherman
United States Army

GENERAL: Your communication reached me today. In it you state that it has been officially reported that your foraging parties were murdered after capture, and you go on to say that you "had ordered a similar number of prisoners in your hands to be disposed of in like manner." That is to say, you have ordered a number of Confederate soldiers to be "murdered." You characterize your order in proper terms, for the public voice, even in your own country, where it seldom dares to express itself in vindication of truth, honor, or justice, will surely agree in pronouncing you guilty of murder, if your order is carried out. Before dismissing this portion of your letter, I beg to assure you that for every soldier of mine "murdered" by you I shall have executed at once two of yours, giving in all cases preferences to any officers who may be in my hands. In reference to the statement you made regarding the death of your foragers, I have only to say that I know nothing of it; that no orders given by me authorize the killing of prisoners after capture, and that I do not believe that my men killed any of yours except under circumstances in which it was perfectly legitimate and proper they should kill them. It is a part of the system of the thieves whom you designate as your foragers to fire the dwellings of those citizens whom they have robbed.

To check this inhuman system, which is justly execrated by every civilized nation, I have directed my men to shoot down all of your men who are caught burning houses. This order shall remain in place as long as you disgrace the profession of arms by allowing your men to destroy private dwellings.

You say that I can not, of course, question your right to forage upon the country. "It is a right as old as history." I do not, sir, question this right. But there is a right older even than this, and one more inalienable - the right that every man has to defend his home, and protect those who are dependent upon him. And from my heart I wish that every old man and boy in my country who can fire a gun would shoot down, as he would a wild beast, the men who are desolating their land, burning their houses, and insulting their women.

Your line of march can be traced by the lurid light of burning houses, and in more than one household there is an agony far more bitter than that of death. The Indian scalped his victim, regardless of sex or age, but with all his barbarity, he always respected the persons of his female captives. Your soldiers, more savage than the Indians, insult those whose natural protectors are absent.

In conclusion, I have only to request that when you have any of my men "disposed of" or "murdered" for the terms appear to be synonymous with you, you will let me hear of it in order that I may know what action to take in the matter. In the meantime I shall hold 56 of your men as hostages for those you have ordered to be executed.

I am yours, etc.
WADE HAMPTON,
Lieutenant General

Ellen finished reading and quietly handed the letters back.

"You can imagine General Sherman's reaction when he received this scathing reply from General Hampton. We believed the three men I questioned you about had been killed, but we didn't know where, nor by whom. I was assigned to find out if they were dead because they were foragers, or if something more had happened."

Arledge put the dispatches carefully back in his jacket.

"The scavengers were at Oak Lane. When you refused to give much information about it, I was suspicious. When I threatened you with arrest, I had no idea what had occurred. Now that I know more, I regret I wasn't the one who shot the bastards myself."

His voice was harsh, his fists clenched. Ellen remained quiet.

"After interrogating the prisoner again this morning, I now know enough to cause me to end the investigation. I'm convinced that whatever happened to the men, they deserved that and more."

For Arledge to mark an unsolved case closed was difficult. He was not that kind of man. Anguish wracked his gut. Physical attack of a woman would not be tolerated.

He was aware of the lawless behavior of the bummers. The hobo soldiers had served long and well, and General Sherman had often remarked that he was so fond of his rag-tag scavengers he would have pardoned them for anything short of treason. However, the hardened general would not countenance the violation of women.

"Is the prisoner you hold an older man, a sergeant from Georgia?" Ellen had to do all she could to help the man. He had risked his life for her sister.

"Yes. He finally talked about the skirmish at Oak Lane. He told me that, on their way back, his patrol was ambushed trying to get through to the Confederate lines. One of the men was killed, one got away, and his lieutenant was wounded. He was not sure how badly."

"Please tell him that the young officer will recover," she said quietly. "I helped nurse him in the College hospital."

"The sergeant's story is as you said, except that when they arrived, the barn was already burning. The bummers didn't hear them ride up because they were engaged in a personal assault upon... a lady. He told me that fighting ensued. Several men were killed and later buried. He would disclose no more. I shall not probe further."

Ellen paled. "You will need to know the full story." She drew a deep breath. Again she recounted only known details of the incident, carefully omitting any mention of Pamela. Her face was without expression, her voice lifeless.

"The scavengers are dead. They were not executed. The men were armed and there was a gun battle. I shot and may have killed at least one of them. Anyway, they are all dead, killed by the Confederate soldiers or by me. If I'm not responsible for their death, God knows I tried." Ellen abandoned all caution.

She pulled away from him and crossed her arms, clutching her elbows. Continuing the tale was difficult. "The scouts couldn't leave the bodies in our stableyard. That would implicate us... me, and give away their own presence in the contested area. The dead men were loaded into our farm cart and taken to a wooded area and buried. It was after dark. No one saw us. No one aided us. The patrol rode away and I drove the cart back to the plantation. I knew nothing about their subsequent ambush until, by accident, I happened to see the young lieutenant here in a hospital ward."

He looked at her proud immobile face. "I didn't have much information when I first threatened you. I beg that you please forgive me. I am so sorry." His voice was strained.

She turned from him. "Are there any more questions?"

"Yes." He reached out to gently touch her face and lift her chin. "May I please start all over again with you?"

Startled, she looked into his tortured eyes. She realized that he thought she had been the woman attacked. He still believed that Pamela was a child. Was this pursuit of her some noble gesture? Was he seeking to make amends?

"Ellen," he whispered gently, "Don't you know I have been strongly attracted to you from the moment I first saw you?"

Disbelief was plainly written on her face.

He smiled wryly. "Why do all of our meetings seem to turn into battles? Yesterday I decided it was best not to see you again. I knew I had become too personally involved in a case."

"I was aware you felt that way."

"Last night was pure hell, so I'm back, as if drawn by some magnetic force. You are important to me. Let's begin again?"

"I don't think that is wise." She was stunned.

"Don't you think you could learn to trust me?" he asked, ignoring her response to his plea. "How long must I keep begging? We have so little time. Why won't you answer me?"

"Which question?"

"Any of them, all of them, some of them, one of them." His smile was disarming, the sudden easy banter completely charming.

"I don't know how to answer you," her reply barely audible.

"The timing is wrong, I know, but this is the moment we have. You can't ignore there are fireworks between us. What we feel is too strong to deny. Each of us has waited forever for something like this to happen." He took both her hands in his, compelling her to face him, hoping to overcome her stubborn hesitancy.

"We have missed so much of life already, Ellen. Let's start over. I want to do all of the right things. Have you located your father? May I ask for his permission to pay court to you?"

Tears began to course down her cheeks. "My father died a week ago… not in combat. He was ill." She felt defenseless.

"Honey," he whispered, "I'm sorry. I'll take care of you."

She tried to pull her hands away, but he continued to hold them firmly. She found his nearness disturbing. "Major, I'm not sure what to do about you. I am accustomed to taking care of myself. I find you overpowering. I agree with your first conclusion. It is best for us not to meet again. Our lives are already mapped out. We have nothing in common."

John Arledge had rarely been rebuffed. He, who never had trouble expressing himself, felt tongue-tied. Professionally he was known for his excellent communication skills. Socially, he was much sought after. Most women were attracted by his good looks and courtly manners. For him, easy charm and light romance had always been second nature. Now, desperately serious, he was fumbling for words.

"I am trying very hard to tell you that I care for you," he said with sincerity. "Why does this surprise you? Why can't I fall hopelessly in love just like any other dumb soldier?"

"John, I have had no experience with charmers like you. I am completely at a loss. I don't have a history of being pursued."

He loved her naive attempts to be honest. "Charmers? From off the western plains?"

"Yes, from there and from out of the ballrooms of Virginia."

"Miss Heyward, I assure you that my intentions are honorable. I do not seek a light flirtation with you, nor a hasty love affair," he softly teased. "I am not a green boy. By age thirty-six a man knows what kind of woman appeals to him."

"Boy? I find you rash, impetuous... and worldly, sir."

"Impetuous? A legal officer! Not likely. As for worldly, mam, I assure you I am very inexperienced at falling in love."

"Major Arledge, I repeat, I don't know how to play games."

"Oh, Ellen," he muttered with a rakish smile, "this is no game. It's very real. I am not trifling with your affections. I seek nothing casual with you." He put his arms around her and gently kissed her lips, his touch featherlike and sweet.

She was powerless to resist. "John, please!"

"You finally called me John," he whispered against her lips. "I take that as a positive sign."

Ellen felt out of control. Unreasonably so. She melted against him. His hard body caused warm and sensuous feelings to envelop her. She could feel his heart thudding against the soft fabric of her dress.

His breathing quickened. His arms tightened about her.

"This minute," he groaned, "I want so much to be gentle and tender, yet my blood races because of your nearness. My arms ache to crush you against me and kiss you. Impetuous, inappropriate, unwise, insane, any way you wish to describe this feeling, Ellen Heyward, I know you were meant for me."

His next kiss was not feather light.

"I was afraid that such a wonderful, maddening, completely overwhelming passion would never come to me," he confessed. "Thank God I found you."

She felt overwhelmed by his nearness. She was conscious of the lean strength of his body, and of her undisciplined response. Intoxicated by the maleness of him, she tried to pull away.

"Sir, aren't you attempting to sweep me off my feet?" she primly inquired. "Am I about to be compromised?"

She felt the rumble in his powerful chest as he chuckled deeply. "That's my girl! Yes indeed, mam, I am certainly doing my damnedest to sweep you off your feet." A roguish grin spread over his face. The tense look was gone. He was still the arrogant Yankee major she easily recognized.

"Would a nice ladylike swoon be sufficient to please you?"

"Miss Heyward, let's sit in the parlor and talk like a proper courting couple. Is there a chaperone in the house? Am I considered a suitor? May I take liberties with you?" His lips brushed warmly on her neck.

"Please, I'd like to be serious."

"Me, too. Deadly serious. Where is your bedroom?"

"John! No," she exclaimed in mock horror. "Besides, every bedroom in this house has a dozen people living in it."

"I love it when you are outraged and berate me, Miss Prim and Proper. I love it when you hotly return my kisses and pretend to resist. I love it when you are shy and coy. In fact, I love everything about you."

"Well, I don't love it when you tease and threaten, or when you make rash statements, and are insulting and outrageous."

"And most of all, I love your acid tongue."

"Please, John. You must listen. The pattern of my life is set. It does not include you. Now that my father is gone, Pamela has only me. We must go home and run the plantation ourselves. I am a woman, not a giddy girl. My home is here. I have responsibilities."

"I understand, Ellen, but you must realize all of that is in the past. We begin now, today. We can work it out."

She shook her head sadly. "Too much has happened."

"Outside events have happened, but all of the real and personal things about our lives and our future are only beginning." His eyes darkened. "Unless there is someone else."

She averted her face. Thick clumps of dark lashes veiled her eyes, hiding from him the wistfulness and hunger buried within.

John framed her face with his strong tanned hands and searched her eyes. "Ellen, maybe you have thought you were in love. Even if you were promised, engaged, married a hundred times over, that was before we met. You and I are different. Our meeting was fated, predestined. Can't you tell that?"

She felt herself drowning in the blue of his eyes. The soft caress of his voice eroded her resistance. She saw him lower his head toward her and she began to tremble.

His arms tightened about her. The illusive soapy aroma about him, his muscular body pressing against her, his masculine tenderness, the combination was hypnotizing. There was a feverish incandescence in his eyes. He must not suspect the depth of her feelings.

He kissed her, gently at first, then long, hard, expertly.

Ellen's resistance was faltering and crumbling. The cold core of numbness, which for so long had insulated her heart, began to melt as she returned each heated kiss. She was suffused by a wondrous awakening of passionate feelings totally new to her. She fought for breath, then began to struggle to get out of his embrace.

He raised his head slowly and searched her face.

"What?" His eyes were bleak.

"What if I really do swoon?" she stammered.

"Swoon away. Surely your aunt has a fainting couch around."

"You! You overwhelm me. I can't think. I can't breathe, but," she smiled meekly, "would you please kiss me again?"

"Lady," he laughed exultantly, "will I ever! Contrary to what you keep saying, I'm the one in danger. Do you realize what you are doing to me? You keep saying you are inexperienced, but no other kisses have ever had such a profound effect on me."

He swung her up easily, sat down on the sofa and held her imprisoned in his lap. "Though you may not choose to admit it, Ellen Heyward, you belong to me."

"No, John, pretty speeches roll off your tongue too fast and easy. You know this is madness. I don't think I'm any good at snatching moments of fire and passion."

"Hush, please," he murmured, "you asked to be kissed. Let's snatch one of those moments you just described." He cradled her against his chest.

Her arms crept shyly around his neck. Her long, full skirt fell softly about his knees. Beneath her, his legs were muscular and hard and her whole body strained toward him.

Her lips softened and parted. Her tongue touched his hesitantly and ignited banked fires. She felt her breasts begin to tingle. She was enflamed by his hunger and the wanton abandon of her own response.

She sprang from his lap, her senses reeling. "Please stop this! I need time to think."

"Think about what," he demanded, exasperated. "You and I are in love. My intentions are honorable. Marry me, Ellen, now, today, this minute. I will find a chaplain this afternoon."

"Are you mad? You know that's impossible. We hardly know each other." She backed away, a frightened doe poised to run.

Arledge looked in her eyes a long moment, then reached out, took her hand and softly pressed a kiss in the palm.

"Mad? Yes, mad about you, but perhaps you're right. I am rushing you. Quiet, thoughtful women probably fall in love slowly, but I'm sure they fall deeply and passionately. Listen to your heart and your body, honey. Beneath that serene exterior of yours there's a glorious woman, one I will never let go."

"Major Arledge," she said heatedly, "You are brash. We are not teenagers stealing kisses under a magnolia tree. I cannot allow myself to be drugged by warm embraces and smooth words."

"Sweetheart," he chided, "stop making excuses for being a normal, red-blooded woman. You can't escape yourself, or me. You and I must dispense with the usual preliminaries. We may not even have time now for the legalities, but that doesn't alter one thing. From this time on, our lives are unalterably welded together. Get that through that hard head of yours, please."

He reached for his hat. "And now, my love, I must report to headquarters. I'll probably put in another long lonely night."

She followed him to the door.

Cupping her chin in his hand, he bent and kissed her softly. "Darling, for both our sakes, do hurry and admit the truth about us." His voice was husky. "I tremble when I think of the fiery sweetness your surrender will bring." With an impudent wink he strode quickly out.

Ellen watched him out of sight. As he turned the corner, he smiled again and waved. Her heart thudded. She kept the hand that he had kissed closed tightly, hoping to imprison the magic.

Two hours later the dishes were restored to the cabinet and Ellen was pretending to read. Her aunt came home filled with news of what she had seen and heard. She failed to notice Ellen's quiet dreaminess. Near dusk the ritual of dinner preparation began.

Mr. Richards returned and announced that he had found a permanent home farther down the block for his daughter and himself. He planned for them to leave soon. Mr. Conrad arrived, and for once, had little to say. When the two Union officers entered they spoke briefly and went directly to their room. The orderlies sat on the porch and talked.

Dinner was a quiet and hurried meal. Each person, buried in private thoughts, soon disappeared. Ellen helped clear the table. Hattie had returned, but Aunt Mariah stoutly refused to allow her back in the kitchen.

"I ain't going to have that no-account Yankee-loving trash underfoot cluttering up my kitchen," she declared and her word was final. Hattie sullenly resumed her duties as maid. Only the certainty of shelter and food brought her back to Laurel Street.

Tasks completed, Ellen went to the chilly parlor to wait for the McCullys to arrive. She knew that John would likely be on duty all night again. Though her fingers and toes felt numb, she was warmed by the memory of his kisses. She welcomed solitude.

Time did not drag. She needed to think, to remember his exciting words and to try to relive the thrill of his touch. The desire to follow the urging of her heart was overwhelming, but her head had always ruled. Southern heritage and rearing had deeply ingrained within her the importance of duty and of accepting responsibility. John, her heart cried desperately, why couldn't we have met at some other time or place?

She heard the girls step on the porch and opened the door. They looked exhausted.

"Grandmother died early this morning and father's condition is much worsened," Sally blurted out as soon as they entered.

Ellen tried to offer comfort, but little could be said that would alleviate their situation. She realized that the few minutes of stolen dreams and happiness she had experienced earlier were completely unrealistic. She locked the door and prepared for bed.

Ten

Soon after four o'clock Monday morning activity began in the city. Two groups of old men, denied war service because of age and infirmity, prepared for an arduous day. The forty-eight hour hiatus of fearful watching and waiting was ended. They were prepared to shoulder the burden of organizing and managing a demoralized population in a ruined city.

Knowing that the Union troops would be gone by midday, one committee went to the Asylum to receive the promised arms and ammunition. Mr. Richards went with the other committee to the College horseshoe to take charge of the cattle.

The Union soldiers encamped behind the College began to move out long before dawn. Behind them, immense wagon trains, half a mile in length, began winding through deserted streets in the gray light of dawn. With bated voices drivers urged their teams past gaunt chimneys standing in black and crumbling brick walls.

Ellen, too, has risen early. For hours she had listened to the solemn rumbling of the wagon trains as they dragged their slow length through ravaged streets, stealing away from the gutted heart of the city.

Chilled dampness clung to everything. The night had seemed endless. The two officers billeted in the house were at breakfast when their summons came to report immediately.

"You still have provisions here," Ellen reminded the men.

"They are for you," said the doctor. "We wish we had more."

Carrying a lighted candle, she followed them to the door. As they were leaving, the clatter of horses' hooves sounded wildly in front of the house. The sputtering candle she held did not shed sufficient light for her to see who approached.

"Ellen," John's voice called from the darkness.

She waited in the doorway.

"Thank God you are awake." He bounded onto the porch, took her by the shoulders and kissed her quickly. "I would have dragged you out of bed if you weren't up yet." He pulled her inside the doorway out of the cold.

"We have been ordered out," he said breathlessly. "I couldn't go without seeing you again. I know I promised to give you time to make up your mind about me. I'm afraid that's no longer possible." Despite the seriousness of his face, a slight smile crinkled the corners of his eyes.

"And why is that?" She shivered in the cold dawn. He was leaving, too She had not thought his departure would come so soon.

"I need promises from you. I want assurances. I find I can't wait patiently. Please admit that we need each other. You can't say that there is nothing between us," he pleaded.

"No, John, I won't try to deny that, but the feelings may not be real. Perhaps they are created by haste, war hysteria, our proximity, loneliness, or any of a million other reasons."

"Lord," he groaned. "With all the women there are in the world, why did I have to fall in love with a thinking one?"

"We hardly know each other, John. We have just met. For the past several years neither of us has had the opportunity or time to get to know anyone else," she reasoned, "no eligible members of the opposite sex, I mean."

"I refuse to listen," he declared. "You make no sense."

"You and I are not the kind to act irrationally."

"So, we fell in love. That happens."

"Under ordinary circumstances, we would never have met at all. I think it's best to forget that we did."

"There's no time to argue." He pulled her roughly to him, snuffing out the light and causing her to drop the candleholder. "No time for formality and nonsense. It's just as reasonable to believe that the war was arranged so that we could meet. As far as I am concerned, it was. It's the only good thing that has come out of the whole bloody mess for either of us."

She attempted to retrieve the candleholder.

"And forget about the damned candle. I don't want everyone to see how thoroughly I intend to kiss you."

Ellen's knees went limp. Blood which had been like ice water became molten lava as his lips crushed hers. Resistance crumbled. Her arms swept around his neck and held him tightly. Her body strained toward his. The brass buttons of his blue frock coat dug into her breast. The stiff wool of his uniform was rough against her skin. He might be a Yankee soldier, but she was powerless against the hot desire consuming her.

Arledge lifted his mouth from hers, breathing harshly. He leaned down to press his face against her neck. His warm breath sent spasms of delight down her spine.

"Ellen, oh, Ellen," he choked. "It's good I must leave now. You wouldn't be safe with me."

He released her slowly and stepped back. "Nothing your beautiful lips can say will keep us apart. Deny the practicality, try to disavow the feeling, if you must, but you are mine and I will be back for you."

He stepped back from her.

"John." The breathless sigh was all Ellen could manage.

"I don't know how long it will take, but be sure that I will come for you. If you aren't willing, I swear I'll kidnap you. In all this miserable world, you and I were meant for each other. Nothing can change that."

With one final hard kiss he was gone.

Ellen stood in the darkened doorway, the sound of fading hoofbeats echoing in rhythm with her pounding heart. Even if she and John Arledge never met again, love had not passed her by. She fought tears, knowing that despite her denials, she would wait forever and hope. The moisture gathering in her eyes felt icy. She was standing coatless on an open verandah in the cold of a February dawn, feeling foolishly in love.

By daylight the mayor was notified that the cattle were in the college enclosure. The elderly gentleman, suffering from nervous exhaustion, sent a deputy to investigate. The report came back that five hundred and sixty head remained there, the part of the herd that the Union quartermaster chief must have known could go no farther. No food or water was available for the animals, and they were in too weak a condition to be driven to the river to drink. Emergency planning was needed.

Mr. Richards voted with the committee to begin butchering immediately. One hundred barrels of salt, which had been hidden in the basement of the new state house, were sent for. Thirty men volunteered to act as butchers, and the slaughtering began. Though the committee worked with haste, one hundred and sixty of the cattle died before they could be killed.

An old shed on the corner of Plain and Market Streets was used as a ration house. From there the men parceled out the tough beef and a portion of salt. The townspeople were told to line up and, as each one testified as to the number of mouths he had to feed, the meat was issued.

When Ellen learned that the beef was being dispensed, she prepared to go for their ration. Mr. Richards insisted that he be allowed to claim their household's share. Ellen refrained from embarrassing him by pointing out that there would surely be a long wait, and that he might be incapable of bringing back what was issued them.

"You have been out in the weather too much lately, Mr. Richards," she protested, "and you are busy preparing to move. I can take Randolph or Hattie with me. We can manage fine."

"No, my dear. You and Miss Sophie have been so kind to my daughter and me. Please permit me to perform this one service for you. I have a servant who can accompany me."

Conscious of his need to contribute, she accepted and thanked him graciously. "Your kindness will help us. Aunt Sophie and Rose are writing notes to relatives and friends, assuring them of our safety, and I am responsible for household tasks today."

"Don't expect me to soon return. I know the line will be long. Perhaps I can get news. There is rumor of a battle."

The house was quiet all day. Time dragged on leaden feet. Over and over Ellen relived the few minutes she had with John. She hugged herself and shivered, remembering his words of love, words she had thought she would never hear.

Mr. Richards returned in late afternoon with beef and salt. "Mariah," he announced, "even you will have difficulty making anything edible out of this! The cattle Sherman left here must have made the march through Georgia with him. They are as tough as his scurvy bummers."

Aunt Mariah rose to the challenge. "I am a cook, suh. You just get that meat in the kitchen to me. I fix us something."

"I know you are exhausted, Mr. Richards," Ellen worried.

"On the contrary," he assured her. "I am relieved to have been of service. I saw several of my friends and exchanged experiences. I learned that most of the guns given to the men's committee were unserviceable, and the ammunition issued will fit only six of them. Also, there was no battle this morning."

The McCully girls came in earlier than usual. Their father had died unexpectedly during the morning, and they were no longer needed as nurses. Mrs. McCully was making arrangements for a hasty funeral. Tonight would be their last at Laurel Street.

"Mother decided this afternoon that since we have lost our father and grandmother, the three of us should go to her sister's for a while. The part of the state where our aunt lives was not badly damaged by the Yankee army. We can stay there until the nonresidents can evacuate the city. We plan to come back here to live."

"My sister and I are leaving, too, as soon as I know Aunt Sophie will be all right."

"We have been told that every road out of the city is filled with people walking to nearby towns and plantations. Small groups band together for protection. Some of them plan to walk as far as sixty to a hundred miles."

"But they can cover only ten miles a day walking, perhaps less. How will children and older people manage?" The trip from Oak Lane was only twelve miles and that had not been easy.

"People can be resourceful when they must. They will sleep on porches or in barns along the way, and when none are available, they plan to rest beside the road or in the woods. Different members will take turns as lookout."

"I have thought about it. Pam and I can walk home in one day. We'll have to start early, but we can make it. Aunt Mariah can't do the twelve miles back to Oak Lane. We'll find a place for her to stay on the way and send the farm cart back for her."

There was little cheer around the supper table on their last evening together. So much had happened to the McCullys that they were numb. Mr. Conrad announced he planned to begin his trip back to Charleston the next morning. The normally loquacious gentleman was subdued by the prospect of the difficult journey.

Mr. Richards, ever courteous, made a few remarks about what must be done to ready the little rental house for his daughter's occupancy. Sophie asked for news from Lexington. She wondered if Miss Gilham might soon be able to get back to Columbia. No one volunteered information. Each person was anxious to establish some pattern of normalcy, no matter what it was, to give their life some semblance of order.

"I shall be lonely when you leave," Sophie told them. "I'm grateful to you for staying with me during this terrible time."

They were astounded by the remark. Each person was painfully aware of how much her generosity had helped them.

Ellen listened, both encouraged and saddened by the plans they each made for parting. Her mind continued to dwell on the sheer hopelessness of having fallen madly in love with a Union soldier. Her heart remembered only the incredible bliss.

Tuesday the sun was shining, the Union troops were gone and Columbians were resigned to their fate. At Laurel Street the McCully girls bade a tearful good-bye. Mr. Conrad departed early and Mr. Richards went to make preparations for moving Rose, and to spend the afternoon in the meat ration line.

With Hattie's sullen assistance, Sophie began to wash linens. Ellen brought in the silver from beneath Aunt Mariah's mattress. As she dawdled polishing and putting it away, her ears picked up the sound of horse hooves nearing the house.

Strange, for the streets had been uncommonly quiet all day. Small wonder. No horses or mules were left in the city. She could hear the rumble of wagon wheels drawing to a stop in front of the house. A male voice yelled, "Whoa!" Stifling the hope that John had returned, she went to the window and peered out. A familiar middle-aged lady was awkwardly disembarking.

"Aunt Sophie," Ellen called up the stairs. "Come down. Miss Gilham has returned." The wagon driver was a teenager.

Together they went outside to greet Sophie's roomer.

"Oh, Miss Sophie, I've been worried to death." Miss Gilham was huffing from exertion. "The firelight from Columbia was so bright on our side of the river Friday night it's hard to believe that any houses are still standing... especially after so many people began to pour into Lexington telling of how they had been burned out." She lifted out a basket of produce.

Ellen and the boy watched as the women tearfully embraced.

"My sister-in-law's family came yesterday, but nobody we talked with had news of you. I wasn't needed there any longer, so I have returned. Your house is home to me now."

"Of course it is. I'm so glad you are here."

"As soon as we heard the soldiers were gone, I began to get ready to come back. When people around us heard I was coming they wanted to send messages and food to family members here. Our neighbor had managed to hide a horse and wagon in the woods before the Yankee army passed through. His son, Stuart Caughman, brought me." She paused to nod toward the gangly lad standing patiently at the front of the wagon holding the horse's reins. He dipped his head shyly.

"Stuart offered to take messages and provisions to their relatives, if I would go along and see that things were delivered to the right places. That's what we have been doing all morning. Now I'm back to stay, if you have room for me."

Sophie embraced the tall spinster a second time. "Room! I wondered how I'd manage until you returned. I have so much to tell you. Things you'll never believe. We were crowded for several days, but by tomorrow the house would have seemed like a tomb."

"Then it's all settled. Stuart, the two packages in the front of the wagon are mine. The others go back to the families who sent them. Tell them the people they asked us to take the food to were gone, home destroyed usually. I labeled the boxes."

"Yes, mam, I think I can keep it all straight."

"Tell everybody I thought it was best to return their food. They sacrificed to send it and, from the looks of things, they will be called on to help give meals to a lot more travelers. Be sure to tell them everything you saw here."

"Yes'm," the boy replied solemnly.

"Give a ride to as many walkers as you can carry along the way back. Start on home now. Your mother will be worried if you are after dark getting back. Be careful crossing on that ferry."

"Yes'm," he repeated snapping the reins. They watched the wagon move westward down the street toward Lexington.

"Thank you, Stuart," she yelled after him. "Watch out now. Don't forget to thank your folks for me. Tell them Miss Sophie's house was spared." The boy was well beyond hearing distance before the lady's instructions ended.

"Let's put Miss Gilham back in her own room, Aunt Sophie. Pam and I have to get home, too. Now that we know she is back with you, we won't delay any longer."

"But, dear, two girls out in the country alone!"

"We are hardly girls any more, Aunt Sophie. Pam has had to grow up fast" Bitterness stung her voice. "Remember we've stayed there alone for the past two years. Nothing will be any different, except that now we know Father won't be returning."

Ellen and Sophie helped to carry the boxes inside.

"I'm sorry to hear about your father's death, Ellen. Do you have good help?" Concern registered in Miss Gilham's voice.

"Probably more than we can feed." She grimaced. "We have at least a dozen slaves who didn't leave. Aunt Mariah and her grandsons and one or two more are all we need. There are some with us we hope will take their emancipation seriously."

"They're the very ones who will likely stay." Ellen knew her aunt was thinking of Hattie.

"Pam and I will be pleased to have the two of you go home with us," she suggested. "We can grow our food."

"No, dear, thank you, we must try to get our lives back to normal, too." Sophie spoke with pride and independence.

"The four of us aren't the only women facing the future alone," Miss Gilham quietly observed. "The whole country is filled with widows with small children to feed and care for."

Once inside Ellen hastily packed her clothes and moved them upstairs. Later she and Randolph went to the convent to get her sister. On the short walk back Pam said very little. When they reached the porch she put her hand on Ellen's arm to detain her.

"Please, Ellen, it's time to talk." Her face was a mask of stoic calm. "Let's sit down on the steps. It's quiet and nice in the sun and there are some things I must know."

Ellen had dreaded this moment. Pam, always honest and direct with others, deserved the same consideration.

"Very well." Ellen sank to the top step. "Randolph, put Miss Pam's things beside the front door, please, and you can go."

The boy followed instructions. After he had gone around back, the sisters sat for a while in silence, each waiting for the other to begin.

Finally Ellen spoke. "What did you want to ask me?"

The younger girl groped for words. "I want to know exactly what happened that day after I passed out, or was knocked out... and what has taken place since. I want to hear it all." She did not have to say which day.

"What do you remember? I need to know where to begin."

"Skip the early afternoon. Both of us remember that clearly. Later when the drunk foragers started to fire the barn you went to get Father's pistol. I realized that even if you shot them, there was not time to save the animals."

"I had told you to stay inside."

"I know, but when you left I ran out back, past the soldiers into the stableyard to try to open the stalls. One of the men grabbed me. He dragged me from the burning barn over to where the other two bummers were." She paused. "They were laughing. 'I might turn your horse out, Pretty Eyes,' one jeered 'if you give me a sweet kiss.' Another said, 'Get the kiss first. Better see if it's worth it.'"

"How awful!"

"I was struggling to get away when one grabbed my dress and ripped the front. They began shouting and shoving me around from one to the other, each soldier tearing my clothing more and laughing. One said, 'The more I see the better I like it.'"

Pam stopped talking.

"I was there by that time," Ellen offered.

"No, you arrived later. I remember scratching and fighting. The men were getting rougher, really hurting me. 'Let's show her we are not only good soldiers, but real lovers, too,'" one said. 'Make her forget her little Reb army boy,' That man hit me and forced me to the ground. He fell on top of me. Ugh!" Pamela tightened her shoulders, shivering in disgust.

"And I remember him breathing drunkenly in my ear, 'Like I'm feeling, Missy, this is going to be something you'll never forget.' He was absolutely correct. I never shall." Her face was white and expressionless.

Tears began to slide down Ellen's cheeks.

"The others were watching, waiting… and urging him on. One of them had started to pull down his pants. I was screaming. The soldier holding me hit me in the face with his fist. I heard you yell, Ellen, and then there was so much noise and shouting… and gunfire, a lot of gunfire. One of the shots seemed to explode right in my face."

"I fired, Pamela, but I believe I shot high. I was afraid of hitting you. I think you were unconscious by then."

"No, I remember hoping that I had been hit, been killed, but instead, the man over me grunted and swore and I felt him go lax. There was a lot of blood. I must have fainted. Then when I came to later I was in my bed with Aunt Mariah hovering over me."

Ellen had hoped she would not remember so clearly.

"Aunt Mariah bathed me and put salve on the bruises. She kept saying over and over that everything would be all right. I asked about you. She said you were busy. Did you kill the men, Ellen?"

"No, Pam. I couldn't kill all three of them. I wanted to and I tried to, but I wouldn't have been able to do it alone. I had help. The scavengers are all dead, though."

"Oh, God, what a nightmare!"

"A Confederate scouting patrol came to our assistance. You heard them doing most of the shooting. When they rode up, the Yankees got their guns and started scrambling for their horses. While they fought each other, I kicked that dying wretch off you and tried to pick you up. Benjamin had seen the smoke and ran to help. He and I took you inside the house to Aunt Mariah."

"And the Confederate soldiers, how many were there?"

"Four. While we moved you they dismounted and searched the bummers. The field hands had come in and were trying to fight the fire. I don't think they saw you. Except for Benjamin and Aunt Mariah, none of the slaves knows what happened. The bummers were all dead. Little was said. The Confederates knew that there were other Yankees in the vicinity. We had to hurry."

"Were any of the Confederates killed or wounded?"

"No one was killed or wounded at the time. They could only guess what had gone on before they got there."

"What happened next?"

"It was too late to save the stable or the animals. The Negroes were frightened. I told them to go to their quarters, and, if any questions were asked, to say that they were in the fields, and all they knew was that the stables had been burned."

"It was a long time before you came back in the house, Ellen. Where were you?"

"Big John had dragged our cart out of the fire. One of our soldiers hitched a mule to it and dumped the three dead Yankees inside. The Confederates said the bodies had to be removed and hidden, so that I wouldn't be held responsible for their deaths."

"The wretched beasts deserved to die. Why should you be blamed?" she asked tonelessly.

"We could be accused of having executed foragers and of aiding spies. Both groups of soldiers were in disputed territory. The scouts had every right to shoot, even if the men had not been attacking us. They were Sherman's official scavengers though, and the lieutenant thought there might be an investigation. He didn't want the incident to be traced to our plantation."

"But it was."

"Yes, later, but there's no need for you to worry."

"So what did you do?"

"I got a lantern and went with the scouts to bury the bodies. We took them to the swamp between our place and Uncle Adam's. I waited while they dug one large grave."

"How awful for you." Pam was breathing raggedly, on the verge of losing her composure.

"One of the men, an old sergeant from Georgia, asked me if, being a religious man, he could say a few words over the dead. I nodded and he prayed, 'Lord, we are sending you some scum. Please see that their filthy souls burn in hell.' The others added amens. They came back with me as far as our lane. Knowing that there were likely other Yankees in the area, they refused food or rest and rode away."

"How much of this does that Yankee major know?"

"When he first questioned me, I denied any knowledge of the soldiers' whereabouts. I told him the foragers came, robbed us, burned the stables and fled with several of our army in pursuit. Later he came back. He had found out that a Confederate patrol was caught in the area that night."

"Was that the day he questioned me?"

"Yes. He had learned that one Confederate was killed, one captured, and another wounded. He knew there was a fourth man who had helped the wounded officer get away, and that they were the ones who had been here. He said it was only a matter of time until he learned the full truth."

"And you fled... but he has continued to hound you?"

"He has been here several times. He couldn't get much information from the captured man, the sergeant from Georgia. Sunday the major came back and showed me a dispatch from General Sherman to General Hampton in which he threatened to shoot hostages, captured Confederate soldiers, if his foragers were harmed. The letter convinced the sergeant that innocent prisoners might lose their lives if he didn't reveal the truth."

"And what will happen now?"

"When John finally learned everything, he decided to close the investigation. He came and told me."

"John?"

"The major. He is a Virginian."

"Some Virginian! And do you think he will drop it?"

"He had no reason to say he would if it isn't true."

"He appears to have kept up more closely with you than duty requires, Ellen. I knew I saw that light in his eyes."

Ellen remained silent.

"Well? Wasn't he pursuing you?" Pam persisted.

"He professed to be attracted to me. He said he would come back. Since I've never had that kind of an experience before, I don't know what to think." She tried to sound emotionless.

"And you? How do you feel about him?"

"I'm not sure. None of it makes sense."

"I know," Pam insisted, "just the fact that you have doubts makes me know that you care about him. You deserve a wonderful man. Too bad this one had to be a damn Yankee!"

"He has gone and I'll probably never see him again. And that is that." Ellen rose with finality from the step.

"Does he still believe that you killed the men?"

"I don't know. The sergeant told him they did it, but I admitted that I probably killed at least one of them."

Pam looked away. "What did he say about me?" Her strained voice was hardly recognizable.

"He still thinks you are my adolescent sister."

"Then he thought you... you let him believe .. that it was you the soldiers were violating!"

"Pam, he didn't need details. The investigation is ended."

"Oh, Ellen, you brave, noble, stupid big sister. Why? I've never known you to be interested in any man before, and you probably threw away a chance for happiness. How did shielding me help? What does it matter now?" Her expression hardened.

"Matter? Your whole life is ahead of you, Pam."

"I hope that another man never looks at me as long as I live. I intend to remain just as nearly sexless as possible." She spoke through clenched teeth. "Thank God we have a plantation, the cattle, and more work than we can do. You and I can isolate ourselves out there and forget the world."

"That's exactly what we have to do."

"At first I believed the worst thing imaginable had happened to me." Pam stared into space. "Then," she continued, "after all I've seen and heard since, I realize we have all been through hell. My troubles are no greater than anyone else's. We have been ravaged by the Yankees. So what? You and I are survivors." She stood and resolutely prepared to enter the house. "Ellen, don't try to assume my disgrace. I shall never deny the truth. I intend to tell your Yankee major exactly what happened."

"Pam," Ellen said brokenly, "you are almost as much daughter to me as sister. I practically reared you, and I've never been more proud of you. With your courage, how can we fail?"

They entered the house together.

Mr. Richards returned at dusk loaded with the beef ration and the day's news. "Colonel Gibbes has aptly summed up the meat situation. He said what at first looked like a great misfortune, was really a blessing. If the beef Sherman left us had been good, it would hardly have been a drop in the bucket toward supplying the city's needs. However, the tough blue sinews are like India rubber and they go a long way. He declares that the more you chew the stuff, the larger it gets."

"How true," Sophie agreed. "Even Mariah's culinary skills can hardly make this meat palatable."

Rose was brought down for supper. They sat late around the table, each making an effort to talk and laugh more and later than usual. This was the last night that they would be surrounded at dinner by congenial friends.

Rose was the first to note the lateness of the hour. She asked to be taken up to her room. Pam went along to help her get ready for bed. The women cleared the table and Sophie and Miss Gilham went to their rooms.

Mr. Richards waited while Ellen checked the doors. When the women had gone he drew a paper from his pocket. "Miss

Ellen, I'd like you to read this, please. Soldiers were staying in the house with the family who rented from me. In his haste to march out yesterday morning, one man left this letter behind. We must save it for posterity. Better still, we will place it in the library when it reopens. Nothing could tell the tale better."

Ellen took the letter from him and moved closer to the light of the candle. He waited patiently beside her, watching her face as she read what had been written.

South Carolina,
February 20, 1865

My Dear Wife:

I have no time for particulars. We have had a glorious time in this State. Universal license to burn and plunder was the order of the day. The chivalry have been stripped of most of their valuables. Gold watches, silver pitchers, cups, spoons, forks, etc., are as common in camp as blackberries.

Officers are not allowed to join these expeditions without disguising themselves as privates. One of our corps commanders borrowed a suit of rough clothes from one of my men and was successful in this place; he got a large quantity of silver (among other things, an old time silver milk pitcher) and a very fine gold watch from a Mr. DeSaussure at this place. DeSaussure is a F.F.V., of South Carolina, and was made to fork over liberally. Rings, earrings, breastpins, etc., of which, if ever I live to get home, I have about a quart - I am not joking - I have at least a quart of jewelry for you and all the girls, and some No. 1 diamond rings and pins among them. General Sherman has enough gold to start a bank. His share in gold watches and chains alone at Columbia was 275; but I said I could not go into particulars. We took gold and silver enough from the damned rebels to have redeemed their infernal currency twice over. This (the currency) whenever we come across it we burn as we consider it utterly worthless. Sometimes we take off whole families and plantations of Negroes by way of repaying the secessionists; but the useless part of these we soon manage to lose - sometimes in crossing rivers - sometimes in other ways.

I shall write you again from Wilmington, Goldsboro, or some other place in North Carolina. The order to march has arrived and I must close hurriedly.

Love to Grandmother and Aunt Charlotte. Take care of yourself and children. Do not show this letter out of the family.

Your affectionate husband,
Thos. G. Myers, Lieut., etc.

P.S. - I will send this by flag of truce to be mailed unless I have a chance of sending it to Hilton Head. Tell Sallie I am saving a pearl bracelet and earrings for her; but Lambert got the necklace and breastpin of the same set. These were taken from the Misses Jamieson, daughters of the president of the South Carolina secession convention. We found them on our trip through Georgia.

Eleven

Ellen and Pamela dressed quickly in the waning darkness. Today, Wednesday, the second day after the departure of Federal troops they planned to be on the road home at daylight. Packing was no problem for Pamela. Nothing had been saved from the convent fire except the childish attire she had been wearing.

Ellen finished buttoning on her shabby wool frock and laid the remaining two dresses, her underwear, the pistol and the last of their money on the bed. They should have spent the money. At the cessation of hostilities it would be totally worthless, and the end was near. Ellen rolled her possessions tightly, wrapped newspaper around the bundle and bound it with string. She made a wide loop at the knot to serve as a handle. Walking home, as they must do, carrying a valise would only be excess weight.

In the kitchen Aunt Mariah was cheerfully humming and stirring hominy. "Good morning, babies, I'm ready to go. I done got my shoe soles patched good with thick papers and I cut me some more to put in when that wears out. I'm going to make this trip fine, same as you two. Don't you all fret none."

"Let us go on alone, Aunt Mariah. We'll send for you soon."

"No, mam. I be evermore glad to be left this here town."

"Twelve miles is a long walk, and you know you have been talking about the misery in your feet for years."

"Miss Ellen, misery going to be misery no matter what," she insisted. "How you girls going to make out without me?"

"We could manage a few days. The trip will be hard."

"I wouldn't want none of them field hand gals in my kitchen, neither. No, mam, I be ready to leave here same as you, and it can't be none too soon to suit me."

The sisters sat down to breakfast.

Sophie's hurried footsteps echoed in the hall. The kitchen door burst open. "Girls! Why didn't you awaken me? There are things I want to fix for you before you leave."

"Thank you, Aunt Sophie," Pam answered. "We have what we need." She pulled another chair to the table for her aunt.

"I know your travel method demands that you pack light."

Ellen smiled. Sophie saw no humor in her stilted remark.

"You are to have your share of the coffee, sugar and beans and staples on hand. There won't be any for you at home."

"The food would be too heavy to carry, Aunt Sophie, and you don't have enough to be giving it away."

"The roads may not be safe," Ellen reminded her. "I prefer not to look as if we are carrying anything of value."

"Your leaving frightens me so. Won't you reconsider? As for provisions, half of this is yours. I may have the opportunity to secure more. Out in the country, I doubt that you will." She went to the cupboard and began to measure out supplies.

Randolph was called in for breakfast. Aunt Mariah had cut strips of beef and made corn pone for their lunch. She packed slices of dried apple. Drinking water would be available along the way. Sophie wrapped the remainder of yesterday's cooked beef allowance in newspaper and handed it to them.

"Please keep that, Aunt Sophie," insisted Ellen. "We really have no way to carry it."

"Leave that to me, honey," soothed Aunt Mariah. "I know what to do. Randolph, finish eating. Go to the carriage house and get me a feed sack and a long pole. I fix a shoulder stick."

Aunt Mariah continued to talk to herself as she made her final preparations. "I fix that stuff so it won't look like much of nothing. Can't tell what kind of folks we might meet. Could be runaways or camp followers out there. Might need the stick anyhow. I seen me some sorry folks lately."

The more the old lady muttered to herself the more angry and determined she became. "I get myself back home and ain't nobody going to stop me. Ain't never leaving that place again."

"I feel the same way, Aunt Mariah." Pam reached out and patted Aunt Mariah's shoulder. "Don't worry. We may go slow, but we will get there."

"You been sick, child. You just walk. You ain't carry nothing but the lunch bag, and when you get tired toting that, we stop and eat. This afternoon your hands be free. Miss Sophie, please, mam, wrap them things in paper. Jars be too heavy. A market basket be good. Between us, we get it all home."

Through the kitchen window they could see the sun rising. The day, dawning bright and crisp, showed promise of warming. Good. None of the four travelers had adequate clothing for February's usually cold weather. They were soon out on the street ready for departure. The ground was still frozen.

Aunt Sophie continued to wring her hands and urge them to stay. "What would your dear mother say!" she kept repeating.

"Right now she would say that we look like a band of gypsies, but she would be proud of our strength and good sense," Ellen spoke with firmness. "Mother was always practical."

"Yes, dear, but if the slaves have deserted, or if you find life out there too hard, come back. We can manage here together. But two young, defenseless girls alone, I just don't know."

"Almost anything that could happen to us already has, Aunt Sophie," Pam answered unsmiling. "We have survived. Ellen and I have been running the plantation alone, and we can continue to do so. If city life becomes intolerable, you come live with us."

Tears streamed down the old lady's face. "You girls seem so grown up now. You have always been the daughters I never had. I can't help but be anxious about you. I know it will be some time before you get back to Columbia."

The ever-tactful Miss Gilham had absented herself to allow family farewells. She appeared to comfort and help disentangle the anxious fretting aunt.

"No, we will be returning soon. I plan for us to have farm produce to sell before long," Ellen assured them.

"Have one of the hands come in with a letter from time to time. I may have something to send you. Let me hear from you."

Embracing their aunt one last time, the sisters started down Laurel toward Main and turned east. The few remaining houses along the block were still dark, the streets deserted. They had to make their way around debris. Upon reaching Gervais Street they paused to look toward the remains of the old State House and the wreckage of the new one which had been under construction.

"This place sure a mess," observed Aunt Mariah. "Everything burnt down and tore up. Ain't never seen nothing like it."

The sights were all too familiar to the others. Already Ellen's arm was beginning to ache from the weight of the basket. She shifted it to the other hand. Aunt Mariah was lagging a few paces behind, Ellen's clothes bundle perfectly balanced on the top of her head. She walked, seemingly unconscious of the burden. Ellen thought of better times, when they had seen her carry a bucket of water the same way, never spilling a drop. Beside her, Randolph skipped jauntily, the tough meat swinging crazily on the stick he carried on his shoulder hobo fashion.

They walked past the College grounds and headed down Green Street. Little activity there. The frost, which had been heavy, was beginning to melt and their fingers were not quite so cold. At the outskirts of the city they began to notice people about.

Increasing numbers of Columbia's overcrowded population were spreading out into the outlying countryside. The four walked steadily, but at a slowed pace, for more than two hours before sitting down beside the road for a short rest.

"Getting through town took a long time. I wonder how much distance we have covered." Even Pam seemed winded.

Aunt Mariah, sitting down heavily, grunted, "I promise myself the night of the fire I won't never going to let you all go off and leave me nowhere again. I mean to keep right up with you no matter what my feet say."

Ellen and Randolph traded loads. After a few minutes they pushed on, walking past the swampy bottom land that towns-people used as the city dump. Soon they started the climb up the gentle hill which led out of town. Aunt Mariah was needing to pause for rest more often. It was mid-morning before they reached Valle Crucis, Bishop Lynch's country place, three miles out of town.

Ellen had set Millwood, Wade Hampton's plantation, as their destination for the morning. They crossed Gill Creek and climbed the high wooded hill on which the house was built. At the entrance to Millwood they looked down the tree-lined avenue leading up to the mansion. All that remained was several large column posts standing proudly in the noonday sky.

"What a blow to the family," Ellen softly breathed. Though she knew that the home of any Confederate general would be ashes, seeing the grand historic manor in ruins was heartbreaking. Only the kitchen house and a few out buildings still stood.

"Randolph, please go up to the kitchen house. Tell anyone you see who you are, and that you are with Miss Pamela and me," Ellen directed. "Tell them we want to rest in their woods for a while, and ask if they will be kind enough to give us some water to drink. Explain that we are walking home from Columbia."

He handed her the basket and dashed down the avenue.

"Where does he get the energy?" Pam sighed. "I'm half dead."

Aunt Mariah, saying nothing, stretched out in the sunshine on a bed of oak leaves and pine needles. The sisters sat beside her. There was a lazy stillness over the woods. An occasional bird flitted near. Already yellow jessamine was beginning to bud. They reveled in the tranquillity. Randolph returned, an oaken water bucket in one hand and water glasses in the other.

"That white lady, she said she the general's sister, she wish she had beds for you and dinner for all of us, or a horse and carriage to offer us, but she ain't. She said help yourself to the woods and the water, good luck on the road, God bless us all, and here is some glasses to drink the water out of." He smiled, pleased to have remembered the entire message.

The cool water was refreshing. They ate their cornbread silently. While Randolph dashed back to return the bucket and glasses they settled down for half an hour's rest. Pam and Ellen shared the clothes bundle as a pillow.

"Pam," Ellen said quietly, "did I remember to tell you I sent that young lieutenant from Beaufort... the one I nursed at the hospital, the one who helped me to find news about father... out to the plantation the day before Sherman's army invaded?"

She watched her sister's face for some reaction.

"I don't know if he was able to get there. He was weak, but I asked Isaac to get him to Oak Lane if he could, and to care for him until he could travel again. He may still be there."

"I hope not," Pamela replied fiercely.

The remark made Ellen uneasy. She had hoped the two would never have to meet, and if they should come face to face, that neither would realize it was not their first meeting.

As they left Millwood they saw another group of travelers resting by the roadside. They stopped to speak. Bound in the same direction, they took comfort in knowing that they were not on the road alone. By three o'clock Randolph spotted the next plantation. They neared it slowly, seeing from a distance another ruined homesite.

"Ellen, do you have any idea what we're likely to find when we get home?" Pamela's expression was grim.

"None." Her voice was firm. "I have thought about it. The main Union force approached Columbia from the other side of the city. Father's role in the war was minor and he was not an ardent secessionist. There is no reason for an outsider to harbor vengeance against him. Our plantation is small and not well known. The house is a good distance off the main road. Foragers have already raided us. I have hope."

The last four miles of the journey were the longest. They passed the Goodwyn place, their nearest neighbors, and were heartened to see the house had not been burned. Since noon they had been walking just ahead of a group en route to Sumter, a forty mile trip. Aunt Mariah, obviously exhausted, straggled a bit behind. They waited as she continued to plod doggedly forward.

"Aunt Mariah, wouldn't you like to stay at the Goodwyn place tonight?" Ellen offered. "You could visit with their people and we'll send someone back to get you tomorrow."

"No, mam. I just as anxious to get home as you. I can rest tomorrow. I work hard all my life. I bound to be just as strong as you girls. If you make it, I make it, too."

"Good girl!" cheered Pam, "spoken like a true Heyward."

Now that it was certain that they would reach home before dark, they slowed to a snail's pace. As she neared the outer boundaries of Oak Lane, Ellen stopped to allow the Sumter-bound travelers to catch up. When she walked past the spot

where the scavengers had been buried she wanted to be surrounded by others.

They renewed their brief lunchtime meeting and tried to
exchange a few optimistic remarks. Gloom was gathering, despite their best efforts. Pam's face was white and set. Ellen held
her shoulders high and stared straight ahead.

After they had cleared the swamp area, all four Heywards
began to search for a glimpse of the house. Half an hour later
the cedar roof of their home could be clearly seen in the light of
the setting sun. The girls looked at each other, relief flooding
their faces. Pam's happy expression was one of the first hope-
ful signs Ellen had seen on her face in more than two weeks.

"We still have a house," Ellen announced to the other travelers, "and we would be very pleased to have all of you spend
the night with us."

"Thank you," one of them replied, "we rejoice with you,
but we are expected at Horrell Hill tonight. Some of our friends
passed this way yesterday and made arrangements for our accommodations. I hope we can get there before hard dark. We
have about three or four more miles to go."

The Heywards turned in at their lane and waved farewell.
A nostalgic sadness at parting with others who had shared the
terrible experiences of the past few days gripped them. Ellen
hid all apprehension. She was ready to face the problems of
their private world.

Aunt Mariah limped far behind. Randolph danced
around her impatiently. The sisters sat down to wait, knowing that for the black woman the indignity of dragging in
last, while the other family slaves looked on, would be harder
than the long walk home from Columbia had been. They
would arrive together.

The house, when they reached it, was enveloped in quiet.
Grateful that they had finally arrived and that they still had a

home, all four sank down on the front steps of the verandah and breathed private prayers of thanksgiving.

With the house, the land, the cattle and a few faithful hands, they could survive. The sun was sinking. Their people would be coming in from the fields soon. After a few minutes Ellen walked around to the back of the house and stood waiting. Big John was the first to arrive, closely followed by Luke and James and the others.

"Lord bless you, Miss Ellen, I some glad to see you home. I worry about you all and about the work." His face clouded. "With Mister Henry gone, it's you and me now, ain't it?"

"Yes. We'll have to talk and make our plans. Thank you, all of you, for staying here." Others had gathered before her. "We are back home now. You may go to the quarters and I'll see you tomorrow. I need to wait and speak to Benjamin."

They all disappeared into the various cabins lined up behind the kitchen house. Three men were approaching from the direction of the lower pasture. They walked slowly, the two black men on the outside adjusting their gait to that of the slender white man between them. Ellen rushed forward, calling a greeting to Benjamin and Isaac, and extending her hands to James Milton.

"You made it, Jim!" she exclaimed, "and you look stronger. I'm so glad. I knew we could depend on Isaac."

"Ellen, how wonderful to see you!" Jim's pale face brightened. "How is your aunt? And Pamela?"

"Everybody is safe. No way to describe the nightmare we endured, but we survived. Aunt Sophie's house wasn't destroyed."

"We could see the light of the fires. The brightness of the night sky was unbelievable. Brilliant red... even from this distance. I kept wishing that you all had come back with Isaac and me. We have been waiting for a message from you."

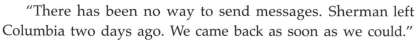

"There has been no way to send messages. Sherman left Columbia two days ago. We came back as soon as we could."

"Willie, the plantation news service, has told us that Mrs. Heyward's home was not destroyed. He saw Hattie in town, so we had that good news. He was there when the army marched in and I have his version of everything that happened. I felt guilty escaping and leaving you to face all that Yankee hostility."

"I am glad you were able to get here, Jim. You would surely have been captured. The College wasn't destroyed, but only because they had Union wounded housed there. Did Willie tell you how the soldiers took or destroyed everything they saw?"

"We know. People began to pass here on Sunday. They were going by all day yesterday and today. I hobbled out to the end of the lane each morning and sat until late afternoon talking with the refugees as they passed."

"The cattle, Benjamin, how about them?"

"Fine, Miss Ellen, everything is fine."

"How about you, Isaac?"

"We been good. Mr. Jim doing better. We set us up a way station by the road. He talks to the people and I go back and forth to get fresh buckets of water. We swap water for news."

Ellen was relieved that Jim had heard everything and they wouldn't need to relive all the details.

"What about food for the cattle?"

"We made do," Benjamin answered solemnly. "Stayed way down in the pocosin, almost to the Congaree swamp. There ain't nothing down there but a few cattle trails and some deer and wild boars. The Yankees couldn't find us."

"How do they look?"

"Mighty lean, Miss Ellen, but the green stuff will be out before long. We can find enough cane and such to hold them over. It will be calving time any day now."

"Thank you, Benjamin, you have done well."

"We heard yesterday that the Union troops left Monday. I told Benjamin that it is safe to graze the herd a little nearer the house now. I knew he missed coming in at night." Jim looked at Ellen apologetically. "I hope I was not interfering."

"No," she answered quickly. "I'm grateful to you. I know Benjamin was glad to have someone help shoulder some of the responsibilities. Ours must be about the only decent cattle in the area now. You should have seen what Sherman left for beef for the people of Columbia to eat."

"We heard all about that, too."

Isaac's deep laugh rang out. "Willie told us he help with the butchering. He said them cows so poor the buzzards fly right past and play like they hadn't even seen them."

"For once Willie told the truth. Where is he now?"

"Lord knows, Miss Ellen. He comes and goes, just drops by here and brings us the news."

"Still trying to make the others feel they are missing all the glories of freedom by staying here, I suppose."

"Yes'm."

"I was hoping that he had decided to accompany the Union army up to North Carolina. Plenty of people did."

"That reminds me," Jim interrupted. "You had a caller from the Union army, Ellen."

She looked startled. "I did! Who? When?"

"Last Sunday afternoon late. I recognized the blue uniform from a distance. Isaac hid me in the attic and John went out front to intercept him. It was a soldier with a loaded pack mule. He delivered several wooden boxes which he said were to be safeguarded, especially for you. Big John stored them in the cellar."

"Did he say who he was and why he came here?"

"He told Big John he was Sergeant Kelly, that the crates were a special delivery for you, and they were not to be touched until you returned. He said you'd know about them, and that

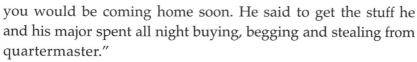

you would be coming home soon. He said to get the stuff he and his major spent all night buying, begging and stealing from quartermaster."

Ellen drew a sharp audible breath.

Jim looked at her closely. "Have yourself a secret lover on Sherman's staff, do you?" he teasingly questioned.

Ellen, feeling color mount in her face made no reply. She turned away and they walked slowly back to the house.

"Benjamin, Aunt Mariah came with us. Please make sure she gets a good night's rest. The walk was hard on her. Isaac, we can look after Mr. Jim. Go home tonight and see your folks."

"Thank you, mam. I be back tomorrow. Mr. Jim and I been walking in the fields some. Need to build up his strength more before he tries to get back to the army. Good night, folks."

Isaac cut behind the house and through the dried stalks in the cotton field, the lean strength of his athletic body as he easily loped across the hardened furrows contrasting sharply with that of the emaciated youth at Ellen's side.

"Jim," she said, her voice low and serious, "there is something I must explain before we get back to the house. Kelly and the major he spoke of are the Union soldiers who came out here to investigate the disappearance of the foraging party. They captured your sergeant. They know that you were wounded. The major ultimately learned what happened, or most of it."

"Has there been trouble for you?"

"He found out that I was in Columbia. My aunt requested guards for her house and he recognized the name. He didn't realize that there were two women involved in the incident here. After he learned the truth, he apologized for threatening to arrest me. He said that he would not continue the investigation."

They were nearing the house. She wanted to finish the conversation before they reached there. "I think this means that you are no longer liable to any charges, also. Evidently he sent some supplies out here to help compensate for our losses."

"Doesn't sound much like one of Sherman's officers!"

They walked around to the front of the house. Pamela and Aunt Mariah were still sitting on the top step, each one leaning tiredly against a column post. Pam rose and looked at the man.

"So this is Pamela," greeted Milton with the false heartiness which the young reserve for those still younger.

Men made Pam uncomfortable. She ducked her head and forced a wooden smile.

"And Aunt Mariah, I know already how much everybody loves you. They have been missing you here."

He had immediately won the old servant's heart.

"All right everybody," Ellen said authoritatively, "this has been a long day. Let's put together something for supper, wash our faces and fall into bed."

"Yes, child," sighed Aunt Mariah, "I am ready. Just let me get in my kitchen."

"No," protested Ellen, "you sit. We'll have a cold supper of the cornbread, beef and apples that Randolph carried."

"Sometimes a body gets too tired to rest right away," Aunt Mariah observed. "Stirring around in the kitchen going to make me feel better. Esther brought up some eggs while you were talking to the hands. We going to have scrambled eggs and hot coffee. That be good for Mr. Jim, too."

Benjamin had already started a fire in the big wood stove. He and Randolph brought in water to heat. Pam lit candles for the table, and the dark and chill of the house began to lift. Throughout the meal Jim worked at maintaining conversation, but the women were tired and had little to say. Soon after finishing their food, more than ready to retire, they made their way upstairs. Isaac had put Jim in their father's room. Ellen hastily washed her face and hands and went to check on Pam. She found that the younger girl had already crawled wearily beneath the bed covers.

"Are you all right?" Ellen inquired anxiously.

"Tired. Please don't worry about me. I am just too exhausted to undress, and too cold."

"I understand. So am I. Let me loosen your clothing and take off your shoes for you." Ellen unbuttoned the neck and waist of her sister's dress and removed her dusty brogans. She tucked the quilts around her and spread the girl's coat over her feet for extra warmth.

Satisfied that Pamela was all right for the night, Ellen groped her way back to her own room, removed her shoes and got into bed. She would worry later about the impropriety of having a young man stay the night in the house with two single unchaperoned women.

For the thousandth time that day she thought of John Arledge and her heart fluttered. Tomorrow the boxes in the cellar would be investigated. He had realized how dire their circumstances were. She fell asleep remembering that he had been thinking of her welfare on his last days in South Carolina.

Twelve

Ellen didn't go down to the cellar until mid-morning. She waited to be alone. Settling into normalcy was going to prove difficult. The isolated day-to-day life at Oak Lane felt lethargic after the quick pace of the past two weeks in Columbia.

With Milton in the house, Pam was uncomfortable and he was at a loss to understand why. At breakfast, clad in a pair of her father's old pants, Pam had been withdrawn and uncommunicative. Jim, ever polite and well-bred, appeared to notice neither her unusual appearance nor her strange behavior. Aunt Mariah, however, was incensed and freely vented her feelings.

"Ain't no lady never wore no man's britches," she kept muttering. "No cause for to look scandalous."

Pam chose to ignore the remonstrations. Ellen made an effort to lend support to her sister and dispel the tension. "We all have work to do. We should dress in whatever seems most appropriate for the task. There is very little clothing here to choose from anyhow, Aunt Mariah, and you know Pam will be checking on the cattle today. Father's clothes are warm and practical."

As soon as the younger girl announced her intention to go to the lower pasture, Aunt Mariah's loud banging of pots and pans on the stove signaled further disapproval. Milton, hoping to help the situation, suggested he accompany her.

Though Pam clearly did not want him with her, there was no way, short of being openly rude, that she could refuse. Ellen watched them moving slowly across the sunlit fields, Randolph tagging close behind. They would be gone for hours. Aunt Mariah, having seen Pam properly chaperoned, elected to order a good house cleaning. Ellen was free. She could go to the cellar.

After her eyes adjusted to the darkness, Ellen saw that the crates John had sent were nailed tightly shut. A small square of folded paper was securely tacked to the lid of the top box. She pulled the paper from the box. It was a note, neatly lettered.

Ellen,

Wait for me, my love. Return, I shall, and soon.

John

Ellen detached the paper and turned it over. On the back was a list of food staples, with a small check beside each item. Beneath the list were instructions to attach Note One to the outside of the top crate, and to see that Note Two was placed inside the box, before it was sealed.

Note Two. Ellen's heart was racing. She took the kitchen ax, and with the sharp edge of the blade, pried the top from the wooden packing case. Oats. A large quantity of oats, and tucked into the top of them, Note Two. She recognized another sheet torn from the small notebook. She had seen John write in the book and fit it into his breast pocket. Stationery, any paper to write on, was another of life's necessities no longer available in the south. She unfolded the paper, carefully shaking the grains of oats caught inside back into the box. Her hand trembled as she began reading the bold masculine handwriting.

My darling Ellen,
As statements of my love, I send to you, not bouquets of roses nor bunches of violets, but the staples of existence. I know you

will face the future with strength and fearlessness. Please remember that, from the ashes of this holocaust, you and I were able to salvage love. My great desire is to protect—no, to always stand beside—you, for you need no protector, my proud, lovely one.

I have entrusted my friend to procure and deliver some supplies for me. These basics, I am sure, will have greater appeal to you, dear, brave, practical, sensible darling, than all the flowers I might have found.

There is so much I love about you, Ellen Heyward—your indomitable spirit, your fierce independence and family loyalty, your stubborn refusal to be defeated, the fading line of freckles across the bridge of your nose. Until I can return, I will treasure in my heart these things, and the memory of your incredibly beautiful face.

John

She pressed the paper to her heart. A love letter. A letter from the one man who could fill the empty spaces in her life, the one man fated to collide with her in the all the cruelty and confusion of war, the man who called her incredibly beautiful. She closed her eyes, forgot her dismal surroundings, and, for a moment, was back in his arms in the cramped parlor on Laurel Street.

One box was filled with oats. Another with shelled corn. No wonder Yankee horses look good! They were better fed than Confederate soldiers. A third box contained a large bag of sugar, five pounds of coffee, a quantity of flour and parcels of rice, dried fruit and peas.

Ellen was stunned by the sight of gifts so costly and difficult to obtain. How was he able to do this for her in the haste and confusion of his departure? Huddled alone in the cold cellar, she was overcome by the futility of their situation and her strong feelings for him. Tears began to flow, tears she had not allowed herself to shed before, tears for herself, for her sister, for the father they had lost, for all the homeless people, for the bereaved, for the South. She shed tears for the past, the present, the future, and then, more tears out of feelings of hopelessness, all the while clutching the letter tightly.

Later, face blotched and eyes still puffy, Ellen left the privacy of the cellar and went to search for her mother's small jewel box. She remembered an intricate locket with a special compartment for a lock of hair.

The baby curl of some long forgotten relative was removed and John's note fitted inside. She fastened the clasp in back of her neck and dropped the locket inside her dress. The silver chain was long enough for the locket to drop down between her breasts. Ellen pressed the cold metal against her skin, warming it with her body, knowing that she would always carry that note close to her heart.

The next hours were spent at her father's desk poring over his account books. She must learn how to best use John's gift. Records of past years were examined, noting planting times and dates. Ellen studied the figures about field size, crops sown, and amounts of seed and fertilizer needed.

Estimates of expected yield were compared to the actual crop records. Costs and the amount of labor involved were analyzed. The careful documentation her father had kept gave Ellen greater appreciation of his meticulous habits. How often she had seen him hunched over his obsessively kept ledger! He had so admired Thomas Jefferson that he tried to practice the same rigorous self-discipline about keeping his own agricultural records.

Supper that night was more relaxed. Jim had walked to the pasture with Pamela, then out to the main road with Isaac. He had talked with numerous people in the steady stream who continued to pass all afternoon. Nothing new was added to their knowledge. Pamela looked tired, but she was ready to report on the condition of the herd and to make recommendations. Ellen wanted to discuss the information she had compiled.

As soon as the dishes were cleared away Ellen told them about the contents of the packing cases. Note Two was not mentioned. Note Two would always be personal and private.

"We have a real windfall," she announced. "I opened the boxes."

"The mysterious ones from the Yankee major?"

"Yes, we were sent at least two bushels of oats and that much or more of corn. I am sure it was meant for food, but we'll use it as seed."

"That should be enough for three acres of oats and about fifty of corn, Ellen." Jim pushed back his chair and looked at her. "Will you have labor to plant that much?"

"I believe so. The disgruntled slaves have left. Those remaining consider Oak Lane their home. Most of them were born here. We still have five prime field hands and Willie, six women and fifteen or so children. Right now I'm more concerned about keeping everyone fed and busy, than about being short of help."

"Did you grow up on a plantation, Lieutenant?" Though Pamela addressed him directly, she did not lift her eyes.

"Yes, but I don't know much about running one. I have two older brothers. They assumed those responsibilities. My father died before the war. We lost our mother two years ago. I was away at school, the Citadel, then went straight into the army."

"Where in the Beaufort area do you live?" This was the first time Pam had shown any interest in the young man.

"On Lady's Island. We planted some rice, but like most lowcountry planters, cotton was the big thing. The sea island long staple cotton was our special cash crop."

"Not our father." Ellen was proud to tell him about their father's ideas. "He foresaw the end of slavery. We planted very

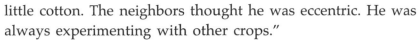

little cotton. The neighbors thought he was eccentric. He was always experimenting with other crops."

"What did he try? Indigo, oranges, sugar beets? My brothers have considered them all."

"No, first it was tobacco, which didn't grow well in our sandy soil, yet it thrives only forty miles away."

"Sunflowers one summer," remembered Pam.

"Several kinds of grain and various breeds of livestock."

"That explains how you happen to have a herd of beef cattle," he observed thoughtfully. "Dairy cows I would have expected, but I was surprised when I first saw the whitefaces." He rose from the table, slid the chair back under, and prepared to leave. "I know you two would like to talk, so I shall bid you good night."

"We need to make spring planting decisions, Jim, but I would welcome your advice." Ellen looked pointedly at Pam.

"Yes, will you stay?" Pam echoed the invitation woodenly.

He looked at her closely. "Pamela, at the hospital Ellen's friendship meant a great deal to me. I asked her if I might substitute for the younger brother she never had."

Pamela frowned slightly and looked down at her hands.

"I have two sisters and I miss them. You are kind to allow me stay here, and I'd like not to be a total burden. I keep feeling that you don't approve of my being here, and I'm sorry."

She glanced up, eyes haunted.

"Do sit down and stay, please. We would appreciate your help. Men... I am not accustomed to being around men."

Ellen breathed a sigh of relief. Perhaps a major hurdle had been crossed. If her sister could begin to gradually accept and trust Jim, then the healing process would start.

"Please get the account book and a pen, Ellen. We can do a cattle inventory to update Father's records. I made a tally."

The older sister went for the necessary materials.

"There are forty grown cows," began Pamela, "two big bulls and two yearlings. I counted fourteen steers and twelve young heifers, a total of seventy head. I think we can expect thirty to forty calves to be born between now and the end of March."

Pam's knowledge of cattle was apparent from the ease and confidence with which she rattled off information. "They are in surprisingly good condition," she continued, "though lean. Most cows are with calf. Two or three are likely to be dropped tonight. There is enough dried grass, honeysuckle and such for grazing two more weeks. They can make it. Grass will green by mid-March."

"At least we know that we have steers to sell, if anyone has the money to buy them." Ellen was relieved.

"If we are to keep the high standards Father wanted, we'll have to get a new bloodline soon."

Ellen leafed back through the records to check the birth dates of the cattle. "Right, Pam, and that could a problem."

"How so?" Jim asked.

"When Father was looking for another money crop fifteen years ago, someone told him about Henry Clay having imported a superior breed of beef cattle from Scotland back in 1817," Ellen explained.

"The first herdbook said Herefords mature early and thrive under adverse conditions. That appealed to Father," Pam volunteered.

"He began to correspond with a breeder. In 1856 he arranged to buy eight heifers, already bred, and one young bull, not related to them."

Aunt Mariah divided the last of the pot of supper coffee between the three of them. Ellen continued the story.

"The cattle were shipped into Charleston. Father took Benjamin with him to see about getting them here. They were sent to Columbia by rail. Benjamin was younger than Randolph then, but he rode back in the cattle car. He has looked after them ever since."

"Do you know how much the cattle originally cost?"

"Over a thousand dollars, plus shipping. The bull alone was two hundred."

"A big investment! How did you get them from town?"

"Father had planned a small western-type cattle drive, but the ocean voyage was too hard on the young cows. After having had no exercise for several weeks, they didn't look strong enough for the twelve mile walk. We couldn't afford to lose any of them. Father came home. Left Benjamin with them in a box car on the railroad siding. That night he had Big John and the others build tall wooden sides on three large farm wagons. They left at dawn next morning and hauled the cattle home. Pam and I will never forget. That was an exciting time."

Her voice trailed off, animation lighting her face as she reminisced. "Remember, Pam, how we stayed up most of the night watching the men work... heartbroken that we were not going to get to go on a cattle drive?"

The younger girl smiled faintly. "The next day seemed an eternity while we waited for them to return."

"Ten years ago! You were very young," remarked Jim.

"Yes," Ellen hastily cut in, "to sum things up, the cattle survived the trip, lived through that first winter and have done well since. Every person at Oak Lane knows we consider them important to our future."

Milton's eyes were shining with interest. His face lost some of its pallor as he fired more questions. "How long does it take for Herefords to mature? How fast do they multiply? What do you feed them? What market price will they bring?"

Pam answered. "Herefords grow faster than other breeds and are hardy. The are said to be doing well in America, even in the harsh winters out west. A heifer will calve at two years, and after that you can expect a calf every spring. They eat any kind of grain or grass. Until this year, we've always supplemented the winter grazing. We lost our hay when the stables were burned."

"Father liked to keep them fat and sleek," Ellen added quickly to cover Pam's sudden pause.

"They are the best looking cattle I have seen in nearly three years. Even the ones we were able to commandeer from the Yankee army didn't look that good," Jim assured them.

"Father heard about a Hereford breeder in Texas just before the war started. He and Benjamin went down there and bought a grown bull and a yearling. It's best to have a new bloodline every third year. Inbred cattle are not as hardy. We are back to that problem with the fourteen young heifers."

"Where could you find cattle like this now? Do you suppose there are any left in the south?"

"Probably not, Jim. And where would we get the money to buy them even if we could locate them?" Ellen answered.

"It's not completely hopeless, Ellen. Father had been corresponding with a Hereford breeder in Ohio. I am sure he saved the letters."

"I noticed them in the back of the ledger this afternoon."

"That man must be having the same problem we are," reasoned Pam. "We are prepared to deal. That's why we have fourteen steers and two bull yearlings, instead of sixteen steers."

"Good thinking, Pam." Jim rose from his chair to walk around. "Barter is the answer. Gold isn't available to us and Confederate money is almost worthless."

"Especially in Ohio," Ellen wryly pointed out.

Jim flexed the injured shoulder and rubbed it as he was thinking. "How to effect the exchange is a real problem, but you do have something to work toward later. Without railroads, transportation will certainly be difficult."

"Barter can help us get some of the things we need in Columbia, too, providing any supplies still exist there."

"Ellen, last night I had an idea that I believe might help." Pam's brow was wrinkled in thought. "Let's consider dividing some of the land we don't need for planting into small family farms. Our hands can choose sites or draw lots, and work their own piece independently."

She rose to take the cups to the sideboard. "They could use our mules and what equipment we have in return for working for us. The more reliable of our people will have the opportunity to try out their new freedom."

Ellen was pleased at Pam's growing interest in the future.

Milton showed amazement at the young girl's maturity of thought. "I am impressed with your fine mind, Pamela. The two of you are remarkable ladies. I wish some of the professors I had at the Citadel could know you."

"We are independent thinkers because we have had to be."

"No, the two of you have a special spark that's rare. One of my history teachers talked constantly about the changes coming, about rights of the small landholder, the demise of King Cotton, the coming industrialization... ambitious immigrants arriving and how each of these things would impact on the South."

"His ideas must have seemed radical to most of you."

"To all of us," Jim admitted. "He went so far as to predict that, if there was a war, outside reformers would descend on the state like a plague of locusts."

"Heaven forbid!" Pam prayed.

"Outsiders have never had much influence in the South," observed Ellen. "We are a proud and stubborn people. If we lose the war, nothing short of a large standing army can enforce radical reform laws here."

"The problem is," Jim said sadly, "that a large standing army is not completely out of the question."

Ellen sighed and picked up the ledger. "Tomorrow I want to walk over the fields. I'll talk with John and Luke and tell them what we are thinking about doing. They can explain to the others and let us know who is interested in your idea, Pam. Do you agree?"

"They will have to make it clear to the others that there will be a lot of work to be done, not much food, unless they grow it, and no money. But they have never had any money, so they should be able to deal with that."

"I just hope we can!"

"We want to give the opportunity to anyone who had rather leave to do so now." Pam stood up, stretching tired muscles. "Randolph and I will go to the swamp for the china tomorrow. Good dishes might help to relieve the monotony of our diet."

Ellen looked at the boyish lieutenant. "You need rest, too, Jim. You've made good progress, but there's still a way to go."

"I suppose," he agreed. "In the morning, when Isaac comes, we'll go out to the main road for news. I have to find out where General Butler's men have gone. I hope to be ready to rejoin my unit in another week."

"It would be unwise to leave too soon. Please ask if there are rumors as to where Sherman's forces have gone, too. Offer shelter to anyone who would like to stay with us for the night."

When the others had gone up to bed Ellen sat thinking. Where is John tonight? Winnsboro, Chester or farther away? She had not heard how fast the army was moving. Without railroads there could be no mail. Should she expect it? Perhaps by now those restless blue eyes of his were gazing hungrily down at another woman.

She remembered the touch of his lean, hard hands, the tenseness of his face, how handsome he became when he suddenly flashed his rare, quick smile. She thought of the deep rumble of his voice hoarsely whispering words of love, words which seemed to force their way through his lips against his will. She savored the exciting feelings for a long moment.

As she rose, Ellen noticed the newspaper which had been used to wrap their beef ration lying open on the table. The editor's words from the February 12th *Guardian* leaped out at her:

"Long before Columbia falls we look for a battle and a victory commensurate in its consequences with the great interests now at stake, one which will prove that God is fighting by our side, although with visor down, and that he has vouchsafed to Carolina the proud privilege of closing as she began the war - in triumph."

More rhetoric, she thought, as she picked up the candle.

"What do you think of this?" Sherman handed Arledge a paragraph to read.

Looking down at the *Journal* page Arledge read. "Having utterly ruined Columbia, the right wing began its march northward toward Winnsboro. Even if peace and prosperity soon return, not for a century can this city or state recover. It is not alone in the property that has been destroyed, it is the crushing downfall of their inordinate vanity, their arrogant pride."

"An apt description, Sir."

The mood of the troops was jubilant, the pace tough and calculated. On the march John Arledge rode near the head of the column. As a key legal officer he was attached to the general's staff. After years of relative inaction on far-flung western posts, the responsibilities of provost were challenging and absorbing. His duties, combating espionage, some responsibility for disciplinary matters and seeing to the security of prisoners of war, were all ones he had experience with. Citizens' requests were routinely funneled to him. He was responsible for posting guards on private property as needed and at army hospitals.

Sergeant Kelly rode up beside him. The two had worked together a long time. Arledge had requested that the trusted veteran come with him when General Grant assigned him to Sherman.

"Major, this country looking like home to you?"

"Not yet, Kelly, but soon. It has been a long time."

"What did you think of that back there?"

"The mess we left behind? Not much. What about you?" Ever taciturn, Kelly merely grunted. He had caught up with the major after being delayed an extra day in Columbia fulfilling the orders concerning the Heyward woman.

"Spent all your money getting that stuff. How come you thinking she is the one… that one back there, I mean?"

"Have you ever seen a thoroughbred horse, Kelly?"

"I ain't from Virginia, major. Seen a Tennessee walking horse once. Pretty sight."

"A real thoroughbred is so beautiful your heart stops… sensitive, high-spirited, small bones, long graceful lines, beautiful flowing mane."

"You remembering her on that porch that day with her hair down, ain't you?"

"I'm remembering. Thoroughbreds are special. Noble, all of them can be traced back to three Arabian stallions in the early 1700s. They have keen eyes, a good memory, great endurance, loyalty."

"We talking horses or women?"

"We are talking thoroughbreds. I know them."

"They good at listening, taking orders, obeying?"

"I have to admit they need a little gentling."

"Thought so. That note you gave me for her ought to do it."

"Damn, sergeant. You read my letter?"

"Of course, never know when I might be needing to use some sweet words myself."

"Don't you ever get tired of tom-catting around, want some commitment and permanence?"

"Not lately."

"Never tired of being alone?"

"All the time."

"God, Kelly, you are hopeless!" The sergeant would never understand his deep hunger for constancy, for intellectual companionship with someone of similar background and interests, his desire to know and love a woman of fire and free spirit.

"In the army, major, moving around, there's always the chance of better pickings at the next post."

"There's that."

They rode for a while in silence.

Since he was drawn into the war, Arledge was glad not to be leading troops in the kinds of senseless destruction he had been witnessing lately. He was relieved that he would likely not be called upon to shoot at former University of Virginia and West Point classmates, and at fellow Virginians, possibly including his own brother. If he had to actively participate in the war in the east, he had drawn the best possible assignment.

Ironic that his responsibilities had led him to Ellen Heyward, and had helped him to relocate her, when she tried to elude him. He smiled to himself, confident that this same assignment would later bring him back to South Carolina. Upon the cessation of hostilities, supervision of occupied territory was also in his province, and he would ask to be sent to Columbia.

"You're coming back here, ain't you?"

"You usually read me right, Kelly."

"Ought to. Been riding right beside you long enough."

"It's hard for anybody to know what General Sherman will do, but I plan to ask to be assigned to the South Carolina district."

"You ask, and you'll get it. Uncle Billy likes you, that is, if he likes anybody."

"If he likes anybody! That's something hard to tell, Kelly. The newspapers call him a loner. He surely gives the reporters and field artists a hard time."

"Don't he, though! Don't trust what they might say."

"That's why he writes everything down in his journal. He wants his campaign to be recorded the way he sees it."

Sherman's army of seasoned veterans followed the railroad north to Chester and turned east. By February 23rd rain was so heavy and persistent that the pontoon bridge the soldiers laid across the Catawba River washed away. General Davis and the 14th Corps, following close behind Sherman, were unable to cross.

Delayed by the weather, the general had Arledge closely question the civilians, freed Negroes and prisoners of war that they encountered. He was able to learn that Charleston had been evacuated by Hardee and that Wilmington, North Carolina, had fallen to northern troops. Though the news was reaching him as vague rumors from rebel sources, Sherman had every reason to feel that his march was reaping the fruits he was seeking.

John had never known a southern spring this cold and wet. By the first of March the roads were so impassable that the men had to corduroy nearly every foot of the way. They moved into Cheraw in drizzling rain. No further great impediment

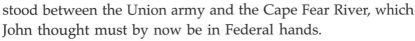

stood between the Union army and the Cape Fear River, which John thought must by now be in Federal hands.

Badly depleted Confederate units were reported scattered from Florence to Charlotte. They posed little threat. The Union forces crossed the border and marched toward Fayetteville. Rain continued to pour relentlessly and artillery and wagons moved laboriously over hastily laid roads of fence rails and split saplings.

Sunday, the 12th of March, was a quiet southern Sabbath.

After six long weeks of hard march, the Union forces rested in Fayetteville. Despite foul weather they were all in splendid health and spirits. A vast crowd of refugees and Negroes had followed the army.

Arledge watched as Sherman, ever faithful in his correspondence and record-keeping, wrote, "I must rid myself of twenty to thirty thousand useless mouths who have clung to our skirts, impeded our movements and consumed our food."

This ragtag train of refugees was sent by land to Wilmington, accompanied by a two-hundred-man escort. Thus disencumbered, the army was prepared for instant battle. The bummers were, Sherman wrote, 'dirty, ragged and saucy,' having marched four hundred and twenty-five miles in the worst of winter. They had crossed five large rivers, captured several important supply depots, completely wrecked the railroad system of two states and devastated most of the countryside.

The general was in a hurry to reach Goldsboro, join forces with General Schofield and prepare for what he felt would surely be the final stage of the war. He was not anxious to meet his special antagonist, Confederate General Joseph Johnston, known to be in the area. Sherman moved, therefore, with greatest caution.

"Major Arledge," he shouted, "get me some hard facts. For weeks we have been cut off from all communication with friends. Lately I have been forced to listen to the prognostications and croakings of open enemies."

"General, their information is about as reliable as ours. The war correspondents are anxious to cover your activities, but you have never been civil to them. We could use their help now. They can keep current through the telegraph system."

Sherman snorted and puffed on his cigar. "I never trusted reporters. I want you to keep the rascals barred from my camp." He rubbed his stubby fingers through his short red hair. Years ago he had been burned by newspaper reports printing that he suffered from mental illness. For a long while only Grant had believed in him. He had been told that the president now closely watched his campaign. Sherman reveled in his current reputation as Lincoln's most successful general. He preferred to continue to write his own accounts of the march through the South.

The two men were piecing together information in an effort to estimate the size of Johnston's forces. There could be as many as forty thousand soldiers, made up of the remnants of Hampton's, Wheeler's and Butler's cavalry, and what troops Hoke, Cheatham and Hardee could muster. The bulk of the southern armies was reported to be collecting near Raleigh.

John knew Sherman was determined to give the Confederates little time for reorganization. His plan was to scatter and separate the various groups of rebels and keep them cut off from the Army of the Potomac. He dispatched orders for the Union forces to meet at Goldsboro by March 20th so everything would be in readiness for the final push. He was certain his army could reach Grant's field of operations by the first of April.

"Uncle Billy is going to put an end to this war, ain't he?"

"This one," Arledge answered solemnly, "and all future wars, it seems."

Sherman's campaign, grand in conception, had sounded the death knell of southern resistance. He had kept his vow to make war so terrible that peace, when it came, would last. The blackened path he forged through the South had left a trail of outraged civilians who swore that the breach between North and South was widened each day by a thousand new atrocities. His tactics were accomplishing his purpose. He was ending the war.

The southern armies knew with agonizing certainty that defeat was at hand. Soldiers and civilians alike felt a sense of having been betrayed. They had not expected so long, so hard, so cruel a war, and they had never expected to have to surrender.

Arledge knew, better than most other Union officers, the far-reaching military and economic results of Sherman's tactics. The captured Confederates that he questioned were all aware of the general's ruthless campaign. They were demoralized by the knowledge that marauding armies had destroyed their homes and left their families defenseless and without food. The end was surely near.

In South Carolina what little war news that did filter back to the people was usually bad. After the sack of Columbia, news of the evacuation of Fort Sumter hit the people like a death blow.

"Through four years of constant bombardment from Federal batteries on Morris Island the fort stood," bemoaned Aunt Sophia. Mr. Richards had stopped to tell her the distressing news he had heard. "For four long years Fort Sumter was a symbol of the invincibility of the Confederacy."

"Now there is only Virginia." Miss Gilham's face was solemn.

Gloom settled over the South like a dense fog. Petersburg and Richmond, shaken and battle-weary, could not be expected to continue to hold out, especially against the North's newest commander, General U.S. Grant, and the thousands of men he was willing to sacrifice.

"I was able to see a fairly recent New York paper," Mr. Richards told them. "Lee's army, poorly clad, underfed and badly equipped, is still fighting valiantly against wave after wave of fresh Union troops. For more than nine months, they have held out against insurmountable odds. Forces greater than twice the number of ragged butternut and gray clad men have laid constant siege to the battered capital of the Confederacy. The article said that, though the hills and riverbanks around the city are often carpeted with the bodies of men in blue, each day fresh Union troops arrive to close the gaps."

"We have no replacements," Miss Gilham reminded him. "The first conscription in March of 1862 applied to all men between the ages of eighteen and forty-five. The army has long since accepted soldiers both younger and older. Men who are sick, maimed and walking wounded keep rallying one more last time. I have heard beardless boys of sixteen write the numerals 1 and 8 in their shoes and swear they are over eighteen."

Together they faced the fact that the tide of battle had changed after May of 1863 and the death of Stonewall Jackson. Much of the heart was gone, not only from Lee's tireless men, but from the whole fighting force. Only the flashing brilliance of the youthful cavalry generals, Jeb Stuart and Lee's son, Fitzhugh "Rooney" Lee, were able to bolster the flagging spirit of Jackson's brigade.

After Gettysburg each casualty list had been longer and more heart-rending. Rooney Lee was captured; the colorful Stuart mortally wounded in May of 1864. Sherman was able to march through Georgia and the Carolinas virtually unopposed, but Richmond had hung on.

The little Columbia group could do little but wait. Lee retreated and regrouped, and despite terrible odds, he continued to hold. Discouragement, hopelessness and grief reigned across the South. Only the certain knowledge that the war was nearly over, and that the men would soon be returning home, brought relief to hearts heavy in defeat.

Most of the world was losing interest, but Richmond still hung on.

Thirteen

As February drew to an agonizing close, the countryside and fields began to brighten. Not so, the war news. Jim Milton's shoulder was slow in healing and his strength not up to normal. He knew he was as fit as some of the men in the front lines, and in early March began preparing to return to Columbia.

"I can't complain. General Butler has lost one leg and has little use of one of his arms," he reminded the Heyward sisters when they protested his plans for departure.

Isaac was constantly at Jim's side, tending him with a nurse's skill, insisting on regular exercise, taking him on daily walks, helping him assume some plantation work. His old loyalty and affection toward Henry Heyward had been transferred to young Milton.

Ellen watched as Pam warmed a little more each day to the lieutenant's gentle friendliness. His courageous smile and fumbling efforts to assist were endearing. As Jim grew stronger he began to accompany Pam through the fields, helping her to lay out future pasture borders, mark likely trees to tie fencing to and supervise rail splitting.

Much of the Oak Lane land lay idle. Grass overran fields once kept immaculate by slave labor. Terraces were washing away, ditches choked with weeds. Aging farm equipment needed skilled repair. As he grew stronger, Jim's broad knowledge, manual dexterity and complete affability was proving invaluable.

Big John, Luke and the field hands who had chosen to stay on the plantation began preparing ground for spring planting. The richer land lying near the creek beds was to be sown in oats. Fields were tilled for seeding with corn in April.

In the late afternoons each former slave tended his own plot and planned for the crops he would plant. A seed of hope began to germinate. Oak Lane, isolated from the main stream, was blessed by insulation from the barrage of gloomy war news.

At supper one evening in mid-March Jim announced that he was ready to return to duty. "I realize that, without a good horse, I have no way of rejoining my outfit immediately. According to rumor, Butler has gone to eastern North Carolina. All the armies seem to be moving toward Richmond."

"You can't get to Virginia in your condition," Ellen warned.

"Until I'm able to get some kind of transportation, I can do military clerical work in Columbia or help in a hospital. Some rail systems must be in operation or Richmond would have fallen."

Ellen regarded him with sadness. "I will be sorry to see you leave, Jim. I know you feel you must go, but you are not strong enough to march or to fight. A few days of sleeping in trenches and going without food and you'll be weaker than ever."

"I realize that. I don't expect to report for combat immediately. Medics, orderlies, couriers and clerks are needed and I am experienced in all of those duties. I don't want to be listed among the dead... or worse yet, as a deserter."

She saw that he was not to be dissuaded.

"There is a problem," he confided. "Isaac wants to go with me. Should I refuse him?"

"Isaac is a free man. He was born free. His father sent him to war with our father out of friendship and loyalty."

"He is insisting on returning."

"If Isaac wants to go with you, he has his own reasons. Have you asked him why? He may see himself as a southern man serving in the way he knows best. He is an excellent nurse. Father trained him. It seems to me that Isaac is volunteering."

"Perhaps you're right. I'll talk with him more about it. He can go with me as far as Columbia, anyhow. I plan to leave Saturday morning."

Pam rose from the table and began to gather the dishes. She had not entered the conversation. Her eyes were downcast.

"We will miss you, Jim," she said and moved away from his sight into a darkened area of the kitchen. His glance followed her narrow shoulders. She worked silently with the dishes. He did not acknowledge her remark.

The next morning Jim indicated that he would not go with Pamela on the pasture rounds. He had been helping each day with the newborn calves. Disappointment was written on her face.

"Aren't you feeling well today?" she inquired.

"I thought I'd walk out to the road early. When I talk to passing travelers, I plan to try to find a way to send a message to my family. I want them to know I'm all right. Perhaps I can send a letter by someone. Benjamin gave me writing paper. He had saved it. And later, I want to go to Isaac's home to talk with his parents."

"Do you know how to find their cabin?" asked Ellen.

"I will find it. I owe my life to their son. Without his help, I would have ended up in a Yankee prison camp. I want to tell them that I appreciate the sacrifice they made in sending him to serve, first your father and then me."

"This afternoon I can show you the shortcut through the pasture," Pam offered hesitantly.

"Would you? That will help. Let's plan to go around four."

She brightened. "I shall be pleased to escort you, sir," she said lightly. Then in a more serious voice added, "You are thoughtful, Jim. In many ways you are like Father. I had almost forgotten that men can be gentle and considerate." She turned and bolted from the room.

Later, when Ellen walked outside on the porch, she was surprised to see Jim sitting there.

"I have waited hoping to talk with you," he confessed.

"Yes?" Her reply a question. She paused beside him.

"It's about Pam." He appeared unsure and embarrassed.

"I had guessed as much."

"She is not an adolescent child, Ellen. I suspected that the very first night. Since then, I have come to be sure. You haven't told me the truth about Pamela, have you?"

"No, not entirely," she admitted. "With conditions the way they were when the Union army went through here, having her masquerade as a child seemed a good way to protect her. I didn't realize that we would get to know you."

"And how old is she really?"

"Why do you ask?"

"I was impressed immediately by her exceptionally bright mind. Later I couldn't help but notice her physical maturity."

"Have you mentioned this to her?"

"No. I thought she would tell me when she was ready. These days of working outside with Pam have helped me. I have become very fond of her... more so than I would dare let her know."

Ellen reached out and took his hand. "You are a fine young man, Jim. You've been good for her. You are thoughtful, sensitive, gentlemanly... qualities that we very much admire."

There was a long silence.

"May we talk about the day you and I first met, Ellen?"

"Talk to me about it," she replied guardedly, "but not Pam."

"When Isaac brought me back to Oak Lane Benjamin recognized me immediately. He didn't say so at first, but when I told him I would be leaving soon, he tried to thank me for helping you and Pamela the afternoon the foragers came."

"Benjamin feels protective toward us. He is too young to try to assume all the responsibility we give him."

"I have felt all along that I didn't know the full story about that day. I think I do know now. I couldn't understand Pam's attitude toward me at first, nor why she hated being a pretty girl. She seemed frightened and hostile. Then I realized she had to be older than the twelve or so she pretends to be."

"She is frightened, Jim, and confused. Why wouldn't she be? She's nineteen. The war years have been long and lonely for her. Mother saw that I went to Barhamville to school, but because of circumstances Pam didn't have that opportunity. She has known few young people, almost no men or boys, and there have been few happy times in her life."

"It's more than that, Ellen. She is the woman who was attacked by the bummers, isn't she?"

He had difficulty asking the painful question.

"Yes," Ellen answered, confirming his suspicion. "She is and I despair for her. I don't know how to help. Rape is a savage, ugly crime. Naturally she is distrustful of all men. Right now Pam despises her femininity and the emotions it can arouse. She will need time to recover."

"Do you suppose," he asked softly, "that she could ever..." He faltered.

"Fall in love? I certainly hope so, with the right young man. He will have to be someone very patient and understanding."

"I'd like to be that man. That is, I am asking you, as head of the family, if I might have your permission to pay court."

"Jim, that is Pam's decision. She is very proud and independent." Ellen cut short the stilted formal phrases. Permission to pay court. His words were the same ones that John Arledge had used. She felt tears standing in her eyes.

"You must examine your own feelings. Some men wouldn't be able to accept what has happened. Be very sure you can."

"My God, Ellen, you know I don't think she's at fault! I am just thankful I came that afternoon before things became worse. I'm glad that I was one of the men who helped rescue her."

"I know I don't need to remind you that the progress she has made so far can be easily undone. She is beginning to accept you. You talked about being our brother. She will gradually realize that you are more to her than a brother, I believe."

"I'm planning to come back by Oak Lane when the war ends."

Ellen stood up and sighed.

"We will be here and we'll welcome you."

"I don't know where my brothers are, nor what the situation is at home. I recently heard about Sherman's Field Order No. 15. All sea islands from Charleston to Port Royal and adjoining islands are to be set aside for the use of the Negroes who have followed the army. If that order stands, our plantation on Lady's Island is included."

"What will your family do?"

"We have some land in upper Beaufort District, too. We may have to try to make a go of it there."

"I had no right to ask the question, Jim. Nobody knows what's going to happen. All we can do is live from day to day. Now I need to see about the plowing." She kissed his cheek. "Thank you for being the kind of man that you are."

"Why do you say that?"

"For Pam. What happened to Pam would make a difference to most men."

"I was there, Ellen, but she must not know. I have Benjamin's word that he won't tell her. Will you give me yours?"

"Yes, unless she asks me directly. I, too, hope she never realizes it. Some day she'll tell you all about it, what she remembers, that is. Pam is too honest to let you begin caring for her without your knowing the truth about that day."

In the afternoon Pam led the young lieutenant to Isaac's home. Though they cut across the field to shorten the distance, he was weak from the exertion. She walked slowly, chatting shyly about everything and nothing. She stopped often to examine budding plants and trees, to ask him trivial questions and to watch as birds flitted through wooded areas.

Jim was aware that her animation, and the pretended interest in so many things, were really tactful subterfuges. She knew he needed time to walk slowly. He was grateful. Ultimately they reached the cabin and Jim talked with Adam about Isaac. The gray-haired father was proud and gracious. He had heard about Jim from his son and was pleased to be visited.

"Mr. Henry Heyward was a fine boy and he grew up to be a fine man. Isaac says you just like him. The Heywards are the only family we got. Whatever troubles them troubles us, and that's why I sent Isaac with Mr. Henry to the war."

"Yes, the Heyward ladies told me that."

"Now Isaac says he can't come home to stay long as the war keeps on. He says he ain't no soldier, but he knows how to look after sick folks. Mister Henry was the best doctor around here anywhere. He taught my boy how to nurse, you know. The two of them been tending to hurt soldiers for the last two years."

"I know. I heard about them when I was in the hospital in Columbia. They were working there. The soldiers had many good things to say about the two of them. Everybody knew your Isaac."

"He says he is going back to help care for the sick long as he is needed… whether you take him with you or not."

"That's what he has told me, too."

"Well, sir, lieutenant, I sure could rest easier in my mind if he stays with you. I know you will look after him, and he could look after you. That way the ones of us at home wouldn't need

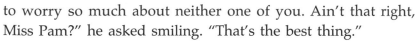

to worry so much about neither one of you. Ain't that right, Miss Pam?" he asked smiling. "That's the best thing."

Pam nodded. "That's right."

"Thank you, Uncle Adam," Jim repeated as he prepared to leave. "I am proud for Isaac to go with me. I plan to stay in Columbia a while. Isaac says it will be another month before I can make the trip up to Virginia to join my unit."

"That boy knows. He been trained good."

"Isaac will let you know when we leave. I wish I could pay him, but I am not being paid either. I owe him a great deal. I have been helping him learn to read and write. His work is teaching him about healing. Those things are worth more to him than money."

"Yes, sir, he told me. I'm proud to hear it. Mister Henry done taught him a heap. Isaac wants to be the black folks doctor around here when he gets back."

"Good-bye. I am much obliged to you." Jim reached out to shake hands with the old man. The gesture was strange and unexpected. Adam hesitantly grasped the white hand, ill at ease.

"Miss Pam, I will send you all some collard greens if you got any way to tote them. Where did Randolph go? He with you?"

"No, he didn't come this time, Uncle Adam. We are busy with the spring work. He is helping in the fields today. Some of our people left us, you know."

"Yes, mam. Soon as I get my work laid by, I come see what I can do for you all. Tell Miss Ellen I'm looking after them seedlings of hers."

"I will."

Down the path a short distance Pam turned to Jim. "Did you hear Uncle Adam reprimand me for being out with a young man unchaperoned? That's one thing the war has done for me. I don't worry about whether behavior is proper or improper."

"Anyone could take one look at me and tell that I am harmless." He smiled weakly at her. "I suppose your reputation is ruined, nevertheless. I shall do the only decent thing and propose to you as soon as I can catch my breath."

Though he clearly spoke with humor, her expression changed. "Don't say that. Don't ever say that, not even in fun." She ran ahead.

When he finally caught up with her, his shirt was damp with perspiration and he was out of breath. "Pam, I'm sorry," he panted, "I didn't mean to offend you."

"I don't like to be teased," she lamely explained.

"Perhaps I was not teasing," he replied softly and smiled. He tried to look at her.

She refused to meet his eyes.

They walked on in silence. When they reached the stile over the split rail fence Jim climbed weakly to the top and reached down to help Pam. He looked apologetic. She hesitated for a moment, then took his hand.

"You know," he murmured, looking down at her, "I'm not sure whether I am helping you, or you are helping me."

She attempted to smile and followed him down the other side of the steps. He continued to hold her hand.

Pam was skittish and uncomfortable. "Jim, I..." she stumbled, "it isn't your fault. The way I behave has nothing to do with you. Please believe me."

"I'm glad," he breathed, "because I get the feeling that you are always trying to avoid me." His steady gaze held hers.

"Also, I should tell you I'm not a child. I am older than you think."

"I have known that from the beginning, Pam. You and Ellen are beautiful young women. I think you were wise to change your appearance when you went to Columbia."

"You knew, and didn't say anything?"

"Ellen was my nurse, remember? She wanted to appear to be a middle-aged woman, but I soon realized that wasn't true. I was not surprised that you had tried to look younger."

"I became a child and she tried to make herself unattractive, but it was already too late to help either one of us." Her voice sounded bitter and she freed her hand from his. She did not explain the remark.

Shadows were lengthening as they headed toward the house.

Supper that night was more solemn than usual.

Early Sunday morning Ellen and Pam walked to the end of the lane with Jim. They had forced him to accept extra food and two blankets. Isaac was there waiting.

"Please," Jim protested once more, "don't give me things I know you need. I find it hard to accept what can't be replaced. You have already been too kind to me."

"Nonsense," scoffed Ellen. "Think how much you have helped us! All that valuable farm advice! We loved having you here. Come back as soon as you can."

"We know how long the walk is, and you are not strong enough to make it in one day," Pam reminded him. "The blankets are so that you can stop for the night. Isaac, please make him rest."

"Yes'm, I watch him."

"Millwood is about half way, and the Hampton family will be glad to have you sleep in their barn tonight. The blankets are for the two of you. They are not to be given away."

"Yes, mam, Miss Pam. We know what to do."

"Be sure your shoulder is completely healed, and that the cough is gone before you leave Columbia," Ellen warned Jim.

"You Heyward women mother me worse than Isaac does," he teased lightly, putting his good arm around Ellen's waist. "I will go and see your aunt and let her know you are well."

"She'll want you to stay at her house while you are in the city. Isaac knows where she lives." Ellen took his face in her hands and kissed his cheek. "Thank you," she said, her voice choked with sincerity. "Thank you for everything."

He turned to say good-bye to Pam.

She looked at him steadily, hesitated and then kissed his cheek quickly, just as her sister had done. "Good-bye," she whispered, "we will all be thinking of you."

To break the silence that followed, Ellen put her arm around Pam. "I am beginning to like you, Jim Milton," she declared. "If only you were ten years older, I'd propose, or ten years younger, I might adopt you. You offered, and now I really wish you were my brother."

"So do I," he replied gravely, looking steadily at Pam.

She averted her eyes.

He stepped back, stood at attention and saluted smartly.

"Look at that Citadel man show off!" Ellen mocked.

"Trying to impress the ladies. Looks like a heartbreaker to me," Pam quipped.

He smiled.

They watched as he walked down the dirt road, worn gray uniform hanging loosely on his wasted frame. The big Negro strolled leisurely beside him, hardly conscious of the weight of the bundle he was carrying.

The two girls stood watching. When he was nearly out of sight by the wooded area at the edge of the swamp Jim turned and waved. He was near the place where they had buried the three Union foragers. Ellen wondered if he was thinking of that awful night, scarcely more than a month ago.

Pam's face was so pale that her budding crop of spring freckles stood out like a sprinkling of tiny copper pennies high on her cheekbones.

After responding to his wave, they watched as James Milton walked around the curve of the road, past Adam's property, on toward Columbia and out of sight. For a long silent period they kept watching. Both girls brushed away tears.

Though the end of the war was near, the worst could be yet to come. Many more men would die. How long, they wondered, before that final battle?

The day was spring-like and perfect, balmy and warm for the second week of March. Jim and Isaac had walked steadily since early morning. They neared the wooded avenue leading to Millwood earlier than expected. Jim was less exhausted than he feared.

"We'll stop here to eat our food. We can refill the water jars at the Hampton well, but I want push on after a short rest."

"All that walking you been doing lately done paid off, Mr. Jim. You got good wind."

The lieutenant knew that Isaac was more lavish with praise than his physical condition warranted, but he appreciated hearing it. He sat down on the ditch bank to rest briefly, thankful for the warmth of the sun and for Isaac's companionship.

Rest time over, the two continued at a slower pace for another three hours, nearing town at sunset. As they approached Columbia from the east side, they stared ahead in disbelief. The normally busy town looked desolate. It was as if a curse had descended, leaving the sacked city suspended motionless in time. There was no sound of street traffic, no shrill train whistles blew. No city lights of any kind pierced the gathering dusk. Few people moved about.

Although Ellen and Pamela had described the night of the 17th, and they had heard numerous accounts of the town's fate from others, the men were not prepared for the devastation they saw.

For a while they stood silently surveying the scene before them. Then, drawn toward the silent shadows of past glory, Jim and Isaac began to proceed slowly toward the State House.

They passed the high brick wall around the College campus and looked down the length of Sumter and Main Streets. Where was the business district? For as far as they could see, only mounds of rubble and ashes were visible in the late afternoon stillness.

"Great God, Mr. Jim," swore Isaac staring in disbelief.

Behind them the College buildings were intact, ahead only Arsenal Hill in the far distance looked familiar. They felt lost in a once familiar city. Turning back, they solemnly retraced their steps and soon approached the confined area of the College.

"I'll go to the main hospital building first to ask for news of Butler's Cavalry, Isaac. You try to find out if there is shelter here for the night for us."

"Yes, sir, and then I wait for you on the horseshoe."

Inside the stout brick walls of the College very little had changed. Jim talked with several people, volunteers and the homeless, most of them listless and elderly. Stacked about the enclosure were contributions of food and clothing sent in from parts of the countryside that had not been ravaged.

He learned that news of action farther north was beginning to trickle in. As the Union army had moved northward from Columbia the greater part of the towns of Lexington and Winnsboro had been destroyed. There was talk of Orangeburg and Camden being burned. Chester was spared.

As always, a thousand unfounded and conflicting rumors flourished. Richmond had fallen. Sherman was dead. Hampton's men had recaptured all of the plunder stolen from Columbia. Hampton was dead. France was going to intervene on the side of the Confederacy. Richmond had been evacuated.

Jim learned that the last of Wheeler's Cavalry had left the area to join Hampton. Cheraw had been burned. Charlotte still stood. Johnston had retreated to Raleigh. And as always, no one knew anything for certain.

It was the news from Charleston which caused the deepest despondency. A few of the city's residents, declaring they were no longer able to endure the fear and degradation, had found their way on foot to Columbia. They described a reign of terror. The city was garrisoned by black troops who moved unrestrained about the streets with such savagery and barbarism that their officers had been forced to interfere. Thirty of the men, it was said, had been executed for violating Charleston women.

Foster's unit, the 55th Colored Massachusetts, had landed in Georgetown and marched through the streets on the night of February 21st singing the March of John Brown's Soul. There was anarchy in the surrounding countryside. The slaves were loose, lawless and roaming from plantation to plantation. Rumor ran rife; fear was high. No one was sure of the exact truth.

Columbians were afraid that a Negro garrison would be sent to govern them. Yankee gunboats were rumored to be coming up the river to complete the destruction of the city by blowing up the still standing granite walls of the new State House. Residents, deprived of newspapers, telegraphic communications, mail delivery and reliable couriers, were seizing avidly every scrap of news from the outside world, both rumor and fact.

Jim reported to the officer at the main desk of the hospital. He was well beyond conscription age.

"I take it you were not in the city while Sherman was here?"

"No, sir, I have heard about it though."

"It has been bad here. People are trying to cope, but it's bad." The elderly man looked at Jim through eyes that were rheumy and vacant. He had said the same words so many times to so many people they were now rote and meaningless.

"Last Friday was a day of fasting and prayer appointed by President Davis," an elderly doctor waiting in the office informed him. "It rained and few people were at church."

"I'm not surprised. Most people have already been fasting. They have been praying for a long time, too."

"But this morning was a bit more heartening," the old man added, brightening, "the church was full. Sitting there with the choir singing and the organ playing, it was hard to believe that so much has happened."

A doctor standing near the desk leaned to sign papers he had been handed. He picked up his bag to leave, "I am concerned about the people here. You and I have become inured to tragedy, lieutenant, but I'm afraid these recent weeks are more than the civilian populace will be able to handle."

"I am James Milton, a member of M. C. Butler's Cavalry, sir," the younger man explained again to the duty officer. "I was one of the wounded moved from this hospital just ahead of Sherman's arrival. I'm trying to locate my outfit."

"We have had almost no official communication here lately. Nothing from the front."

"Until I'm strong enough to get back to my unit, I'd like to volunteer to assist here. I have a servant with me. Isaac and I are experienced in hospital duty. He was Dr. Henry Heyward's aide. We will report for work in the morning. We have been walking all day and tonight we need a place to sleep."

"We can certainly use your help, lieutenant. The College buildings are crowded. The seriously wounded were brought back after the Yankees left. Some of the city's sick are here, too. We are also housing civilians who were burned out, refugees from other places, freed slaves, and the like, but I feel sure you can find shelter within some of the buildings."

Jim found Isaac waiting by the horseshoe well and they found a place on the ward floor to bed down for the night.

Measles, they learned, was still prevalent. At dawn Isaac began tending the needs of the sick. Jim, unable to perform the physical work of nursing, wrote letters for helpless soldiers. He wrote on scraps of wallpaper, the edges of old newspaper, pages torn from the back of small Bibles, on the inside of envelopes. There was little hope of posting any mail, however. He helped to distribute supplies being brought in and to dispense the meager supply of medicine.

In the late afternoon the two men walked to the house on Laurel Street to give Sophie Heyward news of her nieces. She and Miss Gilham were filling candle molds when the they arrived.

"Evenings are long and dismal with no illumination except dim firelight," explained Sophie. "We were glad to be able to procure beef tallow so we can mold candles."

"I'm surprised to learn there was that much fat on the beef you were given."

"Ellen told you about them, I see." Sophie's eyes sparkled.

"Yes, Miss Sophie. Willie was out at the plantation, too."

"Miss Gilham, who lives with me, is a skilled seamstress, and we are keeping busy. She has been fortunate enough to receive several yards of factory cloth… some unbleached domestic. Recently we have been spending our days sewing." She did not reveal that they were making the coarse homespun into ladies underwear.

Isaac went around to the carriage house to visit. As soon as the string wicks were set in the candle wax, Milton and the ladies moved to the parlor to talk. Both women immediately picked up their knitting. The wool appeared to have been previously used. He noticed that they were working on stockings, their hands so accustomed to the movements of the needles that they rarely had to look down.

"Lieutenant Milton, I'm happy that life on the plantation sounds normal. My niece spoke of you when you were her patient. I believe you helped her locate her father. I would be pleased to have you stay with me while you're in Columbia."

"Thank you, Miss Sophie, but Isaac and I can better serve in the hospital if we are living right on campus."

When they were ready to go Jim promised to call again before he left the city. On the walk back to the College, they noticed that lawns were greening. Elm trees had begun to bud, a few birds were about and daffodils and tiny sprays of blue hyacinths were blooming near the blackened rubbish of a former homesite. Down farther, through the tall gothic window frames of the gutted Christ Church, he could see trees struggling into leaf.

A small group of Confederate soldiers had pitched a tent on an open lawn and they were preparing a meal around a campfire. Jim stopped to talk. Two of the men had been in Butler's unit. At last he was able to get reasonably accurate information.

As men of Butler's brigade, they had been ordered to Columbia in late January to procure remounts. Sherman's advance forces started to arrive in the area about the same time. Jim told them that his patrol had been scouting southeast of Columbia for horses, too, and that they had encountered bummers.

"I was wounded and separated from my men," he explained. "I am attached to the hospital now. Where is our outfit?"

The news they relayed was more detailed than any he had thus far heard. Butler's troops had moved out of Columbia just ahead of the main Union forces. They had bivouacked for the night at Dent's mill, eleven miles out on the Camden road.

"General Butler was so wore out he dropped down and went to sleep. He didn't even know til next morning that Columbia had been burned," one soldier informed them.

"Some people told us," another reported, "that you could see the glow from the fire as much as seventy miles away."

Butler's Cavalry, they had been told, moved on toward Charlotte. There were rumors of daily light skirmishes and engagements with enemy flankers and pockets of bummers. The remnants of their unit were merged with Hampton's men. General Joseph Johnston had assumed command of the army. The latest report was that the bulk of the Confederate army was now near Fayetteville.

Jim and Isaac worked at the hospital while March dragged to an end. By April of 1865 it no longer mattered whose army was able to outmaneuver whose. Winning or losing, the lifeblood of the South was being rapidly drained away.

Fourteen

Mary Whilden was the first to learn about the Union Army's spectacular fourth anniversary program at Fort Sumter. Major General Robert Anderson raised and planted the United States flag on the ruins of the Charleston fort, the very same flag he had been forced to lower when he evacuated. The flag was saluted by one hundred guns from inside the fort, and by a national salute from every fort and rebel battery which had fired upon Fort Sumter.

Henry Ward Beecher, special guest speaker, orated in his famous glowing rhetoric. Mary was told that only a very small group of Union soldiers attended the ceremonies, while a few disinterested Negroes shuffled their feet and looked on.

"Thank goodness my dear husband never had to hear this horrendous tale." Aunt Sophia shook her head in disbelief.

Miss Gilham was rendered speechless.

"Kelly," Arledge shouted, "look in my field desk and get the best map we have of this area. I'm going with the general and two other officers to the big supply depot at City Point." It was the afternoon of March 25th.

"What's happening at City Point?"

"General Grant is there, and possibly the president."

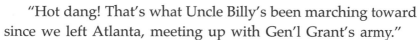

"Hot dang! That's what Uncle Billy's been marching toward since we left Atlanta, meeting up with Gen'l Grant's army."

"Looks like the reunion is about to take place, all right."

Kelly located a recently drawn sketch of the Goldsboro area and spread it out on Arledge's precisely made army cot. He watched the seasoned officer study the markings.

"You 'bout home, ain't you, Major? You know this country."

"Pretty well," he nodded, leaning to peer more closely. "We'll ride to New Bern, then to Morehead City. We are to put to sea there and go to Fortress Monroe. Should take us two days."

"All that territory in Union hands now?"

"Most of it. There's some concern about Johnston and how many Confederates he may be gathering to bring up to Lee's aid."

"Sure can't be many Rebs left from what we done seen."

"I agree. From Monroe we'll proceed up the James River. That, Sergeant, is really Virginia and home. We've had word that Grant and his staff are waiting there to meet with the general."

He knew the steamer River Queen lay at anchor in the harbor at Port Comfort. President Lincoln was aboard and, according to the latest newspapers, anxiously awaiting a briefing on recent action in the field. It was common knowledge that, hungry to hear of successes, he eagerly followed Sherman's campaign.

The first afternoon, after their arrival at Port Comfort, the president met with Grant and Sherman for two hours. They adjourned to continue the discussion the next morning.

Later General Sherman recounted the meeting to members of his staff. Arledge, knowing he might be responsible for implementing terms of the treaty, listened carefully.

"General Sheridan is at this time crossing the James north of us with a large cavalry force," Grant said, "and matters are drawing toward a crisis. I only hope that Lee will wait in Richmond long enough for us to converge on him."

"And, I added," color was high in Sherman's cheeks, excitement flashing in his eyes, "within two weeks my army can be there. Together we can starve Lee inside his own lines, or make him come out from his entrenchments and fight. I agree with General Grant that we will have to fight one more bloody battle, the last one."

President Lincoln did not agree. "Gentlemen, enough blood has been shed," he insisted. "I want everything possible done to avoid another battle."

"We can't assure that, sir." Sherman told him. "I have made a study of Confederate tactics. Control rests with our enemy. I'm of the opinion that Jefferson Davis will have Lee fight one more desperate battle. I am returning to my troops today. Are you ready for the war to end, sir?"

"More than ready, General," was his reply. "I have been ready for a long while now."

"Have you decided what's to be done with the rebel armies when they're finally defeated?"

"All I desire is for us to bring them to defeat. Then I want to get all the Confederate soldiers back to their homes and at work on their farms or in their shops."

Back in Goldsboro by March 30th, Sherman began to reorganize and resupply his army. On April 2nd Petersburg fell and on the following day, Richmond. April 9th, at Appomattox Courthouse in Virginia, Lee surrendered the Army of Virginia, and Armies of the Potomac and James to General Grant. That day 27,805 men surrendered and were paroled. A scout reported that there were no dry eyes in the ragged lines of gray when their white-bearded General Lee, sitting ramrod straight on Traveler, rode past them to surrender his sword.

General Grant described it as a moment unblemished in history. His men were forbidden to cheer in celebration of their victory. Full rations were issued to everyone by the Union quartermaster. Most of the Confederate soldiers had their first food in three days.

Formal surrender and the stacking of arms was on April 12. Grant, Meade and Sheridan had left Appomattox but Lee remained. The gifted writer, Union General Joshua Chamberlain, minister, Bowdoin professor and hero of Little Round Top, was in command. Describing the day he later wrote 'before us in proud humiliation stood the embodiment of manhood: men whom neither toils and sufferings, nor the fact of death, nor disaster, nor hopelessness could bend from their resolve; standing before us now, thin, worn, and famished, but erect, and with eyes looking level into ours, waking memories that bound us together as no other bond; was not such manhood to be welcomed back into a Union so tested and assured?'

"Ain't the old man ready to march yet?" Kelly was growing restless.

"Not yet. Intelligence reports from Richmond have changed his plans. Instead, he has decided to move toward Raleigh. At long last, he will meet Johnston's army near Smithfield. We think he has around thirty-five thousand men. Scouts are reporting that both Hampton's and Butler's Cavalry have arrived to support Johnston's left. A big battle seems to be looming."

The night before he was to move out, Sherman received the message from Grant that Lee had surrendered at Appomattox. Immediately he announced the news to his troops. The enlisted men celebrated; at headquarters an uneasy quiet prevailed. Most of the officers felt relief that the long bloody mess was ending.

Arledge had known surrender was inevitable, but he was stunned by its finality. His face mirrored the strain he had been under for so long. "I think I'll go see some of the men."

The major would seek out a few of the other southern-born officers. Together they could talk, men of like heritage comforted by the fact that more than 300,000 other men of southern birth had also served in the Union army.

Sherman received word that Confederate General Johnston wished to meet and surrender by the Appomattox Court House terms. The battle it seemed was going to be averted. As Sherman and his staff were boarding the locomotive to take them to the meeting point, the telegraph operator in the depot building caught Arledge by the arm.

"Please, Major," he implored in a state of great agitation, "have the general delay his departure. I'm in the midst of receiving an urgent dispatch in code from Morehead City."

Arledge notified the engineer to stand by. The train was held while Sherman fretted. After more than half an hour the clerk returned, pale and shaken, to confer alone with the general. The translated message from Secretary Stanton announced the assassination of President Lincoln.

"Operator," Sherman ordered, "I charge you not to reveal 'by word or luck' the contents of this telegram until after my return in late afternoon." The general dreaded the effect that the news would have at such a critical time. The surrender conference must be given the chance to succeed.

Arledge stood outside the train wondering what message could be more important than meeting for the Confederate surrender.

Johnston, accompanied by Butler and several aides, awaited the Union general's arrival. They met just after eleven o'clock on a farm near Hillsboro, North Carolina. Although the rival generals had served in the regular army together for thirteen years, this was their first actual meeting during the course of the war. Each man knew much about the other. Each had great respect for the other. Both generals had been preparing for this ultimate encounter for nearly four years. They had thought to meet on a battlefield.

Wade Hampton, who had accompanied Johnston, waited outside. Arledge and his small group of Union officers waited with the southerners. Sherman and Johnston went into the farm house alone. Once inside, the Union officer handed the dispatch announcing Lincoln's death to Johnston.

Perspiration covered the southerner's forehead. He made no effort to hide his distress. "This is a disgrace, sir. I hope you do not charge it to the Confederate government."

"I do not believe that you or General Lee, or the officers of the Confederate army could possibly be privy to an act of assassination. I will not say as much for Jefferson Davis and others I could name," replied Sherman, ever suspicious. Hatred and distrust of the President of the Confederacy was widespread.

"This act will have a profound effect on the country at large and on the armies. I realize, also, that it makes your situation extremely delicate," Johnston worried.

"General, you are the first to know. I have not yet revealed this news to my own personal staff or to any of the army. I dread the effect it will have when it is made known in Raleigh. Mr. Lincoln was peculiarly endeared to the Union soldiers. Who knows what acts of retribution might ensue."

"I pray that we have seen the end of bloodshed and destruction."

"Yes, General. You must realize that you cannot effectively oppose my army. Since Lee has surrendered, you can do the same with honor and propriety."

Johnston nodded in calm acceptance. "Asking my men to engage in further fighting would lead to senseless slaughter. Instead of surrendering piecemeal, I should like to have terms arranged that will embrace all of the Confederate armies."

"Do you have control of armies other than your own?" Johnston was faced by Sherman's penetrating gaze.

"Not at present, but I believe that I could get authority from Mr. Davis. I want to pursue the idea of universal surrender and include not only my army, but those of Taylor in Louisiana and Texas, and Maury and Forrest in Alabama and Georgia."

"May we continue this meeting tomorrow at noon? I am anxious to get back to Raleigh before the news of the President's death is known."

"Tomorrow is good. I believe that I may be able to procure authority during the night to act in the name of all of the other Confederate armies now existing. I shall certainly do my best."

On the return trip Sherman passed the telegram among his staff officers. Stunned, Arledge read through the telegram twice. Subdued, the war temporarily forgotten, he wondered what would happen next. Peace suddenly seemed more uncertain. Upon reaching Raleigh Sherman had the news published in a Special Field Order.

Peace negotiations were resumed the next day.

"I would like some assurance of the political rights of the men and officers after their surrender," General Johnston insisted.

"Mr. Lincoln's proclamation of amnesty made December 8, 1863 is still in force enabling Confederate soldiers and all officers, below the rank of colonel, to pardon by simply laying down their arms, and taking the oath of allegiance to the United States."

"What about the general officers, sir?"

"General Grant, in accepting General Lee's surrender, extended this principle to all officers, Lee himself included."

"Do you know the conditions of the pardon?"

"The pardon, I understand, restores the rights of citizenship. I am willing to submit these terms to the new president, Mr. Johnson."

Clerks were summoned to prepare copies for signatures. The lengthy signing process completed, the two groups parted. They waited almost a week for word from Washington.

The days of waiting passed slowly for Arledge. He wanted to write to Ellen, but no mail or courier service to the south had been established. He didn't expect to hear from her. He hoped that the grain and food supplies he had been able to send had helped. Falling in love was an unsettling experience for a disciplined man.

Service with Sherman was the most important assignment of Arledge's career. Although his mind was challenged, since February his heart had constantly tugged southward. He planned to request reassignment to the South Carolina Military Garrison when peace terms were final.

It was time for celebration of the Union victory. War Department Special Order No. 239 directed that there be a grand review by the new president and his cabinet of all the armies then in the Washington area. General Meade's troops were scheduled to parade on Tuesday, May 23rd. Sherman's day was to be Wednesday, the 24th.

Tuesday was a spectacular day. The air was filled with excitement, the pageantry superb. The streets of Washington teemed with strangers in holiday mood and dress. Flags and bunting decorated every house. The President and his cabinet observed the parade from a large stand built directly in front of the White House. By division, in close column, Meade's army marched around the Capitol, down Pennsylvania Avenue and past the reviewing stand.

Sherman's 15th, 17th and 20th Corps bivouacked in the streets around the capitol during the afternoon and night of the 23rd. Arledge, temporarily attached to the 14th Corps, camped near Long Bridge. The 24th was an ideal spring day, and by early morning the streets were lined with spectators carrying bouquets for the heroes of their favorite regiment.

The signal gun to begin the parade fired punctually at nine and General Sherman, attended by General Howard and the officers of their staff, rode slowly down Pennsylvania Avenue. John, although long a member of Sherman's staff, was uncomfortable in his role in the victory parade. Men, women and children crowded beyond the sidewalks and into the street, nearly obstructing their passage. The generals were followed by Logan at the head of the 15th Corps.

Sherman paused to look back. "A magnificent sight," the general breathed softly, "truly the finest army in the world."

Arledge, behind his commander, followed the general's gaze. The glinting muskets of the compact column resembled a mass of well-oiled steel swinging with the regularity of a pendulum. Seasoned veterans every man, four years of hard campaigns behind them, and they strutted proudly. Large reviewing stands, overflowing with cheering people, flanked both sides of the avenue.

The officers rode past the President, saluting with their swords. Everyone in the stands stood and acknowledged the salute. The general's party turned into the gate of the presidential grounds, left their horses and joined the group on the reviewing stand to watch the men pass. Mrs. Sherman sat with General Grant and the President. Sherman took his post to the left of the President. Arledge stood some distance behind them. Uppermost in his mind was the thought that this was the final act of the terrible struggle. He longed for the time he could be reunited with Ellen. Tomorrow morning he would submit his request for transfer.

For more than six hours they watched while their four corps passed in review. Sixty-five thousand men, battle-hardened and splendid in physique, men who had just completed a two-thousand-mile march through hostile country, were closely scrutinized by their fellow countrymen. Division after division marched triumphantly past. The commander of each unit came to the stand during the passage of his men to be presented personally to the President.

"Mr. President, you are, in my judgment, viewing the most magnificent army in existence," emphatically declared Sherman. "Many good people have until now looked on our western army as a mob. Look at them!" he urged, voice choked with pride, "the steady firm tread, the uniform intervals between the companies, all eyes directly to the front, tattered, bullet-riddled flags festooned with flowers. Everyone can see that is an army. No wonder it swept through the South like a tornado."

Throughout the day, the crowd of spectators did not leave their places, and when the rear of the column had finally passed, people still lingered to express admiration. Spectators had laughed and cheered as each division was followed by its baggage train... ambulances and wagons loaded with gamecocks, poultry and ham, followed by herds of goats, cows and strings of mules.

Some groups had freed slaves parading with them, including women and children. Each division had a corps of black pioneers, armed with picks and spades, in the lead. They marched abreast in double ranks, keeping perfect dress and step.

To those who were watching and those who were participants, the grand review seemed a fitting conclusion to the final campaign of the long war. The work was done. The armies of the South no longer defied them. They were victorious. They could go home.

Fifteen

Sophie Heyward and Miss Gilham did most of their sewing on the front porch of the brick house on Laurel Street. While they took advantage of the bright daylight, they could also talk to neighbors passing by. Since the surrender at Appomattox they had waited to learn what effect this would have on the civilian population.

Mr. Richards always stopped by to share news. General Q.A. Gillmore was now in charge of the state. As Federal commander at Hilton Head Island, where 40,000 Union troops had been permanently garrisoned since early in the war, he had immediately assumed military command of all of South Carolina. Rumors were rampant about his plans.

"Good afternoon, ladies." Mr. Richards was approaching from the direction of Main Street. He swept off his hat and stopped before the walkway. "I'm returning from my men's meeting. The news is not good, I'm afraid. The steps Governor Magrath has taken to restore the state's government will not be recognized."

"Good heavens! Does that mean we are powerless?" Sophie tucked the homespun ladies bloomers she was working on down beside her in order to spare the old gentleman embarrassment.

"South Carolina is virtually prostrate. As a group, the men generally support what the authorities are trying to do. The small contingent of Union soldiers that was sent here recently has helped us to re-establish public order."

"Please come in and sit with us for a while, Mr. Richards," Sophie invited, indicating the rocker beside her. "We so look forward to your reports from the discussion group."

"The men know very little," he admitted, easing himself down on the feather pillow. "We pool our information, you know, and the snippets we collectively hear are often far from factual."

"Any news is better than none." Miss Gilham rarely lifted her eyes from her work. "Forewarned is forearmed. The McCully girls saw an advertisement for teachers posted in front of the Bureau office. More schools being set up?"

"Oh, yes. The Union government wants schools, businesses, shops, everything open again. They will certainly try to get churches and schools functioning first."

"I encouraged the girls to apply. Women are accustomed to work. We've just never been paid for it. Many of us are going to have to support ourselves, and I see nothing wrong with that." Miss Gilham believed in a woman's right to independence.

"Many homes have no head of household, but is it safe for women to be on the streets unaccompanied? How can they look for employment?" Despite the economic realities, both custom and present conditions precluded women being out alone.

"The most disturbing thing to me is that the army plans to turn control of such concerns over to 'suitable civilians.' They have not spelled out exactly who will be considered suitable."

"That will not include southern supporters. Am I correct?"

"Yes, Miss Gilham. The consensus is that we are about to be lorded over by a conglomeration of scalawags, carpetbaggers and former slaves, with a military force standing by to back them."

"Lord help us!" moaned Sophie, "I'm glad my dear Marion is not here to see that happen." Her stomach churned as she thought of scalawags and carpetbaggers. These derogatory names described people considered to be the lowest of human dregs. Scalawags, southern white collaborators, were the most despised. Carpetbaggers, so named because they arrived carrying all their worldly possessions in a sack made of carpeting, were usually predatory northerners looking for ways to profit from the misery of others. These opportunists could be spotted regularly on the streets. More arrived daily.

"I've been worried ever since the first blue uniforms reappeared here in mid-May. That Freedman's Bureau authorized to administer and secure the rights of former slaves they established near the College campus is ridiculous." Miss Gilham was not one to mince words.

They knew that legislation for the bureaus had not easily passed the Congress. When it was first debated, there was fear that such offices might become resting places for 'broken-down preachers and played-out reformers, too lazy for work and slightly too honest to steal.'

"The talk is," Mr. Richards placed one foot firmly on the bottom stair, "to provide money to run the Bureau, authorities have begun confiscating and selling property that belonged to the Confederate government. Captured blockade runners, storage warehouses, iron foundries, government cotton, war materials, and hospital buildings and equipment are being auctioned. I hear that Bureau Offices are being set up in towns across the state and hordes of freedmen and some poor whites are being fed."

By the end of May the first of the southern troops began to come home. Church congregations, once almost wholly female, were sprinkled with veterans. Men, who had dreamed of returning home triumphant came back as burned-out shells. Loose hanging gray uniforms could not mask their shrunken bodies and stumbling gaits. Energy and strength spent, the Confederates were soldiers of a defeated army coming home to a ravaged land.

"Today the news is that Jefferson Davis has been captured. The days for weeping have passed." Miss Gilham's tone was emphatic. "The new watchwords must be stick, hold and preserve."

"The state is not without material resources, ladies. Eleven of our eighteen cotton factories were not damaged. More than a hundred thousand bales of cotton have been saved. Cotton will help many who are penniless." Mr. Richards climbed the stairs to sit in one of the porch rockers. "However the money situation is desperate."

Today's outward despondence was uncharacteristic. "The ending of the war has created a mania for speculation," he informed them. "There is panic to exchange southern securities for gold."

"I'm surprised that anyone has securities to exchange." Sophie had become accepting of their plight. "Exorbitant prices and heartless swindlers have already taken everyone's money." Her steel needle continued to stab in and out of the rough fabric of her sewing at a regular pace while she talked. "We have heard that a few people are profiteering from the extravagances of Union soldiers and the gullibility of the freedmen."

"Confederate securities absorbed the South's gold and almost every other holding of value. The greatest loss, however, is the money that was paid for slaves." Mr. Richards leaned his head against the back of the rocker.

The women waited for their faithful neighbor to continue. "We estimate that at least two hundred million dollars was invested in the state's more than 400,000 slaves. That is money totally lost. Only the land remains and no way to work it. Now United States land taxes dating back to 1861 are said to be due."

Sophie frowned in the fading daylight. How would she manage to pay five years of back taxes on her house? And there was the loyalty oath. Attitudes varied. Some regarded it as the ultimate humiliation, others as a bitter pill to be swallowed.

High-ranking military officers, government officials and any person who owned more than $20,000 worth of property were excepted. They would have to apply individually for pardons. Though there was quiet acceptance of Federal rule, a pall of bleak uncertainty hung over the state. Would they be abandoned by the government in Washington, or should they expect occupation? Which would be preferable? The absence of national patriotism in South Carolina created the strong likelihood of occupation.

The status of women, if they had status of any kind, was unknown.

Oak Lane was an island remote and lost in time. The aftermath of war, little different from the preceding four years, manifested itself only through continued scarcity, loneliness, fading memories and endless work. Time moved on leaden feet. Travelers still drifted past and stopped in occasionally to talk and to rest. Food was offered when food was available.

"Northerners are pouring into Columbia," one passerby told Ellen. "Trade in the city is beginning to become brisk again."

"Are the merchants local citizens, or charlatans?" She had heard tales of the carpetbaggers.

"There are a few honest businessmen and entrepreneurs among the newcomers. You have to know who you are dealing with, they say. Not many locals, though. Most of them lost everything."

"I could see signs that the city is starting to come back to life," a traveling companion added, "but I wouldn't call what's happening progress."

"I'm glad to hear recovery is beginning. Any Union soldiers on the streets?"

"Didn't see any, but heard there are a few around and more coming. Washington folks are planning all kinds of missionary projects for us."

At the plantation the corn and cane crops were growing. Oat fields were thick and green. The cattle had put on weight and the new calves were thriving. For Ellen and Pamela each day was the same and filled with mind-numbing, backbreaking work.

"You girls get your pretty selves out on the verandah and catch a breath of fresh air," Aunt Mariah ordered. "We done worked enough for today."

The June afternoon was hot and humid. Ellen, Pamela and every plantation woman and child not in the fields, had picked blackberries all morning. Ellen insisted that the freed women be included in work projects. They must learn the skills needed to see to the livelihood of their own families.

The fruit, now washed and prepared for preserving, simmered slowly on the back burners of the iron cook stove. Because of the heat, the doors and windows in the big house were thrown open. The cloying smell of bubbling berries drifted outside and clung, perfuming the still air. Ellen and Pamela idly watched the slow progress of a lone traveler on the dusty main road. When he reached Oak Lane he turned in toward their home. Their interest quickened.

"Another foot-sore, vermin-covered veteran en route home, I suppose." Ellen squinted, closely observing the approaching male. "Wonder why he's by himself."

"I hope that's not a bad sign." For reasons of safety, returning men rarely traveled alone. Pam watched him closely.

"We'll probably need to boil the clothes he's wearing. I hope we have enough supper to offer him a decent meal."

"I don't like to see a man by himself. That one appears to be in better health than most we have seen pass," Pam worried. "Could be trouble. Should we close the house and get the gun?"

They had been warned to be on the lookout for danger. There was the threat of stragglers from the Union army, thieves, deserters, carpetbaggers, guerrillas, ex-slaves on the run and even Confederate soldiers who might be temporarily deranged.

"No, there is still plenty of time. Let's wait until he gets a little closer."

The gray of a Confederate uniform was clearly discernible. The man's step was too strong to be that of a recently released prisoner of war. As yet, few of the veterans from the Virginia campaign had passed their way. Being alone, the man would have to have been serving some place near. As they watched, the approaching traveler began to vigorously wave.

"I think it's Jim," Pam said, wonder in her voice. She had not once mentioned his name in the past two months, but Ellen suspected that Milton had often been in her sister's thoughts. "You go and meet him, Ellen, while I tell Aunt Mariah he's coming. By the time you get back, I will be out to sit and listen to everything he has to say."

She dashed inside. Ellen smiled, suspecting that Pamela really wanted time to smooth her hair and compose herself. She ran down the lane to greet the young man.

"Jim, how wonderful to see you!" she shouted as they neared each other. "And you look so well."

When they met, his arms encircled her in a giant bear hug. He hung on to her for long minutes and then kissed her cheek.

Ellen warmly returned the embrace and leaned back to examine him closely. The young lieutenant's face, pale and haggard when they had last seen him, had begun to fill out and was deeply tanned. He stood erect, no longer favoring the injured shoulder. His clothing was worn looking, but clean. He didn't appear to have been on the road a long time.

"Ellen," he whispered, still holding her close, "it's so good to be back. And Pam, how is she?" His voice sounded choked.

"We are both well, working hard. And you, how about you?"

"Isaac and I got back from North Carolina two weeks ago. We were needed in Columbia so we have been there since. Now I'm on my way home. I wanted to come by here first."

They turned and walked toward the house arm in arm. When they reached the verandah Pam was waiting. Her golden hair, no longer a mass of short stubble, curled softly at her shoulders. She was wearing a dress, faded and worn, but a dress that fitted around her slender waist and accented her small shapely figure.

"Welcome home, Jim." Pam smiled up at him shyly.

He looked at her, heart in his eyes. "It seems like forever since I was here," he said.

"Come in. Would you like some water? Are you hungry?" Pam sounded breathless.

"Later. I had my canteen with me. Let me look at the two of you."

"Then we will sit and talk." Ellen led him up the front steps. "We want to know everything since we last saw you."

Ignoring the big rocking chairs, they sat down together on the wide second step, just as they had often done in the past.

"Isaac and I stayed in Columbia and worked in the hospital three weeks. The first day I went by to tell your aunt that you were well."

"Yes, Uncle Adam got word and he let us know. Thank you."

"When I was stronger we headed for eastern North Carolina, following Butler and Hampton's men. Travel was slow, but we caught rides on an occasional army wagon. A few trains were still running. A week or so out we heard about the surrender, so we turned around and made our way back. Since then we have been helping to get patients home and close out the College hospital."

"Tell us what's happening in Columbia. We've heard that strangers are setting up businesses, that gangs of unruly blacks are roving about town, and that occupation troops are arriving. How much of that is true?" Ellen was asking all the questions.

"Some. I only know about the College, not the other things that are happening. They hope to get the school in operation again."

"Where would the young men come from… not to mention their tuition money?" Ellen shook her head in doubt.

"When the Confederate medical officials took over the school in '62 they agreed to pay rent. I understand that the amount owed is nearly $100,000, none of which has been paid."

"Nor ever can be."

"The faculty members who continued to live on campus during the war are anxious to open up in September. They hope to collect some of the money. With boys coming home and the country in turmoil, the professors say education is more important than ever. They are making tentative plans for a fall semester."

"I expect most returning soldiers will feel they've outgrown college?" Pamela made her first comment. "And what family could possibly spare a male member at this time to attend?"

"I agree, Pam. Not many veterans will be thinking of college any time soon." Jim turned to look directly at her. "Nevertheless, we have been working feverishly for the past two weeks to get the College buildings emptied. As of two days ago the classrooms are no longer wards. Not everything looks good, but I think the place is operational."

"What other problems do the professors face?"

"In February when Sherman was approaching, Professor Rivers was unable to find transportation for the books in the library, but Professor LeConte packed all the chemical and scientific equipment and shipped it to Greensboro for safekeeping. Strange how things happen." Jim stretched his long legs out before him and, placed both elbows on the top step behind him. "The books were not damaged. They say a Yankee major, who happened to be southern-born, was on duty the night of the fire. He helped to save the library and the other college buildings."

Ellen's felt her heart racing. She remembered the tired lines in that particular officer's handsome face when he sought her out the next morning. That was the time she began to realize that she cared about him. So now he had become a local hero.

"The lab equipment disappeared. Nobody knows anything about it. They have even had the Union officials in Greensboro try to trace it down."

"The lab tables were used in wards. Chairs, too," Ellen reminded Jim. "They should be able to round up most of those."

"You would think so, but they are gone now. Stolen or used for firewood, I expect. The work and planning may all be in vain. The military arrived and claimed the buildings May 25th."

"How awful! Whatever for?"

"For housing, to start a Negro college, to serve as barracks for an occupation army, nobody knows. Rumors were wild, as usual, and things seemed pretty gloomy when I left. A Freedman's Bureau has been set up across the street from the horseshoe."

"Has all college planning stopped?" Pam finally asked him a second question.

"They have switched to other projects. Everybody is trying to keep busy. One of the history professors was beginning to compile statistics about the role of the college in the war. Did you realize that it furnished twenty Confederate generals?"

"And General Butler? Did you ever get to see him?"

"The general passed through Columbia day before yesterday. He was on his way home. The last big battle the unit fought in was at Bentonville, a little place in northeastern North Carolina. He was among the Confederates paroled at Greensboro."

"How was he?" Ellen had not forgotten the young man's hero worship of his general.

"Still an inspiration to everyone. I wish you could have seen him, the way he sat so straight in his saddle. You should have heard him when he said, 'Men, I'm returning from war, twenty-nine years old, one leg gone, a wife and three children to support, seventy freed slaves I feel responsible for, fifteen thousand dollars in debt and exactly one dollar and seventy-five cents in my pocket.' He will succeed. I'm proud to have served under him." He paused.

Neither woman broke the silence.

"Yesterday afternoon," Jim continued, "I called on your aunt to tell her that I was coming by to visit you. She wants you to know that she is well, the pace is picking up in town, more goods are available, but everything is more expensive than ever."

"What do people use for money?" Pam asked. "I mean, I assume that only United States currency is recognized."

"Barter. Most people trade service or swap goods."

"What is Aunt Sophie doing? Is she having problems?"

"I was asked to tell you that she and Miss Gilham meet with other ladies to devise moneymaking schemes. At first they were embarrassed. Their work had always been for charities, but now it's necessary for most women to help support their families."

"But those women don't have marketable skills." Ellen was astounded. "And they all have the same skills, don't they? Running a home, teaching small children and the like."

"You will be amazed at their ingenuity. They plan to make straw hats and baskets, keep bees, can fruit, churn butter for sale and grow flowers. I can't remember all the things she told me. Women young and old are preparing to offer private music and art lessons in their homes. Those ladies are versatile!"

"Tell us what Aunt Sophie has in mind," Ellen prompted. "We know life must go on for her, too."

"Your aunt is calling what she is planning her 'adventure in rank commercialism' and, since you are her only living relatives, she wanted me to make you aware that she will be baking goods to sell, renting rooms to any respectable person able to pay, and offering to do clothing alterations. She and Miss Gilham will work together. She hopes that you'll understand that her outrageous conduct is prompted by necessity." He delivered the phrase of the message in Aunt Sophie's stilted diction.

"Poor dear Aunt Sophie." Ellen was laughing. "Despite her apparent humiliation, when it comes to ladylike behavior, what she is doing beats working in the fields the way Pam and I do."

"Everybody has to live the best they can." Pam's voice was assertive. "We are doing whatever work it takes to hold this place together. I wish someone would pay to room or board with us. Ellen would take in Sherman himself."

"No, I might stop just short of that. I don't want to risk being tar-and-feathered by the neighbors, but with the Union army returning, we are certainly going to try to sell beef to them."

"I had the same idea, Ellen." Jim's voice rang with enthusiasm. "The military are prospective cash customers. Trade with them and then you will have hard money to shop with. You can buy what you need for less than if you try bartering."

Jim shifted his position to look more closely at Pamela.

"Now you must tell me about your life here." He wanted to hear directly from the younger sister. "I came to make sure that everything is all right with you before I go home. How many calves do we have? As you see, I feel like part of the family."

"Tomorrow," answered Ellen, "we'll take you around and you can see for yourself. We are encouraged. Planting time was hard, but crops are satisfactory. Pam will show you the cattle."

Milton turned to face the girl sitting less than two feet from him. So conscious of her presence was he that he could hardly restrain himself from touching her soft hair.

Jim's nearness was making Pam uncomfortable. She leaned away from him. "We gave up hope on a new bloodline for this year." Pam spoke nervously. "We are counting heavily on finding customers who can afford the kind of beef we have."

"They will have to be carpetbaggers, scalawags or members of the occupation army," Jim replied grudgingly.

"We know that, but if they can buy, we are selling. They will be helping us."

"Jim, we've learned how to rationalize. I hope Aunt Sophie won't be ashamed of us." Ellen was honest about their intention to survive.

"Your planning is sound. You'll need cash to pay the back taxes that the federal government is going to impose. And the final count on calves this spring, what was it?"

"We have thirty-eight," Pam answered proudly, "and twenty of them are heifers."

From the open doorway Aunt Mariah shouted, "Lord, Mr. Jim, I am some more glad to see your face again. You are looking good! Come on in this house. Soon as I heard you was coming down the road I started making you some good eating for tonight."

After supper they talked by candlelight only a short while. The first rush of news was over and they had each had a full day.

"Your same room is waiting," Ellen assured Milton. "I know you are exhausted from the walk."

"Twelve miles a day is not much for a seasoned soldier," he protested smiling. "For an ex-cavalry man accustomed to riding,

I'm catching on to this walking business pretty well."

"It's nice to have you back," breathed Pam softly.

His gaze sought hers, but she refused to look at him. Later as Ellen was undressing she heard a hesitant knock at her door. She knew immediately that it was Pam.

"Ellen, may I come in?"

"Of course." She opened the door and smiled.

"I want to talk… to talk about what both of us have avoided mentioning. I think it might help me."

"All right, you begin while I brush out my hair."

Pam crawled into the big bed and tucked her feet under the covers. "You have fallen in love with John Arledge. Are you going to do anything about him?"

Ellen stopped brushing. Pam was always direct. Ellen had not thought they would be talking about her problems, however.

"Pam, what do I know about falling in love? I never expected it would happen to me. I am not sure how I feel about him. In any case, there's nothing I can do. I sent him away. After all, he is a Union soldier."

"I don't think that when you fall in love something like that matters. You don't stop to weigh all the consequences."

"No, but parents and friends usually participate in such decisions. They approve or disapprove, give advice… and if they are convinced that the choice is too wrong, I understand they pack you off to visit relatives living in some far away place."

"Don't tease, Ellen. You know your mind. How do you feel?"

"What do you mean?"

"I mean feel. Nervous, excited, giggly, stupid, shy, what?"

"Hopeless and overwhelmed, mostly, and despairing. John is completely different from anyone I have ever known, and he's a long way from here. Why should I think that I made an indelible impression on him? I really know little about him. He may be a scoundrel, a predatory rake, perhaps even a married one."

"When you were with him how did you feel?"

"Rather frightened of him, and of myself, too. I couldn't predict or control my emotions when he was near. I was most uncomfortable with how I felt. Passion scares me, his and mine. I felt ashamed, indecent, disloyal." She smiled slowly. "You asked for honesty."

Pam silently studied her older sister as she talked.

"I have tried to stay busy and not think about John. He said he is coming back. Perhaps he has told women all across the country that. If he comes, I can decide what to do then." She continued to brush her hair. "There must be many ways of knowing if you are in love, but I'm not sure what they are."

"There must be. So much is said and written about it."

"Constant unrest and indecision are surely a part of it... and dreams and sleeplessness. Do you wonder, too, little one?"

"About what?"

"About your own feelings. About love? About Jim?"

"Ellen, is it that obvious? Around him I am either shy and tongue-tied or too excitable and talkative. I hate the way I feel and the way I behave. It frightens me."

"While he was here recuperating you had time to get to know him. I'm sure you have found him to be thoughtful and gentle. They are necessary qualities in a man."

"I know. I almost hated him at first just for being male, and now I have grown to trust him."

"You both come from similar backgrounds and so you should think alike, be able to understand each other. That's very important."

"I had thought I despised all men. Gradually I found that I liked him and enjoyed his company. Does that make sense?"

"Of course and I'm sure he has some of the very same feelings for you. Why do you think he's here now?"

"I know that he is fond of us and he feels indebted to you."

"I think you suspect it's more than that," Ellen reasoned.

"Yes, but I can't let him get too involved. I will have to tell him what happened. The sooner he knows, the better. I hope I can find the courage I need."

"It's your decision, Pam, but you don't have to tell him just yet. Many bad things have happened to people in the last four years. Most of us have as much we want to forget as we have worth remembering."

"I have to tell him. I know he may lose interest in me."

"He is a fine man, Pam. The past will not matter to him."

"I know men expect purity and virginity and all of that when they fall in love. Oh, Ellen," she moaned, "what should I do?"

"You said you are beginning to trust him. Before he left to rejoin his unit he formally told me, as head of the family, that he has serious intentions toward you. Isn't that reassuring? He knew right away you weren't an adolescent. Wait. Let things develop naturally."

"I can't. I must tell him." She began to sob.

Ellen put her arms around the girl's shaking shoulders. "Don't torture yourself this way, honey. John believed that I was the one who was assaulted here that day. It didn't make any difference to him. Tell Jim, if you must, and if he cares for you, he will continue to do so."

"How can you be so calm and sure with your advice to me when you are willing to make such a muddle of your own life?" Pamela demanded to know. "I don't know how good your advice is."

"Dry your eyes, Pam," Ellen comforted. "Let's go to sleep."

Ellen lay awake long after Pam returned to her room. Her resolution to forget John Arledge had met with little success. The silver locket lay warm between her breasts. In secrecy she had read Note Two a thousand times. Since she couldn't force him from her mind, she relived the moments they had shared. Their times together were not all tender memories. Many meetings had been emotional, threatening, angry and argumentative. Some were passionate and explosive. All were filled with maddening innuendo, unanswered questions and unfulfilled dreams… and usually with more heat than innocent sweetness.

She could give her sister no helpful counsel. She did not know how to advise her about men, or love, or life. Worse, she was not even able to read her own heart… or her mind.

"No, Pam, I can't go with you to show Jim the new calves this morning." Ellen looked up from the pot of melted beeswax. "I'm busy sealing preserves and I have to pack the jars away." She dispatched the young pair toward the pasture, noting the look of gratitude that Jim's eyes flashed, and the one of terror on her sister's frozen face. They wanted to come to some kind of understanding with each other. Neither wanted further delay, and for both, the prospect was unnerving.

Randolph was summoned, as Aunt Mariah always required, to serve as chaperone. The sky was bright, the air was clear, and a light summer breeze was stirring. Randolph, never one for procrastination, was circling around them, flitting back and forth, indicating that the pace was much too slow.

They had barely crossed the first field when Pamela stopped and blurted, "Jim, please stop. There is something I must say. I…" she stammered, "want to talk while I have the courage."

Her palms were clammy. Her stomach churned.

His calm gaze met hers squarely.

The fierce hammering of her heart was making her ears throb. She was breathing too fast. "Could we sit by the rail fence?"

"Of course," he answered easily. "Randolph, I see Benjamin by the stream ahead. Go and talk with him while Miss Pam and I rest. We'll catch up with you in a few minutes."

"Yes, sir," the boy sang out, skipping off happily to join his older brother. He was accustomed to Mr. Jim having to rest.

Adults seemed to need a lot of rest.

The couple sat down in the triangle of green grass formed by the zigzag of the split rails. Pam could hear the dim buzzing of bees. The sweet smell of honeysuckle blossoms surrounded them. She gathered her courage.

"Please don't look at me while I talk, and don't say anything until I have finished," Pam requested.

"May I interrupt now... before you begin, I mean."

"Yes, but briefly. I want to get this done."

"Pam, whatever you are about to say seems to be painful to you. You don't owe me any explanations about anything."

"Jim, please hear me out first."

"Very well." He waited resolutely for her to begin.

"I have not told you why I was concealing my age when you first came. I am nineteen." She faltered, groping for words.

"I'm pleased to hear that," he said quietly. "At first I thought you were a disturbingly precocious child."

"I spent most of last night trying to figure how to tell you this quickly and yet include all the details." She took a deep breath and began. "More than a week before Sherman's main forces reached Columbia there were Yankee bummers already in this area. A foraging party came to the plantation and set fire to our stables. A heifer I had raised and one of the family horses were shut up in stalls. We had to let them out."

He leaned against the rough rails and tried not to see the anguish so evident in her face.

She swallowed roughly and struggled to continue. "Ellen went to get Father's pistol. I slipped out the back door. I thought I could run to the stables, open the doors and get the animals out before the men noticed me. They had been drinking. I was wrong. They caught me... and I was assaulted."

She was having difficulty maintaining her composure. Determined to complete the story, she forged ahead. "By how many, I hardly know. I was struck several times and thrown to the ground. I saw Ellen coming with the pistol. About that time a Confederate patrol rode up. God knows what would have happened if they had not come! There were shots. I was knocked unconscious... or I passed out."

She gulped air as if drowning. "Much later I learned that the Yankees were all killed. Ellen had me carried into the house to Aunt Mariah and then she helped to bury the bodies that night."

Having told the worst part, Pam's rush of words began to slow. The pitch of her voice lowered, her panicked breathing calmed. "A few days afterwards a Union major showed up here asking questions about the missing men. In order to protect me, Ellen convinced him I was a child and ill. He threatened to arrest her and insisted on questioning me. I had to look like a child and to continue the masquerade as long as he was a threat to us."

"Is that all?" Jim's voice was quiet.

"No. The story has become more involved. The Yankee officer saw Ellen two or three times during the time we were in Columbia. I am sure that he has fallen in love with her... and she with him, although she wouldn't dare admit it."

"Getting to be a tangled web, isn't it?"

Pam ignored the remark.

"He continued the investigation until he found out most of the truth. She let him believe she was the woman violated, and that she probably killed the men. Most of the Yankee major's information came from one of the Confederate soldiers who was captured later that night. The lieutenant in charge of the patrol was wounded... Jim," she suddenly stopped, jerking her gaze around to his face. She paled.

"Yes?" He turned to look directly at her.

"Where, when and how were you wounded?" she demanded.

"In the shoulder by a Yankee bullet," he replied with calculated calm.

"You were here." Her words were delivered with stony conviction. "You let me go on with this story when you already knew everything."

"You asked me to listen and not interrupt."

"That's why Ellen has been so devoted to you. I should have suspected. How could you keep this a secret from me?" She jumped to her feet and started to run toward the woods. With one long stride he caught her and gathered her in his arms.

"Pam, we didn't want you to know I was one of the men here that day," he explained. "You were suffering. I hoped you wouldn't try to tell me what happened. The past doesn't control the future."

She attempted to struggle, but he held her firmly. Securely pinioned, she buried her face in his chest and started to weep.

"Don't cry, Pam. Like so many others, you were wounded by the war. It's over. You are well and strong. That is all that is important now."

"Don't say that," she sobbed. "It isn't over. You know that. You were here. You won't forget and I won't forget."

"You are wrong. At the time I felt great sympathy for the girl who was attacked and hatred toward the men. As soon as I met you, I began to adore you. I never associate you with what happened. Don't you know you are not to blame. I helped to kill the foragers. Instead of feeling any guilt about that, I'm thankful I was here."

"Oh, Jim, what am I going to do?"

"Do? You are going to get on with your life. Many people were victimized by the war. You aren't the only woman who was ill-treated. War is always filled with hardships, indignities, and suffering, especially a civil war. For us, it is over."

"I wish that were true, but it isn't."

"Look at me, Pam," Jim demanded. "You know I am in love with you. You are the dear, sweet girl I adore. The only one in the world for me."

"Jim, please don't say that."

"I shall say it regularly. Every time I see you I will rerpeat it until you believe me and start to think of me as important in your life. And please get hold of yourself, woman. This is the only shirt I own and you are soaking the front of it with your blasted tears."

She looked up and sniffed, trying to dry her cheeks with the back of her hand. "To stop the tears is easier said than done."

"I'm serious, Pam. No weeping about the past. You and I are young. I won't allow what happened long ago to intrude upon our lives." He released her, waiting until she regained composure.

"It wasn't long ago."

After a few quiet minutes he answered. "It seems a million years ago, another lifetime ago. Do you think that now you could learn to care for me? Please know that, at the moment, I have nothing to offer you except my complete devotion."

"Who could not love someone as kind and thoughtful as you?" she responded, trying to smile.

"That's not what I asked," he reminded her gently.

"I know, but I'm not sure, Jim. I need time. Thoughts of love frighten me."

"I won't rush you. I'm only asking for hope. For you, I can wait an eternity." He kissed her forehead softly.

She looked up, timidly raising a hand to touch his cheek. "There's no one else, if that is any comfort."

"I am asking you to wait for me. I must go home. I came by here first to see if I have a chance with you. You've made me very happy, Pam." His eyes were shining.

Pam searched her pockets for a handkerchief, and finding none, wiped her face with her sleeve and smiled ruefully.

"I don't know how things will be when I get home, but now that you and I have this understanding, no obstacle will be too great." He took her hand. "Let's go see the calf crop."

Late that afternoon Ellen walked out to meet Jim and Pam as they neared the house. They were holding hands. Soft radiance suffused their faces. Their talk had been satisfactory.

"Miss Heyward," Milton called from a distance, "do not be concerned. Our young chaperone still accompanies us."

"He tends to dawdle a bit and then rush ahead, but he has most diligently attended his duties." Pam's mood was light and playful, too. Blessed be the Saints!

"What's more, I've proclaimed my serious intentions to this lovely lady beside me and, while not accepted, neither was I totally rejected. Therefore, I shall begin to hope that someday I am to have the distinct privilege of becoming your esteemed brother-in-law."

"Well, that takes a load off my mind," Ellen scoffed and sighed dramatically. She then kissed them both warmly. "Jim, I was determined to keep you in the family. I am glad my sister is somewhat agreeable to the plan."

Two days later Milton was ready to leave for Beaufort and the Lowcountry. He and Ellen talked quietly on the verandah.

"I don't know what things will be like at home or how long it will be before I return. My brothers may need me."

"Perhaps there will be mail service soon. Write to us in care of Aunt Sophie. We'll be going to Columbia, or sending someone in from time to time."

"I'll be back. Please plead my case with Pam, Ellen."

"Plead your own case. You can come back and become our overseer at any time you wish. We can't pay you, but the garden is starting to thrive. We will be able feed you well." She attempted to lighten his mood.

"I don't want to come here a pauper." His proud face looked strained, his eyes bleak. "A prospective bridegroom who is unskilled and penniless is not what this plantation needs."

"We are all penniless, Jim," she reminded him gently, "and all learning the skills we must have."

"Opportunists are arriving in Columbia daily who aren't broke."

"Then I shall certainly look for a wealthy speculator or a greedy profiteering merchant next time I go into town."

"You have already found your man, haven't you?"

An interruption from inside the house shielded Ellen from having to answer his question.

"Soldier boy," Pam's voice rang out cheerfully from the doorway, "I have here your lunch for the road." She dangled a small package before him. "It has been prepared and packed lovingly for you by our own Aunt Mariah."

His eyes lighted as the younger sister moved toward him through the sun-splintered morning. He took the lunch and tucked it in a worn uniform pocket. Looking very solemn he kissed first Ellen and then Pamela. The kisses he bestowed were safe, sweet, brotherly ones.

Ellen looked at him. James Milton, vanquished, shabby twenty-two-year-old warrior, recently wounded and newly in love, was marching home. They watched him out of sight, just as they had done once before.

"He won't be alone, Pam. In no time he'll meet up with others returning home. He will have companions along the way."

"I hope so."

"And they will be made welcome by the widows and children in the homes they pass and generously offered whatever meager hospitality the people can afford."

"Heaven knows we have done it for other soldiers often enough!" Pam agreed. "Surely he will be treated well."

The sisters worked doggedly all afternoon, saying little. Each was buried in private thoughts. Although the day was filled with the quiet and shining promise of summer, acute loneliness settled around them like a dense enveloping fog. Spring, oblivious to the desolation everywhere, had arrived early in 1865. There had been no frost since late March.

"We will plant nothing," Ellen had ordained, "except those things that we can eat and easily barter or sell."

New ground was spaded early for gardens. The seeds which had been entrusted to Adam were carefully planted and expertly tended. Old garden spots were left untouched in the hope of volunteer seedlings.

Daily Uncle Adam walked over to inspect the plantation gardens and the small plots behind the Heyward slave cabins. He watched for young random shoots of beans, peas, corn and mustard greens. Isaac or Randolph accompanied the old man, carrying water for the plants and pulling weeds under his supervision.

"I knows them little seedlings when I see them. Once I find some, I work around them with my short-handled hoe and we going to nurse them along. I believe the good Lord sure going to bless us this season."

Sixteen

By late June simple food was plentiful once again at Oak Lane and for most South Carolinians living in the unscorched rural areas. In July the Heywards had field peas, asparagus, mustard greens and new potatoes growing. The difficulties involved in saving fresh produce had forced Ellen to experiment with every method she knew of canning, drying and preserving food. Daily she blessed Mason for the glass canning jar and lid he had patented a few years earlier.

"Ellen, studying again? You must have Father's old records memorized by now."

The sisters were sitting on the front verandah steps.

"This book is Mother's… her recipes and notes on food and herbs. She kept a journal on medicinal plants. Each thing she learned from Adam, Aunt Mariah and the older plantation people is carefully written down. She was almost as thorough as Father."

"I wonder if our parents ever imagined that our survival might depend on the information they recorded?"

"Perhaps. I know that our grandfather started a journal because he read about Thomas Jefferson's habit of recording agricultural and horticultural information and Father grew up thinking that it was important. By reading what he wrote I can predict when to expect the first frost, about how much rain we will have, and when and how much produce certain plants will yield. We would have a hard time without these records."

"I doubt that they thought we'd be farmers instead of planters, small farmers... not so great for a southerner... and women farmers, at that."

"Ironic, but we're going to make it." Ellen was determined, stubborn, tenacious and positive. The land was sacred. The farming profession called for intelligent management. She searched for ways to eliminate waste and to use every natural resource to advantage. They were two women rebuilding their future, and they would succeed.

"Father used to list his plans. We need to do that, Pam. Small things, goals to work toward."

"I only want to talk about things that are possible. No dreams. Facing reality is what will save us."

"You have started fencing old fields so we have more pasture land. We have planted oats and corn and garden crops. We're not trying to grow cotton now. That's reality."

"It's a start. When there is money, we'll buy machinery... mowers and rakes. If we need skilled labor occasionally, we'll hire someone. No more families as tenants. That way we can dismiss anyone whose work doesn't please us."

"Good thinking, Pam. Father would be proud of you."

"You're the one he trained, Ellen, the son he never had."

With Adam to advise her, Ellen had watched each plant as it matured. The seeds were of more concern to them than the produce.

"Next year, Miss Ellen," Adam promised, "we have plenty of garden vegetables for sale. Need to start more peach trees and pecans, grow watermelons. Sell that produce in Columbia, too."

All across the south there would be short crops. The war had ended too late in April for returning soldiers to plant their fields. Few women had the skills or saw the necessity for the energetic resumption of farming. Fewer still were able to take the initiative.

Land, because it was the principal resource left to most southerners, would be exploited in every possible way. Cotton and large estates might continue to dominate agriculture, but Ellen was determined that, if they ever grew cotton again it would be planted and raised according to the best practices.

Whatever profits they might realize this year would go toward buying commercial fertilizer for next year. Peruvian guano was said to be the best. She was interested in getting some of the phosphate rock found near Charleston. They would try lespedeza for hay purposes and for its potential as a ground cover and soil builder. The cultivation of sumac, which grew wild in their woodsland, might be worth attempting. She read that dyers and tanners were using it.

Work and planning dominated Ellen's life. Neither she nor Pamela talked of private dreams. The long days of July and August lessened the necessity for constant work and supervision. Food, such as it was, had become plentiful, monotonous but plentiful. The intensive cultivation had paid off in all the fields. The sisters could take time now for themselves. There was business to be attended to in town.

Crops laid by, accompanied by Isaac and Randolph, the Heywards were on their way to town. The faint sparkle of early morning dew was still shining on the grass as they pulled out of the lane in the big farm wagon. Before first light Ellen had supervised the loading of produce from the gardens and fields. Summer had been bountiful at Oak Lane. In addition to fresh vegetables, they were carrying sun dried plums and figs, late summer grapes, elderberry wine and salted fish. Beef was still too precious for them to eat.

Of late there had been conflicting rumors about the Union troops. Passersby had little information as to how many soldiers were stationed in the capital or how long they were to remain. Though maintaining order appeared to be their only duty, there was no doubt that the army stood ready to enforce whatever new regulations were sent down from Washington.

Ellen and Pamela planned to arrange the sale of cattle to the military. They wanted to be paid in gold, but would barter for supplies from the army commissary, if necessary. They knew that southerners must take the loyalty oath in order to transact legal business or to send and receive mail. They were unsure whether the regulation also applied to women. Probably not.

Ellen intended to locate the post office as soon as she arrived. She had tried to discourage John Arledge, but that did not keep her from hoping that letters from him would be waiting for her.

For the past six months both sisters had worked from sunrise until dark, falling into bed each night exhausted. Ellen's tanned face was thinned to fine patrician angles. The soft curves and milk-white skin of the past were long gone. Her body, beneath the faded dress, was as trim and hardened as that of a muscular teen-ager. Sitting straight and confident on the wagon seat, she handled the mules with strong, work-roughened hands and the skill of a man.

Pamela, thin and alert, rode confidently on the stiff board seat beside her. A gun and a stout buggy whip lay between them. Although they were accompanied by a black male, the sisters could not be mistaken for two insecure, defenseless women.

As they neared the Goodwyn plantation they could see smoke rising from the chimneys. The place looked changed since they had last passed. Numerous former slaves were stirring in and about the house and yard. Ellen slowed to look.

"I believe the family has returned." Pam studied the signs, searching for someone she recognized.

"Should we pay our respects?" Ellen halted the mules.

"You keep right on driving, Miss Ellen," Isaac called from the rear of the wagon. "You don't want to stop there. A bunch of freedmen done took over the big house at the Goodwyn place. So many folks there now they living and cooking in every room. That place going to be a mess. Ain't none of that sorry crowd studying about going to work in the fields neither."

Ellen snapped the reins and urged the mules on. "If they don't work, they won't eat," she said grimly.

"I know that, and you know that, Miss Ellen," Isaac called from the back of the wagon, "but they don't know that. They say the land is theirs. Yankee soldiers done promised it to them. They don't much want no land, though. Land means you got to work. Only thing they want to own is a horse and buggy and a dog and a gun."

After bumping along for ten more miles the group approached the outskirts of town. Ellen handed Isaac the reins and directed him around the northeast side of the city. She wanted to avoid the burned-out center surrounding the main street. Rolling slowly down Laurel they marveled at the nearly perfect tranquillity which seemed to have returned to that part of Columbia.

Aunt Sophie's effusive greetings were hardly over before she launched into her confession. "I must tell you the worst before you discover it for yourself, girls. I have taken in a Yankee boarder. What's more, she is one of those schoolteachers sent down here by some kind of holier-than-thou Boston society."

"Then I'm sure she has the money to pay her bills, Aunt Sophie. That's wonderful!" Ellen's immediate support brightened the older woman's face.

"No telling what the neighbors are saying!"

"They are saying that you are a fine Christian lady working to help support yourself," assured Ellen. "We are pleased that you are coping so well with changed circumstances."

"How did she happen to find you, Aunt Sophie?" Pam was surreptitiously rubbing her aching backside and wondering if the neighbors might have something to say about that, too.

"The woman presented herself at my front door one day a few weeks ago. She said that a Yankee officer who knew the family suggested that she ask for lodging here. I refused her at first but, with typical New England persistence, she kept coming back."

"I think you were wise to accept her, Aunt Sophie. Stop worrying about it."

"She is Miss Elizabeth Rice, a refined young person... stiff, prim and a bit misguided, but very pleasant."

"Sounds like a perfect roomer to me."

"Also, she vowed she had looked everywhere and there is no proper place in town for a lady to stay. I know she's correct. So, after much soul searching, I decided to take her in."

"She's fortunate to have you and Miss Gilham to look after her," declared Pam. "Being able to live here must be a great comfort to her and to her family. I'd hate to be working in Boston, friendless and alone."

"She is very dedicated to her cause, comes in late each afternoon exhausted. She never says much about her work and retires early. I am surprised that a woman so young and attractive chose to accept a position this far from home."

"Missionary zeal, I imagine. We have been hearing about that," Ellen answered. "Or, she may have to work and support herself, the way we do."

"Who do you suppose sent her, Aunt Sophie?" asked Pam.

"Oh, I expect it was either Colonel Corley or Doctor Calahan," Ellen speculated.

"That's what I thought, too, dear, but she said it was a Major Arledge. Miss Rice assumes he's a close family friend. I haven't dared to admit that I can't even recall who he is."

"You remember him, Aunt Sophie. It has just slipped your mind. He knows Ellen. He was here when Sherman came through." Pam interceded to save Ellen from having to make explanations.

"Yes, I think I do remember the young man now. He is the Yankee officer who came here the night of the fire, isn't he, Ellen? So much happened that night. Miss Rice said he's a southerner, which I found hard to believe. He and her brother, also a Union officer, are good friends, West Point graduates."

"Perhaps they were classmates."

"They served together out west and they met again recently in North Carolina. When Miss Rice was on her way down here to accept her teaching position she stopped and visited with them."

"Then is Major Arledge still in North Carolina?" Ellen tried to make the inquiry sound politely disinterested.

"No, that was months ago. They were ordered to Washington when she left. This was just after the surrender. She seems impressed by the major. He is a handsome man, as I recall. Miss Rice said that he has requested assignment here. I believe she expects to see him before long. She sounds pleased by the prospect."

Pam noticed that Ellen was strangely silent.

"Oh, my goodness gracious!" Sophie finally had time to direct her attention to the loaded wagon. "Look what you have brought! How wonderful. Let's get these things in the house."

Isaac drove around back to unload the wagon contents. Hattie was told to assist. As soon as the wagon disappeared around the side of the house Sophie hurried the girls inside out of the late afternoon heat. Neither sister was surprised by their aunt's next remonstration.

"You girls have not been wearing a sun bonnet. You are ruining your skin. It's indecent to be burned the way you are. You will have to wear a hat in town, and a veil, too."

"Because we are tanned? Ellen said you wouldn't approve."

"It's more than that. Young ladies are wearing double veils and carrying parasols to further shield their faces now. Yankee soldiers and all kinds of riffraff are on the streets."

"Aunt Sophie, we are working women. When you manage a plantation, there's little time or money to devote to the trappings of ladylikeness." Pam addressed her aunt with adult firmness. "We like being strong and self-reliant... and tan."

"Such talk!" the old lady exclaimed. "I know Aunt Mariah must be beside herself."

"She spends a lot of time fuming about what's 'fittin' and what's not. Little we do is fitting anymore, I'm afraid." Ellen quickly dismissed the topic. "How is life in the city?"

"Things are improving. The Union army has guards posted and Mr. Richards says its safe to go out now. Women are beginning to walk about more freely. It is necessary to get out occasionally, but, girls, you must hold your skirts back when you pass soldiers on the street. Women are careful to make sure that they don't allow their clothing to touch those men."

"Our skirts no longer stand out enough to create a problem, Aunt Sophie," laughed Pam. "The dress material is limp and we have worn out all of our petticoats, or had to use them for better things. The stiff ones were too much trouble anyhow."

"Most of the time we wear Father's trousers." Ellen further scandalized her aunt. "Pants are better suited to our life."

"How shocking!" Sophie gasped. "I never know how much to believe of what you girls tell me."

"Since the women in town are so concerned about maintaining propriety, it sounds as if some semblance of normalcy is returning. Who is in charge of the troops?" Ellen asked the question realizing that, with Miss Rice living in the house, her aunt did not have to depend on hearsay for information.

"A Colonel Houghton of the 25th Ohio Volunteers is the Commandant. We never see him. I understand that the troops stationed here usually behave in a courteous manner. Townspeople absolutely avoid any kind of social contact with the military."

"I'm interested only in business contact, Aunt Sophie. Do you know the location of army headquarters?"

"The regiment is bivouacked behind the college campus and a number of the government offices are housed in college buildings. Surely you don't plan to go there!"

"I certainly do, first thing tomorrow morning. We're here to trade with people who have money."

"Northerners are the only people who can afford to buy anything." The old woman spoke with resignation. "The Federal garrison has brought money to the town. They are spending it on Freedman's Bureau programs and the Negroes are being paid salaries. You won't believe the prices of things! With goods to sell, you will be able to find customers easy enough."

"That sounds good to us," declared Pam. "We intend to keep our land and having Yankee money is the only way we can do it."

Sophie was stunned by the young girl's hard realism. "What about the mail service?" Ellen inquired. "Has that been restored?"

"I don't know. Miss Gilham and I don't have anyone writing to us. Our families live near. The trains used to carry the mail, but they're not running yet. The military, of course, uses the telegraph. So much faster. I'm not even sure where the post office is located now. Miss Rice might know."

Ellen's felt her heart sink. No mail. She changed the subject and began to relay the plantation news.

"I'm so proud of you girls," Sophie declared when Ellen finished her accounting. "We are the last of the Heywards. I wonder if the others would even recognize us now."

"We have improved. I was never good at being decorative," admitted Ellen, "nor was Pam. We three Heyward women are too strong to be conquered, Aunt Sophie. Think of it that way."

"I suppose so, dear, but it isn't easy."

"Never was, never will be," Pam stated matter of factly. "Now let's discuss what we hope to get accomplished tomorrow."

They were reciting a list of minimum needs when the front door closed sharply. The business-like staccato of sensible heels in good repair announced the arrival of the Yankee school-teacher.

"Miss Rice, do come into the parlor for a minute, please," Sophie called. "I'd like for you to meet my nieces. Miss Ellen Heyward and Miss Pamela Heyward, Miss Rice."

"How do you do. Your aunt has spoken fondly of you numerous times." The prim stranger smiled. "I am pleased to meet you."

The clipped New England speech grated harshly on ears long accustomed to hearing only the slow drawl and slurred consonants of South Carolinians. Elizabeth Rice was tall, trim and stylishly dressed. Her skin was pale, eyes light blue. Soft blonde hair was pulled into a neat bun high on her head.

"How are you?" Ellen responded with careful politeness, surprised to see that the teacher was quite young, probably still in her twenties. "Aunt Sophie has been telling us how delighted she is to have you living here with her."

"Thank you. I'm afraid I forced her to accept me, and I am most grateful that she finally did." The young woman turned to go. "I hope I shall have the pleasure of seeing you both again at dinner this evening." She walked out and disappeared up the stairs.

"She is attractive," admitted Pam grudgingly. "I had pictured her as more the horse-toothed old maid type."

"I'm truly sorry for her," said Sophie. "She has few friends. The other northern teachers are much older women."

"What about the military? Didn't the officers bring their families with them?"

"Some of the army wives are beginning to arrive, but I have heard they are a world unto themselves. I'm not sure she will have much in common with them."

"Since her brother is a Union officer, I thought perhaps she had grown up in that life."

"No, her father is a minister in Boston."

"She can make friends through the church then," Pam reasoned.

"That's hardly likely. Columbians refuse to recognize that the northerners even exist. No local person will have anything to do with her socially. The outsiders don't understand our bitterness, of course. People who have just arrived here don't know what life was like for us during the war."

"I can't imagine why not?" Ellen was surprised. "Surely they have heard about it."

"Most of the people coming here now had little contact with any of the fighting. People up north never felt the war like we did. They arrive here, overflowing with that missionary spirit you mentioned, but they are treated like the Yankee do-gooders and opportunists that they are."

"You are right. She must find life hard," Ellen agreed.

"I am sure Miss Rice had no idea what she was getting into when she volunteered to come south and teach freed slaves. She said she had never seen half a dozen black people in her life!"

Suppertime in the summer was always late. Sunset was after seven and the hot August air did not begin to cool until much later. Sitting on the front porch would have been pleasant, but hordes of voracious mosquitoes denied them that option.

When Miss Rice came down to the dining room the crisp daintiness of her frock reminded the Heywards how threadbare their clothing had become. Soft ruffles framed the young teacher's face. She was from another world. The others had not seen bright prints and delicate fabrics for four years.

"I do hope your summer is nearly over. I did not dream that the heat could be so oppressive." Miss Rice's precise diction was as stiff as the frock. "I seem to accomplish very little in the school room. I'm beginning to think it is a mistake to try to teach on warm days like today."

"I don't wish to disillusion you, Miss Rice," Pam replied blandly, "but July heat, as I'm sure you have noticed, is only surpassed by that of August. And September is the worst of all."

"Perhaps we are so weary of the heat, that by the time September comes, it just seems worse," temporized Ellen.

"Oh, how dreadful," the teacher moaned. "You mean it will be worse! I shall surely expire. I have felt so indolent myself I can hardly criticize my pupils for their indifference."

Miss Gilham bustled in to join the group. "Ellen and Pamela, I was in the kitchen and saw the fresh vegetables and fruit you brought. How can we ever thank you!"

They talked of life at Oak Lane. Elizabeth Rice listened intently, surprising Ellen with her apparent interest. "I do admire you ladies," the New Englander declared. "Being able to manage a plantation is truly remarkable. Southern women impress me as strong and capable, not at all as I had imagined."

"What had you imagined?" Pam sounded testy.

"I am sorry," she apologized, "I did not mean to sound rude. I meant I had pictured hoop skirts, magnolia trees and servants everywhere. The romanticized view of womanhood, I suppose."

"Romanticized is the correct word." Ellen's voice was even and pleasant. She was determined to show no animosity toward the young woman. "You should have known our mother.

She was on call for the sick day and night, was a pillar of the church, and served as a regular fountain of knowledge for the whole neighborhood. She also hosted social events and was always a devoted wife and mother. She taught, supervised and nursed our slaves far more than they ever served her."

"You loved and admired your mother very much," Miss Rice said with sincerity. Tact was another of her attributes.

Lest misunderstandings concerning southern womanhood become a sore point, Pamela interceded. "Please tell us about the work you are doing, Miss Rice."

"Are you sure that you are interested?" She seemed surprised by the invitation.

"Of course." Ellen wanted to learn more about the woman. "Mother maintained a plantation schoolroom - a rather unusual practice, and Pam and I often helped with the teaching. We know the kinds of difficulties you must be encountering."

The teacher hesitated a moment before beginning to speak. "I realize that I, and the others like me, must be the subject of much ridicule. We have undertaken a job that is monumental in scope and, under present conditions, virtually impossible. The black people, I have decided, are not yet ready for the progressive ideas of the societies which have sent us."

"As you become more accustomed to your pupils you will be able to adjust your program," Sophie suggested kindly.

"The confinement of a school room is as tedious to these grown-up children as it would be to three-year-olds. I have never felt more helpless than I did the first morning when I stood on the teacher's platform and faced that large crowd."

"You are teaching adults?" Pam sounded surprised.

"I'm afraid I hardly teach at all," she confessed dismally. "Emancipation to the Negroes appears to primarily mean two things. They are at liberty to roam around as they please, and they are free to be educated like white men. A first impulse for many has been to come to school. I certainly admire them for that."

"What do you find most discouraging?" Ellen was disarmed by the teacher's frankness.

"The curriculum we are expected to use is more suited to industrially proficient people than to a race just emerging from slavery," she answered quietly.

"What do you try to teach, Miss Rice?"

"When we organized the school the teachers drew lots. It fell my duty to instruct those applicants who have had no acquaintance with the alphabet. I teach beginners, and that has turned out to be almost everyone. I have a large school room. Four hundred seats have been crowded into it. When they are all filled we have to turn people away."

"Four hundred!" gasped Sophie. "An impossible situation!"

"What is worse, I have a constantly changing group. I'm ashamed to admit that most of my pupils never come back a second time."

"I had no idea your task is so difficult," sympathized Miss Gilham. "I am sorry we have not talked about your work before."

"I would like to try teaching only small children. Many of the women bring their babies with them. The students also bring their other possessions. Pigs are a favorite with the men."

"Pigs!" Pam exploded. "In your classroom?"

"Pigs," she nodded, attempting a feeble laugh. "You can't imagine how disruptive it is to have several people roaming around the room with a squealing pig tucked under each arm."

The young woman's dismay was apparent, as was her sincerity about her mission. "Much of the time I'm frightened," she admitted. "Some of the people don't understand what I am saying, and I can decipher very little of their speech."

Everyone waited for her to continue.

"I have an armed guard outside my door. I often have to call on him for help. Keeping order is very difficult."

"Perhaps, as more schools are set up and more teachers hired, conditions will improve," Sophie suggested.

"I hope so." Miss Rice rose from the table. "Thank you for telling me about your work and allowing me to talk about mine. Ladies, please excuse me. Before I came here I had imagined I would spend evenings marking papers. Instead, each night I work on a journal I'm keeping for the Society about my experiences. Tomorrow will be another busy day. Good night, everyone."

Ellen and Pam soon followed Miss Rice upstairs to a bedroom.

"At least this room is warmer than it was when we last slept here," Pam commented dryly as she yawned.

Ellen didn't reply. John Arledge had not been out of her thoughts since she arrived. She realized that she felt less sure than ever about him. The secret locket hung heavy on her heart.

Pam watched her sister with understanding.

"Why don't you ask her about him?"

"Who?"

"You know who."

"I can't."

"Why don't you write to him then?"

"Not unless he writes me first." She tried no subterfuge.

Pam could read Ellen's face and sensed distress.

"Anyhow, I have no idea where to write. I did everything I could to discourage his attentions. What almost was, ended. Perhaps it never really existed."

"You refused him because you feel responsible for me. I know you wouldn't let the fact that he is in the Union army cause you to close your mind to him. I won't let you sacrifice your chance for happiness for me. It has not ended. You aren't the kind of woman a man could easily forget. If you won't do anything about him, Ellen, then I shall," she declared.

"Pam, no!" Ellen was aghast. "If he has forgotten me this quickly, then his interest was only superficial."

"Why are you so sure he has forgotten you?"

"This Miss Rice. You heard what Aunt Sophie said."

"You have only Aunt Sophie's imagination that there may be something between them. You know better than to rely on that. He's a man who knows his mind. I'll simply ask that teacher lady what, if anything, is going on between them."

"You do that and I will strangle you."

Pam merely chuckled and pulled the bed covers up high around her ears. She was exhausted.

Ellen had difficulty falling asleep.

Ellen and Pamela, with Randolph in tow, were accomplishing little as they struggled to make their way through the business district. On every side workmen were vigorously applying hammer and trowel. The rebuilding of Columbia, however, was progressing at a snail's pace.

"This place will still be a sea of ruins for years to come." Pam's face reflected the dismay she was feeling.

"What's more distressing, the stores being rebuilt are hastily constructed shacks. Main Street looks like a raw frontier town. Less substantial, I imagine."

Ellen seldom expressed pessimism, never defeat. Today she was discouraged. During the morning they were able to make only limited inquiries. Nobody knew anything. Nobody was in charge. Nothing was near completion. Obviously little of their planned shopping was going to get done.

Traffic into the city from the Lexington side was limited. Since all bridges had been destroyed, the Congaree River could be crossed only by flatboat. The normal flow of produce and trade with the thrifty, industrious Lutheran farmers from the other side was no longer coming in regularly.

Heavy August rains continued to cause the river to be high. Many of the city streets were tangled mires of sticky red mud. No paving or hard surfacing of any kind existed. Each new rain turned the main street into one long clay bog. Only a few of the adjoining avenues, where the sand was deep, were any better for travel. Pedestrian progress down the street was difficult. Except at the front entrance of hotels, and at the steps of a few public buildings, there was no stone flagging nor any pedestrian sidewalks in the business district.

"Life for the city's residents is drastically changed," Mr. Richards had told them earlier, as they were starting up town. He was outside sweeping leaves from his front walk. "Formerly wealthy citizens now repair their own homes, open their own gates and drive their own carriages. Their once fine horses are spoiled by plow service."

Mr. Richards was correct. The refined dignity of yesteryear had vanished. The hustle and bustle was confusing. The temporary nature of everything Ellen and Pamela saw made them feel alien. Plantation life, though caught in poverty, was essentially the same as it had always been. Change there gnawed away gradually, creeping in almost unnoticed.

"Would you look at that!" Pam pointed to a hastily lettered sign advertising hay at four hundred dollars a ton. The price of potatoes was sixteen dollars a bushel; butter was listed at three dollars and fifty cents per pound.

"Even if we had money, those prices would be unaffordable."

Ellen took a firm hold on Pam's arm to thread through clusters of coarse looking people, mostly males, milling around. Much of the language they overheard was illiterate and crude. At the Freedman's Bureau, when they finally located it, a crowd of black people had gathered.

"This must be some of the school population Miss Rice was describing last night," whispered Pam.

"No doubt," Ellen agreed. "Inspired libertarians have been saying for years that the government must instruct the backward South. The time is now, it seems... and the freedmen are

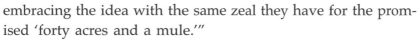

embracing the idea with the same zeal they have for the promised 'forty acres and a mule.'"

Inside the Bureau office few of the military were in evidence. The clerk nearest the door motioned to them as soon as they entered.

"Ladies, we do not hire teachers, nor set up schools. The Bureau merely aids established schools. If you are here about jobs you will have to contact the American Missionary Society or the Freedman's Union Commission."

"We're here to speak to someone about selling fresh farm produce."

Ellen was quickly informed that the Bureau office bought no foodstuff. He could not, or would not, direct her to an army purchasing agent. The clerk seemed to suspect that, despite her stated business, the two women were really there to apply for a job. Poverty-stricken gentry were easy to recognize. The southerners, he had been told, feared the kind of education that northern missionaries and teachers would provide. They all needed gainful employment to support their families, and saw the wisdom of applying to teach the freedmen themselves.

A call for South Carolinians to take up the work of the Freedman's Bureau had been issued and Confederate widows, their children, and even Confederate veterans themselves were applying to become teachers in the schools for Negroes.

Schools were proliferating. Through the sponsorship of Christian missionaries, Congregational churches and Bureau offices, a haphazard variety of poorly organized day schools, night schools, Sunday schools and industrial schools were beginning to spring up all across the state.

At dinner that evening Ellen, tired and dispirited, revealed her dismay at how little she and Pam were able to accomplish during their day in town.

"We need cash," she explained. "We had hopes of arranging to sell produce to stores and perhaps a few cattle to the military garrison. I talked with any number of people today, but I didn't accomplish a single thing. I suppose I will have to keep making inquiries."

"Were you able to locate an information office?" Aunt Sophie was distressed for them, but could offer no help.

"I'm not sure which office I should go to, nor how to make an appointment. Few of the old merchants are still in business. People don't communicate. The southerners can't help me, and I don't seem to be able to get past the clerk at the door in any of the government offices."

"Perhaps I can locate the information you need tomorrow," volunteered Miss Rice.

"Thank you," Ellen replied humbly. "I would be very grateful for your help."

"I am pleased to assist you." Her smile was genuine.

"I did learn that a few Florida cattle growers are shipping their beef to Cuba to be exchanged for coffee. We need coffee, too... and sugar and flour. We hope we can trade farm produce for that."

"I'd like to find yard goods for new dresses. We couldn't locate a dry goods store. Surely there must be some calico or homespun available." Pam looked beseechingly at Miss Rice.

"I know I can help with that," declared the teacher, shedding some of her stiff dignity. "I have been around and met most of the new shopkeepers. Some of them operate in homes away from the downtown area. The best store for ladies clothing I have found is owned by the wife of one of the mission workers. Please allow me help you shop. I can get the material for you at better prices."

The young teacher hesitated, drew a sharp breath, and looked from Ellen to Pamela. She was afraid that she might be guilty of some breach of etiquette. "Do forgive me!" she stammered. "My New England thriftiness and enthusiasm for sewing prompted me to intrude. I do not wish to be presumptuous. It's nice to talk with women my own age again, and I am merely offering you my assistance."

"You are kind. Thank you, but our shopping will depend entirely upon whether we make sales of our farm products," Ellen explained.

"Miss Rice is too modest to tell you girls about her talents," Sophie revealed. "She's a marvelous seamstress. She brought her own sewing machine with her, and she has the most divine pattern books up in her room that you ever saw."

"I have been admiring the lovely dresses you wear, Miss Rice," confessed Pamela.

"She allowed me to examine her books. Did you know that the hoop skirt has vanished... collapsed like a parasol!" Miss Gilham was hardly a hoop skirt wearer.

"They disappeared at our home some time ago." Pam's laugh was infectious. "You can't do much field work with those things popping up behind you each time you lean down over a freshly plowed furrow."

Ellen was pleased to see her sister conversing happily and showing interest in clothing again. Somehow she must get Pamela a few new frocks.

"Miss Rice designs and makes all of her garments, and she is much in demand as a consultant. Her acquaintances know that she has excellent taste. That's why she is so well informed about the shops and all of the best fashion buys in town," Sophie continued.

"I have to sew for myself," the teacher acknowledged, trying to cover her discomfort at the lavish praise. "A teacher's salary is quite modest. I must struggle to make it go as far as possible. I look for bargains and use what I believe you southerners call my Yankee ingenuity."

"We'll be pleased to accept your help when we are ready to make our purchases." Ellen welcomed the offer.

"In the meantime, may I suggest that for selling your cattle, the army is the best prospect." Again Miss Rice offered advice with characteristic knowledge and efficiency. "There are not many soldiers in Columbia yet. Fewer than eight thousand military men are on duty in the whole state at this time. Since this is the capital, more troops will come here soon. Your potential market is certain to improve."

"I had expected to find a larger garrison in the city." Ellen hoped that Miss Rice might have specific information to volunteer about returning military troops.

"Tomorrow I suggest you begin your inquiries at the College. I believe that is the best place to start. Look for the First Military District headquarters."

"Thank you. I will ask Isaac to go with us. He knows the campus well."

"You might try the office of the Freedman's Bureau again. I know you were discouraged today, but I'll get the name of someone there for you to talk with. I have heard that charitable organizations are feeding large numbers of former slaves daily. I don't know how much longer their funds will last, but they are having to buy farm produce from some place. You might prefer to deal with the army, though. Try their headquarters first."

Later, as they readied for bed Pam idly remarked, "I find it very hard not to like her."

"You are right," her sister agreed, without asking to whom she referred.

The next morning Isaac accompanied them on their rounds. He was so familiar with the College grounds that by noon Ellen had located and talked with several of the quartermaster procurement officers. Suitable terms were arranged. They agreed to buy two head of cattle per week and some garden produce, so long as their present Columbia garrison was maintained. Isaac found the storage areas. They were able to make tentative plans for regular delivery and payment.

Conversation at the dinner table that night was more relaxed and cheerful. Markets for Oak Lane's surplus for the next few months were set. One or both of the sisters would be coming to Columbia regularly.

"Miss Rice," Ellen announced as soon as the teacher reached home in late afternoon, "we were more successful today. Your suggestions were good. Pamela and I sincerely appreciate your help."

"I am so glad. I asked around at school and I have some other contacts for you that might prove worth while. Here's a list I made." She handed Ellen a neatly compiled roster of new merchants. Ellen recognized no names, titles, and store addresses from Columbia businesses of the past.

"You are very efficient, Miss Rice. We'll have to consider making you our city agent," Pam was looking over Ellen's shoulder at the precise and orderly rows of figures and script.

"I expect your remark was in humor, Miss Heyward, but it isn't a bad idea. I'd be pleased to be your factor. I see people who are your potential customers fairly often. They could place orders with me." Her manner was totally serious and businesslike.

"We will explore the idea," Ellen gravely replied. "We'd happily pay a commission to a good representative." She wondered if they would be branded scalawag collaborators if they did employ the teacher.

"Thank you, Miss Heyward, we can discuss that after you have completed some sales. I didn't offer my help to be paid." She paused and then soberly added, "I am a long way from my family. Your aunt has kindly allowed me to live in her home. I am indebted to her for that."

"She told us when we arrived that you have become a very welcome addition to the household," Ellen assured her.

"I'm aware that southerners are not quick to accept outsiders nor to dispense with formality, but it would make me happy if all of you would please call me Elizabeth."

"It's nice to have your permission," Ellen hastily replied, "and Pamela and I hope that you will refer to us by our given names, also."

Elizabeth smiled gently. "Thank you. After supper I'd like to bring my pattern books down and engage in some girl talk, please. I have missed my sisters."

"Tell us," Pam innocently asked, "how it was that you knew about Aunt Sophie."

"It's a rather long and involved story."

"We would love to hear it," Pam insisted.

"Very well." She folded he hands precisely and began. "As the recent hostilities were ending, we had news that my brother had been slightly wounded and was in Greensboro, North Carolina. By then I had decided to accept the teaching position in Columbia, so I was able to stop and visit him on the way down. A close friend of his, a man with whom he had served in the Western Campaign, Major John Arledge, happened to be there."

Ellen's heart stilled.

"Did you know the major previously?" Pam inquired.

"No, but I felt as though I did. My brother had mentioned him often in letters. He had known John at West Point. They were happy to see each other again. The war was over, both had dangerous assignments and both of them had survived. The whole story sounds almost like a novel."

"Please continue," Pam urged.

"Major Arledge is a very interesting and charming man. He is well educated, handsome, gallant and unmarried. The few days I was in Greensboro he kindly served as my escort."

"Sounds like the answer to a maiden's prayers." Pam continued to probe.

Ellen speared Pamela with an intense glare.

"I might easily have thought so," Elizabeth admitted.

"Why do you say you might have thought so?"

"Bob, my brother, has known John for ten years or more and greatly admires him. Right away he warned me not to become too interested in the major. The man is one of those courtly Virginians that women find most attractive wherever he goes. Bob declares women always chase after him. He might have exaggerated a bit, but if you met Major Arledge you would know that some of what Bob says is probably true."

"I can easily believe it," Pam nodded in solemn accord, "I have met him."

"Then you know him, too?"

"Not really, Elizabeth, he was conducting a military investigation and I had to answer some of his questions."

"He is a legal officer, and thought to be a confirmed bachelor, completely impervious to the charms of most women. Now, Bob thinks, the gentleman has fallen in love."

"Oh, something that has happened recently?" Pam's voice was filled with innocent curiosity.

"Bob thinks so. He said that in all the years he has known John, the man has never been this seriously interested in anyone before. He met her in the South. She evidently spurned him."

"And how is he taking that?"

"Not well, Bob says. He declared that neither the Indian wars nor the secession of Virginia hit the man so hard. John Arledge is not the kind to give up easily. Where do you suppose there is a female so foolish as to send a man like that away!"

"I can't imagine," Pam wondered dramatically.

"It does sound romantic," Miss Gilham ventured.

"Bob insists he knows the trouble. The woman must be some stiff-necked southern aristocrat, they are his words not mine, that is looking down her nose at John because he is a Union officer. He thinks it would serve her right if John chose to forget her. I know he won't, though. He is the one-woman kind we read about and dream of… and rarely find."

"Oh, Miss Gilham, you are right. This does sound romantic!" Pam gushed, clearly enjoying the discussion. "And so what happened with you two?"

"Not anything, Pamela. Sherman's column was ordered to Washington, Bob was leaving with them and I came on to Columbia. I am not foolish enough to let girlish dreams ruin a friendship. Major Arledge did say that he will be stationed in South Carolina, and that he might see me again soon."

Throughout the interrogation Ellen had kept her eyes averted, studying her plate and saying nothing. Pam, however, looked amused and extremely pleased with herself.

"Ellen," Sophie asked, "wasn't he the officer that walked us to Mary Whilden's house the night of the fire?"

"Yes, Aunt Sophie. That's how he happened to know you and where to send Elizabeth to find a room. Now," she reminded them, "it's getting late. Let's look at the pattern books. Pam and I will have to go home tomorrow."

"Oh, no, dear, I was hoping you all could stay longer."

"Not this time, Aunt Sophie, but we'll be coming back soon. Our first cattle delivery is to be in two weeks."

"With so many homeless blacks about, it's not wise for us to be away from Oak Lane very long. We saw trespassers at the Goodwyn place. Aunt Mariah can probably defend the house better than we can, but we still worry." Pamela rose, ready to end their discussion. A night's rest was needed to prepare for the journey home tomorrow.

Seventeen

September colors were beginning to stain the parching countryside. Sumac and dogwood leaves blazed red. Goldenrod and ragweed swayed lazily as the hot sun continued to beat down. Day-to-day life at the plantation rarely changed. After Ellen and Pamela returned from Columbia they began preparations for delivery of their first load of cattle to the Federal garrison.

A loading chute had to be built. For two days John and Isaac hauled dirt to make an earthen ramp beside the pasture fence. Soil was piled in a gradual grade four feet wide to the height of the wagon bed. They fenced the ramp with sturdy cedar posts set close together and made gates to control each end.

Pamela supervised as the men doubled-lined the bottom of the farm wagon to make the flooring strong enough to hold the weight of the cattle. Stout side rails were attached to the main frame and makeshift stanchions added to the middle of the wagon to help steady the animals during the ride to market.

On the day of departure Ellen was up early loading the front of the wagon with freshly gathered baskets of yams, greens, field peas and late sweet corn. Pam drove the wagon to the pasture and backed up to the high end of the loading ramp. Benjamin led two steers single file up the chute and into the back. The animals were securely penned in. The sisters, accompanied by Isaac, were ready to begin their journey.

"Aunt Mariah, we know to be careful. We will deliver the goods today, spend the night with Aunt Sophie and buy supplies tomorrow morning. We will be home by late afternoon."

"I ought to be going along with you. Girls ain't got no business out by theyself." The old lady would not be comforted.

"We're not by ourselves, Aunt Mariah," Pam assured her. "You know Isaac will be with us every minute."

The ride to town was uneventful. Upon arrival they went directly to the commissary holding area on the College campus to unload. The army cooks, pleased with the cattle, agreed to purchase part of their produce. The Heywards were given vouchers and directed to the quartermaster's office for payment. The gold dollars handed them were the first they had seen in years. Ellen held them out in her open hand so Pam could examine them, too.

"The sight of hard currency that belongs to us makes all that work over the past year seem worthwhile." Pamela listened to the clink of the gold pieces dropping into Ellen's reticule.

"Father paid sixty Confederate paper dollars each for the last gold dollars we had," she reminded her sister.

"Let's not spend these. We'll try barter instead."

"No, we should buy what we need now." Ellen took a deep breath and drew up her shoulders proudly. "We know how to earn money and we can look after ourselves in the future."

"Let's find the post office next," Pam suggested. They were both hoping for mail.

Outside, the campus was a beehive of activity. Military authorities were housed in the east wing of Rutledge Building, and the post office, they were told, was located in the west wing. Legare and Pinckney were filled with refugees. The center section of DeSaussure had been converted into a military prison.

Their inquiry at the post office proved futile. No mail could be found for either of the sisters, nor for any of the ladies residing at Laurel Street. The look of disappointment apparent on their faces, prompted the clerk to suggest that Ellen and Pamela use the telegraph service in the future.

"You cannot depend on the postal service these days, ladies. There are no railroads in operation within thirty miles of Columbia. Consequently, we receive very little mail."

The sisters completed their business at the college and by late afternoon arrived at Laurel Street. Aunt Sophie, delighted to see them again, bubbled with small talk.

"It's nice that you girls are here again so soon. I hope visits every two weeks will become a regular pattern." Sophie didn't need, nor did she allow, time for responses between her remarks.

"You look too thin and you're burned black by the sun. I do hate to see Henry's daughters arrive here mounted on a common wagon seat... so undignified for ladies. Please take my buggy home with you this time. It has not been out of the carriage house since the army took the horse."

"Please slow down, Aunt Sophie," urged Ellen. "We are well. We have made a delivery to the garrison at the College. We also made inquiries at the post office and there was no mail for any of us. We'd like to spend the night with you and we have brought you some sweet potatoes and a jar of honey."

"Something sweet. How marvelous!"

"Naomi has several bee hives now. There should be more. Aunt Mariah said to tell you that soon the sugar cane will be processed we'll have syrup and brown sugar. How is everybody?"

"Especially Miss Rice?" inquired Pam. "We were paid today. We have money and I'm ready to consider new dresses."

"I am delighted to hear about your interest in clothing, Pamela, and about the money, of course. It's time to get you looking more like a young lady! We'll talk about it after supper."

Some of her sister's intense interest in new clothing, Ellen suspected, was because she wanted to look pretty when Jim Milton returned from the Lowcountry.

"How are you managing, Aunt Sophie?" Ellen inquired.

"Life here is slow. Quite dull really, after the work committees and the wartime gaiety. Columbia was criticized by the rest of the state for all of the parties we had, but they were for the war effort. We were so lively at first... concerts, picnics, balls... marvelous soirees and the great Bazaar! Our merriment may have caused ill will, but those occasions were excellent fund-raisers and they kept up morale."

"I know you miss the activity," Pam tried to sympathize.

"Staying busy constantly was the only way we could manage to get through those dark days," Sophie confided.

"Aren't you and the ladies working now?"

"I do a bit of volunteer work occasionally at the Board of Relief. There are still homeless refugees in the city. Many Columbians are without adequate food, too. The distribution of meat by the citizens group after the big fire only lasted three months."

"How do city people manage to get the food they need?"

"Other towns around the state continue to be very generous with their provisions. We were sent wagonloads of food by the people of Georgia, and they were hit almost as hard as we were."

"How are the homeless blacks surviving?"

"I hear that the Freedman's Bureau and the army both work to relieve physical distress. They give rations to hundreds of people, and many of them white, I understand. Of course my friends would rather starve than accept Yankees' help."

They moved to the front porch.

Isaac had long since unhitched the mules and fed them.

"Things are getting better in the neighborhood," Sophie continued. "I see signs of that every day."

"Have your friends who weren't burned out started to come back yet? And what about the others?"

"The Whildens are back in town, Ellen. I hope you'll have time to see Mary. She is her same wonderfully positive self."

"You were glad to welcome Mary back, I'm sure."

"Get her to tell you about a recent party she attended. They called it a 'calico ball.' Only one fiddle to dance to, rather than an orchestra and for refreshment the hostess served cold water, but they were determined to be gay for the returning soldiers."

Ellen could think of nothing to add but the usual cliché, "The spirit is what counts, Aunt Sophie."

"We keep telling each other that, dear. We are starting to plan ladies' historic societies now. We intend to record and preserve accounts of all the heroic deeds of our brave men."

"Sounds like a worthy project."

"The more we talk, the more ambitious we become. We want to gather our dead for proper burial and decorate the graves. We plan to eventually raise money for monuments to mark battle sites and to erect statues to honor the men."

"That may take a while, Aunt Sophie." Pam felt that the past was past.

"Yes, dear, but over the next few years that work is going to be our major patriotic undertaking. We are determined to preserve our heritage. It's a project for our children and grandchildren to carry on forever... a major, major war effort. We are thinking of calling our organization the Daughters of the Confederacy. It will be important all across the south."

"I am sure it will be," affirmed Ellen.

"Oh, my yes! Women throughout the Confederacy are beginning to unite. We are unshaken in our patriotism. We will honor the sacrifice of our dead. You girls know how strong the will of southern women can be. We plan to begin celebrating Confederate Memorial Day next year."

Ellen was aware of the strength of southern women. She and Pam personified it daily. The energy of all the women was sorely needed for the rebuilding the south must undertake. Mourning, honoring heroism and cherishing the past was an important part of the healing process. Many women had suffered major losses. Defeat was a sobering experience.

"You will be successful," she assured her aunt, "and we want to help. Let us know which committees need us."

At supper, with most of her news related, Sophie was ready to hear more from Ellen and Pamela.

"We loaded and left at dawn this morning." Ellen explained everything in detail. As mundane as the facts were, they were interesting news to their aunt. "The Goodwyns appear not to have returned yet."

She turned to look directly at Elizabeth. "They are our nearest neighbors. At Millwood life goes on. Somehow the Hamptons are coping with the loss of the big house."

"We stopped once to rest the mules and water the cattle," Pam took up the recital, "and experienced no trouble. The worst part of the whole trip," she ruefully admitted, "was parting with the steers, after we got them here. We had raised them so carefully."

"Benjamin's face was a woeful picture this morning when he told them good-bye." Ellen, too, wore a wistful expression.

"I'll remember those steers with thanksgiving every time I wear the new frock I hope to get," declared Pam, struggling to put a weak smile on her face.

"Please tell me the fabrics and colors you like and I will look in the shops to see what's available," Elizabeth offered.

"That's going to be a major decision requiring extensive time and thought," laughed Pamela. "Let's begin after supper with the pattern books."

"Tell us how your work has been progressing, Elizabeth. Are your classes still as large as ever?" asked Ellen.

"No, they are smaller now. Thus far I have had more success with music than any other class. I've been able to teach several hymns. My pupils can't read, but many of them sing beautifully and they have strong religious backgrounds."

"That reminds me," interrupted Sophie, "Ellen, I didn't tell you that the slaves have withdrawn from our churches. The balconies were practically empty last Sunday."

"Are they going to stop attending church? That is hard to believe. Aunt Mariah would certainly disapprove."

"There are plans to start black churches." Elizabeth was always well informed. "They are to open an African Methodist church soon, I hear. Societies like the one I work for are supporting sixty teachers. We instruct, or at least try to instruct, over thirty-five hundred pupils. Churches are next on our agenda."

Dark circles ringed the young teacher's eyes. Daily struggle with an almost impossible task was telling on her.

"Perhaps you'll be able to get an aide."

"The Society has set eighty schools as our goal. We are anxious to receive white children, too, provided they are willing to associate with colored pupils. Thus far none are forthcoming."

No one would tell the Boston native that there was little likelihood of white pupils attending the schools of the freedmen.

"When families of the troopers start to arrive, perhaps their children will be enrolled in the freedmen's schools," Miss Gilham offered.

"All in all," Miss Rice continued, looking dejected, "I feel like a failure. I reach a very small number of the colored population who are actually of school age. Only five or six per cent of my pupils are children. Interest in acquiring an education seems to have waned."

"That will change with improved classroom conditions." Pam felt sympathetic toward the young teacher. "Ellen teaches in our kitchen at night. Her pupils, she has two, are doing well."

"I fear that the fatiguing exercises necessary for academic progress are too exacting."

Ellen wondered if Elizabeth attempted to instruct in the same stilted style in which she regularly conversed.

"Have you been sending your reports back to Boston? Your experiences may convince the authorities to accept your recommendation for more manageable age groups," suggested Ellen.

"I do hope so. I send reports and continue to keep my journal. I think it would be helpful if they chose to have it published. My observations should be informative to others."

Conversation moved to downtown growth, new store openings and ultimately to clothing and what materials and notions might be available. The hour grew late as the women continued to talk.

"We really must retire," Pam finally said. "Elizabeth has an idea of what material we need for our new dresses, and I can hardly stay awake. Ellen and I have to go home in the morning. Gathering the fall crops is a busy time on the plantation."

"There will be regular visits," Ellen explained over Sophie's plea for them to stay longer, "now that we have made one successful delivery. Our future trips will be easier."

The next week at Oak Lane moved on magic feet. There was produce to be gathered and prepared. The prospect of regular trips to Columbia spread optimism throughout the plantation. Pam, returning at sundown from the lower pasture, heard her name being shouted. She spotted a lone horseman galloping down the live oak avenue toward the big house. She immediately recognized the familiar figure.

"Jim," she yelled, running forward to meet him.

He jumped from the horse, caught her to him and swung her from the ground. "I'm so glad to see you." His voice was husky. "I have thought of you constantly." He searched her face as he set her back on her feet.

She smiled, this time not trying to avoid his eyes.

A positive sign. He reached for her hand and together they walked toward the front of the house.

Randolph came to take the horse's reins.

"This sure a fine mount, Mr. Jim."

"Not very, Randolph, but keep telling him that he is. Maybe he will start to believe it and act that way. He has been eating regularly, though, and that makes a difference." He turned back to Pam. "How is everyone?"

"I'll go get Ellen." Pam pulled away shyly, self-conscious about her disheveled, straight-from-the-field appearance. "She will want to hear all you have to say. And we can share our news together."

Ellen had heard their voices.

"Jim!" she exclaimed "You look well." Though she kissed him warmly, Pam had been more reticent.

Milton's slim frame was beginning to fill out. The sickly pallor had completely disappeared.

"Tell us about your family and things in Beaufort district?"

"Everything at home was about as we had pictured. Thomas, my oldest brother, returned a few days before I arrived. Tom is only thirty, but he looks like an old man. He has been attached to the Army of Northern Virginia. He was at Gettysburg, a bad time then and after for the men."

"I know. We were still getting occasional newspapers at that time. Stonewall Jackson was killed, Vicksburg fell and Lee suffered a defeat, all within a three months period."

"Many of Tom's men had four years of almost constant fighting. The worst thing for them was hearing of Sherman's exploits in South Carolina. He said it was especially demoralizing for them to have to worry about the safety of their homes and families while they fought so far away in Virginia."

"How is Tom now?" Ellen's heart filled with compassion.

"Hardly the brother I remember."

"Then neither are you," she reminded him.

"That's what he said." He smiled broadly. "Tom seemed surprised to see that his little brother was just another thin, ragged veteran returning home. He served longer than I did, and his experiences were much harder, of course. He teased me unmercifully when I told him about Pam."

"What about your other brother?"

"Rutledge. He was at home. We can hardly believe that all three of us survived, a rare thing. He's not well. He lost an arm two years ago. He was in a Yankee prison for a long time, one of the last of the prisoners exchanged. He wasn't able to go back to active duty, so he reached home first. I found both of them at Rut's wife's plantation. They were waiting for me. Our place was taken at the beginning of the war."

"I'm so happy your family could be reunited," whispered Pam.

"Martha, Rut's wife, tried to keep our plantation going at first. We lived in a rather isolated section out on St. Helena Island. There was no way to ship our cotton so she stored it."

"I hope it didn't all fall into Yankee hands."

"No, that's another miracle. When she heard that the Union navy had sailed into Port Royal and that all the landowners had to evacuate, Martha had the cotton moved to her father's plantation further inland. No fighting took place near her home.

She continued to plant throughout the war years. Our cotton is still there, nearly seven hundred beautiful bales of long staple sea island cotton, the most valuable kind, and most of it is undamaged."

"Unbelievable! Can you all keep it? Will you be able to sell it?"

"We think so. We're having to move carefully. The Federal authorities may think of some way to claim it, or to levy more taxes, if they realize how much we have."

"What's happening on the islands now?"

"When the landowners had to flee, nearly two hundred plantations were abandoned. That left ten thousand slaves on their own. The Federal authorities sent what they called labor superintendents down there in '62. They tried to put the slaves to work producing cotton... which the north badly needed."

"How did that work out?" Ellen was filled with questions.

"We don't know. The federal government also sent overseers. We heard that Quakers in Philadelphia started schools for the black people, too, but that was at the beginning of the war. I don't know if they are still operating."

"They have opened freedmen's schools in Columbia. Aunt Sophie has a teacher from Boston living with her, a paying guest." Knowing how her aunt felt, Pam thought she had better volunteer the information early on.

"Good for Aunt Sophie! That's an excellent way to earn money and keep up with what the authorities are doing at the same time." Jim was not in the least disturbed by Pam's revelation.

"How did things stand when you left home? We want to hear the rest of your story," Ellen prompted.

"Nobody knows what will happen next. This year, in January, Sherman's Field Order Number Fifteen was issued. The sea islands and the bordering rice plantations up to thirty miles inland are to be set aside for the use of the Negroes who were following his army. If that order is enforced it may include our land."

"There were hundreds of slaves following the troops when he left Columbia." Ellen thought again of that bleak February morning. "I don't know how he could allow all of those people to tag along behind him all the way to Washington."

"I suppose you have heard that landowners in the south owe back taxes to the federal government since 1861. General Rufus Saxon has taken possession of most of the island land. He divided it up among forty thousand blacks. Planting started this spring. There are a few white people left in Beaufort, but all southerners are prohibited from going on the island preserve."

"Then you have no way to find out what has happened to your home. Surely that order won't remain in force with all hostility ended!" Ellen had paled at the thought of losing family land.

"Tom and Rut heard that President Johnson is providing some means for property to be restored to landowners, if they can show land titles and proof they have been pardoned."

"I am pleased to hear he is that reasonable."

"The catch is, former owners will have to pay the squatters for 'improvements' which have been made. Even if we do redeem the plantation, we won't have blacks to work it. There's talk of trying to induce immigrants from Europe to come here to help solve labor problems next year."

"European refugees will never come south. Father tried years ago to interest some in settling here. They have heard too many rumors about ill-health and the discomforts of life in a near-tropical climate."

"You are probably right, as usual."

"Besides, newcomers tend to go where relatives and friends have already migrated. The north never needed slaves. They had access to plenty of cheap white labor." Ellen tried to speak without showing bitterness.

"What about labor contracts with former slaves? We plan to offer them to our best people. Father never bought slaves. Ours were inherited from our grandfather and from his. Some of them have been in the family for two or three generations."

Pam listened as Jim talked. The situation at Oak Lane might be better than the Milton family's, despite the large cache of cotton Martha had saved.

"Rut and Martha are staying on at her family place. She's an only child and her father is getting old. Tom is thinking of going to Beaufort to try to make something of Mother's property in town. The house there was being used as a Yankee hospital, but it is supposed be vacated soon."

"The town of Beaufort is intact?"

"Only because it was occupied from the very beginning. Tom plans to start a business. He hopes the money we'll get from the cotton will be enough to set up a store. Hardware and building supplies are what he is considering. He should be able to make a go of it. Tom is a quiet level-headed man. He believes that anyone who is not too proud or too stubborn will be able to succeed."

"It sounds as if he's ready to start over."

"He's a wonderful big brother, a fine man. I know how hard all of this has been for him. He deserves a chance for happiness. I wish he could meet someone like you, Ellen."

"Thank you." She accepted the compliment graciously, never doubting Jim's sincerity.

"I told the family I have become interested in cattle raising, and that I hope to make a home here."

Pam drew a sudden deep breath.

"They approved and wished me luck." He looked at Pamela and smiled. "Tom insisted that our cotton money must be divided into four shares. Martha was included since she saved the original cotton and grew more. Tom will pay us for our share of the Beaufort town property."

He paused and looked from one sister to the other.

"And so, to make a long story short, I told my brothers that I was coming back here and camp on the Heyward doorstep until Pamela decides to marry me. And," he said with finality, "here I am. I knew whether you were glad to see me or not, you'd make my new horse and my two strong arms welcome."

"You, and most especially the horse, are very welcome, sir." Ellen did not look at her sister. "Now we can finally use Aunt Sophie's buggy. Pam remodeled the farm wagon to haul cattle. Aunt Mariah says we disgrace her every time we drive around in it."

Ellen, conscious that Pam and Jim needed some private time together, excused herself to see about the evening meal.

Jim had waited patiently to be alone with Pamela.

"Pam, we need to talk. You know I am in love with you."

"I... is this where the girl says 'this is so sudden'?"

Dismay was written on his face. "I practiced a lot of pretty speeches on the way here and I forgot to use them."

"It's just as well. I wouldn't know how to handle them."

He had not heard her gay laugh before.

"Please, show respect. I prepared some very persuasive words."

He cleared his throat.

"In the aftermath of war, when everything is a struggle, convention and custom are often ignored. I know that young ladies reared as you and Ellen were are conscious of propriety."

"Don't forget Aunt Mariah." Pam grinned up at him impishly.

"Most especially Aunt Mariah. Aunt Sophie, too, I'm sure."

"You can depend on it. So what is it we are talking about?"

"About being realistic. I have come back to Oak Lane, as I told you I would, and I'd like to stay."

Pam sighed. While she was unsure where the discussion was headed, his return to Oak Lane was a safe beginning.

"You know Ellen and I both hoped you would return."

"I am trying to say that I want to remain here, to work here, to invest in the cattle and land here, to make my home here, and to wait here in hope that you will learn to love me."

"You can stay here, Jim, but for investment, you need to talk with Ellen. That's a decision we will have to make together."

"There's no other plantation near where I can stay. We both know that an extended visit with young ladies, in the absence of their parents, is improper."

"You stayed here before."

"I was a convalescing soldier and that was different. Now I'm a suitor. You do not have a father here to protect you. Unmarried girls do not allow men to move in with them."

"I believe you know that it's late to be so formal about protecting my honor," she said stiffly.

"Pam, please. You and Ellen are alone. I am in love with you. You need someone to look after you and help with the work. I want you to agree to marry me now."

She looked frightened. "I... you promised. I'm not ready."

"I intend to honor my promise. You and I can be married and our relationship need not change until you say you want it to. I know how you feel and I respect your wishes. I realize that I could lose you by trying to rush. I will not take that chance."

"I haven't thought about marriage yet, Jim," she replied hesitantly. "Things are moving too fast. Ellen needs time to make decisions about her life. I think she is in love."

"Do you know with whom?"

"I think so."

"Does she know if he will be returning?"

"She's not sure." Pam was careful to reveal nothing about the identity of the man.

"Will she marry him if he does come back?"

"I don't know, and I don't think she knows either. She will be concerned about my future, as I am about hers. We need time."

"I think you should agree to marry me now. I want you, Pamela, as any normal man wants the woman he loves, but I will wait, a whole lifetime, if necessary, for you to come to me willingly. Won't you consider my proposal?"

"I wonder," she said, her voice catching with tears, "what I did to deserve a wonderful man like you."

"You haven't answered my question. Can you give me one good reason why we can't be married right away?"

"I surely can," she laughed shakily. "I don't have a decent dress to my name. I absolutely refuse to be married in Father's old trousers."

"That can be easily solved," he laughed happily. "I hear new stores are opening every day in Columbia. I am sure we can find dressmakers there anxious to sew for two ladies as lovely as the Heyward sisters. We'll go tomorrow, purchase the material, engage a seamstress, give her your measurements and press for immediate delivery."

"Jim, we don't have money to spend on clothing yet."

"I'm ready to start my herd. I plan to buy four purebred heifers and a bull of the Oak Lane strain right away. I'll pay exactly what your father paid for his original stock, one hundred dollars a head. You and Ellen will have the money for shopping."

"We can't accept money from you. In the first place, cattle aren't selling for that much now. Think of the seed, fertilizer, plow points, nails and such that could be bought with that much money. If we are to be married, what is mine will be yours, you know that. You won't have to buy cattle from us."

"I am taking that as a 'yes'. Let's talk with Ellen. It's mid-September. If she agrees, we will plan an October wedding."

"October!"

"October is a beautiful month, although I really prefer September." He leaned down softly kissing the top of her head.

"October! That's less than three weeks away."

"I know. How will I ever be able to wait that long!" he whispered in mock seriousness.

"Give me time to think about it."

"Oh, I will, and while you are thinking, get ready to go to Columbia. I'll take you and Ellen to your aunt's. Stay there a week or two. You will have time to get the shopping, sewing and planning done. I can stay here without compromising you two. Then I shall expect to pick up my future bride, her trousseau and the maid of honor at the end of that period."

"Jim, we can't be gone that long," Pam protested feebly.

"You won't need to worry about the plantation because I'll be here. I will have to work every minute to keep my mind off you, anyhow. A few pretty dresses and a long holiday will be good for Ellen. She's much too thin and serious."

"I know. While we're in town she can visit all of the new stores to buy supplies and see what other kinds of produce we can market. She will like that."

"You can leave me instructions. I will make the next cattle delivery. I'll come by to see how plans are progressing and take back the supplies she has bought for the plantation."

After supper Jim, Pamela and Ellen sat on the verandah lingering over contented conversation. Jim asked again to make sure that he had Ellen's approval.

"Pam is her own woman, Jim. She makes her decisions," she told him firmly. "I approve of you, but remember I'm not the one thinking of marrying you."

Pam shyly told her the tentative plans they had made. The quiet radiance of her sister's face delighted Ellen. Happiness was shining through. At last the healing process was beginning. James Milton was the perfect young man for Pamela.

"Aunt Sophie will love planning a wedding. When we were there last she was complaining about how dull life had become. Elizabeth Rice and Miss Gilham will help with the sewing."

"Elizabeth? Is she another relative?"

"Hardly! You don't mean you have forgotten?" Pam frowned. "Some husband you'll make! She is Aunt Sophie's prim, stylish Yankee roomer. I'm sure you will like her. She has offered to be our fashion consultant."

"A Yankee teacher? I doubt I will like her. And you have accepted!"

"Accepted! We were overjoyed," Pam assured him. "Wait until you meet her."

"First we need to search to see what material we have that can be reused," Ellen cautioned. "We can't afford to make many purchases. It wouldn't be seemly to do so, even if we could."

"This is starting to sound wonderful." Pam was losing the look of stoic endurance she had worn for six months. "We'll go to Columbia this week to enlist the help of Aunt Sophie."

Eighteen

Two days later, bouncing excitedly on the seat of the farm wagon half-filled with produce, Ellen, Pam and Jim set out for Columbia. Although this was not a regular delivery day, Ellen would not forego an opportunity to market vegetables.

"Anything we can't sell," she reminded them, "Aunt Sophie or her neighbors will be able to use."

"I imagine they all have gardens. How can they manage otherwise?" Pam was learning to be as frugal as her sister.

Randolph sat on the tail gate, smiling and swinging his feet. He loved the high adventure of going to town and was fortunate that his primary duty was to accompany the Heyward women wherever they went. Anymore they were doing interesting things. They went to town so often the distance seemed short.

As they were approaching the heart of the city, Ellen could see additional signs of returning life since their last visit. "They have erected more ugly structures of that raw fresh-sawn lumber."

"I count as many as twenty stores now open for business." Jim stood up as he slowly piloted the wagon down Main Street. He was having to exercise great care. Though much of the debris had been cleared, evidence of the earlier carnage still remained.

A confusing assortment of wagons, buggies and pedestrians moved about, slowing their progress. The easily recognized blue uniforms of Union soldiers flashed often among the crowd.

Jim was wearing gray and butternut parts of his old uniform. He had removed the Confederate buttons and braid, as Federal pardon regulations required. He, like all Confederate veterans, had to continue to wear his uniform. No other clothing was available, nor could most of them afford anything else.

The few Rebel soldiers they saw on the street held their thin bodies proudly erect. No longer listless and shuffling, the returnees were accepting the defeat with less animosity than most civilians in the south, particularly the women.

Jim slowed the wagon as they passed a small cluster of idle Negroes gathered on a street corner. A few were laughing and gesturing boisterously, while a flashily dressed carpetbagger regaled them with a wondrous tale.

"I imagine the people in that group are hearing how easy it is to get an instant education." Ellen hated the cruel delusion and sly entrapments in which many innocents were easily caught.

"Or to own forty acres and a mule in the Lowcountry." Jim's voice sounded bitter. He maneuvered the length of Richardson Street, now usually referred to as Main, successfully and turned right on Laurel.

The street was quiet. On either side large granite carriage blocks lined the sedate residential avenue, most of the blocks now marking spots where houses once stood. The muted golds of September were beginning to color those trees that had survived the winter. No carriages stirred. No pedestrians darted about. Far down the street the pointed gables of the tall brick house near the end of the third block beckoned them.

Sophie was overjoyed when she opened the front door to them.

"Girls, what a wonderful surprise! And Lieutenant Milton! I hope you are fully recovered from your wound." She watched from the porch as Jim helped Pamela and Ellen from the wagon.

"Yes, mam," he shouted to her, "not only have I recovered, but you are looking at a deliriously happy man."

"Wonderful! Do tell me what has happened. I need to hear good news."

"I persuaded your beautiful niece to accept my proposal."

"Marriage? A wedding in the family! That really is news. I am so happy for you and... ," she looked expectantly from Ellen to Pam, and then back to Ellen again.

"Aunt Sophie, don't you dare be looking at me," Ellen protested with laughter. "As charming as he is, what in the world would I do with such an exuberant youth?"

"Pamela, dear," the old lady squealed, "so you are the bride to be! You have accepted the offer of a fine young man."

"Yes," she answered confidently, "I think so."

"Lieutenant Milton came to call when he and Isaac were working at the hospital. I was completely taken with him. When is the wedding to be? Come in. We have so much to talk about."

Inside the house Sophie's barrage of questions continued.

"Did you find your family well, James? You were concerned about your brothers. Have they returned? How are things in the Lowcountry? Do Union troops still hold the sea islands? And Port Royal, is there still a Union navy presence in the area?"

"Yes, thank you, Mrs. Heyward, my family is well. Both brothers survived the war and are at home."

"And Beaufort, was that beautiful old city destroyed?"

"Slow down, Aunt Sophie, your questions are backing up. We will have several days to talk."

"Oh, how wonderful! Pamela, you do plan to stay a while this time. I have so much to ask about that I am almost breathless. Miss Gilham and I are starved for dependable, firsthand news about other parts of the state. We need to go to the back now, so you can tell Randolph how to store your things for the night."

"I'll attend to that. You all go in the parlor and talk." Ellen had decided to leave the wagon loaded so she could be ready to get to the market early. Jim followed her to the kitchen.

"I'll go with you tomorrow morning," he offered.

"No, Randolph and I can handle it. I will be going to the Farmer's Market on Assembly Street. It's not far, and I like selling directly to the shoppers. We get better prices that way, and the people get fresher produce."

"You handle the produce sales and I'll move about the market. That will give me the chance to find out about prices and things in general. I want to know what new laws have been passed in Washington, especially what's happening with land taxes."

Once they were back in the parlor, Jim attempted to respond to those of Sophie's questions he could remember.

"Across the state, from here home, I found conditions pretty much alike. Except for the wide swath carved out by Sherman's troops as they came through, people who try will be able to survive. There are few crops in the fields. Poverty and general deterioration are widespread and much hard work must be done. That pretty much sums up the situation. I haven't heard anything about conditions in the western part of the state. I don't think they were hard hit."

"Please tell me about Beaufort."

"The city is intact. The citizens endured more privations than most, since they were occupied early. They seem to have struggled through it bravely. A large contingent of Union troops is still stationed in the area. They've been there since the beginning of the war to hold the sea islands for the blacks."

"Good heavens!"

"There was little destruction in the town. The big homes were used as hospitals. A good number of Union sick and wounded are still there and hundreds have been buried in the town cemetery. The people don't like that."

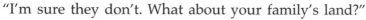

"I'm sure they don't. What about your family's land?"

"Seized in the beginning and still being held."

"How terrible!"

"My brothers are at an inland plantation, but I plan to live here. Knowing Ellen and Pamela caused me to want to become a cattle man."

"Henry would be pleased to know that. I am relieved that there will be a man with the girls out at Oak Lane."

"For goodness sakes, Aunt Sophie," Pam feigned disgust. "I should think that the past four years would have convinced you that Ellen and I are pretty self-sufficient."

"Yes, dear, they have. Even I am learning to solve my own problems." The old lady's solemn acceptance spoke volumes.

The tap of approaching footsteps caused them to look toward the front entrance. Miss Rice swept purposefully into the hall.

"Elizabeth," caroled Sophie. All signs of the awkward stiffness between them months ago had disappeared, "Please come into the parlor. Ellen and Pamela are here for another visit. I want you to meet Mr. James Milton, Pamela's fiancé."

The school day was over and Elizabeth looked worn.

"Jim, this is Miss Elizabeth Rice. Miss Rice is a teacher from Boston who is rooming and boarding with me. Miss Gilham and I have become very fond of her."

Jim, unusually stiff and diffident, acknowledged the introduction. Though Ellen had carefully described the young woman, he seemed surprised by her youthful, attractive appearance. She did not appear at all formidable.

Elizabeth reached out and firmly shook hands with him. Highly unusual behavior for a woman. Despite her look of feminine vulnerability, she was likely prim Yankee through and through.

"How nice to meet you, Miss Rice," he said, bowing slightly. Generations of gentlemanly behavior were bred into James

Milton. He would never fail to be courteous, but he was not prepared to like the New Englander, nor to find her attractive.

"How do you do, Mr. Milton. I am pleased to make your acquaintance. Please accept my warmest congratulations. Pamela is a lovely young woman. I hope you two will be very happy."

"Thank you."

She turned to face the girls and, discarding some of her customary reserve, exclaimed, "Ellen and Pamela, how wonderful to see you again! Pam, you did not prepare me for this wonderful news. I hope you are going to stay longer this time."

"We definitely will. I know nothing about planning weddings and you ladies at Laurel Street must assume the task," Ellen answered for her sister. "Pam is still in a state of wonderment. I am better prepared to deal with this wedding than she is, and that isn't saying a lot!"

"I am a minister's daughter. Don't worry about a thing. I am very experienced...as a spectator, of course. I hope you will allow me to help. Do you plan to marry soon?" Her tired face lighted with excitement.

"In October, we think. No exact date has been set. We will surely need your assistance, but everything really depends on what Aunt Sophie can help us work out." Pam lost all reticence.

"We happily accept the wedding assignment," Sophie beamed. "Tomorrow I'll ask Mary Whilden to come over. When Mary, Miss Gilham and the four of us put our heads together, marvelous plans can be made despite the shortages."

"I am here mainly about a wedding gown. I don't want to be married without a suitable dress." Light tinges of embarrassment colored Pam's cheeks. "We haven't had anything decent to wear in such a long time. I need advice and help with that, Elizabeth."

"I will be pleased to assist," the teacher willingly agreed.

"Now," said Sophie, "on to other matters. We can discuss these details later. I'm sure that Lieutenant Milton doesn't find our discussion of wedding attire very stimulating."

He smiled boyishly. "On the contrary, Mrs... Aunt Sophie, I'm delighted with the sound of it."

"More good news, Aunt Sophie," Ellen announced. "Jim has a horse. He will bring the animal next trip. We can use your buggy for shopping trips. I know that will make you feel better."

"Yes, indeed. I must go attend to supper. I'll see if I can find Hattie." As she stood to go to the kitchen, Sophie put her hand on Jim's arm. "James, Columbia has a newspaper being published regularly once more, the *Phoenix*... out of the ashes, you know. I have saved every issue. They are all stacked on the library table. Would you like to take them out on the piazza to read? You might want to escape this women's talk."

"Thank you, mam. I want very much to see them." Jim asked to be excused and went to get the papers.

After a night on the parlor sofa Jim rose early to accompany Ellen to the market. Other farmers were already there hawking vegetables from the back of their wagons. In less than two hours Ellen had sold most of their load, and traded her surplus greens and field peas for radishes, carrots and apples. Randolph stayed by her side. He counted or parceled out the produce for Ellen and put it in the basket all shoppers had to bring.

Jim disappeared into the crowd, but soon returned.

"More federal troops are expected. Nobody is sure what that means. Most of the people at the market are from outlying areas. They don't know any more than we do." Jim's face wore a look of disappointment.

"I did learn something important. The man two wagons over said firewood sold for one hundred dollars a load by the end of last winter. That may be another source of cash for us."

"When I return to Oak Lane I'll tell Big John to set the men to cutting wood during slack time." Ellen was pleased.

Immediately after midday Jim prepared for the trip back to the plantation. Pam walked outside with him for a private good-bye. Through the parlor window Ellen noticed the young man's hand resting lightly, but possessively, at her sister's waist. Before he climbed up to the wagon seat he leaned down and kissed Pamela softly on the lips.

"I'll be back a week from Friday to deliver the cattle. Don't worry about things at home. Benjamin, Isaac and I will follow all of your instructions. I'll be coming to see what kind of progress has been made on that wedding dress."

"Take care," she whispered.

Pam waited by the carriage block and watched him out of sight. When she returned to the house a soft look of wonderment suffused her face.

The days sped past in a whirl of planning, looking and careful buying. Sophie searched through every chiffonier and clothespress for materials to recycle. Old lace was removed from worn garments and bleached. Homespun material was washed repeatedly to soften and whiten it. Aged silk was sponged and set aside to be used again. Trips to stores confirmed that muslin was still ten dollars a yard, while calico prices ranged from twenty to thirty dollars. No organdy was available. Pamela and Ellen purchased very little.

"Aunt Sophie, can you believe that the price of a tallow candle is two dollars?" moaned Pam. "And it wasn't even white!"

"We will make our candles, honey. I can get beeswax and tallow. We'll scent them with herbs from the garden. Rose petals would be better, but it's too late in the season. I do have mint in abundance. There is plenty of time to make candles and put them outside for the sunlight to bleach."

"There will be no talk of hiring dressmakers," Elizabeth decreed. "Miss Gilham and I are both experienced seamstresses. We will design and make the most beautiful gown you ever saw."

After much discussion Pamela decided the dress would be made of plain off-white muslin. "I can wear it as is for a time, then later remove the trim and dye it with indigo. A dress as expensive as this one will be has to be serviceable."

They could find no white illusion for the headpiece.

"Don't give it a thought," consoled Sophie, "I have exactly the right thing, the parlor curtains. They have been serving this family well for years. Just lately I have used them for a church reception and several parties. Remember they covered the tables at the Great Bazaar! My sheers will be perfect."

"No, Aunt Sophie," protested Pam, "it may be years before you can replace them."

"We can work around the problem." Elizabeth spoke with calm assurance. "I will gather and tuck the material, but do no cutting. When the wedding is over, I can remove the stitches, wash and iron the curtains, and they will be ready to hang back at the windows... until the next grand occasion occurs."

"Until Ellen needs them!" Pam cast a knowing look toward her sister.

"Or until we need a christening gown," Ellen retaliated.

They bought soft printed calico for Ellen's maid of honor dress and enough similar fabric for one other frock for Pamela. Aunt Sophie would wear an old silk gown freshened with new trim. "These homespun undergarments we have made look very much like clothing Mother used to sew for the plantation slaves, except for the tucks and French knots." Ellen was saddened that there were none of the dainty articles of a pre-war trousseau.

During the afternoons the women sat on the front porch tucking, gathering and sewing on what seemed like endless miles of lace and ruffles. Neighbors stopped to visit, discuss their progress and admire their handiwork.

"Girls, for the first time I feel like the war is really over and life is returning to normal." Sophie greatly enjoyed the work.

"For the first time since I left Boston I am feeling contented." Elizabeth bent her head to examine a thread she was clipping with embroidery scissors. "It means a great deal to me to be useful and wanted. My schoolwork is often not rewarding. Not being accepted by the local people has been hard."

When Elizabeth lifted her head, tears were shining in her eyes. "I can't thank you enough, Pamela, for being so kind as to include me in your happiness."

"And for the first time in my life," confessed Pamela, "I have had the opportunity to feel like an adult and to be completely feminine."

She was sitting in a sea of ruffled petticoats, trying valiantly to learn to sew a fine seam.

"And this is the first time in my life I have had the opportunity to sit and listen to so much sentimental drivel."

Ellen smiled irreverently at them.

⁂

Jim and Isaac arrived Friday with two more steers for the army quartermaster. They brought the sale money to Laurel Street.

"Land sakes, Lieutenant, has a week already gone by?" Hattie was not around. Sophie greeted him at the front door.

"Is it safe to attempt to enter this female stronghold?" he inquired. "Are you ladies going to meet the deadline I set?"

"Everything is on schedule," Ellen assured him.

"In two more weeks the girls will be ready to go back to the plantation with you. We have been making wonderful progress."

Aunt Sophie would not be rushed.

"May I safely notify my brothers about the date and start to invite guests?"

"Yes, you may," Pam's eyes were bright with merriment, "unless you are getting cold feet."

"Not a chance." His steady gaze glowed with tenderness. "I'll telegraph my brothers."

He had, as promised, brought his horse to leave with them so they could use the buggy in their travels about the city.

"Between the oats we brought with us and the overgrown yards along the street, I suppose Survivor will have enough to eat. Randolph helped me name that superb piece of horseflesh. Isaac came to stay and be your driver."

"Oh, my! That does sound lovely." The suggestion delighted Aunt Sophie. "Almost like old times."

"Aunt Sophie, Pamela and I can drive as well as any man." Ellen's voice was emphatic.

"I know you can, dear, but it doesn't look right."

"Isaac is needed at home. If you insist, we'll take Randolph with us. Apparently he and Survivor are friends. He can hold the reins while we are inside the stores, but we are capable of managing a horse and buggy ourselves."

"But what would your mother say?" Sophie got intense pleasure out of fretting.

"She would agree. Aunt Mariah is the one who disapproves."

Jim listened to them argue and tease, his adoring glance rarely straying from Pamela's face.

"The wedding date is set for three weeks hence," Pam said.

"Be glad you are not at Oak Lane, ladies." Jim confided. "Aunt Mariah has the women in such an orgy of cleaning and sprucing up about the house and yard that everything has been disrupted."

"I am glad to hear she has gone ahead with that. I should have known she would take charge."

"Take charge, Ellen, you'd think she was the bride! She has all of us whipped into shape. Eggs and honey are being hoarded for important baking. I am to bring back white flour and sugar for the wedding cake. Will you be able to find them for her?"

"Already bought! My gift to the bride," said Miss Gilham, pleased to have located not only flour and sugar but some vanilla beans, also.

"I hope this is the last time I will ever have to tell you goodbye," Milton whispered softly to Pam as they stood outside the next morning, "and the last time I have to sleep on that damned short sofa."

"I hope so, too." She stared up into his eyes and rose on tiptoe to boldly kiss him.

His heart raced, but restraint was necessary. Though Pam had made great strides in her acceptance of him, she was still as skittish as a colt. Sighing audibly, he shoved his hand through his blonde hair and grimaced. The two weeks until time to come back for her would seem interminable.

"I'll stop at the telegraph office on the way out of town. I'm glad we have a date fixed. Tom will have time to get here to be my best man. I never thought I'd get married before he did. I feel certain that Rutledge isn't well enough to make the trip."

The two weeks in town flew by lightning fast.

Elizabeth and Ellen were sitting on the front porch sewing the last few seed pearls on the coarse muslin bodice and skirt of the wedding dress. They had fashioned an underskirt from mosquito netting to make the gown bouffant. The tucked head-piece and long lace curtain train was spread across a rocking chair. Earlier Mr. Richards had brought Rose by to see Ellen again, admire their handiwork and extend her best wishes to Pamela. Jim was expected to arrive soon to take the sisters back home.

"Ellen, do you have a special young man?" Elizabeth posed the question casually. They had been sewing in silence for a while. "If I am prying, please forgive me. You never talk about yourself. I hope the war didn't . . ."

"No," Ellen answered hastily. "I am afraid I am destined to be an old maid. In the south, once you have passed the age of eighteen the relatives start to give up all hope."

"In New England, too, only we are usually called spinsters." She laughed easily. "The trouble is, I don't feel like a spinster. I'm twenty-eight. Being unmarried hasn't bothered me. I must confess my mother has had many anxious moments about it, though."

"I'm twenty-seven. And," Ellen added with emphasis, "despite conventional wisdom, I doubt that I passed my prime ten years ago. In fact," she lifted a wooden spool to her mouth and with strong even teeth bit off a strand of white thread, "I have never been more energetic, nor felt more self-confident."

"Interesting that you should say that, Ellen. Despite the frustrations of my teaching, I feel exactly the same way."

"Elizabeth Rice, you and I are not timid women. May I immodestly say, I think our best years are still ahead."

"I believe you are correct. And to be even more brazen, I also think I would make a good wife, if the right man asked me. I am very sure that you would. And," she added with typical New England candor, "I would hate to miss the experience of having a husband and of being a mother."

Ellen stared down at the work in her hands.

"Have you met the right man, Elizabeth?"

"I don't know. Perhaps I have. I may have met several men who could have been right. The trouble is," she explained, "he, or they, never seemed to recognize me as their right woman. It doesn't seem quite fair, does it?"

"What?"

"That women never get to select. They can only wait around to be discovered, and then to either accept or reject."

"I am pleased that Pamela has found happiness." Ellen wanted to lead the conversation in a more comfortable direction.

"Pam is young. Have she and Lieutenant Milton known each other a long time? Were they childhood sweethearts?"

"No, they met near the end of the war. He was wounded last February and a patient in the College hospital where I was a volunteer."

"You haven't told me about that."

"We came into town when General Sherman's army was approaching. Jim would have been a prisoner of war if I had not arranged for him to convalesce at our plantation. He stayed with us until he was strong enough to rejoin his unit. After the surrender, he came to see us again on his way home."

"He impresses me as the kind of young man your parents would have approved for Pamela."

"Yes, he's a part of our way of life. He is thoughtful and gentle, also, just the kind of husband I want for my sister."

"Ellen, where did the lore about the helpless, clinging, over-protected southern woman originate? Look at Mary Whilden and Miss Sophie, and Pamela and you. Towers of strength, every one of you." Elizabeth spoke with obvious sincerity.

"Thank you, but I doubt any of us would be brave enough to accept a position and move into a strange unfriendly world alone, as you have."

"Oh, but I came here to be a teacher, something I'm supposed to know how to do. Not succeeding too well at the moment, I admit, but it is a known world to me. Your task has been more difficult. You have been forced to take responsibility in a man's world, and you have survived."

"We have done what we had to do. We had no choice."

"That's not true. I have enjoyed hearing about your study and the experimentation you are trying. Your aunt is proud of your accomplishments. She has told me a great deal about you."

Ellen was embarrassed by Elizabeth's positive clear-eyed praise. She tried again for a different topic.

"These wonderful traits you are citing are not ones generally admired by young men, Elizabeth."

"I have never thought young men to be especially bright."

"Nor have I. Sour grapes, do you suppose?"

"Possibly, but I don't think so. Wisdom born of keen observation, I'd say." She tried to hide a chuckle.

Ellen nodded thoughtfully and expanded her confession.

"I never learned to flirt and simper and flutter my eyelashes. In the company of males I'm not given to docility and quiet adoration. I am more inclined to be argumentative, than to engage in polite conversation. Nor am I a great beauty...or an excellent dancer. Totally hopeless, wouldn't you say?"

Elizabeth did not reply immediately.

"I sometimes think that not being subject to fits of girlish giggles may be one of my great shortcomings," she volunteered.

"Common sense, spirited determination and a fiery tongue never helped me much in a ball room."

They looked at each other, smiled ruefully and, in behavior totally unlike either of them, dissolved into fits of giggles.

"Perhaps we are not hopeless after all." Elizabeth wiped her eyes daintily with a lace-edged handkerchief.

They worked together another half hour in dignified silence.

"There, that's the last bead," Elizabeth announced with satisfaction.

They held up the completed dress for inspection. Soft rows of delicate lace encircled the high neckline. Scrolls of tiny seed pearls were patterned across the fitted bodice and near the hem of the long full skirt. Together they carefully spread the gown across another chair beside the lace headpiece and train.

"I'm sure that Miss Sophie's sheers never looked prettier."

"Nor graced a more important occasion," Ellen agreed.

They stepped back to admire the full effect of the beautiful work they had completed.

"Absolutely lovely," breathed Ellen. "This wedding will add another illustrious chapter to the saga of the lace curtains."

"Perhaps we should write their biography." Elizabeth made the suggestion with a hint of a grin.

"A gigantic sweeping epic covering both the northern and southern perspective, I presume." Ellen was enjoying the gentle sparring with her usually serious new friend.

They were interrupted by the rumble of iron-ringed wagon wheels rolling down Laurel Street. Jim and Isaac were approaching from the direction of Main.

Ellen picked up her sewing basket hurriedly.

"Elizabeth, please delay Jim out here. Pam wants to be wearing the new calico dress you made for her when he arrives. Give me time to help her with the buttons. I'll hurry. Make small talk. Tell him the history of the wedding headpiece and train. He will enjoy that, and it will take a few minutes."

Ellen disappeared inside.

"Good afternoon, Miss Rice." Milton leaped from the wagon and bounded up the porch steps. "Have you ladies completed the necessary sewing?" His pale blue eyes were shining happily.

"Indeed, yes, Mr. Milton," she assured him. "We barely made it, though. You will be pleasantly surprised at what we have accomplished. Ellen has gone to get Pamela. Please allow me tell you about everything and display the finished products. You are going to have the most beautiful bride imaginable."

He glanced toward the open doorway, impatient to go inside.

"Pamela wants to surprise you. She knows you are here and she will be down shortly." Elizabeth paused, watching a lone rider who rode up and stopped beside the hitching post in front of the house.

Jim turned to look, stiffened and stood erect. A tall Union officer had dismounted. The man removed his felt slouch hat and walked up the walk toward the porch.

"Major Arledge!" Elizabeth was flustered, her voice bright with surprise and pleasure. "How nice to see you again."

Jim appraised the well-muscled length of the stranger. He and the Boston teacher must be acquainted. The immaculate blue braid-encrusted uniform was in stark contrast to the gray and butternut remnants Jim wore.

"Won't you come in?" she invited.

"I hope I am not intruding," the major said, looking toward Jim. "I have been reassigned to the Columbia area. I'm calling to pay my respects to Mrs. Heyward and to you, Miss Rice," His keen glance shot past Jim and fastened on the wedding dress and train spread upon the chairs.

"Not at all. We just were discussing an upcoming happy occasion," she explained. "Major John Arledge, may I present Lieutenant James Milton."

The men nodded warily to each other. Arledge did not come up on the porch, but remained standing on the ground, gaze fixed first on the white gown and then back on Jim. Each man was trying to assess the role and connection to the family of the other.

"Lieutenant Milton is engaged to Mrs. Heyward's niece." Elizabeth rushed to fill the awkward void. "They are to be married next week."

For a moment Arledge looked stricken. His lips tightened into a firm line. The bright blue eyes became glacier cold.

"The two met last February. He had been wounded and Ellen Heyward was one of his hospital nurses. She invited him to convalesce in her home. After the war ended Lieutenant Milton came back to visit and…" Elizabeth foundered, sensing that somehow her explanation was going badly.

There was a protracted strained silence.

"It was all very romantic," she continued lamely. "As you see we have just completed the wedding dress." Elizabeth's sputtering attempts to ease the situation finally died. She felt inept, totally baffled by the unexplained air of hostility.

Neither man uttered a sound.

Footsteps sounded and Ellen rushed out on the porch.

"Jim, dear," she sang out happily as she ran to kiss him. "I am so glad you are here. Pam will be out in a few minutes."

With Milton's arms embracing her, Ellen looked down into the grim face of John Arledge, standing at the bottom of the porch steps. Her heart began to pound.

"Major," Elizabeth said politely, "I'm sure you remember Miss Ellen Heyward."

"Yes, I remember Miss Heyward very well." He bit out the words hoarsely through whitened lips.

Ellen's hand went up to clutch her throat. She grasped the locked chain. She was suddenly rendered speechless.

"Congratulations, Lieutenant," Arledge said stiffly to Jim, and began to back down the walkway toward his horse. He turned toward Elizabeth and Ellen. "I must go. I have just arrived in town. Please give Mrs. Heyward my regards. I will be stationed here for a while. I will call again later."

Though he seemed to be speaking to Elizabeth, the handsome officer cast one last tortured look toward Ellen. "Good afternoon," he murmured. Then bowing slightly, he crushed his hat back on, strode to his horse and hurriedly galloped away.

Jim, unaware of the continuing tension, looked into the hallway and gave a long, low appreciative whistle. Pam was descending the stairs. His fiancee was a breathtaking vision and he had eyes only for her. Pam's joyous rush toward him and their happy greetings helped to cover the strained uneasiness and confusion which existed.

Ellen was numb. She had been overwhelmed when she looked down and saw John standing at the foot of the steps. His appearance was totally unexpected. In the split second, when she first looked into his eyes, she knew she was willing to forget everything she had said about their differences. The blue uniform no longer mattered. All she wanted was to be wrapped in his strong arms once again.

She realized that Arledge had asked no questions. He had sized up the situation and jumped to wrong conclusions. He had rushed away, not waiting for any explanations. Her heart urged her to run down the street calling after him, but he had disappeared.

Or perhaps it was not her, but Elizabeth, he had come to visit. John had no reason to expect to find her at Laurel Street. If he cared to learn the truth, he could easily have done so. Investigation, after all, was his specialty. If he cared to see her again, he knew where she could be found. This time using common sense did not help; rationalizing failed to ease her aching heart.

Jim slowly circled Pamela, eyes filled with adoration. Her hair was brushed into soft shimmering curls. Loose tendrils framed her face. Slight color stained her cheeks as she endured his close scrutiny. The dainty frock of tiny flowered print hugged every slender feminine curve. She looked delicate, lovely, ethereal. He sighed softly, beaming total approval.

"Pamela Heyward," he declared solemnly, "I admired you in children's clothes, I loved you when you wore your father's old breeches, but this new Pamela will take some getting used to. You are a beautiful young woman. I'm glad you never looked this stunning before. I would never have been able to summon the courage to propose."

"Isn't Elizabeth talented?" She turned slowly so he could admire the garment from every angle. "I'm glad you approve of the new dress she made for me."

"Dress? I completely forgot to look at the dress!"

Pam playfully slapped him on the shoulder. "Stop teasing. Go inside and speak to Aunt Sophie, Jim, and if you are not exhausted from the trip in, please walk with me to the Preston mansion. I'd like to introduce you to Mother Baptista and Mother Ursula. I want them to know that we are all well. I shall invite them to our wedding."

"Nothing would give me greater pleasure, Miss Heyward," he said with exaggerated gallantry, "than to escort you up and down every street and show you off to the entire city."

Nineteen

Jim drove Sophie's buggy around to the carriage block in front of the house while Ellen and Pamela made preparations to leave. The wedding dress and train had been wrapped in sheets and folded carefully. Isaac pulled the big farm wagon behind the buggy and loaded the valises. The grocery staples Aunt Mariah had ordered, and the recently purchased plantation supplies, were already stowed inside.

Hattie and Aunt Sophie stood at the rear of the wagon ready to hand up the boxes of crystal and silver being sent to supplement that at Oak Lane. Refreshments at the reception would be in limited supply, but Sophie insisted that food, served properly with an abundance of beautiful dishes and serving pieces, would give the affair an air of lavish hospitality. Two large potted ferns were beside the street, ready to go into the wagon, their first outing since the Grand Bazaar.

"Isaac, I want you to be sure to drive slowly and carefully. I didn't save my dishes from Yankee soldiers so they could get broken rattling up and down on a bumpy road. There wasn't enough newspaper to wrap them well. Fine china is very delicate, so you watch out for any ruts along the way."

"Yes, mam. I'm putting them dishes on top of the quilts and blankets you sending. I wedge them good with bags of rice and flour and sugar all around. Don't you worry none, Miss Sophie. Ain't nothing short of a hail storm from above could bother them dishes. They resting soft and I be real careful."

"Elizabeth, I wish you didn't have to teach next week," Pam repeated once more. They were lifting the wedding dress to carefully place it in the back of the buggy. "We would like for you to go home with us now."

"Thank you, but I have responsibilities I cannot shirk."

"We'll send for you and Aunt Sophie Friday. Leave school as early as you can."

"I'll be ready. Most of the weddings I have attended were small, and in a parson's parlor. I'm really looking forward to a big southern wedding."

"We need you to help us decorate the house. We may want to have the ceremony outside. There are still many things to be decided, but I'm trying not to fret over details."

Pam wore a faded dress. Her hair was pulled back with a ribbon. Frown lines creased her forehead. Gone was yesterday afternoon's stylish young woman. Another working day had begun.

"And, Aunt Sophie," Ellen called, as she brought out the last of the boxes, "with the wedding planned for four o'clock Saturday afternoon you know people will start to arrive soon after dinner time. Please have your day organized so you'll be free to greet early guests and keep them entertained."

"Stop your worry, dear. Mary Whilden is coming to help me. She is wonderful with people on any occasion. Since travel is so difficult for everyone these days, I feel sure the crowd won't be so large that we can't manage everything nicely."

Big John had been instructed two weeks ago to ride to the neighboring plantations with a handwritten invitation Aunt Sophie had prepared for each family to read. Pamela, Ellen and Sophie had traveled about the city and personally invited their friends. Jim's family had been telegraphed. They were hoping some of them could make the trip. On the wedding day everyone would be expected to stay for supper, and the people coming from any distance were invited to spend the night.

Food shortages during the last few years had made it a custom for guests at social events to bring 'a dish' to add to the food table. Ellen had already been told of casseroles, stews, pickles, preserves and fruit that would be arriving. Extra quilts would be brought along so small children could take naps. They would make pallets on the floor later for overflow wedding guests who would be staying for the night.

All morning Ellen had been unusually quiet. She worked steadily. Her hazel eyes, further darkened by the circles beneath them, were lifeless. Throughout the night she had replayed in her mind the disturbing scene on the front porch. Too unsure of the Yankee major's intentions, too reserved to try to explain anything in the presence of Jim and Elizabeth, too proud to go shouting down the street after John, and much too self-controlled to permit herself to cry, Ellen's emotions had been in turmoil ever since the debacle.

Pam's exuberance this morning was heartening and Ellen was content to assume a retiring role. During her life she had rarely allowed herself to be engrossed in personal concerns. There had never been time for that luxury. On the ride home she could examine her personal and very private problems with calm logic.

"Elizabeth, thank you for everything." Ellen tried to inject a cheerful lilt in her voice. "We could never have managed without your help."

Discarding her usual stiff dignity, the Bostonian hugged first Ellen and then Pamela. "I thank you. The past three weeks will always be among my happiest memories. Your friendship is very dear to me. I hope you'll soon number me among your kissing cousins, whatever they are." The expression on Elizabeth's face was so serious Ellen could barely repress a smile.

"You have helped make a traditional wedding possible for me. Forget cousin, you are a full-fledged adopted family member now." Pam was no longer the withdrawn child of seven months ago.

"Indeed you are," Sophie agreed. "This wedding is a godsend for all of us. We needed a happy occasion to bring us together."

As soon as final good-byes were said and they pulled away from the house, Pam snuggled beside Jim. The two began to review for each other the things that had happened while they were separated. They were oblivious to the unusually quiet Ellen riding with them.

What could have been done to change the course of events yesterday? John knew that the Heyward family was small. He believed Pamela was an adolescent. He had no reason to think that the bride-to-be niece could possibly be the younger sister.

She had rushed out and embraced Jim…and there was a wedding dress spread out on the chair behind her. He had no way to know that hers was a sisterly embrace. John's eyes, as he had looked up to her, seemed to accuse her of betrayal. He had asked her to wait until he could return. He looked angry and hurt, or perhaps she had seen in his eyes what she wanted to see.

In February she had insisted that they were wrong for each other. Now she knew that nothing could be more right than her feeling toward John Arledge. He had returned, as he said he would. She should have invited him inside, let him see Pamela again and realize that she was not a child. He would have learned that she had deceived him about her sister's age. Would he forgive her for never telling the full truth about the bummer incident?

Ellen was thankful that Jim and Pamela were engrossed with each other and did not notice how uncharacteristically silent she was on the buggy ride home.

Back at Oak Lane work helped to deaden Ellen's heartache.

In the camellia garden she pruned unsightly late summer shoots from the shining green bushes. John Arledge is only twelve miles away. That thought was uppermost in her mind. She staked chrysanthemums, already heavy with tight coloring buds. She divided large clumps of iris, looked for late blooming varieties of day lilies and trimmed dead blooms from the perennial beds. She worked for physical exhaustion.

Another day was devoted to landscaping the backdoor herb garden. Ellen fashioned an intricate geometric design, latticed and criss-crossed with narrow brick walkways. She worked on her knees, savoring the heavy scent rising from the crushed leaves of the various mints, glad that she could seek the sanctuary of outside work. She did not want the others to be aware of her preoccupation. Aunt Mariah was in charge of household chores and Pam and Jim spent their days outside wandering dreamily in each other's company.

"You keep on making them fancy designs out there, Miss Ellen," cautioned Aunt Mariah from the kitchen door, "and you better fix yourself a hex sign in the middle of the bed. Some of them plants you working with got strange powers. You best take pains to ward off evil spirits."

"I plan to do that. I found a design from an old English garden in one of Father's books. Randolph is getting me more bricks."

Aunt Mariah looked thunderous and shook her head. The ends of the triangular kerchief tied over her hair flapped violently. She brooded as Ellen tucked lush green knots of feverfew and rosemary between bunches of lavender and thyme.

"I know you worried about something, and I know you ain't going to tell nobody til you get whatever it is worked out, but ain't no need to kill yourself while you doing your worrying. What you think you going to look like when all them folks get here for the wedding? Bag of bones with big, dark eyes look like a raccoon, that's what."

"I will soon be finished with the gardening."

"Then you just be start something else. Your hands going to be a mess, and I ain't got nothing to soak them in. That wedding just two days away. How come you can't rest some?"

"I'm working off nervous energy, Aunt Mariah. I'm fine."

"You think I ain't seen them puffy eyes, girl? How come you crying and missing your sleep?"

"Has all the silver been polished? Aunt Sophie will be here tomorrow. No telling what else she has in mind for us to do."

"You know good and well everything been done. You don't fool me none. You just trying to keep me from asking you any more questions about yourself."

Ellen looked up and smiled, reminded once again how wise and loving the dear old lady was.

Jim left in the buggy Friday morning to go for Sophie and Elizabeth. Isaac would return early the next day for Miss Gilham and the two sisters from the Ursuline Convent. Mary Whilden and Frank were coming before noon in the Richards carriage with Rose and her father. The McCully girls had a cousin who was bringing them.

Jim's brother Thomas had telegraphed that he would arrive by Saturday morning. Rutledge, as Jim had feared, was not well enough to travel the distance.

Sophie began issuing a flurry of last minute orders the minute she descended from the buggy. Jim was instructed to bring in a box containing the last of her candles. She was carrying a large crystal water pitcher filled with white chrysanthemums.

"For the bridal bouquet," she announced with satisfaction.

Elizabeth proudly displayed fresh white satin ribbon she had been able to find. "And look," she shrieked girlishly, dangling a frilly garter, "this is one of mine... something borrowed and something blue."

"I have begged every white blossom there was on Laurel Street." Sophie set the flowers on the marble-top table in the hall. "Mary and Mr. Richards will be bringing several bottles of homemade wine that friends are sending. We will be festive!"

Although the family church was less than three miles away, Pamela preferred to be married at home. From the beginning she had quietly insisted on a simple headpiece and a short wedding train, rather than a bridal veil. Aunt Sophie assumed she was trying to protect the parlor curtains. Ellen knew that it was Pam's way of making a painfully honest statement to Jim.

Elizabeth was everywhere that night as final preparations were made. Her quiet competence extended to many fields. Unsure about the possibility of a late afternoon shower, they collectively decided that the ceremony should take place inside.

"We will bank green branches of magnolia leaves on the mantel around white candles to form an altar. The mirror there will reflect the service beautifully."

"And we will be able to see the faces of the bride and groom, Elizabeth." Aunt Sophie loved the idea. "I'll put the fern stands on either side of the hearth."

When the flower urns were in place, the graceful fronds of Sophie's ferns hung to the floor. Like the curtains, the ferns had a distinguished history of having beautified many important events.

The piano was moved into the hallway.

"Since you know how to do everything, Elizabeth, I suppose you play piano, too," Ellen scoffed.

"Of course I do. I play very precisely, very correctly and very stiffly, just exactly what you would expect from a Yankee school teacher. I have heard Miss Gilham play. She is far better than I am, plays with soul, as you would say. She is to be the designated pianist for this wedding. I'll wait and play at yours, Ellen."

The rosewood sofa and velvet upholstered chairs were pushed tight against the walls to make room for guests to stand in the parlor during the ceremony. The open space would be needed for dancing later in the evening.

Doors from three of the upstairs bedrooms were taken off the hinges and laid across rough saw horses to make extra serving tables. The linen and lace tablecloths were needed in the dining room, but crocheted bedspreads and white sheets, mended and threadbare, were set aside for use on the tables outside. Afternoon refreshments would be served in the flower garden, weather permitting. A special food table was being set up for the plantation servants.

Saturday morning preparations began at dawn.

"I ain't never seen nothing like that little Yankee school teacher lady," Aunt Mariah confided to Ellen. "You and Miss Pam bad enough, but that lady a whirlwind. Good thing she do everything herself. I can't hardly understand a word she says."

Ellen was leaning over the kitchen table smoothing white icing on Aunt Mariah's freshly baked wedding cake. Sophie stood nearby, absorbed in fashioning mosquito netting to tuck around the tall crystal cake stand.

"Ellen," her aunt absent-mindedly remarked while she concentrated on pleating the stiff material, "in all the excitement I nearly forgot. I have a rather strange message to deliver to you."

Ellen straightened up to look at her aunt.

"As we were driving past the College yesterday, Elizabeth recognized that Major Arledge among the officers standing by the main gate. You recall he is the one who told her she might be able to rent a room at my house."

Ellen waited, body suddenly very alert.

"Elizabeth asked Jim to stop so she could speak to him. I know that he was here with Sherman and I, of course, would not be stopping to speak to the man, but he is Elizabeth's friend. He walked over to the buggy and they chatted briefly. I'm sure it was uncomfortable for Jim, but he is a gentleman. She introduced the major to me again, and, to give the devil his due, I have to say that he is a handsome man and very well-mannered."

"And exactly what was the strange message?" Ellen was hardly aware that she was holding her breath.

"First Elizabeth told him that we were on our way to Oak Lane for the wedding today. Then he looked straight at me with those startling blue eyes of his and said 'Mrs. Heyward, please convey my best wishes to your niece and tell her that I sincerely regret any pain that I may have caused her.' This struck me as such an unusual wedding message that I asked him which niece he was speaking of. He seemed puzzled and said, 'The bride, of course, Miss Ellen.' Don't you think that is strange?"

"What did you say?"

"Well, Elizabeth and I were both shocked that he could be so misinformed."

"And?" Dislodging information from Aunt Sophie was worse than extracting teeth.

"Oh, Elizabeth straightened it out. She told him that he was mistaken about the identity of the bride, that it was Pamela's wedding we were going to. He was dumbfounded. You would have though that lightning had struck the man. The entire conversation was strange, if you ask me."

"Is that all that was said?"

"No, indeed. He looked at me again and said, 'Mrs. Heyward, I'd like to change my message. Please tell your niece, Miss Ellen Heyward, that I will see her tomorrow, perhaps at the wedding.' Now, Ellen, I want you to know that I did not invite the man, but I suppose that if he is a friend of Elizabeth's we can't prohibit him from coming. What do you think?"

The wooden spatula which Ellen had been using to smooth the icing clattered loudly as she suddenly dropped it on the table. She felt her heart begin to sing.

"Move out of the way, child," her aunt admonished. "You haven't finished icing the cake, and now you are about to mess up the trim I'm fixing. It's not like we have more of either, you know. I do believe you are as nervous as the bride."

"Yes, mam, Miss Sophie," Aunt Mariah agreed. "You watch out about that cake. We ain't got nothing but that one little bitty cake and some apple cider to serve at the reception. Going to have to slice the thing paper thin. Ain't hardly got enough wine to toast the bride with neither."

Ellen was no longer listening.

"Only thing we got for the younguns is molasses cookies. Got a good supper for later on, though, and that make up the difference...but, tonight, folks sure going to have to drink well water at the dancing for refreshment."

In the afternoon as Ellen dressed she noticed the slight tremor in her usually steady hands. Fits of breathlessness were attacking her, followed by erratic pulse beats. How would she survive! Her customary serenity was gone. All morning there had been too much to do to allow herself to dwell on John's message.

"Honestly, Ellen," Elizabeth fumed, "you are only the maid of honor! Why so nervous? Let me do the buttons for you. You are not the kind to be in a such a state of panic."

"And you, Miss Busybody, are beginning to sound like Aunt Sophie. Actually, I'm trying to hurry so we can go help Pam."

The cold knot which had settled in the pit of Ellen's stomach a week ago had been replaced by a spasmodic fluttering that was hard to deal with.

"Everything will be perfect." Elizabeth was always so calm and organized.

Buttons fastened, Ellen took two deep breaths to still the wild beating of her heart. Only she knew that the strange mixture of elation, apprehension and anxiety choking her was not all due to the wedding. She felt as if she had swallowed a swarm of butterflies.

"You look quite nice, Ellen. Your new frock is most becoming, but I never dreamed I would have to dress both of you Heyward girls! That is a lovely locket you have on. I haven't seen you wear it before."

"Elizabeth, you are getting prim and officious again, bordering on nosy." Ellen's eyes had darkened until they were shining. Beneath the smooth tan of her face high excitement had spread rosy stain across her patrician cheekbones.

"Had I not come south to teach, I wonder if this wedding could ever have taken place."

"Yes, I'm sure it would have, but certainly not with such precision and efficiency. I shall try to repay you."

"No, Ellen!" She was appalled. "I was attempting to jest."

"I know you were, dummy. I plan to repay you in kind."

"Perhaps you had better tell me exactly what you mean."

"Jim has an eligible brother. He will be here today. How does a thirty-year-old former Confederate artillery colonel sound to you? Don't you expect that he would make your icy heart go pitter-pat...and give your parents apoplexy?"

"Without a doubt. And I know the gentleman is anxious to meet a genuine New England spinster. I would say that we make perfectly suited candidates for marriage."

Ellen giggled merrily, the first time since their afternoon of confession and stitching on the porch at Laurel Street.

"I do hope," Elizabeth added solemnly, "that you will have the common decency to leave him alone until he has had the opportunity to discover what a multitude of charms lie buried beneath this nosy officious exterior of mine."

"Why should I give you an advantage?"

"Because I suspect you already have found your man."

Ellen stilled.

"Last week I was puzzled by John Arledge's strange behavior. He left too abruptly. Jim's presence could not have disturbed him that much. And his unusual remarks to Miss Sophie yesterday. Something else is there. Just how well do you know him, Ellen?"

Elizabeth's keen eyes studied Ellen's face. The beginning of a smile tilted the corners of her mouth. She shook her finger at Ellen knowingly.

"Ellen Heyward, you are the one! You are the stubborn, stiff-necked southern aristocrat, the one my brother said had stolen Major Arledge's heart. You are, aren't you?"

"Obstinate, perhaps and maybe even stubborn, but surely not stiff-necked. That sounds more like you."

Elizabeth put her arms around Ellen and hugged her close. "You know, I half suspected the night Pam kept questioning me about him. You were entirely too silent. I hope you will have the good sense to be more receptive to him this time."

"I am scared to death. I have no idea what to do or say when I see him again."

"Don't be an idiot. Put the poor man out of his misery. Run straight into his arms."

"Now you're giving advice to the lovelorn. Do be quiet, Elizabeth. I'm in enough of a dither as it is."

"I hope that means that I will have clear sailing with the dashing Reb colonel."

"I never said dashing. I haven't met him. I only said eligible, meaning wifeless."

"Well, that's certainly a start. Why did Pamela have to invite those Ursuline sisters? Might be competition, you know."

The playful exchange was helping to ease Ellen's tension. Together they walked across the hall to Pamela's room to find the prospective bride dressed and calmly waiting for their assistance with the head-piece and train.

"I thought I had better get dressed by myself. With no doors on the rooms up here, I was able to hear every word you two were saying. I take it there won't be time for any advice about how to be a dutiful wife." Pamela's cool blonde composure reflected such inner contentment and certainty that Ellen had difficulty stemming the tears that tightened her throat.

"At least you are going to be a wife, little sister! That's more than either of us can claim. Our advice would be worthless. Let me pin the headpiece for you and attach the train."

The sounds of the grand piano drifted up from the hall below as Miss Gilham began to play the first bars of the wedding music.

"Quick. We must hurry. I have to get back downstairs lest I be mistaken for the bride when I descend." Elizabeth became all efficiency. She straightened the lace panel so it would trail properly behind the bride, handed the sisters their small bouquets and dashed down the wide stairway to join the others.

Mary Whilden and Aunt Sophie had the guests positioned about the parlor. Rose's wheel chair was by the window, a McCully sister on either side. The family minister was standing amid the magnolia boughs with his back toward the fireplace.

Ellen and Pamela waited at the top of the staircase. Each girl clutched a small nosegay of white late summer daisies and fall chrysanthemums. The guests were looking expectantly toward the stair landing. Mary glanced to the top of the steps and signaled that it was time for the maid of honor to proceed.

Ellen began slowly descending the stairs. She searched discreetly among the group of friends and neighbors who were gathered below. Arledge's tall form was not among the guests. The wild singing in her heart had not slowed. She reached the last step, walked across the room and took her place at the left of the altar. He said he would be here, and he will be here.

Jim, face aglow, waited beside the fireplace looking up. His brother stood stiffly erect at his side. Both men wore the Confederate officer's yellow military dress sash over their plain gray uniforms.

The bothers closely resembled each other. Thomas, still pale, was much taller than Jim and far too thin. He had none of Jim's boyish look. Touches of gray glinted at his temples. His somber expression and the deep age lines around his eyes and mouth gave mute testimony to the four years of constant hardship that he had endured.

When Miss Gilham struck the first notes of the wedding march all attention was on the bride. Pam slowly descended the stairs, coarse muslin wedding dress sweeping past portraits of ancient relatives more elegantly attired. Her unveiled face radiated happiness. She looked first at Jim and then briefly at Ellen, seeking and giving each of them reassurance. The satisfied sniffs and sighs of the plantation folk could be heard. They had all gathered at the end of the hallway.

Soft vows were whispered in a quiet hush, broken only by Aunt Mariah's loud tearful sniffles. When the ceremony ended it was Elizabeth who caught the bride's bouquet.

"Don't touch these flowers." she whispered fiercely in Ellen's ear. "You don't need them. See what I mean." She nodded toward the front door.

Ellen looked out into the hallway. Standing tall against the door-frame, well outside of the parlor, John Arledge waited for her to see him. The impact of his riveting gaze sent shock waves through Ellen's body. She felt the smoldering flame in his bright blue eyes electrify the air around her. Noticing Ellen's stricken expression, Aunt Sophie turned to see what had her so transfixed.

An uneasy quiet spread across the room as others became aware of the blue-uniformed man in their midst. Would there be trouble? Though Elizabeth had given her a slight shove forward, Ellen's feet refused to function. John waited quietly as she struggled to regain her composure.

Then guests suddenly began to talk, all at once. They politely pretended to be absorbed in other interests, but each surreptitiously watched, waiting to take their cue from family members as to how they should behave. Perhaps the groom or his brother would challenge the brash Yankee.

Finally Ellen advanced toward him. He bowed slightly, extended his bent elbow toward her and said in a low even voice, "Miss Heyward, please walk outside with me. We must talk."

"I... I can't go outside," she faltered. "We have guests."

"Come outside with me, Ellen," he muttered hoarsely, "or, by God, I will carry you out of here kicking and screaming." The guttural tone of his deep voice, though quietly spoken, clearly indicated that he meant every word he was saying.

She took told of his arm.

Once they had cleared the front verandah he turned to her.

"I thought I had lost you," he whispered between clenched teeth. "This time I'll not let you out of my sight."

"Dragging me out the way you did, sir, you'll be lucky if that crowd doesn't come out here and lynch you."

"Still the sweet, agreeable girl I remember," he growled.

She smiled demurely at him and nodded pleasantly to the guests, some of whom, despite the cake-cutting going on inside, had strolled out to see if all was well. Ellen led him around the side of the house toward the relative privacy of the hexed herb garden.

They had barely reached the path when John pulled her behind a large camellia bush and crushed her against him. He bent his head toward her. The searing kiss that followed was filled with all the longing and anguish of the past months.

"Ellen, darling," he choked, "I should strangle you. If you only knew how I have been suffering. Until last week I had been sure that I could eventually win you. I died a thousand deaths when I saw that wedding dress, and you in young Milton's arms."

"You can't hold me responsible because you jumped to the wrong conclusion," A teasing half-smile lit her face.

"I thoroughly understand why lawyers are taught not to represent themselves. I had a moment of total panic… didn't have enough sense to ask the first question." He shook his head in disbelief, remembering the afternoon.

"As I recall, you once tried to intimidate me with tales of how objective and thorough you are as an investigator."

"I saw that dress and the man in Confederate uniform. When I heard he had been wounded and was at Oak Lane, I immediately knew he had to be the lieutenant who rescued you. I also knew that, regardless of how you and I felt about each other, you would marry him out of gratitude, if he was in love with you."

"So you rode away without asking a question, and let a whole miserable week pass. Exactly when were you going to get around to doing something?"

"I told you it's a mistake to get involved with a client. Clouds the judgment." He nuzzled her ear. "What was there to do? You had lied so convincingly. I believed that your sister was a child. You had to be the bride."

Ellen had both arms around him, clinging tightly.

He buried his face in her hair, inhaling the fresh herbal scent of her. "This has been a week of hell."

"It has been a nightmare for me, too," she confessed. "I was surrounded with happiness, and filled with misery. I thought I would surely die."

"Honey, I'm so damned glad to be back and to be able to hold you in my arms again. I didn't know I could be so much in love," he groaned, "so desperately, wildly, madly, besottedly in love. I can't count the number of times in the past six months that I feared you might have been a dream."

"I have felt the same way." Ellen's voice was husky with unshed tears.

"I know you must go back inside." He slowly released her.

"Yes. Everyone is wondering about us."

With the fingers of one slim, tanned hand John tilted her face up. "Before I let you go, you must promise to marry me."

"Yes." Ellen answered with no hesitancy.

He pulled her back in his arms. She could feel the hard muscles of his chest pressing into her body and, despite the stir among guests it was likely causing, she loved being held by him.

"We have problems to work out, but my answer is definitely yes. Yes, yes, yes." Ellen pulled his head down and kissed John once more with surprising boldness and ferocity.

"Ellen, our life won't be easy. People here may ostracize you for marrying a Union soldier. Can you live with that?"

"I can try."

"Army pay isn't good and army quarters are often miserable, but if you are too unhappy I will resign from the service. We can live in Virginia, or South Carolina, or any place you wish. I am willing to do anything you ask, except give you up."

"John, we can work out our problems. This is Pam's day. Come back inside. Our family and friends have accepted Elizabeth. Despite the uniform, you will be safe... that is, if I decide to protect you."

"Sweetheart," he said with a confident smile. "I am definitely coming inside." His strong jaw was set with determination. "I'm going to talk with that minister before he gets away. There is to be another wedding at Oak Lane tomorrow."

"John, you can't be serious!"

"Never more so. Remember I grew up in Virginia. I know all about southern weddings. Soon you'll serve supper and there will be dancing until all hours. Nearly everyone will stay for the night." He took her arm and started toward the house.

"In the morning there will be a big happy breakfast. I have brought enough coffee and sugar for a multitude, and the flour to make griddle cakes. I intend to ask your aunt and your sister... and your new brother-in-law, if I must, for your hand. There is going to be another wedding at this house tomorrow."

"You don't need to ask all my relatives about marriage. I believe I have reached the age of consent."

"I have made enough mistakes. We are doing this right."

"In that case, you might ask Aunt Mariah. She will expect that."

"Ah, the Aunt Mariah you told me about that first day."

He looked down and smiled. "Is she likely to disapprove?"

"Not if I look happy."

"You look radiant, my darling Miss Heyward."

"Some of the guests are sure to make you uncomfortable, but you are welcome. My sister knows that I am in love with you."

"You must go now and tell her not to spill any punch on that wedding dress and to remove it very carefully tonight because you will be wearing it tomorrow."

"Don't be absurd, John Arledge, you are moving too fast."

"Absurd! The guests are already here. Aren't these the people you would invite? Tomorrow afternoon they will get to attend another wedding... ours."

Ellen gasped.

He raised an eyebrow and smiled rakishly.

"Don't argue with me, woman. We have things to do."

"But I am taller than Pam, Elizabeth and I will be up half the night letting the hem down."

"So? Neither of us will be able to sleep anyhow."

"And no griddle cakes in the morning. Aunt Mariah will want to use the flour to bake another wedding cake."

"You think you have problems! I have to go and try to charm my way into your aunt's good graces."

"If she has trouble accepting you, I will tell her you are the Yankee officer who saved the College buildings the night of the fire. Are you aware that you are a local hero?"

"I am certainly pleased to hear that. I'll remind you the next time you are disrespectful."

"What will you do about a best man?"

"I can ask young Milton. Just last week I was considering challenging him to a duel. Now I want him for a brother-in-law."

Ellen was dazed. For years, time had dragged slowly past. Now everything was happening too fast. "These wedding guests will certainly have a wild tale to tell when they get back home."

Before they reached the verandah steps John swept Ellen in his arms, swung her around happily and kissed her once more.

"I will sleep on the floor with the other guests tonight, Miss Heyward. But that is it! Tomorrow night things will be very different. Most of the people will have left, and I shall see that the bedroom doors are re-hung. A house as big as this one is bound to have enough room for at least two bridal suites."

The End.